THE WIELDER OF THE
TRISHUL

Deva-Asura Katha — Book I

SATYAM

INKSTATE

ISBN 978-93-90463-41-1

First published in India 2021 by Leadstart Inkstate
A Division of One Point Six Technologies Pvt Ltd

119-123, 1st Floor, Building J2, B - Wing,
Wadala Truck Terminal, Wadala East,
Mumbai 400022, Maharashtra, INDIA
Phone: +91 96999 33000
Email: info@leadstartcorp.com
www.leadstartcorp.com

Editor: Roona Ballachanda
Cover: Mihir Joglekar
Layouts: Kshitij Dhawale

This book is for you, Dad.
I wish you could have held it in your hand

Author's Note

Dear Reader,

This book is a journey into Hindu Mythology with an effort to bring out one of the greatest war stories between *Indra – the King of Devas* and *Vritra – the mightiest of all Asura warriors*. The story has influenced me deeply and I was surprised to know that the legend is relatively unheard of. This inspired me to tell this tale in a manner by which we can connect with the characters. For that reason, the *deva* and *asura* are laid out in flesh and blood. I must admit that writing a book series related to Indra was tough as the King of *Devas*, also known as the God of Thunder is one of the most misunderstood gods in present times and is very wrongly portrayed in serials, movies, and even in some books. It has to be appreciated that Indra is praised as the highest god in 250 hymns of the Rig Veda and he is one of the most celebrated Vedic deities. This book is an effort to tell this legendary tale – the reason he was so famed.

I have taken many creative liberties in telling this tale and also altered character names to keep the storyline intriguing. A part of the story incepted in my dreams, literally! As I began writing, the question that kept me going was – what if there is another parallel world, where tales like Mahabharata and Ramayana unfold in a different way? Therefore, you will find similarities with famous characters of these epics, but they are in entirely different situations.

The story poses questions: Were *devas* noble? Were *asuras* evil? Was it circumstances, or was it their choices that defined them? Who was right and who was wrong? The reader should seek their own answers.

Also, I have taken the creative freedom to imagine a different world altogether with its own societal structures. The most glaring of them all is that there is no caste system, but something else. I hope you enjoy the possibilities thrown up by this new world.

Personally, it's a tribute to our rich heritage and numerous mythological stories that I deeply admire, which unknown to us, may be true...or may be incepted in someone else's dream!

This book wouldn't have been what it is without my editor Roona Ballachanda, who has been more like a Guru in teaching me the writer's craft.

I thank her for being extremely patient with me. I will forever be grateful to her. My sincere gratitude to Swarup Nanda, Malini Nair, Ananya Subramanian, as well as the team at Leadstart for their support.

My parents, my lovely wife, and my adorable children: I can't thank you enough for your love and support while I was authoring this book. I also thank my sisters who have always been my source of strength.

A special note of appreciation to my friends Bhargava, Aditi and Saurabh for their sincere and valuable feedback.

Satyam

TABLE OF CONTENTS

Dhruva-Lok

Prologue

Part I

Chapter 1 Smrti (Memory) 19

Chapter 2 Nakshatra (Constellation) 27

Chapter 3 Samaya (Time) 32

Chapter 4 Prativāsin (Neighbour) 36

Chapter 5 Lobha (Greed) 47

Chapter 6 Maitra (Friendly) 51

Chapter 7 Agnipath (The Path of Fire) 55

Chapter 8 Shivalik (Tresses of Shiva) 61

Chapter 9 Vidyā (Knowledge) 69

Chapter 10 Śubhavārtā (Good News) 74

Chapter 11 Vikalpa (Choice) 82

Chapter 12 Vadhaka (Assassin) 92

Chapter 13 Jananī (Mother) 100

Chapter 14 Bhāgya (Destiny) 105

Chapter 15 Krātha (Murder) 111

Chapter 16 Druhī (Daughter) 117

Chapter 17 Hrīkā (Shame) 120

Chapter 18 Nirnaya (Decision) 122

Part II

Chapter 19 Śrēṣṭha (Best) 129

Chapter 20 Devaprayāga (Godly Confluence) 135

Chapter 21 Aśruta (Unheard) 140

Chapter 22 Nirvṛtta (Ready) 145

Chapter 23 Sparśa (Touch) 149

Chapter 24 Upakāra (Favour) *151*

Chapter 25 Anuchit (Unfair) *157*

Chapter 26 Pratikāra (Revenge) *167*

Chapter 27 Mitra (Friend) *171*

Chapter 28 Agni-Maru (Fire-Duel) *177*

Chapter 29 Vīra (Brave) *182*

Chapter 30 Prathama (The First) *184*

Chapter 31 Asi (The Sword) *190*

Chapter 32 Upaśāntin (Tame) *195*

Chapter 33 Sarvaśrēṣṭha (The Ultimate) *199*

Part III

Chapter 34 Gurudakṣiṇā (Preceptor's Fee) *211*

Chapter 35 Yātrā (Journey) *220*

Chapter 36 Pratyāgata (Returned) *226*

Chapter 37 Heraka (Spy) *231*

Chapter 38 Bhasma (Ash) *235*

Chapter 39 Upakṣepa (Hint) *239*

Chapter 40 Prastāva (Offer) *252*

Chapter 41 Mṛtyu (Death) *259*

Chapter 42 Sahāyatā (Help) *263*

Chapter 43 Sabhā (Meeting) *269*

Chapter 44 Preraṇā (Inspire) *276*

Chapter 45 Varaṇa (Selection) *280*

Chapter 46 Trishul (Trident) *288*

Chapter 47 Netrapaṭa (Blindfold) *299*

Glossary of Indian Terms

Dhruva - Lok

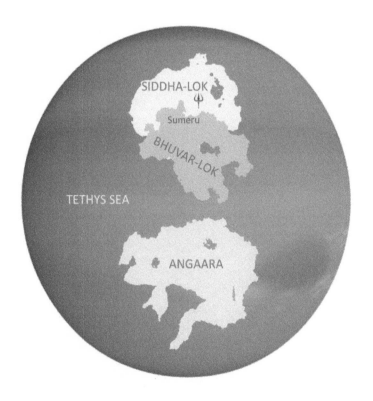

SIDDHA - LOK

BHUVAR - LOK

Prologue

"Son, open your eyes."

The austerity of his *tapasya* (meditation) was so strong that it shook the heavens. Lord Vishnu residing in his celestial abode, Vaikuntha-Lok, was compelled to appear before his youngest devotee ever – a five-year-old, Dhruva.

All that the young Dhruva wanted was to sit on the lap of his father, King Uttanapada. But his stepmother Suruchi scolded him. She told him that he should not aspire to what belonged to Uttama, her son, and his younger half-brother. Uttanapada was disturbed by what Surichi had done, but he loved his wife so much that he did not open his mouth against her. Seeing that his father was silent at his treatment, Dhruva burst out crying and ran to his mother.

Suniti, Dhruva's mother, consoled him, telling him to accept things as they were. All men and women suffer or prosper depending on their *karma*, their deeds of their past lives. She advised Dhruva to do good deeds in this life and to practice all virtues. She explained that the fate and future of a person depended on what they did in their lives.

Suniti's words convinced Dhruva. But he replied, "Mother, it's true that father loves *Maa* Suruchi more and I am not Maa Suruchi's son. But I am your son. Let brother Uttama have the throne. I do not want it. Through my own hardwork, I will achieve a place that no one has ever achieved before."

With these words, Dhruva left the palace and all the comforts of royal life. Renunciation of all desires is regarded to be essential for eternal peace – which Dhruva achieved at a very nascent age.

Wandering in jungles, he met many sages who were surprised to hear that a Prince was unhappy. He told them that he neither desired wealth nor kingdoms. He simply wished to reach a place where no one had ever been before. The sages advised him to pray to Lord Vishnu. They also taught him the *mantra* that was to be used for praying to Vishnu:

"Om Namo Bhagavate Vasudevaya"

"Om, I bow to Lord Vasudeva"

As advised, Dhruva started his meditation, and went without food and water for six months, his mind fixated on the image of Lord Vishnu. He saw nothing else except the Lord, as described by the sages.

His firm resolve forced Lord Vishnu to appear before him. But even the words from the Lord himself were not enough to break Dhruva's deep meditative trance. Such was his conviction – uncorrupted and pure.

Lord Vishnu touched his right cheek with his divine conch and that sparked off Dhruva's speech. Out poured forth a beautiful poem in praise of the Lord in twelve powerful verses, which came to be known as *Dhruva-stuti*.

"Son, what is it that you want?" Lord Vishnu asked his devotee.

Having spent such a long time in the Lord's remembrance, Dhruva even forgot the purpose of his *tapasya*. He replied, "All I desire is a life spent in the memory and praise of God."

Any other person would have asked for worldly or heavenly pleasures, or for *moksha* at most, but Dhruva had no such desires. Many devas and asuras had come to see what this human might ask from Lord Vishnu, and even they were bewildered.

Lord Vishnu was so pleased that he granted Dhruva's wish and further decreed, "Son, you will be a guide to everyone in the *Brahmand* (Universe). You will attain the 'highest heaven' and become a celestial body which would not even be touched by the *Maha Pralaya* (final cataclysm). You will shine as a star in the sky guiding others. From now on your planet will be called Dhruva-Lok. Go and establish *Dharma* and become a symbol of true devotion."

Since then the path taken by Dhruva has been called *Dhruva-pada* – a path of true faith.

An innocent Dhruva said, "But Lord I only wish to be with you."

Lord Vishnu smiled. "I will always come to Dhruva-Lok in various *avatars*, whenever needed, sometimes to fight and sometimes to guide."

Dhruva shines brightly at Dhruva-Lok in the sky, guiding everyone – a symbol of true devotion. His descendants on the planet came to be known as Dhruvanshis. The rule of the first Dhruvanshi happened in *Satya Yuga*.

In *Treta Yuga*, when dark forces fuelled by ego, greed, arrogance and anger rose, destabilising the wheel of dharma, Lord Vishnu took birth as the righteous King Satyavrat. He re-established the rule of dharma and liberated Dhruva-Lok of its many evils, which had crippled society. He was the greatest and noblest ruler on Siddha-Lok, and indeed one of the great Kings of Dhruva-Lok.

Now, the cycle turns to *Dvapara Yuga...*

✦

PART I

1

Smṛti (Memory)

SIDDHA - LOK

Sunbeams floated like freshly minted souls in the mist. A gentle breeze from the east made the trees rustle like living beings. Vishamadeva expected it to be chilly. But something was amiss. His heart pounded like that of a frightened animal, his legs shook and fear slowly invaded his senses. He repeatedly opened and closed his fists. Jittery and suffocated, he opened the window of the carriage and leaned out to get some fresh air.

The Neelkanth peak loomed before Vishamadeva in the Sumeru mountain range. As their destination drew closer, his anxiety grew and he drew back into the carriage. He drummed his fingers on the window. It did not help. To calm his nerves, he folded his hands in prayer, closed his eyes and prayed to Lord Shiva silently. Simham was seated next to him keeping a sharp watch on the surroundings.

As the *Lok-Rakshak*, Simham, a heavily built, bald man with an angular face framed by a sharp, pointed beard, was the recently appointed chief protector – the commander-in-chief – of the military forces of Shivalik-Rajya. The title, second only to the King, sat heavy on his shoulders. Honoured by this responsibility, Simham reminded himself that legendary ruler Satyavrat had served as the Lok-Rakshak before he became the King.

He bent down and looked at the sky and laid eyes on the snow-capped Neelkanth peak, for the first time in his life. "It really looks blue," Simham said and broke Vishamadeva's train of thoughts. Vishamadeva opened his eyes. "Yes, it really is," he replied calmly, swallowing his temper.

Simham let out a deep sigh in awe. "Is it true that Lord Shiva took rest on this peak after drinking the poison, *Halahala*, giving it the colour blue?"

"Hard to say but that's the common belief."

Simham was a man of thirty-five years, yet he was behaving like a five-year old. "I have also heard people say that the peak signifies the separation between the asuras and devas. With Lord Shiva in between, no asura will ever dare to climb or cross this peak."

Vishamadeva did not respond.

"The towering Sumeru separates us from them, the asura," Simham said in a gloating tone.

Not impressed, Vishamadeva replied, "Some say it joins us with Bhuvar-Lok, else we would have been separated by the enormous Tethys Sea exactly the way the island of Angaara is separated from us."

Simham felt it was impossible to please Vishamadeva. "But I am sure no one can touch us as long as we are protected by Lord Shiva."

"Yes, Siddha-Lok is truly blessed that it has nature's ultimate protection. We, at Shivalik-Rajya, should thank mother nature." Vishamadeva folded his hands, yet again, in prayer and tried to calm his turbulent thoughts.

Simham sighted the approaching ashram. The ashram was in Nandi valley. He continued with his prattling and stated, "A very strange place chosen by the *Saptarishis* as their home."

Annoyed, Vishamadeva opened his eyes. "Strange! I call it perfect. It is in a valley looking up at Neelkanth peak. The valley is called Nandi valley for that very reason. Just like Nandi looks towards Lord Shiva in temples. They are in the shadow of Lord Shiva, away from the bustle of cities and politics of kingdoms."

"It is truly amazing how the Saptarishis survive in such harsh weather and limited resources," Simham said in astonishment.

"Well, they have magical yogic powers. In fact, they are not just yogis or sages, but much more. They have earned the title of the Saptarishis."

With some hesitation, Simham asked, "Do they die? I mean the Saptarishis. Do they?"

Vishamadeva was a man of few words. He had seen too much in life. In spite of his irritation, he continued to answer, "The seven sages represent a position, a title, not an individual. They are named after the seven moons of Dhruva-Lok. Like each moon they will stay on Dhruva-Lok till the end of time...forever."

"Is it true they can predict the future?"

"I believe they can. With the grace of Lord Shiva, the Saptarishis can even transcend time and see the past, present and future. They guide and bless all irrespective of class, creed, *vansha* or birthplace. Since time immemorial they have shown the *Dhruva-pada* to the worthy ones."

Simham didn't really believe it. "It will be an honour to meet them." He gave a mirthless smile. "You must have met the Saptarishis before?"

"Yes, quite a few times." For a moment, Vishamadeva had forgotten his troubling thoughts but the sad musings of his earlier visits returned that made him deathly nervous. *What will they say today?*

"They must be very old and weak. What do they look like?"

"Yes, they are old. But they are like all powerful sages. Old does not mean weak."

So, they must be like you, Simham thought. "What did they say to you?" he asked naively.

"STOP!" Vishamadeva screamed at the coachman, "We have reached the ashram. Let's get down." There was barely suppressed anger in his tone. He did not look at Simham.

Simham wondered if he had touched a raw nerve. Vishamadeva was the *de facto* King though he served as the *Lok-Sevak* who was officially the Chief Advisor to the King. For three generations he spoke as the King's voice, decided disputes, drafted the King's laws and implemented them. He commanded respect from everyone. He was consulted on military and security related decisions. Simham knew very well that it was not Maharaja Dhananjay's rule but the reign of the righteous Lok-Sevak Vishamadeva in Shivalik-Rajya.

"Lok-Rakshak, please escort the Maharaja and Maharani." Vishamadeva referred to Simham by his official title.

"Yes, Lok-Sevak," Simham replied in a prim voice.

"Remember it is going to get dark very soon today. We should be ready to leave within a short while from now."

How does he know? Simham was a born warrior, not a man of science. He never understood why the duration of daytime and nights were so different during the year. It was beyond him and he never made any effort to understand it.

"Certainly, Lok-Sevak," he muttered.

Simham jumped down from the carriage and surveyed the jungle around the ashram in Nandi valley for any possible threats. The valley was deep in the woods in an idyllic setting. Short grass covered the entire area. Tall Deodar and Alder trees stood straight like disciplined students, but Simham still had an uninterrupted view of the Neelkanth peak. Flowering trees were in full bloom. Leopards, wolves, bears and poisonous snakes were common in this area. Sometimes even elephants were sighted here. And yet, the atmosphere was one of peace and calmness. The melodious chirping of birds added to the charm of the holy place. Time stood still in peace and harmony. It was paradise.

Simham felt no fear. He scanned the paths leading to the ashram. The ashram was small and not as grand as he had imagined it would be. There were seven wooden huts in a circle around an old lone, banyan tree, just like the seven moons encircled Dhruva-Lok. The huts were made of wood with a conical straw roof. It had a small door and no windows. At some distance from the seven huts, there was one more hut. Outside, near the entrance, it was written, *'We are the artist, karma is our brush and life is the art'*.

The seven sages were deep in meditation under the tree. White hair, long beards, *rudraksha mala* around their neck and three horizontal lines of *chandan* were on their foreheads. A plain, single coloured cloth covered their body, but each had a different colour. He realized it represented the seven colours of the rainbow. Together, they were the light on Dhruva-Lok.

Simham called out to the ten soldiers accompanying him, who were part of the King's *Suraksha-Kavacha* – his defensive shield. He instructed them, "Secure the ashram from all sides. Keep watch for wild animals especially wolves and bears."

"Yes, Lok-Rakshak," replied Talish – a stout man of above-average height, long face and dark complexion. He was the senior-most among the men. The other nine men nodded in agreement.

"Remember that today the daytime will be short. So, we need to be prepared to leave very soon."

"How do we know that the daytime will be short today?" Talish asked.

"Lok-Sevak says so," Simham replied. There was no need for any further questions.

However, a young inquisitive man in his early twenties, with a medium build, square shoulders and calm eyes, dared to ask, "Lok-Rakshak, I have a question?"

"Yes," Simham replied in a harsh tone, "what is it? Wait. First tell me your name and the unit you belong to." He never appreciated questions.

"Lok-Rakshak, my name is Hetan, son of Karthik. I belong to the archer unit." Simham felt happy that he no longer needed to reveal his name as *son of*. Those who didn't have a vansha name, introduced themselves this way. He now had the title of Lok-Rakshak to say it all.

Simham knew Karthik was the *Anga-Rakshak* (bodyguard) of the Maharaja. It was on Karthik's insistence, he had agreed to let young Hetan accompany them. Simham softened and said, "Hetan, what is it that you want to ask?"

"Lok-Rakshak, why do we have such variations in duration of days and nights? Sometimes daytime is very short and sometimes it lasts for nearly two days. Yesterday, it lasted only two *pahars* (parts) and today you are saying it will be even shorter. Why is that so?"

All eyes turned to Simham.

Simham was caught in a fix. He had to say something. His nostrils flared. He asked, "Do you blink your eyes at equal gaps?"

"No," Hetan answered.

"Exactly! Sometimes you blink slowly, sometimes you blink fast. Sometimes you keep your eyes closed for a long time. *Surya-deva* is also doing the same. Whenever he opens his eyes, it is daytime. Whenever he closes, it is night. We can't expect him to do it at equal gaps. The gods do as they wish. We can just pray to them to be merciful." Impressed at his own spontaneous thinking, Simham grinned proudly.

"Excellent answer, Lok-Rakshak," Talish said loudly. Hetan nodded. The remaining men appreciated this and gave admiring glances. Only very elite gurus understood the science behind it. The common folks developed their own explanations.

Delighted, Simham said, "Now, get going. We don't have much time. Be vigilant."

Simham rushed to assist Maharaja Dhananjay in getting down from his two-horse driven royal chariot. The blue carriage with a golden border was made of wood and metal. A golden Trishul was fitted on both sides of the body, as a symbol for Shivalik-Rajya. It had a back seat wide enough for three persons. An enclosed seating chamber at the back had curtained glass windows on all sides. In the front was a seat for the coachman and two more seats behind that for the Anga-Rakshak. All the seats had blue cotton cushions. He opened the doors of the carriage with a loud, *"Maharaja ki jai ho!"* Hail the King!

The 107th Dhruvanshi, Maharaja Dhananjay, a man of average height and build, stepped out. He was dressed in an exquisite, golden attire: a full-sleeve artistically woven woollen tunic with a belt around the waist and baggy pants. His carefully trimmed beard covered his square face, making his frog eyes appear a lot bigger. He had a fair complexion with bluish-black hair. The golden crown of power on his head had one hundred diamond jewels studded around a big blue sapphire in the centre. The Dhruvanshis ruled Shivalik-Rajya, the biggest and mightiest kingdom on Siddha-Lok in size, population, army and influence on the Lok. It was nearly three times the size of the neighbouring Kailash-Rajya.

Simham held the Maharaja's right arm as he got down with some difficulty, his non-responsive right arm resting on his stomach. Dhananjay initially tried to shrug off Simham's assistance in a peevish manner, but he accepted help as always.

"How are you feeling, Maharaja?" Simham asked.

"Much better now." Dhananjay stretched, rubbed his left palm and blew air in it.

"Finally, we have reached. It's been a long journey with four days of rigorous travel deep into the woods."

Dhananjay said, "I know. An arduous journey but it is tradition. After the wedding it is customary for the Dhruvanshis to come and take blessings of the Saptarishis."

A beatific smile creased his face at the thought of his marriage to Padmini. He still remembered the day he had met her. The early morning sky was lit up in hues of pink and orange when he walked into the Grand Shiva Temple for *pooja* and accidentally collided with her at the entrance. He had seen her before, but it felt different this time. She was dressed in his favourite colour – a blue sari. It was love at first sight for him. His eyes had instantly turned pink. She noticed the change in the colour of his eyes. It was the colour of romance. Before her eyes could respond, she shied and rushed away. However, before she disappeared, she turned and gave him a smile. His mind was made up at that very moment in the presence of the Gods. There were no accidents in life; there was a purpose behind everything – he had taught himself to believe that. The path after that wasn't easy. He had faced stiff opposition in marrying Padmini. She was not a princess, but the daughter of their royal priest *Rajguru* Kashyap. It was unheard of, especially for the King of Shivalik-Rajya, the biggest kingdom on Siddha-Lok, to marry someone outside the *Vanshaj* class. She belonged to the lower *Utkrisht* class. But Dhananjay was adamant. He trusted his heart and even went against the counsel of Vishamadeva in marrying Padmini. The smile stretched across his face.

There was a knock from inside the carriage. Dhananjay opened the door on the other side. He offered his left hand to help Padmini get down.

Padmini stepped down carefully. She was excited and nervous at the same time. It was going to be her first meeting with the Saptarishis and she could feel her heart thumping at every step that took her closer to them.

Dhananjay drank in the beauty of his wife as if he were seeing her for the first time. *She may not be a princess, but she is more graceful than many.* Being a newly married woman, she looked perfect in her crimson red saree. It stood out with its intricately beaded border and like Dhananjay, she had paired it with a matching golden blouse. Her opulent black hair with tangerine tints was parted in the centre and braided in a long and fashionable plait. She had a slightly darker complexion compared to Dhananjay. A small red *bindi* sparkled on her forehead and her wide, penetrating eyes were outlined with kajal. Golden diadem and diamond nose pin accentuated her gorgeous features. A golden plastron necklace with red sapphires graced her long neck, supplementing a jewelled cummerbund on her waist. The scent of the henna on her bangle covered hands could be smelled from a distance.

The Saptarishis – Sage Agastya, Atri, Bhardwaja, Gautama, Jamadagni, Vashistha, and Vishvamitra had not realized the arrival of the royal consort. They continued to remain in their deep meditative trance.

Simham asked, "Shall we go inside, Maharaja?"

Padmini looked towards Vishamadeva's carriage and replied, "*Jyeshta Pitashri* (elder father) is yet to come."

Dhananjay added, "We will wait for him to join us."

Simham felt a surge of jealousy. The Lok-Rakshak and Lok-Sevak were the right and left hands of the King. Right is always the stronger arm. But at Shivalik-Rajya, the left hand was a lot stronger than the right, very much like their crippled King's arms.

In his carriage, Vishamadeva was lost in the memories of his earlier visits, especially the first one when he was three years old. He had come with his father Sudarshan, the 105th Dhruvanshi, and adoptive mother Nayantara, after their wedding. The day was fresh in his mind. He loved his father more than anything in the world even though he was Sudarshan's adopted son prior to his marriage to Nayantara. All good, bad, right or wrong, whatever he had done was towards the unquestionable love for his father. The memory shifted to his last visit with his father and stepbrother Heramba after the latter's wedding twenty-one years ago. Finally, he recalled the day Sudarshan left this world. A wave of loss gripped Vishamadeva as he thought of his late father and his eyes teared up.

Suddenly, a dreaded memory echoed in his head!

"… *the curse of Dhruvanshis …*"

The painful words from memory shocked him out of his reverie, and he opened his eyes. He shuddered. Breathing heavily, he wiped the beads of perspiration on his forehead.

Memories haunt, they really do!

✦

2

Nakshatra (Constellation)

SIDDHA - LOK

Weak sunshine filtered in through the window of his carriage. Vishamadeva looked out, only to realize that Maharaja Dhananjay and Maharani Padmini were waiting for him. Hurriedly, he placed the silver crown of Lok-Sevak, his burden, over his head and stepped out. Even at this age, he had the aura of a powerful warrior and a true yogi. Tall and strong, his muscular body was wrapped in a white shawl that was draped over the shoulder, with bare minimum jewellery. Since birth his black hair had a silver tint – a very rare hair colour. He had a long grey beard, but his body showed no hint of ageing or weakening. Many referred to him as *Shvetaveera* – the heroic one in white. As his bare feet touched the ground, a gust of wind rushed through the air and the sages opened their eyes realizing the arrival of a pure soul.

Vishamadeva bowed and touched the feet of the seven sages.

The sages blessed him, *"Chiranjeevi bhava!"* Wish you eternal life.

Dhananjay followed him. The sages blessed, *"Ayushman bhava!"* May you live long.

Padmini gracefully moved and touched their feet. The sages blessed, *"Sada Saubhagyavati bhava!"* Good Luck always.

Simham folded his hands and bowed his head from where he was standing. The sages nodded and silently blessed him.

Vishamadeva brought his palms together in respect and uttered, "O Divine Sages, nothing is hidden from you. Maharaja Dhananjay and Maharani Padmini have started their married life. They seek your godly blessings and words of wisdom. Shower them with your blessings and guide them."

The seven sages together raised their right arms with palm facing towards the couple and gave them silent blessings.

Vishamadeva continued, "Bless them with a worthy heir to the kingdom, the 108th Dhruvanshi."

Sage Vashistha smiled, flamboyant eyebrows capping streaks of light coming from his piercing eyes. He spoke, "O Great Dhruvanshi and Noble Queen – Brahma, Vishnu and Mahesha – the *Trimurti* have showered their blessings on you. The Queen is already carrying the heir to the kingdom. She will give birth during *Shivratri* next year."

Dhananjay and Padmini exchanged stunned glances. As the news sank in, their faces lit up in happiness. The jubilation felt by the visitors knew no bounds. All of them could barely control their delight at this wonderful news.

Sage Agastya's words were even more astonishing. "The time has come for the Wielder of the Trishul to be born. The 108th Dhruvanshi is destined to wield the Trishul."

Wielder of the Trishul! No one had wielded the mighty Trishul, since legendary King Satyavrat had received it from Lord Shiva. Centuries had passed, but it had remained unmoved. The prophecy from the Saptarishis would spread like fire across Dhruva-Lok, and beyond.

The joy of the newly married couple skyrocketed, hearing two such great news in such a short span of time. They could barely decide on how to respond. Gratified, both Dhananjay and Padmini fell at the feet of the sages.

"But…" Sage Vashistha became quiet and looked concerned. He closed his eyes. His mind was in turmoil.

Vishamadeva knew something more was coming. He pursed his lips hard. He knew that the curse would change everything.

A worried Padmini rose in alarm. Her heartbeat raced. Her lower lip was pursed between her teeth. An expression of fear enveloped her face.

Their happiness vanished.

Sage Vashistha opened his eyes and said, "*Nakshatra* (constellation) are aligning in a manner which has never occurred before. It will be changing from *Dhruva Nakshatra* to *Ugra Nakshatra* around the time of birth."

Sage Gautama read the visitor's concerned faces. He explained, "Dhruva Nakshatra occurs when all the seven moons of Dhruva-Lok are visible in the sky at the same time. That is a rare sight. Even rarer is Ugra Nakshatra, which happens when the shadow of Dhruva-Lok falls on all of them. Seven lunar eclipses at the same time happens only once in a century."

"Do you know about the *Navgraha*?" Sage Jamadagni asked.

Dhananjay shook his head mutely. Padmini remained silent. As the daughter of a royal priest, she knew about the Navgrahas.

"As you know there is no other planet orbiting the sun in our solar system. So, the sun and seven moons are the eight grahas. The ninth graha – *Shesha* – is a comet. Whenever it pays a visit, it is considered *Uttam Nakshatra*," Jamadagni said.

"What does Shesha represent, Divine Sages?" Padmini asked.

"It represents the *Shesha-naag* on which Lord Vishnu rests. It passes Dhruva-Lok once in a millennium in a non-periodic manner. Shesha implies the 'remainder' – that which remains when all else ceases to exist. Its arrival marks either the change of Yuga or the arrival of a Lord Vishnu's avatar. King Satyavrat was born in Uttam Nakshatra – which is the rarest of nakshatras," Sage Atri answered.

Dhananjay's chest swelled with pride. King Satyavrat, a Dhruvanshi, was indeed an avatar of Lord Vishnu.

Simham now understood the symbolism of the outside hut at a distance. It represented Shesha.

But both Dhananjay and Padmini wondered why the sages were explaining Nakshatra in so much detail.

After a momentarily silence, Sage Vashistha continued with his prophecy, "If the child is born in Dhruva Nakshatra, he could become the saviour and bring prosperity to this entire Lok. But if the birth takes place in Ugra Nakshatra, he could be the destroyer."

Saviour or Destroyer! All eyes snapped to attention.

The words made Padmini strangely uncomfortable. She closed her eyes as tears filled in them and threatened to spill. The wind picked up, and sent a chill through her. The surroundings suddenly felt cold and hard.

Dhananjay's feet trembled.

Vishamadeva's heart skipped a beat. Yet, he remained calm. He had come prepared.

Sage Vashistha added, "This change of Nakshatra will happen at midnight of Shivratri next year."

There was a frightened calm for a long time. The thought of a destroyer sent shock waves to everyone present. It was a kind of prophecy no one had ever heard before. A gust of wind swept the area and wrapped its icy fingers around them. Questions were flying fast and furious in their heads. Still, no words were spoken.

Confused and short of breath, Dhananjay finally asked, "What does it mean, Divine Sages?"

Sage Bhardwaja replied, "We have both Light and Darkness inside us. The alignment of different graha controls our thoughts and behaviour. Which part – Light or Darkness – prevails, decides destiny! Your son will have the power, how he acts will determine the future."

Padmini scrambled for words. At last, she asked the sages in a shaky voice, "W-w-why will the Trimurti bless us with a child that is destined to d-d-destroy everything?" A tear managed to escape the corner of Padmini's left eye. Her mouth felt dry, lips bloodless and lungs short of air.

Sage Atri answered, "Creation and destruction is a cycle which goes on and on. The beginning could be the end, or the end could be a beginning – that depends on perspective."

"What is born, shall die. What is dead, shall never die! Whatever happens, it will be the wish of God." Sage Vishvamitra completed the answer.

There was a long silence.

Sage Bhardwaja eventually said, "Difficult choices lie ahead. May the Gods bless you all."

Sometimes, seeking answers only unearths more questions. Dhananjay had no idea how to respond. Whether to rejoice or mourn – he couldn't decide. At that moment, he wished he hadn't come. Sometimes not knowing is better than knowing!

"May the Holy Trimurti give us the strength to face the testing times ahead and guide us through the difficult choices we may have to make," Vishamadeva said with a brave smile. Many secrets were sealed in his heart. One could close all the doors to it but there was always someone knocking on them. Memories were not going to stop haunting him.

The seven sages smiled at him knowing that this Lok-Sevak was born to make tough choices. "*Tathastu!*" Amen. They all said it together and closed their eyes, in dismissal.

The weather turned gloomy and the wind stopped blowing. Even the birds had stopped chirping. It felt as if life had been sucked out of the atmosphere.

An eerie calm enveloped them. As they turned back to their carriage, the tension on their faces was palpable and increased with every passing second. No words were exchanged. What could they do, except wait! Nothing is more terrifying than the fear of the unknown.

It was the longest walk of their lives.

✦

3

Samaya (Time)

BHUVAR - LOK

The landscape of Bhuvar-Lok was vast and diverse. The scorching hot Kharan Desert bordered by the Amargosa Mountain ranges dominated the arid west. The mighty Sumeru stood in the north and the massive lake Manasa Sarovar sat in the middle of Bhuvar-Lok. The sacred Indravati River rose from the Amargosa in the west and emptied into Manasa Sarovar and the Tethys Sea in the east. Its numerous tributaries ran through the landmass and were a lifeline for the millions who lived along their course.

More than half the population of Bhuvar-Lok lived in the west, in the kingdom of Jambu-Rajya. It was ruled by the Vardhan-vanshis – they were among the oldest vansha on Dhruva-Lok.

With a fondness for jewelled clothing, the popular Samrat Srivijay, a short man with red-black hair, a round face, and a thin lip-sized black moustache, was the King of Jambu-Rajya. One morning, he woke up early, shaved and bathed and went to his room to get dressed. It was a significant day for all the kingdoms of Bhuvar-Lok as a meeting had been scheduled to discuss important matters pertaining to their trade and commerce.

On this day he chose to wear a dark yellow, heavily embroidered, knee-length *angarkha* with an asymmetric opening knotted by thread loops on the left side. He paired it with a white pyjama and a jewelled turban. His sheathed sword hung prominently at his waist. He looked down at himself in the mirror with self-satisfaction.

Long ago Bhuvar-Lok had always faced foreign invaders across the Tethys Sea until the seven kingdoms, with the leadership of the Vardhan-vanshis of Jambu-Rajya, united and helped them to see through a peaceful last century.

The Vardhan-vanshis were legends – it was believed that his ancestors got a boon from *Indra-deva*, the god of Rain and Thunder, that their kingdom would continue to grow. As a young King of twenty years, Srivijay felt a heavy burden on his shoulders.

His wife Kaushiki was barely nineteen years old; she had a wheatish complexion, average height and a svelte figure with hair colour exactly like her husband – a strong reason behind their marriage. She raised the upper part of her body, and after a lick of her lips and a yawn, slowly crawled out of the bed. She rubbed her eyes so hard that it looked like she may pull out one eye. Her sleepy eyes fell on her husband. "Why didn't you wake me up?" she asked, rushing towards him.

Srivijay cared a lot for her. Unlike regular Kings, he understood what her wife was going through. She was still recovering from her second miscarriage. At some level, he blamed himself for that. "Only I need to go for the meeting. You take rest."

And she blamed herself. "It's been two years and I haven't been able to give you an heir. I wish you hadn't married me." Tears filled her eyes ready to burst the floodgates open.

He pulled her close with a strong grip and looked straight into her eyes. "I married the lady I loved from the moment my eyes fell on her. I will never regret marrying you; no matter what!" His pupils dilated, and a flutter ran through his body. He put his free hand on her back and pulled her very close. He gave her a passionate kiss. One long kiss that left her breathless.

They embraced each other in a tight hug. She let out a deep sigh of relief. Not yet allayed of her fears, she said with a heavy heart, "Maybe you should consider second marriage."

He cupped her cheeks and said, "You will be the only one in my life, the way one sun shines in the sky. No one will ever take your place."

Kaushiki looked outside the window at the sun surrounded by a thin veil of clouds. The solacing sunrays took away her self-guilt. She turned to her normal self – intelligent but argumentative. "The sun looks really big," she said to change the conversation.

"Yes, it's summer season and it's always bigger in the summers."

"Still it's really big."

"This is the day the sun comes closest to our planet. That is why this day is fixed for our annual meeting."

"Does the sun change in size? Or is it an illusion?"

"You know our planet revolves around the sun."

"Who says that? My grandmother used to say it is the sun that revolves around our planet."

"No, it's the other way."

"You men can never accept that a man can move around a woman. It has to be a woman who has to move around you," she said in a tone that made him catch his breath.

"Men and women?" a confused Srivijay asked.

"You call this land your mother, so it's a woman and the sun is a god, not a goddess. So, it is about men and women."

"No, it has nothing to do with man and woman. It's just the way things are. Believe me."

"How do you know? Have you seen from the heavens that our planet is revolving around the sun? Why can't it be the other way around when it is clear to the eyes that it is the sun that moves?!"

"I don't know. Guru Sridhar says so."

"Another man!"

He joined his hands in apology. "Don't get angry, dear. Let us assume the sun goes around us. Gurudeva said that the shape of the path that the sun takes will be like," he moved around and picked a fruit and continued, "a grape. So, in one round it will be closest and farthest twice. It will appear big when it is nearest and small when distant. That is why in a year we have two summers, and two winters."

"You mean to say in one year, the sun completes one round."

"Yes."

"That's so simple. How come very few know about it?"

"It is difficult to accept what you don't see directly. Many say that our planet is flat like a disc, and many say it is like an orange. Who knows the truth?"

"Explain this to me – is this the reason that even the duration of daytime and night-time, though different across days, are the same across the same days every year?"

"No, even I don't understand it properly. Gurudeva used to say that it has something to do with the axis of spin and rotation of our planet which keeps changing but it follows a pattern which repeats every year."

She looked confused. "Spin! Maybe that's why my head spins every morning when I wake up!" she laughed.

"Won't we fall if the planet was spinning?" she asked.

"Even I wonder the same. But for some reason we don't."

"Who came up this?"

"I think it was Acharya Brihaspati of Siddha-Lok. He divided time into years, days, pahars and hours, and invented," he pointed to the corner as he said, "that sand clock for keeping time."

"Hmm…"

Looking at the clock, Srivijay said, "It's time for the meeting. I should get going." He kissed her on her forehead and left in a hurry.

Times were changing. The century-long peace could end today.

✦

4

Prativāsin (Neighbour)

SIDDHA - LOK

An uneasy silence settled on the group. The departure from Nandi Valley was a slow and painful expedition. The clatter of the horses' hooves and the wailing sounds of a gusty wind accompanied the silent group on their return journey. The King and Queen sat rigidly in the carriage, neither looking at each other nor exchanging any words.

It turned dark by the time the King's party reached their guesthouse. A modest two-storey structure made of bricks; this place was maintained by Shivalik-Rajya but used by visitors from all over Dhruva-Lok when they arrived to meet the Saptarishis.

A hand carved wooden double door led into an entry room. There were side tables with three shelves in the corners. To one side, there was a bedroom with a dark wood double bed under a circular net canopy and two exotic-looking chairs placed near the window, which looked out into the mountains. Many lamps were scattered across the room but only two were lit, giving the room a dim, ambient look.

Padmini went straight to the sleeping quarters, followed by Mitasha, her personal maid. Short and lean, Mitasha was dressed in a plain green sari and her hair was neatly tied up in a bun. She was the daughter of the head cook in the palace. She was quick to read the Queen's mood and without asking any questions, she assisted Padmini in changing of her clothes. At a sign from the Queen, she left the sleeping quarters.

Padmini lay down on the bed, but sleep eluded her. She tried not to think about the prophecy and closed her eyes hoping for some relief. But, the happenings of the day were playing in her mind again and again. Events happen once, but they are re-lived a million times in the head.

Lightening flashed, momentarily illuminating the room. Then thunder rumbled, shaking the windows and doors. Rain hit the structure, a soft, steady sound.

Lagging behind the rest of the party, Dhananjay walked in with the caretaker Ravikiran, who was holding an umbrella for the Maharaja. It was the first time he was meeting the Maharaja. Ravikiran was a short man of fragile frame with a fair complexion, a clean-shaven long face with a wide forehead, on which was smeared a bright white *tilak*.

Dhananjay removed his crown and handed it to Ravikiran. "This weather is so unpredictable," Dhananjay murmured.

Ravikiran nodded mutely. He admired the crown and the precious jewels on it. Without wasting time, he quickly placed it on a side table in the entry room.

Dhananjay looked at the sand clock kept in the entry room and asked, "Does this clock work?"

"Yes, Maharaja."

"How do you ensure its accuracy? Do you regularly align it with the central clock in the capital?"

"Maharaja, twice a year, I visit the capital to fill the food stock. That time I align it. Daily I keep turning it."

"Alright."

Ravikiran asked, "Maharaja, at what time should I serve dinner?"

"I will call for it…not feeling hungry right now."

"Anything else, Maharaja?"

"Is it going to be very cold in the night?"

"No, Maharaja. It is summer season, but the weather will be cooler than the plains. Also, it is raining, so it might be cooler than usual days. There are blankets on the bed."

"How long you have been here? Do you stay alone?"

"No, Maharaja. I stay with my wife and two daughters. We have been taking care of this guesthouse for the last four generations."

"You are doing a good job. Thank you, Ravikiran," Dhananjay said in a pleasant tone.

Ravikiran joined his palms, bowed to the Maharaja and left the room. Dhananjay made his way to the sleeping quarters.

Padmini got up, looking visibly tense and worried. Her eyes were blue indicating nervousness. He noticed the colour, but he avoided the topic uppermost in their minds. "We shall leave tomorrow morning for Kailash-Rajya. Vishamadeva says that tomorrow daytime will be much longer."

She nodded slowly.

As per the royal tour plan, they were to spend two days at Kailash-Rajya and one day at Himalia-Rajya.

She asked, "Maharaja, can't we cancel the visit to neighbouring kingdoms of Kailash and Himalia? I want to return home."

Dhananjay had already discussed this with Vishamadeva. He had advised in very clear terms, "We can't, Maharaja. Any sudden change in plans after meeting the Saptarishis might lead to a lot of speculation."

He tried to put on a reassuring face and replied thoughtfully, "It will be better if we continue the tour. You have never been to the eastern side of Siddha-Lok. The route is very beautiful. Fragrant yellow sunflowers cover mile after mile like a golden carpet. Their iconic bloom is reminiscent of the Sun-god. Himalia is nature's paradise."

She said, "Tell me more about Kailash-Rajya. How many pradesh (province) is it divided into?"

"None. This practice of division of a Rajya into Pradesh is only at Shivalik. This was created due to its huge size, population and variations in geography, and it makes our administration easier. We have one hundred pradesh, with each one representing a jewel in my crown. Kailash-Rajya is about one-third the size of Shivalik. It is not densely populated, so there is no need for divisions into pradesh."

"Who is the king?"

"It has been ruled by the Yavana-vanshis for the last twenty generations. King Yuyutsu is the present King. He is about eight years older than me, but he doesn't have any children."

"What sort of King is he?"

"Vishamadeva says he is an ambitious King. He has dreams of becoming a *Chakravarti* King (World Emperor)."

"Really? How powerful is the kingdom?"

"His biggest strength is that Kailash-Rajya commands the most powerful navy on Siddha-Lok and thus controls the entire sea trade. They are lucky that they are on the eastern coast where Tethys Sea is calm. Our kingdom is primarily on the western coast where Tethys Sea is very turbulent, making it unsuitable for any navigation or trade. As it is said – *the west is the doorway to hell*. We have a part of the eastern coast as well, but it is not suitable for port development. Due to this advantage, Kailash-Rajya has emerged as a trading hub with Bhuvar-Lok kingdoms in recent years – making it a prosperous kingdom."

"Do we need to fear them?" she asked, sounding apprehensive.

"Not at all. They stand no chance against us. We have an army which is roughly three times their army. Moreover, they don't have any warriors who can defeat Vishamadeva or even Simham. His dream will remain unfulfilled." He smiled and added, "Now, our son will become the Wielder of the Trishul. We have nothing to fear about our future."

The words reminded her of the prophecy. She started to fiddle with a lock of her hair, twisting and turning it around her index finger. She had one pressing concern about the visit. "What are we going to say to them on what the Saptarishis told us?"

"Vishamadeva has already spread the news that the Saptarishis have predicted that you will be delivering the 108th Dhruvanshi next year and our child is destined to wield the Trishul. Nothing further needs to be told."

She glanced around uneasily, shook her head and muttered, "I can't lie."

"We are not lying. We are saying the truth, but not the complete truth. There is a big difference. Revealing the full prophecy won't help anyone."

"What about eyes? They reveal everything about the mood. We can't control them. They will sense I am hiding something."

"No one will suspect anything. Any lady, that too with child for the first time, is expected to be nervous and scared. You are unnecessarily thinking too much."

She bit her lower lip and kept quiet. It made sense. He hesitated to ask, "Ar...Are you with child?"

She shrugged her shoulders. "I don't know. I don't feel anything, yet."

He put his left arm around her affectionately. "Then let us not think too much... let's wait and watch."

We don't have an option, she thought. The prophecy had sown a seed in their mind. It was bound to grow with time.

✦

They arrived at Kailash-Rajya after four days to the welcome of beating drums and were greeted by King Yuyutsu and Queen Devayani. The flags of Kailash-Rajya – a roaring red lion on a golden flag – were fluttering.

Dressed in a golden sherwani, King Yuyutsu was a tall and thin man with a fair complexion, brown hair and a thick moustache. His eyes had a searing gaze. "Welcome King of Kings, Dhruvanshi, Maharaja Dhananjay." He welcomed his counterpart with open arms.

The attendants showered flowers on them as they both embraced each other.

Queen Devayani welcomed Padmini with a similar honour. She had fair complexion, rosy lips, perfect white teeth and a slender build. Her hair was braided with fresh jasmine flowers. The Queen was draped in a black sari over a golden blouse, and it was embellished with jewellery. Padmini felt a pang of jealousy seeing Devayani's elegant dressing sense.

Yuyutsu said loudly with a fake smile, "We have heard the good news. We are blessed that the Wielder of the Trishul is going to arrive soon. He is destined to take the friendship between our kingdoms to greater heights." The news had spread rapidly.

"It is all due to the blessings of Brahma-Vishnu-Mahesha. The Gods have humbled us." Dhananjay tried to hide his anxiety.

King Yuyutsu noticed Vishamadeva and rushed to touch Vishamadeva's feet. Over time, Yuyutsu had come to realize that it was more important to please Vishamadeva. He had more influence on Shivalik-Rajya.

"Please come to our small palace. It stands on a low hill we call Kasar. It took four generations and nearly seventy years to construct it," Yuyutsu said proudly. After the grand welcome, the guests were given a tour of the palace.

The palace was grand, artistically carved on yellow coloured sandstone. The complex was set in an area of nearly twenty-five acres of land including fifteen acres of gardens. The central dome rested above the inner dome, which was inlaid with wooden panels, set one beside the other, touching at the centre. They were chiselled in the most alluring manner and ornamented with colour and carving of the gods. External walls had carvings of many animals, with the most prominent being lion, elephant, unicorn and snake. The entry led to the lobby which had polished black granite flooring. The passages were long. The lounge area had pink sandstone and marble floors. The palace had one hundred and thirty-six rooms and several courtyards.

"The palace is even more spectacular than what I remember," Dhananjay expressed his appreciation warmly.

"Yes, the palace has been recently renovated," Yuyutsu said.

The sea-trade must be booming, Dhananjay thought.

◆

Dhananjay and Padmini walked to the grand hall for dinner, followed by Lok-Sevak Vishamadeva, Lok-Rakshak Simham and Anga-Rakshak Karthik. They were escorted by Baladeva, the Lok-Rakshak of Kailash-Rajya. Karthik did not enter the hall. He stood guard near the gates.

Padmini looked around the hall in admiration. The room was glittering with a central chandelier and many lamps on the walls. Gold – the colour synonymous with kingdom of Kailash – reverberated through the room. In the centre, there was a low rosewood dining table with chairs without legs. The windows of the hall were closed and covered with full-length curtains. There were many paintings with golden frames on the walls. *Were they framed in real gold?* Padmini wondered.

A small band of musicians were accompanied by a tabla player and flutist. The muted soulful rhythm of songs in praise of the Gods added to the atmosphere, arms and legs moving to the beats.

Only high-ranking officials were invited for the special dinner. Yuyutsu and Devayani were joined by Kalindi, younger sister of Devayani.

The chair for the Lok-Sevak of Kailash-Rajya was empty. Padmini signalled with her eyes at the empty chair and whispered to Dhananjay, "Why is this chair empty?"

"After the death of the Lok-Sevak, King Yuyutsu hasn't selected one. He continues to hold this post."

On the table, a lavish vegetarian *chappan bhog* (fifty-six dishes) dinner was kept for the guests. Clearly, no stone was left unturned in welcoming the Dhruvanshi, especially after the prophecy. The Dhruvanshis have traditionally been vegetarian. Simham felt disappointed.

Yuyutsu pointed his hand towards Kalindi, "Maharaja Dhananjay, do you know Kalindi?"

Dhananjay shook his head. "No, I have not had the honour."

"She is the younger sister of Devayani. Her marriage has been fixed with my distant cousin Madhav from Mayura-Pradesh."

Vishamadeva raised his left eyebrow. "If I am not wrong, Mayura-Pradesh is the recently created pradesh to which Kailash-Rajya has granted independence. Isn't it?" His voice was stern.

"Yes," Yuyutsu replied firmly.

"That sets a very wrong precedent for other kingdoms. Other provinces may start demanding independence. It puts us in a difficult position."

Yuyutsu replied in a scornful tone, "It is our internal matter. We don't need approval from anyone."

"It is not about approval. Your decision affects us. We should have been informed about the reasons for doing so."

This news came as a surprise to Dhananjay.

Dhananjay tried to calm down the rising tempers. "I am sure there must be a very good reason for doing so."

"The region was controlled by dacoits for many years. These dacoits were running a parallel rule. Due to the difficult terrain and dense jungles, even we were helpless. My father had announced a reward for anyone who got rid of these dacoits. It was a promise my father made. And Madhav completed the task. I merely fulfilled the promise. I am sure Vishamadeva understands the meaning of promise. They are carved in stone," Yuyutsu explained.

The word 'promise' silenced Vishamadeva. If there was anyone who would go to any extent to keep a promise, it was Vishamadeva.

Yuyutsu elaborated, "The independence has been granted on very strict terms. Mayura-Pradesh will never ask for any additional land. It can maintain an army of no more than five hundred soldiers and that too only on the condition that it will maintain neutrality and never take part in an armed conflict on Siddha-Lok under any circumstances. Madhav has sworn to it, and I trust him. He is a man of his word."

There was a long silence.

"The food is very lavish, and it looks delicious. I heard Queen Devayani has given personal attention to this," Padmini praised the food in an effort to lighten the mood.

Devayani replied, "Thank you, Maharani."

The servants started serving the food on gold plates. Vishamadeva and Dhananjay shared a look. Kailash-Rajya was not missing any opportunity to show-off its wealth.

"Please try this soup. It is our specialty," Devayani requested the guests.

They all took a sip.

Everyone liked it, except Simham. He had to cover his eyes to hide his true feelings. His stomach rumbled. He gulped down a glass of water. His eyes scanned through the remaining dishes hoping they would taste better. It had salads, various dals, vegetables cooked into many delicacies, three rice dishes and around ten sweet dish items. He identified *rajma* which was a dish for Raja and Maharaja and was named accordingly. Many types of juices, honey water and *chaas* were kept in small glasses. Out of the 56 dishes, he could recognize only half of them. *Apupa* – a form of cake prepared by frying barley – was the one he kept staring at for a long time. His mouth watered.

There was not much conversation, except by Padmini who continued to compliment Devayani on the choice of dishes.

The next morning, talks were held in closed chambers. Apart from Yuyutsu and Baladeva, it was attended by Nageshwar, the *Koshadhyaksha* (treasurer) and Rajguru Brahmagupta as *Dharmadhikari* (royal priest). Baladeva was a tall, muscular, broad-chested man with a thick bushy moustache – exactly the way a Lok-Rakshak should look like. Nageshwar and Brahmagupta both were stout men, in their fifties.

The Shivalik side was represented by Dhananjay, Vishamadeva and Simham. Vishamadeva also held the post of treasurer. Rajguru Kashyap, Queen Padmini's father, had not accompanied them as matters relating to religious laws were unlikely to be discussed.

Dhananjay started the meeting, "We are very thankful to the kingdom of Kailash for a grand welcome. We are honoured by your hospitality, King Yuyutsu. The Yavana-vanshis truly have a heart of gold!"

Yuyutsu nodded his head acknowledging the praise.

Dhananjay looked at Vishamadeva, who continued with the negotiations.

Vishamadeva said, "Thank you, Maharaja. There are three serious matters that need discussion. The first issue is that Shivalik-Rajya is having a trade deficit which is steadily increasing over the years. This is a growing concern. We are importing spices from Bhuvar-Lok kingdoms. As all trade happens through your ports, we have to depend on you for that. Also, you are rich in gold mines and we buy a lot of gold. It is putting a heavy burden on our treasury."

"It is our luck that we are on the eastern coast. The western coast regions have to face the turbulent Tethys Sea; it is not our fault. We don't know how we can help," Nageshwar responded on behalf of King Yuyutsu.

"Well, you can increase the imports from Shivalik to balance it out," Vishamadeva replied sharply.

"Why should we do that?" Nageshwar scoffed.

"That is what friends do! Help each other." Vishamadeva made an effort to placate him.

"In matters of trade, there is no friendship. It's business, pure business!"

"Let me remind you that we also have some part of the eastern coast. We can always develop a port there – it may be difficult but not impossible. As we are friendly nations, we never made an effort to have unnecessary competition. That can always change," Vishamadeva threatened.

Nageshwar had not anticipated this challenge. He swallowed a lump in his throat. He looked to Yuyutsu for guidance.

Yuyutsu knew Vishamadeva made no idle threats. Their bluff did not work. It would be disastrous if they were to build a port. It was time to concede. "Koshadhyaksha, is that any way to talk to a friend?" Yuyutsu asked loudly. Nageshwar lowered his eyes. Yuyutsu turned to Vishamadeva and said, "I am sorry for his language. We are friendly nations and it will always stay that way."

Vishamadeva did not waver. He looked at them with stony eyes.

Sensing no response, Yuyutsu continued, "Kailash-Rajya promises to buy weapons, especially swords and spears, and armours from Shivalik-Rajya. Your region is rich in mines of iron, copper and bauxite and swords made by your blacksmiths are known for their prowess."

Dhananjay replied, "A good gesture, King Yuyutsu. We are both victors."

Vishamadeva added, "Thank you, King Yuyutsu. Your words mean a lot to us. We can work out the pricing and other modalities later."

Yuyutsu made a surprise request, "There is something more. We are hoping you can provide us the technology behind swords made from Wootz steel along with the weapons. We are ready to pay any price."

Vishamadeva furrowed his brows. He knew that the technology behind the powerful Wootz steel sword was only with Shivalik-Rajya. The mining of iron ore, the thermo-mechanical process for forging Wootz steel and the heat treatment were only known to a handful of Shivalik's blacksmiths. Such rare swords were difficult to forge.

Dhananjay started to reply, but Vishamadeva interrupted him, "Yes, King Yuyutsu. We will consider your request." Dhananjay exchanged glances with him.

Dhananjay always trusted the judgement of Vishamadeva in such political and defence matters. No one could question his loyalty. Dhananjay altered his response and stated, "It is a big request and we need to give it some thought. I need to discuss with other pradesh in my kingdom as well before making any such decision."

Vishamadeva was relieved.

Yuyutsu's jaws stiffened hearing it. He felt Vishamadeva had again sabotaged the request. "I understand, Maharaja. I know decisions at Shivalik-Rajya are made after consulting everyone," Yuyutsu replied. The sarcasm in his tone was evident.

Dhananjay gave an awkward smile at the taunt. He needed to come out of the shadows of Vishamadeva and take control of matters.

Simham remained a mute spectator to the entire discussion even in matters involving military issues. He was used to this. But he admired the skills of Vishamadeva in negotiations.

At the end of talks, in a private conversation, Dhananjay asked Yuyutsu, "You have been married for some time. What did the Saptarishis say to you?"

"No, we don't have a tradition of visiting the Saptarishis after marriage. Instead, we visit when the Queen is with child to seek their blessings."

"Ohh. But they stay quite high in the mountains and deep in the woods. Is it advisable to take the Queen in that delicate condition?"

"No, ladies don't go. Only, I will go."

"Let me formally request you that whenever you visit, please give us an opportunity to return the hospitality."

"Of course, Maharaja. But," Yuyutsu said, "I must admit – the thought of visiting the Saptarishis makes me nervous. One does not know what they may say!"

"Yes, that is there."

"I always wonder, why tell the future? Is it appropriate on their part to bias our minds by telling so?"

"Umm...They are powerful yogis. Whatever they tell, they must have reasons for doing so. Still I feel it is better to know what to expect."

"You must be feeling really proud. It is not every day you hear such a prophecy. I always felt that it has to be a Dhruvanshi who will wield the Trishul someday. How does it feel to know about the bright future?"

Dhananjay did not answer straightaway. After a while, he replied in a measured tone, "It helps us to be mentally prepared. The Gods must have chosen us for a purpose."

◆

5

Lobha (Greed)

BHUVAR - LOK

It was a circular, common meeting hall, closed from all sides, with a domed ceiling, no windows and a single entrance. There was a round sandalwood table in the centre where each King had a personal seat. The tall chairs were as grand as thrones. It was a well-lit room, with statues of various nature gods sculpted on the surrounding walls. Indra, Vayu, Bhumi, Agni, Varuna, Yama and Surya were carved at seven equidistant points. At top-centre there was a statue of a young Dhruva meditating. The people of Bhuvar-Lok prayed to the nature gods and not the Trimurti.

On the wooden table, a map of the entire Bhuvar-Lok was carved in three-dimensions including the geographic features of the landmass.

The seven kingdoms of Bhuvar-Lok – Jambu, Plaksha, Salmala, Kusha, Kraunca, Saka and Pushkara had assembled for their joint annual meeting. After a tumultuous period of invasions and infighting, the seven kingdoms had entered into a peace deal in which one kingdom would not interfere in the internal dynamics of the other kingdoms. The annual meetings were introduced for resolving disputes and discussing inter-kingdom problems.

The voice of King Bali of the coastal kingdom of Salmala echoed in the Hall of *Sapta-sabha*. "As coastal kingdoms, we provide ships for trade with Siddha-Lok and Angaara. We depend on Siddha-Lok for textiles, weapons and raw materials for weapons, and Angaara for their timber, charcoal, medicinal herbs and other minor forest products. In turn, we supply them spices, mulberry silk, cotton and agricultural products. In addition, we guard Bhuvar-Lok from foreign invaders. We are the first line of defence against them." He paused to allow his words to sink in. "We have been performing this duty for close to a century for a meagre price. Now, we want our rightful share."

King Bali's dissent was seconded by King Ugrasena of Saka. "I strongly agree. We ride through the turbulent sea against all odds; we take all the risk. We face the growing pirate threats. We deserve more money!"

Both the Kings were muscular men in their early thirties, their red-brown bodies covered in leather tunics, pants and big boots. Their weather-beaten faces were hard and cruel with drooping mustachios. They dressed alike except that Bali wore a black outfit whereas Ugrasena preferred a dark brown coloured tunic. King Bali was taller than Ugrasena. Strikingly, Ugrasena had no neck and he made up for that with a tricorn hat. Bali had a crown of seashells, pearls and seed beads. Their friendship was strengthened by the bonds of marriage – each one was married to the other's sister.

King Surajbhan of Kusha, a man in his late thirties, his face adorned with battle scars, stood up to convey his disapproval. "Meagre price! You already charge a heavy rate just for transportation – it is more than fifty percent of the profits. Our farmers toil hard on the land, they fight against weather uncertainty and they labour at each step. Just because rainfall has been good in the last two years, it does not mean that we are making easy money. Our craftsmen, blacksmiths and miners too work in the most gruelling conditions and they already have small margins. It is we who face the real risks."

The Kings of the other three kingdoms thumped their fists in support.

"It costs a lot to maintain ships and to mount a defense against pirates. If they succeed in their attacks, we have to bear the entire loss. What does he know about our problems? He doesn't deserve a seat here. Look, he doesn't even wear a crown," Bali thundered pointing his hand towards Surajbhan.

Surajbhan, the firebrand, jumped up ready to draw his sword.

"How dare you show your sword against us?" Bali said furiously.

"What can you expect from someone who grabbed power by killing his own king? He knows only the language of the sword," Ugrasena said in a scornful tone. His eyes conveyed disgust.

Bali chortled.

"If you have any problem, let us settle it here, once and for all," Surajbhan challenged breathing heavily.

"One day we will," Ugrasena retorted.

Srivijay stepped in and called them to order, his voice strong with authority.

Surajbhan clenched his fists until his fingernails dug deep into his palm. The pain did little to taper off his frustration, but he sat down.

"We are here to work out issues peacefully, not to fight among ourselves. Let us respect the rules we made," Srivijay said in a calming manner. He knew he was a respected King even at his young age due to his vansha. Except for his navy, he commanded the most powerful kingdom on Bhuvar-Lok. "We need each other. Maintaining peace is our duty. I propose a compromise."

All heads turned towards Srivijay. They waited in silence. Salmala and Saka kingdoms controlled the sea, and had a strong navy. Srivijay's kingdom, Jambu, was practically landlocked. He needed these two kingdoms. The other kingdoms did not have deep pockets to shell out more money. He remembered the words of his late father – *Peace is our natural state, war may appear to do good, but the good is only temporary; the evil it does is permanent.* War was not an option.

Srivijay spoke in a firm voice, "King Bali and King Ugrasena, on trade with Jambu-Rajya, I will pay you twenty-five percent more for the transportation costs for spices and agricultural products, but not for other products. In return you must drop your demands from other kingdoms. I think it is more than a fair deal."

Bali and Ugrasena were surprised by the offer. The kingdom of Jambu was the most populated and trade with it was nearly seventy percent of their trade value. They were getting a lot more than they had anticipated.

Their eyes glistened dark green in greed. They signalled their acceptance to each other.

Looking at their signal, Srivijay thought he had given away more than he should have. But there was no turning back now.

"Fine," Bali said controlling his happiness. Ugrasena nodded with a crooked smile.

The compromise was sealed.

Srivijay knew that he couldn't sell this deal to the farmers and traders of his kingdom; he would need to cut the taxes which meant cutting down his own share of the wealth.

By being magnanimous, the other kingdoms owed Jambu-Rajya. Srivijay had something in mind. *Now it would be easy to get their nod.* The deal was a calculated move by him.

The peace deal was struck but no one knew how long it would last! Greed is a demon with a big mouth that is always hungry.

✦

6

Maitra (Friendly)

A shimmering dawn broke through the purple clouds when the royal contingent left Kailash-Rajya.

The countryside was warm, peaceful and gloriously beautiful. The lush green fields were blanketed in soft waving grass, punctuated by tiny frills of yellow, pink and purple blossoms. The intoxicating breeze and enchanting fragrance spreading out from the freshly ploughed fields added to the seductive charm of the atmosphere.

To their left, at a distance, the small hills were covered by a grove of stately swaying trees. The beautiful fir trees with their long leafy branches undulated softly in the gentle gusts of cool air that wafted through them. Padmini had only seen such scenery in her dreams. The soothing warmth of nature's beauty dissolved into her and made her both drowsy and energized.

They reached Himalia kingdom by dusk.

The royal carriage was escorted from the city gates to the fort by Jayanto, the Lok-Rakshak of Himalia-Rajya.

Padmini took in the view of the fort standing on a huge steep cliff. "This is impressive."

"Yes, it is. Even though it is built for defence, its grandeur is breath-taking. The fort is constructed of stone, lead, and wood, five hundred meters above sea level. Strategically, its location is a big advantage for the Himalians as they can see their enemies coming up the hill. The only main pathway to the fort passes through a network of narrow stairs to the huge door. The fort has conical tops and thirty-six rooms spread across two levels in the main tower," Dhananjay explained.

"Is it true that Himalia is ruled by a lady and she is not married?" Padmini asked. She knew women were allowed in the army, and many brave women fighters participated in battles. A woman as a Queen, without a King, was unheard of, for her! This was not possible at Shivalik-Rajya, she thought.

"Yes, Himalians are unique. It is presently ruled by Queen Maitreyi. The kingdom has broken barriers in many aspects. It has seen even an adopted son become King. They don't believe in bloodlines unlike the rigid rules we have."

Padmini was impressed. The only reason Vishamadeva was Lok-Sevak and not a King was because he was an adopted son. It was unfortunate that such traditions were not followed at Shivalik. Vishamadeva deserved to be a King.

"To which vansha does Queen Maitreyi belong?" she asked.

"I don't know. They don't follow vansha system anymore. They elect a King or Queen based on talent, not bloodlines. Would you believe that?!"

She cleared her throat and replied, "It sounds interesting. A bit idealistic but it can work."

He replied, his tone shrill and high-pitched, "Such idealism doesn't work in the real world. No one cares about talent. Vansha gets you immediate respect; getting the same from talent may take a lifetime. It is just the way we are. Vansha system gives stability. Talent will only lead to chaos in the long-term."

Padmini nodded without lending any credence or acceptance to what Dhananjay was conveying. She understood her husband became King despite his disability only due to his vansha. Even the Lok-Rakshak's selection rules were bent for this vansha system.

Dhananjay continued, "You won't believe it but even Mother Vaidehi was an adopted daughter."

"Vaidehi, the wife of King Satyavrat?" she asked.

"Yes. Himalia was the birthplace of Queen Vaidehi and later she married King Satyavrat. She designed this fort. It is because of these bonds we have the best relations with Himalians. It may be the smallest kingdom on Siddha-Lok, but it is known for its brave and skilled warriors. You will see that Himalians don't believe in lavish lifestyles or big palaces. They live in harmony with nature."

Their carriage reached the entrance of the fort. As they stepped out, they could immediately feel the warmth of the air change. The warmth felt good and inviting.

Maitreyi welcomed the guests at the entrance to the fort. She was dressed in a simple green silk saree, with very little jewellery. Her big kohl-rimmed eyes, high cheekbones, and pearly white teeth made her look statuesque and awe-inspiring even in her modest attire. Her crown was set with many colourful pearls and stones.

No beating drums and flower showers greeted the guests during the welcome. Only a small chandan tilak was put on the forehead of the visitors.

"Welcome O Great Dhruvanshi, the descendants of King Satyavrat and Queen Vaidehi to our heavenly abode. The kingdom of Himalia is proud to welcome Maharaja Dhananjay and Maharani Padmini," Maitreyi spoke firmly, with pride.

Dhananjay replied with affection and in a soulful tone, "It is a great privilege for us to visit the birthplace of Mother Vaidehi. Shivalik-Rajya is truly blessed that she was married to King Satyavrat."

Maitreyi gave a smile and turned to the Queen. "I hope the journey was peaceful, Maharani Padmini."

"Yes, no trouble at all," she replied.

Maitreyi touched the feet of Vishamadeva. His reputation was second to God and he was respected like one.

"Before we go inside let us take blessings of Lord Shiva from the temple," Maitreyi requested her guests.

Dhananjay inched towards the temple. His gaze fell on the statue of Lord Shiva and Goddess Parvati under a tree. Confused, he asked "Why is the statue outside the temple?"

Maitreyi explained, "There is a small tale behind it. The statue was carved out of the rock from the Grand Shiva temple at Shivalik. The temple was not complete, so the statue was placed under a nearby tree. When the construction of the temple was completed, the statue was installed inside. But the then King had a terrible accident. There were heavy rains and floods. It was taken as a bad omen that the Lord was not happy."

Padmini listened attentively and covered her mouth in shock.

"We went to the Saptarishis and consulted them. They told us to move the statue to where it was initially kept. Lord Shiva doesn't like to be moved once he takes his place. And since then Lord has been worshipped here."

"Is the temple without God?" asked Padmini curiously.

"Temples can never be left empty," Vishamadeva smiled as he said those words.

"Then who took the place of Lord Shiva?" As a Shiva devotee herself, Padmini was engrossed in the fable.

Maitreyi replied, "We also asked the Saptarishis the same question. They told us that no one could take Lord Shiva's place except his own sons. A father can never get jealous or offended of his own child. Lord Ganesha and Kartikeya are the gods in the temple."

They prayed at the temple and went inside the palace.

There was no mention of the prophecy by Himalians. They did not know if the prophecy had not yet reached the ears of Queen Maitreyi or if she was merely indifferent to it. Himalians did not believe in prophecies or bloodlines. Merit superseded everything else. Anyone could aspire to become the King or Queen here, unlike Shivalik which was tangled in the web of orthodoxy, in the name of traditions.

No trade talks were held with Himalians. The small state had learned to be self-reliant and it did not trade with outside kingdoms. It had a huge lake – Brahma Sarovar – at its borders which sustained agriculture.

Surrounded by natural beauty, they called the small mountains around it as Sahya Parvatam – the benevolent mountains. It had gorgeous views of the ghats with lush green forests, serene lakes and waterfalls plunging down. There was a hill visible from the fort, with a rock formation that resembled an elephant.

Padmini had a peaceful time there. She loved the cool breeze caressing her face and the wind blowing through her hair. She wished they could have stayed for a few more days, but the one-day visit to Himalia was only a courtesy, keeping in view its size and influence in the region.

She had almost forgotten about the events of the past few days. But like everything else, happiness never lasts.

◆

7

Agnipath (The Path of Fire)

ANGAARA

A ngaara – remote, rugged, inhospitable! A secluded island in Dhruva-Lok, where the wilderness was enchanting and the temperatures soared to the highest levels possible, despite intermittent rainfall throughout the year.

The island had the densest of all jungles. The jungles had grown here for nearly 130 million years, making them the oldest on Dhruva-Lok. Left in isolation, the island housed more than one million unique species of animals, birds, insects and plants, which could be found nowhere else! Its turbulent geographical past shaped this vast island into a dramatic landscape of mountains and valleys. Every corner of the island had its own distinctive geography. The north-west corner had a sweltering hot desert Kantaraya whereas the north-east part witnessed tremendous volcanic activity. The central highlands divided the island into different climatic regions. The grassy plains dominated the western landscape with stony massifs, deciduous forest, and baobab trees, while the south and the east were characterized by dense evergreen forest. The west was known for its pungent smell of leaves rotting on the jungle floor and the crash of stubborn rhinoceros covered in mud, while the east was known for its colourful parrots, leaping lemurs, unsettling crocodile heads floating in rivers with the mingled scents of moisture, soil, creepers and decaying plants giving out the smell of life!

A loud thunderous sound shook the island of Angaara. It was not lightning, something much scarier and more devastating. Fresh lava and volcanic gases erupted from, as the locals call it – Agniparvat – an active volcano towards the north-eastern side – the only one on the entire Dhruva-Lok. Agniparvat belched again today and the river of fire flowed smothering everything that came in its path. The landmass got its name due to this volcano which caused forests to burn like *angaara* (coal).

Fire was revered on this island – a dominant, unparalleled power. In the night, Agniparvat looked nothing less than a mighty god. Many dangerous animals and tribes lived in the evergreen forests surrounding it. Dreaded animals feared the fire and normally stayed away from the Agniparvat.

Tribals lived close to the Agniparvat to stay away from dangerous animals, but they had to be continuously on the move to avoid the river of fire. A multitude of ethnic tribes, groups, classes, and physical types abounded on this island. The tribes were among the oldest on Dhruva-Lok. They spoke diverse languages and dialects. There was no concept of kingdom or King in this part of the planet, only tribal lords. Compared to Siddha-Lok or even Bhuvar-Lok, the tribes were unorganized and continuous infighting left them weak, though they were much better fighters owing to their superior physique. It was believed that the asura powers had blessed the inhabitants of Angaara – making them physically sturdy. Their skin was thicker, and it was more fire-resistant than the skin of outsiders. In fact, their skin had an olive green undertone. Agniparvat emitted a radiation which brought out this aberration in their bodies. They had pointed ears and comet-styled eyebrows as distinctive features.

No outsider could defeat them on this island. This remained true until Satyavrat The Conqueror arrived here.

"Where are we going, *pitaji* (father)?" a four-year-old Vritra asked his father. The boy had a medium complexion with shoulder-length brown-black hair tied tightly behind his neck. He had a visibly long neck, thick eyebrows and enigmatic wide eyes.

Tvashta replied, "To the ashram of Guru Shukracharya." His build was slight but muscular. Stubble on his long face looked very attractive. His hair was short, making his high forehead look bright and lustrous. A white loincloth covered his waist and legs. A loose-fitting, v-shaped pullover shirt with embroidered neck and sleeve lines covered his upper half. He wore a black thread with seashells around his neck. His earlobes were pierced with long brass earrings that dangled as he spoke.

They were sitting inside their hut on a thin jute carpet. The hut was a rectangular wooden structure made of bamboo with gable roofs, a single entrance and windows on the longer sides. Inside, it had a single room which was divided into a small kitchen and a sleeping area. There were two wooden boxes kept in the sleeping area for storage. The hut was in a small settlement of the surviving Shikavan tribe on the western side of Angaara, where jungles were not so dense.

"Who is Guru Shukracharya?"

"Guru Shukracharya belongs to the oldest tribe of Angaara – the revered Bhrigu tribe. His ancestors learned yogic and astra-shastra vidya from powerful sages on Siddha-Lok. They brought this knowledge to our island and established gurukul here. After the Great War of Paulastya with Satyavrat, there was chaos and the gurukul tradition got lost. We started praying to Asuras as they are the possessor of powers. This was until Guru Shukracharya emerged and restarted gurukul. He is the most skilled of them all; he has surpassed his ancestors. He is called a *brahma-gyani*, a knower of everything. But now he is retired."

"If he is retired, why are we going then?"

"Hoping he will come out of retirement. A worthy student can always make a teacher reconsider."

"Where does he live?"

"He is very mysterious and lives deep inside the uncharted jungle towards the south-west. It will take two to three days to reach there."

"So far! I don't want to go anywhere. I want to be with you." Vritra gave a petulant look.

Tvashta replied in a reassuring tone, "Vritra, mere strength is not enough to defeat Raakh. Real skills lie in knowing how to use your strength! With the right techniques, your strength will become manifold. Only then, we can get back our land and avenge the death of your brother. You can be more powerful than Paulastya."

"Who is Paulastya? You mentioned his name earlier."

"He was once the Supreme Lord of Angaara – the only one who earned this title and dared to walk on *Agnipath*. He was trained by the ancestors of Guru Shukracharya. Paulastya did what no one could imagine. He was able to unite many tribes and raise a strong army. His military skills were unparalleled and his army was ruthless. He wiped out a few tribes from Angaara who refused to follow him. His legends were not forgotten the way history treats the defeated."

"He lost? How?"

"He was the only tribal lord who crossed the mighty Tethys Sea to attack and occupy kingdoms in Bhuvar-Lok. He succeeded to some extent. He nearly became the most powerful King before he locked horns with King Satyavrat from Siddha-Lok. It was a war worth remembering."

"Why did he lock horns with Satyavrat?"

"Paulastya believed that Vaidehi, wife of Satyavrat, was his daughter who was lost when she was an infant and he abducted her. This made Satyavrat and Paulastya battle it out in an awful war."

"Was she really his daughter?"

"He thought so. The bonds of blood are the ones that no power, not even time, can break. It makes us blind."

"Tell me more father: why did he lose?"

"Facing imminent defeat in the war, Paulastya refused to make peace due to his arrogance – the chief cause for his demise. The best fighters from Angaara island died in that dreadful war. The defeat was so bad that it ended the unity of tribes in Angaara. It left such a void that it couldn't be filled in centuries."

Tvashta placed his hand on Vritra's shoulder. "You have to become greater than him. You have to get back our lands and avenge the death of your brother Vishvarupa."

"Who took our lands?" Vritra was listening attentively. This was the first time he was hearing stories about their past.

Tvashta, with a faraway expression on his sad face, told his tale, "We belong to the Shikavan tribe; the dominant tribe on Angaara. This was until five years ago when Raakh from Asrasya tribe, taking assistance from Jambu-Rajya of Bhuvar-Lok, attacked and overthrew us. They killed your brother in a shameful manner. Many of our tribesmen lost their lives and we have been living in exile since then." His voice became heavy. He could still hear the screams and shrieks from that horrific night. Writhing in pain, he closed his eyes and ears. It was like someone was pricking him with pins and needles over his entire body. He exhaled heavily and opened bright red eyes – the fire of vendetta was still raging inside him.

He continued, "I performed a rare ritualistic sacrifice of ten elephants to please *Vritrasura*, the most powerful Asura warrior, to avenge the brutal murder of your brother Vishvarupa. From the sacrificial fire *Dakshinagni*, a terrific being emerged. The creature was dark and terrifying with immense energy and power. Agniparvat exploded at that moment and strong winds uprooted the trees. He was none other than the all-consuming form of Death appearing at the time of total destruction – the *Pralaya*. It was as if the sky would fall. He blessed your mother. A year later, your mother gave birth to you. You are no ordinary child. You are born with the combined strength of ten elephants."

Vritra realized the reason why he had outgrown others of his age very quickly. Even at the age of four years, his muscle power was unmatched, and he had defeated boys much bigger than him with his raw strength. Many called him *Vichitra* (strange).

"Now you understand why you need to go and train under a Guru," Tvashta said.

"I am getting training here. Everyone says you are the best teacher here in yogic *vidyas*. You have taught me meditation and many powerful mantras. I am also getting weapons training from teacher Prachanda. I won't leave you."

"Son, what you are getting here is very basic training. The schooling system we have, especially in weapons, is rudimentary. Our best fighters and teachers died when we were uprooted. Guru Shukracharya is the best teacher known. No one can match him in skills. He is the one who taught your brother. He can teach you the ultimate *astra-shastra* (the knowledge of weapons) and *yuddha vidya*... and much more powerful mantras. All of which will make you invincible."

"But as you say I have the strength of ten elephants. I am already invincible; I can defeat anyone." The child was adamant; he needed more convincing.

"No, son. Strength makes you powerful but not invincible. It's the right technique and strategy that will make you the best warrior known. Don't underestimate your enemies."

Tvashta took him out of the hut. Pointing towards a huge rock, he said, "Try to push this rock."

Vritra went and applied his full strength, but the rock was too big to budge. After a while he gave up.

Tvashta now tied two big ropes around it and told Vritra, "Now pull instead of pushing it."

Vritra was sure it wouldn't make any difference. Yet, he obeyed his father. To his surprise, the rock moved a few inches with ease.

"You see pulling is far easier than pushing. More than strength, the right technique is more important. That is why you need a Guru to teach you how to harness your power. You have been gifted with immense power, but it needs to be channelled correctly."

Now, Vritra had no reason to object.

His mother Dana was a tall, lean woman dressed in the traditional outfit of Angaara women. Her dress had three parts – a black tube cotton skirt with one seam, a loose long-sleeved waist-length cotton blouse with no buttons and a long piece of silk about a foot wide draped diagonally around the bosom through one shoulder. The blouse was red while the skirt was black with embroidered borders and had significant amount of beadwork and silver coins. Her long, black hair, silky-soft and heavy was pinned up in a bun and adorned with a *champa* flower. She had put on a silver nose pin with septum piercing, earrings and a necklace.

She finished packing the bags and came out of the hut. Tvashta took the bags from her. Dana kissed Vritra on his forehead. "You are destined for greatness. When you return, there won't be anyone equal to you in this whole world. Everyone will be at your feet."

"I will miss you, *maa*."

She suppressed her emotions and said, "We will wait for you to return."

"Please come with us."

"No, son. I have to stay here." It would be harder to see him off and come back alone.

Vritra touched her feet. She gently moved her hands over his hair and uttered: "Angaara is our birthplace. Agnipath, we shall tread."

With these words, Vritra started his walk on Agnipath – the Path of Fire – to fulfil the purpose for which he was brought into this world.

✦

8

Shivalik (Tresses of Shiva)

SIDDHA - LOK

It was cloudy with a hint of moisture in the air.

"How much more time?" Dhananjay asked Karthik through the front window of the carriage.

"Maharaja, we shall reach the city gates shortly," Karthik informed.

"That is earlier than I had expected."

"Yes, Maharaja. The road has been repaired by Raja Samvaran of Chumbak-Pradesh after they heard that Your Highness will be using it."

Dhananjay closed the window and sat back in his seat.

Padmini said, "Raja Samvaran is the one who gifted us the golden Lord Ganesha idol at the wedding."

"Yes, he is the one. He administers Chumbak-Pradesh – the second biggest pradesh in Shivalik."

"Then shouldn't we visit him?"

"Yes, we will visit them when we tour our one hundred pradesh over the next year. And we need to visit Pampa-Pradesh first, as it is the biggest."

"Aren't one hundred sub-divisions too much?"

"The idea is to keep them divided so that chances of anyone conspiring or rebelling against us are minimal. Moreover, the Lok-Rakshak appoints the Pradesh-Rakshaks at these pradesh. They serve as our eyes and ears in these pradesh. They can be removed or changed any time we want."

"I heard that the Pradesh-Rakshaks are shuffled once every two years as well?"

"Yes, it was Jyeshta Pitashri's idea. He said something. Umm… What was it? Let me remember… Stagnant waters stink!"

"He is really a blessing for Shivalik-Rajya. We owe him for everything," she said in a heartfelt tone.

"Yes, he thinks only about the welfare of the kingdom and nothing else. That is his oath. And I know he will never break it. He serves as the Lok-Sevak but handles everything. Shivalik is safe in his hands."

Padmini had always heard praise and admiration for Vishamadeva. He was a living legend. Curiously, she asked, "Are you sure he has the best interests of Shivalik at heart? He must hold a grudge for serving as the Lok-Sevak when he could have become the King himself."

"It was entirely his decision. Why will he hold any grudge?" Dhananjay dismissed it immediately.

"Making a decision is easy, but to live with it every day could hurt."

"He has made sacrifices which none of us can even imagine. That is why he is called Vishamadeva – a terrible god – for taking oaths beyond the realms of imagination. He is a blessing – a role model for all of us. He never hesitates to say what he feels in the interests of the kingdom. After that, whatever I decide, he obeys without question."

"As if you will ever go against his decision!" Padmini gave a small laugh.

"Is that so? You won't believe it, but he advised me not to marry you."

"What!" She swallowed a lump. "Why? Does he not like me?"

"Don't take him wrong. To him, marriages are for forging and strengthening political alliances. It has never happened at Shivalik that a Dhruvanshi has not married a Princess. So, he wanted me to marry the daughter of Raja Nimi of Pampa-Pradesh – the largest pradesh."

He read her worried face, so he continued, "But I took a stand. And after that he supported me."

She breathed easier. "Was *Jyeshta Matashri* (elder mother) also against our marriage?"

"No, she was the one who supported me throughout. I still remember her words: These divisions of class or vansha, are artificial boundaries created by us. The universe came into existence out of love and for love alone. True love is higher than the heavens, stronger than any weapon known, and mightier than any law of nature. It is the only thing that unites two souls. No one should come in the path of love."

"Nice thought! She has been very helpful to me in getting used to a Queen's ways."

"I was very young when my father, mother and younger sister left me in that terrible accident. It was Jyeshta Matashri who raised me like her own son and Jyeshta Pitashri ensured that the kingdom stayed together. He is the one who made me King even after this." He punched his crippled right arm – his daily reminder of that accident. The memory of the accident shook him for a second.

"We are blessed that we have such elders to guide us," she said. "Raja Nimi must have felt very bad for being turned down. I hope he is not carrying any bitterness."

"Jyeshta Pitashri himself went and explained it to him. I think he is at peace now after his daughter's marriage was fixed with the handsome son of Raja Samvaran. Jyeshta Pitashri played a key role in arranging that marriage."

"But still, it can't be enough. How powerful are these pradesh? Do they maintain an army of their own?"

"Yes, they are allowed to have an army. But they have to contribute double the number of soldiers to the army stationed at the capital, with us. Jyeshta Pitashri has already thought of this."

"What if they keep all the good fighters with them and send us the others?"

"To keep this under check, the Pradesh-Rakshaks are there and even they are routinely shuffled. Everything has been thought of."

A knock on the window interrupted their conversation. Dhananjay opened it. "Maharaja, we have reached the city gates," Karthik informed the King.

The city was sophisticated and technologically advanced, and it spread across an area of one thousand acres. It housed nearly one lakh people which comprised nearly twenty-five thousand soldiers. The city was known for its planning – two or three-storey brick houses, wide access roads, elaborate drainage and water supply systems, clusters of large non-residential buildings and the Palace in the centre. The city was fortified with brick walls shaped like a defensive crescent. The external boundary walls were made of smooth stone to hinder climbing. River Jhanavi flowed through the heart of the city. There were five entry gates to the city and sixteen watch towers.

"Thank you, Karthik. We will go to the palace directly."

Padmini hesitated for a brief moment. "I want to go to the Grand Shiva Temple first," she blurted.

"It's late in the evening. We all are very tired. Let us go to the temple tomorrow." Dhananjay tried to change her mind.

As the daughter of the head priest at the temple, Padmini had spent a large part of her life there. Whenever her mind wavered, she went there. She needed to talk to Lord Shiva. She couldn't have spoken to anyone else. Padmini insisted, "Please, Maharaja. Others need not come with us, but I need to go."

"Alright." Dhananjay relented without much argument. He turned to Karthik and ordered, "Take our carriage to the Shiva Temple. Others can directly go to the palace."

"Yes, Maharaja."

The temple was on the banks of River Jhanavi. The river rose from Sumeru and drained into Brahma Sarovar in the east.

After reaching the temple, Karthik along with five of his soldiers went inside to prepare for the arrival of the King and the Queen. They cleared the place of visitors.

Karthik's son Hetan stayed beside him while the other soldiers surveyed the temple premises. There was a sweet scent of chandan lingering in the air.

Awestruck at the sight, Hetan asked, "Father, who constructed this temple?"

"The temple was constructed after the legendary King Satyavrat The Conqueror – the 49th Dhruvanshi – received Lord Shiva's Trishul. He was an ardent Shiva devotee."

It was a megalith temple carved out of one single rock, undoubtedly the most remarkable and astonishing structure on Dhruva-Lok because of its size, architecture and sculptural accomplishment. The temple was built by digging out from the sloping basalt hill two massive trenches, joined with a connecting trench. This resulted in a high structure that appeared to come out of the ground.

The temple had a three-storey tower with an octagonal dome and two huge free-standing columns flanking the mandapa entrance hall which had sixteen columns set in groups of four. Most of the deities to the left of the entrance were of Lord Shiva while on the right side the deities were related to Lord Vishnu.

"He must have spent a lot in building it," Hetan uttered.

"He must have. But mark my words – Satyavrat The Conqueror did not build this structure to show-off his wealth. He wasn't that sort."

"Then why?" Hetan wondered.

"It is a common belief that a saint was not offered food by the residents of Shivalik-Rajya. Angered, he cursed that a famine would fall upon the region. Shivalik saw a serious drought which lasted for more than three years. To save the people, Satyavrat decided to provide much needed employment to thousands of people during the famine. He nearly emptied his treasury and food stock to save his *praja* (citizens)."

"Is that the truth or a made-up story in the glory of the Dhruvanshis?"

"What are you saying? Why will they make up such a story?" Karthik was horrified at his son's tone.

"To glorify their vansha. Look now the same Dhruvanshis have appointed a crippled Maharaja. They have changed the rulebook to suit themselves."

"Shut up! Don't ever utter such words. If you want to rise, you better fall in line and start controlling your blabbing mouth."

"But father I was just…"

"Enough! With much hard work, I have risen to become an Utkrisht. What will happen if anyone hears your nonsense?"

Hetan swallowed his words.

They moved to the entrance hall where Nandi was sitting on the porch in front of the central temple staring in the direction of the inner sanctuary as is traditional in Shiva temples.

"Father, why is Nandi made to sit outside in the open without any roof? That's so unfair," Hetan said.

Karthik remembered the words of Rajguru Kashyap, and he answered, "Nandi is a symbol of eternal wait. One who sits and waits without any desires is naturally meditative. Nandi does not expect Lord to come out today or tomorrow. He just waits. Before one enters the temple, the devotee must have this quality of Nandi."

Hetan pointed to the right side of the entrance hall. "Are these the ten avatars of Lord Vishnu?"

"Yes. I have heard from Rajguru Kashyap that the order of ten avatars of Lord Vishnu represents the stages of humankind evolution." Karthik pointed to each statue in turn and explained, "*Matsya* – the Aquatic animal at the start of life; *Kurma* – Amphibian who could stay in both land and sea; *Varaha* – the Mammal who lived on land; *Narasimha* – Half-human, half-animal; *Vamana* – the Dwarf Man; *Parashurama* – the Early Human with an axe; *Rama* – the Noble King and the Conqueror; *Krishna* – the Teacher; *Buddha* – the Enlightened One and the Liberator; and *Kalki* – the Machine-man and the Destroyer of darkness."

"Interesting perspective."

"King Satyavrat The Conqueror is said to be the Ramavatar of Lord Vishnu, though Satyavrat never acknowledged it in his lifetime. Well, to be fair, no one had asked him or imagined it during his reign, but there were many resemblances with the story," Karthik added.

"What about the deviations, father? Looks like another glorification attempt by the Dhruvanshis."

"To you the glass will always be half-empty! Why are you such a cynic?" Karthik shook his head in disappointment.

Karthik and Hetan stood at attention when Maharani Padmini entered the temple. Karthik whispered, "Hetan, keep your mouth shut. In peacetime, perception is everything."

Padmini had a harried look on her face. Her eyes remained blue in nervousness as she entered the temple.

After the worrying prophecy, she needed guidance from Lord Shiva. She was a staunch Shiva devotee. In her haste, she didn't take blessings of Nandi.

Dhananjay followed her into the temple.

When Padmini was fifteen years old, she had saved the powerful Sage Angiras from a deadly snake bite and had been granted a boon in return. She wished to be the mother of the Wielder of the Trishul. Sage Angiras blessed her and granted her wish but warned her that it would lose its effect if she did not keep it a secret. From that day, she prayed to Lord Shiva for the wish to come true.

She now knew that her wish would be fulfilled. But she wanted her offspring to be a saviour, not a destroyer. Today she realized what her father meant when he had told her to be extremely careful with what one wishes for, because it might come true in ways one cannot imagine.

She went to the central shrine housing the lingam and prayed fervently in her heart, "Respected Lord! Bless me. I want to be the mother of a saviour, not a destroyer. Punish me but not my child or the kingdom. I want my child to be the Wielder of the Trishul but I never wished for this."

She closed her eyes and intoned the sacred mantra – *Om Namah Shivaay.*

Dhananjay placed his hands on her shoulders. "Don't worry. It will all be fine. He will be a Dhruvanshi, a descendant of Satyavrat. Lord Vishnu had promised Dhruva that he will come whenever the time comes. I am sure our son will be born in Dhruva Nakshatra and make us proud."

There was doubt, hence, there was fear. Padmini embraced him to calm her trembling thoughts. "I feel scared."

Looking at the statue of Lord Shiva, he said, "The city is the tresses of Lord Shiva. He will protect it and destroy all evil in its path. Remember how he came as Lord Bajrang, the *sankat mochan*, and removed all the obstacles from the life of King Satyavrat."

It was a common belief that Mahabali Bajrang was an avatar of Lord Shiva.

Damping his own apprehensions, he tried to calm her. "The Wielder of the Trishul can be no ordinary one. Only a worthy one can lift it. The Gods must have some plan. We need to stay strong and keep faith."

Padmini blinked back her tears at his effort to lighten the mood. Dhananjay said, "Just imagine our joy if the child is born in Dhruva Nakshatra. And we don't know. It's just a prophecy. Who knows, it may not even come true."

That thought brought a small sign of relief to Padmini's face. *It's just a prophecy!*

Dhananjay had succeeded in consoling his wife for now but in his heart, he knew that any prophecy from the Saptarishis had always come true. It couldn't be ignored or taken lightly. Something needed to be done, but not today. That day was still far away.

He muttered, "Let's go back to the palace."

Padmini prayed one last time. *Bholeshankar! Please send someone as Lord Bajrang to stay with my son. If the Lord is on his side, there is nothing to worry about. Please remove all the evils from his path.*

Om Namah Shivaay.

She hoped for one more boon at that moment. If only, she had one! Were the Gods going to listen?

◆

9

Vidyā (Knowledge)

Dusk settled in, turning the sky into a deep blue. The four moons rose, bathing the landscape in silvery moonlight. Tvashta and Vritra lay on the ground resting after the day's travel. It was quiet and peaceful, everything Vritra wasn't at that moment. He recalled his father's words from the morning. The things he had never heard. The things he did not know. "Pitaji, who taught Guru Shukracharya?" Vritra asked.

"He received training under the Saptarishis. Some say he became even more powerful than them. They wanted him to stay but he chose to return to Angaara and continue the tradition of imparting knowledge to us. We are blessed that he came back here."

Vritra had never heard of the seven sages. "Who are the Saptarishis?"

"They are the revered and most powerful seven sages who live on Sumeru mountains at Siddha-Lok. They are said to be the guiding light there; and Guru Shukracharya is the guiding light here."

"Is Guru Shukracharya very knowledgeable?"

"Knowledgeable? It is said that he even knows the *mritya-sanjeevani vidya*."

"What is mritya-sanjeevani vidya?"

"It is the knowledge to bring back the dead."

Vritra's eyes widened. "That can't be possible, can it?"

"Yes, he has learned this rare vidya from none other than Lord Shiva."

"Lord Shiva." Vritra memorized the name in his mind. Curiously, he asked,

"Does that mean he will never die?"

"I don't know. Let's hope he agrees to teach you."

"What other powers does he have?"

"He knows all kinds of astra-shastra vidya. You won't believe it, but it is said that he can talk to animals and even control them. He is difficult to find, forget meeting him. Even more difficult is to become his *shishya* (student). He hasn't accepted one in years. The shishya has to be equally worthy for him to even consider it."

He can talk with animals, Vritra frowned. As the silence stretched, he asked, "How are we going to find him?"

"Such a powerful Guru has a strong aura. Your father has yogic powers too and I can trace his chakra. We will find him."

"Pitaji, who is Raakh you told me about in the morning?"

Tvashta sucked in a deep breath and his nostrils flared. A vivid memory crept through him; the one he hoped he would never forget. He tightened his fists. He buried his rising anger and answered, "Raakh belongs to a rival tribe Asrasya. Raakh is the best fighter alive. He is nearly seven-foot tall and his skin looks like that of a wild bison. His skin has hardened over the years and has many burn marks from playing *Agni-Maru* – the dangerous challenge game of Angaara to decide the tribal leader. He earned the name *Raakh* due to his unique ability in the game."

"Which unique ability, pitaji?"

"Raakh kills his opponents in a manner that others run scared. He has a reputation that he turns anyone who challenges him into *raakh* (ashes) in *Agni-Maru*. It is Raakh against whom you have to stand up in order to get our land back. Mere power is not going to be enough. You will need to learn yuddha and astra-shastra vidya from the great Shukracharya himself."

"And my brother Vishvarupa, how did he die?"

"Your brother was also a student of Guru Shukracharya. He became a powerful yogi. He was one among the few people who could invoke a *Narayana Kavacha* (Vishnu's Armour) which is an impregnable armour. He wanted peace. He trusted others and that was his mistake. He was betrayed. Scared of his powers, they assassinated him in cold blood." Tvashta's eyes burned and he balled his fists in impotent rage and looked up to the sky as if God was looking down and would tell him what to do. But all he saw was darkness.

"Who assassinated him?" Vritra enquired with a tinge of anger.

"Assassins from Bhuvar-Lok who call themselves as the people blessed by Indra-deva." He burst into floods of tears; he couldn't take it anymore. The stress of the past had been too much.

"Indra-deva," Vritra repeated the name in his mind as he dozed off.

◆

This journey through the mystic evergreen jungles was the first experience for Vritra outside his home. There was anxiety as well as excitement. From grasslands to waterfalls, riverbanks to jungles, mountains to valleys, he saw it all. He was astonished by the magical sunrise at a valley where the mild rays of the sun became sandy golden, then turned to reddish-purple, and again turned blue like a chameleon changing colours rapidly. The illusion was so powerful that he wanted to pause the moment forever.

Deep inside the jungles, the whole atmosphere was different – the air, the smell, the sounds – made him feel a stranger. The variety of trees with their sheer height, huge canopy, and dominance baffled him. He realized that in these jungles, trees were the true Lords who had defeated even the Sun-god. These mighty Lords did not let sun rays reach the ground. He spotted tigers, jaguars, tuskers, rhinoceros, lemurs, wild dogs, and many other species he couldn't recognize. *These jungles are filled with weird and absurd characters.* His oddest experience was when his father showed him a meat-eating pitcher plant swallow a mouse. Vritra was befuddled; it was something beyond his imagination.

The scariest moment for Tvashta was when his son stepped on a magnificent twelve-foot long King Cobra. Its elegant, prideful stance and sharp hiss stunned Vritra. The cobra stared at him. Vritra did not step down but instead gazed right back at him. The cobra waited for Vritra to step away and then turned tail and glided deeper into the jungle. Tvashta was scared but the boy was nonchalant. Tvashta felt his son was exceeding his expectations.

After four days of travel through the dangerous jungles, they finally reached a small ashram. The ashram was in a valley surrounded by three small hills. Tvashta thought that Shukracharya must have chosen this place as it was the union of Trimurti. A hut stood there with a well dug up within a few metres from it. The hut was rectangular in plan, with a barrel-vaulted roof that reached down to the ground. The hut was constructed from bamboo that was fastened with rattan and thatched. Thicker bamboo canes were arched to give the roof its bent shape. Over this frame, thinner bamboo canes were tied in pairs running parallel to each other. Dried grass was used for the thatched exterior. The entry door in the front was small and the back had a small window. The hut was designed to protect the inhabitant from the weather and wild animals.

Tvashta knocked on the door of the hut. There was no response. The door was not latched, so he pushed the door open and peeked inside. No one was inside.

As Tvashta came out, he did not find Vritra. His heartbeat raced up. He moved quickly, looking around. Not able to find his son, he went behind the hut.

His nerves calmed as he saw Vritra behind the hut sitting with folded hands in front of Shukracharya, who was meditating under a tree.

There was something intellectual about the Guru; probably the mop of curly white hair, a long beard, deep chest matted with greying hair, saffron cloth covering his body, a curved, beak-like nose set in a round face, and the high forehead with three horizontal lines of chandan contributed to that impression. The most intriguing part of the face, though, was the black eye-patch that the sage wore over his left eye.

Tvashta also folded his hands and said, "Guruji."

Shukracharya opened his eyes and looked up. His peaceful light green eyes rested on Vritra. The child was an enigma – his eyes, his personality, his aura, everything! The Guru was so captivated that he even stopped blinking.

Vritra was meditating. The boy had the body of a serpent. This was not a normal child. He had been blessed with unmeasurable powers. Shukracharya could see that.

Tvashta introduced, "Guruji, this is my son Vritra."

Shukracharya had not noticed Tvashta till now. He came out of Vritra's spell and his penetrating gaze slowly shifted to Tvashta.

"What brings you here, Tvashta?" Shukracharya asked. His face had a mild and quiet disposition.

"Vritra, my son, is four years old and seeks to become your shishya. He can achieve true greatness if he is guided properly." He added, "He is the brother of Vishvarupa, your former student."

Shukracharya looked at the boy more carefully. "The child has a strong aura of himself. When was he born?"

"He was born four years ago in *Ashvini Nakshatra*. I had performed *Das-Gaj-Bali* (Ten Elephants Sacrifice) ritual to please Vritrasura before his birth."

"He has immense strength. He will do what no one has done before."

Tvashta knew his son was special but these words coming from

Shukracharya meant a lot more. He went down on his knees and bowed his head to be blessed.

"With the right intentions, he can probably wield the Trishul."

Not many knew about the Trishul in Angaara but Tvashta had heard stories. He never believed them. "Does this Trishul really exist, Guruji?"

"Yes, Lord Vishnu received it from Lord Shiva who had given it as a gift to Dhruva-Lok. It is kept at Siddha-Lok. Anyone whom Lord Shiva or Vishnu blesses, will be able to wield it."

"But why will Lord Shiva or Vishnu bless us? We don't even pray to them. We only pray to the Asuras."

"They are the Supreme Gods. All prayers reach them. They bless everyone without any discrimination. They only see devotion of the devotee. A true devotee can get extraordinary powers from them. It does not even matter whether the devotee prays to Deva or Asura." Shukracharya himself was a staunch Lord Shiva devotee.

Shukracharya added, "Dhruva was blessed by Lord Vishnu. He shines above all of us and would not even be touched by the Maha Pralaya. Anyone who treads on Dhruva-pada will achieve greatness."

It was Agnipath in the mind of Tvashta and not Dhruva-pada. "Guruji, will you accept Vritra as your shishya?"

Shukracharya looked at Vritra who was still in deep meditation in the aura of his Guru. In his mind, he already had. *He is the worthy one. He will wield the Trishul.*

The Guru smiled and closed his eyes.

✦

10

Śubhavārtā (Good News)

The day dawned warm and humid in Siddha-Lok. The city officials had gathered in the courtroom for a meeting in which important judicial, administrative, and financial matters were heard by the King and Queen. This happened once every five days.

"The King of Kings, the Conquerors, the One True King of Shivalik-Rajya, Dhruvanshi, Maharaja Dhananjay is arriving. All rise," announced the gatekeeper in a strident voice. There were some whispers in the courtroom as there was no announcement of the Queen's entry along with the King.

Dhananjay entered the courtroom dressed in a navy blue long, fine sherwani with a gold border worn over a kurta. An embroidered golden shawl was draped over his right shoulder with the other end elegantly draped around the opposite arm. The left side of the sherwani had the Shivalik emblem – Dhruva star in the background with Trishul and Om symbol co-joined at the centre. Dhananjay walked through the hall followed by his Anga-Rakshak and the ten elite soldiers forming a protective shield around him. The people assembled in the hall bowed their heads in respect.

The courtroom was a monumental hall with a high ceiling and hammer beam roof. Abundant light filtered through the eastern side of the hall which had plenty of glass windows. A network of stairs led to the two-tier elevated platform on the north side of the hall with a grand throne on the top. The chairs for the Lok-Rakshak and Lok-Sevak were on the right and left of the King on the first level. Anga-Rakshak Karthik stood next to the Lok-Sevak with a sheathed sword and a spear in his hand. He was supported by ten soldiers, five on each side with their weapons. Hetan was one of them.

At the bottom of the platform, there were chairs for other high-ranking ministers like the *Dharmadhikari* (royal priest), *Koshadhyaksh* (treasurer), *Vrajapati* (in-charge of agriculture), *Athapati* (chief judge) and *Bhagadugha* (revenue collector). Most of these officials reported to the Lok-Sevak and Lok-Rakshak. The great hall could accommodate five hundred members.

Dhananjay sat down on his throne, conspicuously alone. Three steps led to the two-seater main seat with a canopy of a golden umbrella. The throne was carved out of fig wood and decorated with ivory plaques. It was decorated with jewellery, gold, precious stones and silver figurines. The four sides of the throne were decorated with the Lion in the North, the Horse in the West, the Bull in the South and the Elephant in the East. The royal seat had cloth covered cushions and pillows studded with precious stones. The hand rests were carved in a half-lion and half-eagle art work. The back of the seat had artwork depicting birds and flowers. At the top of the backrest was a carving of the royal emblem and below it was inscribed the King's Dharma – 'Protect and Serve with Honour'. Above the royal umbrella was a celestial bird called Huma, a swan with an emerald gem on its beak, showering blessings on the royal crown.

Everyone followed the King and were seated.

Dhananjay gestured towards the *dwarapala* (gatekeeper).

The dwarapala came forward and announced the agenda, "There are twelve matters to be heard by the Maharaja today. Out of twelve, eight relate to disputes among the residents, farmers, and traders; three relate to murder trials; the last matter pertains to a corruption complaint in recruitment into the army."

Athapati Brinda, a timid woman in her forties, rose from her seat, bowed to the King and spoke, "Maharaja, the first matter is a dispute between two residents of the city – Mangal, son of Kalavati and Aatmaram, son of Kashiram."

Both Aatmaram and Mangal were escorted by the two soldiers. They walked in with folded hands.

"To which class do you belong?" Dhananjay asked.

Mangal answered, "Maharaja, I am an Utkrisht. I am a landowner and businessman."

Aatmaram replied, "Maharaja, I am a Yukth. I have a sweet shop."

"Hmm... What is the dispute?" Dhananjay asked, looking at Athapati.

Brinda took out a small leather bag used for carrying coins. "Maharaja, they both claim to be the owner of this bag of money."

"Both?" Dhananjay exclaimed.

"Yes, Maharaja. They both are able to tell the contents of the bag."

"Let each of them tell their version. We will start with the Utkrisht."

Mangal stepped forward and recollected the events. "Maharaja, I had placed a big order of twenty boxes of sweets for a function at my house. Yesterday morning I went to his shop to collect the sweets. I took out my money bag and counted the coins for making payment. Before the payment was done, I saw him making jalebis. They looked fresh and delicious, so I decided to eat them first. I put the coins back in the bag and placed it on his counter. After I finished eating, I reached for my bag but he claimed the bag belonged to him."

"If it's your bag, how does he know the contents?" Dhananjay asked.

"He must have seen it when I took out the contents to make the payment," Mangal replied.

"What is your version, Yukth?" Dhananjay asked.

"Maharaja, he came to collect the sweets he had ordered. I gave the sweets and he paid me the money in form of one gold coin. I took out my bag to give him the change. Before I could settle the payment, he asked for some jalebi. So, I kept the money back in the bag, left it on the counter, gave him the jalebis first and waited for him to finish them. After finishing, to my utter shock, he tried to take my money bag saying it was his," Aatmaram narrated.

"Hmm." Dhananjay took a deep breath. "Athapati, is there any witness?"

"Maharaja, they both have Nihsv as employees who were present. But their statements are not reliable as both support the version of their employer."

"Athapati, what is your judgement?"

"Maharaja, in the absence of any witness, it is a question of Mangal's word against Aatmaram's. The money bag is a very common type with no marking. In such a situation, we have to go with the word of the higher class which in this case is an Utkrisht," Brinda replied.

Aatmaram begged, "No, Maharaja. I am not lying."

Brinda added, "Also, the bag had ten gold coins, twelve silver and forty-six brass coins. It is improbable that a Yukth will have so many gold coins."

Aatmaram cried, "Maharaja, that was the money for the upcoming wedding of my son."

Brinda differed, "The rule is that the word of an Utkrisht carries more weight than that of a Yukth. Yukth should be punished with a penalty equal to the contents of the bag and two weeks of imprisonment for lying in front of

Your Highness."

"Punish the poor. That's the law of the Vanshaj," Hetan scoffed, louder than he should have.

Vishamadeva heard it. He asked calmly pointing his hand, "Son, is there something you want to say?"

Karthik shook his head in despair. "Maharaja, he is my son. He is new to the city and does not know the court decorum. I apologize on his behalf."

Vishamadeva spoke, "He is old enough to answer for himself. Step forward and introduce yourself."

Hetan stepped forward, bowed his head and said, "Maharaja, I am Hetan, son of Karthik. I am an archer and currently part of the ten soldiers of the *Suraksha-Kavacha*."

Dhananjay asked, "What do you have to say?"

"Maharaja, I may have a way to tell who the real owner of this bag is!" There were whispers in the courtroom.

Dhananjay said loudly, "Silence." He asked, "How will you do that?"

"I need a big bowl of boiling water," Hetan said in a confident voice.

Both Mangal and Aatmaram wondered if he was going to put their hands in the water. Was he going to torture them?

Admiring the conviction of the young man, Vishamadeva signalled the gatekeeper. He had an idea of what was going to happen.

The gatekeeper rushed out and brought a bowl of boiling water.

Hetan moved and took the bag of money from Brinda and dropped it in the boiling water.

He waited.

Dhananjay furrowed his brows. "What is going on?"

Brinda moved and looked in the water. She saw nothing. She sneered, "Are we waiting for Varuna-deva to appear?" and followed it with a loud laugh.

The laugh was joined by many others in the courtroom.

Hetan said, "Maharaja, I was expecting a layer of oil to appear in the water if the bag belonged to Yukth, who is a sweet shop owner. His hands must touch oil many times in the day which should leave stains on the money bag. However, it hasn't happened. It appears that the bag belongs to the Utkrisht."

Mangal was relieved and he said, "Yes, Maharaja, this proves that I am speaking the truth."

Aatmaram said, "No, Maharaja. It is not my regular bag. I had brought a new bag for the upcoming wedding of my son."

Vishamadeva got up. "The absence of oil does not prove that the bag belongs to the Utkrisht. The result is inconclusive."

"Then how are we going to decide, Lok-Sevak?" Dhananjay asked, confused.

Vishamadeva was prepared with his line of questioning. He went close to Aatmaram and instructed, "Take the Yukth outside and see to it he can't hear anything."

The soldiers obeyed.

Vishamadeva's forceful voice echoed in the hall as he announced, "Utkrisht, narrate what all you did backwards after coming to the shop."

Mangal was nervous as Vishamadeva was looking straight into his eyes. In a shaky voice, he spoke, "I picked up my money bag from the counter... I finished eating jalebis... I asked him to give me fresh jalebis... I made payment for the sweets... I collected the order of sweets I had placed... I took out money for making payment... I reached the shop."

Mangal took a deep sigh when he finished recollecting the events.

Vishamadeva said, "Now, bring the Yukth."

The soldiers did as commanded and Vishamadeva repeated his instructions.

Aatmaram narrated, "I picked up the money bag to give him the change... I waited for him to finish jalebis... I gave him jalebis... I put all the coins back in the bag... I counted the coins in the bag... I took out my bag of coins to pay him the change... I gave him sweet boxes as per his order..."

Vishamadeva turned to Mangal and said, "Utkrisht is lying. In telling the story backwards, Utkrisht narrated the events as they actually happened and forgot to mention about taking out the bag and counting of coins. Whereas, Yukth has told the events correctly and it matches with his earlier narration. Yukth is telling the truth."

Mangal wiped beads of perspiration from his forehead realizing that he had been caught in his own web of lies. His heart thundered.

Dhananjay was delighted. "Excellent." He turned to Athapati and asked, "Athapati, do you concur?"

Brinda pursed her lips hard. She conceded, "Yes, Maharaja."

Mangal fell to his knees and pleaded, "I am sorry, Maharaja. Please forgive me."

Dhananjay looked at Vishamadeva and said, "Lok-Sevak, announce the punishment."

Vishamadeva said, "It is a case of cheating in money matters. Mangal, an Utkrisht, tried to cheat a Yukth, a person lower in class to you. The punishment is double what would have been given to a Yukth. You shall pay him double the amount of money in the bag as penalty and spend four weeks in jail for lying in this courtroom."

Vishamadeva continued to speak sternly, in a warning tone, "Athapati, you carried out no inquiries whatsoever to verify their versions of the story. In the rulebook it is clearly mentioned that the statement of a higher class is to be given higher weightage only when nothing else is possible. It should never be taken as an easy way out and used to cause injustice. Remember that. The mistake should not be repeated in the future."

Brinda swallowed hard on hearing the warning from Vishamadeva. She nodded quietly.

Next, Vishamadeva turned to Hetan and said, "And, you Hetan will be personal assistant to the Lok-Sevak from this day onwards." Clearly, Vishamadeva was impressed with him for his intelligent thinking and courage to stand up for a lower class.

Hetan beamed in delight. He was getting a rare opportunity to work under the one and only Vishamadeva.

Karthik's face lit up in pride.

The matters of the court resumed.

After having heard three matters, Dhananjay felt that it was enough for the day. Whenever he felt tired, he delegated the responsibility to Vishamadeva. The visitors were used to this. In any case, Dhananjay consulted Vishamadeva on every matter. So, this, in fact, made things move faster.

Before he could delegate, Mitasha, Queen Padmini's personal maid hurried into the courtroom and whispered in the gatekeeper's ears. His eyes lit up and he stepped to the Lok-Sevak and passed on the message.

Vishamadeva approached the King's throne. "Maharaja, your presence is requested in the Queen's chamber."

Dhananjay stood up and everyone in the courtroom rose in unison.

He announced before leaving, "Lok-Sevak Vishamadeva will administer the matters in my absence and his decision will be mine."

✦

Dhananjay walked swiftly to the Queen's chamber where he was greeted by Sanjeevani, the *Varishtha Vaidya* (Senior Doctor), *"Pranam, Maharaja."* Greetings, great King. Sanjeevani, a woman in her early thirties, was dressed in a white sari, with an amber border and a matching amber blouse. Fair complexion, aquiline nose and a certain aura on her face marked her personality. She wore no jewellery except a nose pin and earrings. Her demeanor conveyed simplicity and knowledge. Her noble profession made her an Utkrisht.

"Pranam," Dhananjay said with excitement and concern.

"The Maharani is blessed with child."

The words echoed in Dhananjay's ears. He was overjoyed. "Say it again," he said.

"The Maharani is carrying the heir to Shivalik-Rajya," she said, a bit louder this time.

Delighted, Dhananjay pulled his favourite diamond ring from his left middle finger and presented it to the vaidya.

Sanjeevani was not used to taking such gifts. Though young, she was already a senior vaidya. But in that delicate moment, unable to refuse, she accepted it quietly. *"Dhanyavad,* Maharaja." Thank you, great King.

With these words, she bowed and left the Queen's chambers.

Dhananjay dropped a kiss on Padmini's forehead and held her hands tightly. She was resting. She tried to get up, but he stopped her.

He ran his fingers through her hair. "Does it feel any different?"

"A bit of fatigue and a slight dizziness."

"You take complete rest. I am here."

She gripped his hands.

"We will cancel our visits to the different pradesh. When is our heir expected?" he asked.

"Vaidya Sanjeevani was saying around Shivratri next year."

"The Saptarishis were right then."

She tightened her hold in his hands.

"You did not say anything to her, did you?" he asked nervously.

"No, nothing more than she is supposed to know."

"We can't tell anyone. You have to remember that."

"What are we going to do?"

He smiled softly and replied, "The Gods will decide for us."

Her smile stretched wider.

But deep under their smiles, there ran an undercurrent of fear, the fear of the unknown.

✦

11

Vikalpa (Choice)

SIDDHA - LOK

Seven months had gone by since Hetan had started working under the Lok-Sevak as his personal assistant. A modest but prestigious post. Vishamadeva made him read a lot, especially the various laws used to govern the kingdom.

Vishamadeva had a second office next to his personal chambers which was a small, makeshift room; more like a study. A number of books were arranged on shelves covering three walls of the room. There was a tidy table in a corner near a big window giving way to abundant sunlight, which lit up the room during the day. It overlooked the colourful gardens of the palace – the smiles of nature. On the table, to the left, there were many blank scrolls with a quill pen and an inkpot. The seal of Shivalik-Rajya with its emblem and a sand clock were placed on the right side. There were three chairs facing the Lok-Sevak's chair across the table, one of which found Hetan there, reading, on most days.

Today, Hetan was alone in the room reading a book on *Dharmashastra* (legal rules). Vishamadeva had not come.

It was close to dusk. Hetan yawned and closed the book. He got up and stretched when Vishamadeva entered. Hetan fumbled to look attentive and folded his hands in a greeting, "Pranam, Lok-Sevak."

"Pranam." A faint smile creased Vishamadeva's face. He was glad to see his protégé working so late. He asked, "You are here so late?"

"Yes, Lok-Sevak." He pointed to the book and spoke, "I finished Dharmashastra today."

"That's good. You are a fast reader."

Hetan was restless; repeatedly opening and closing his hands. He wanted to ask questions.

Vishamadeva guessed his intent. He asked, "It appears you have some questions?"

Hetan relaxed and said, "Yes, quite a few actually."

"Let's see what they are. I will try to answer whatever I can," Vishamadeva said in a humble tone.

"I was wondering how this class system came into being?"

"Interesting question. Difficult to say precisely but I think we humans are looking for ways to identify ourselves and measure our capabilities. We want to take pride in what we do. If we do good work, we want to be recognized with a title or a reward. This is an inherent need. As we ascend to higher notions of identity, such abstractions emerge on their own. Also, to bring some order in the society, some grouping is required. This led to divisions based on profession and social status, and probably that's how it emerged."

"Who made these rules for defining different classes?"

"They have been there for a long time. It remained unwritten until King Satyavrat codified it. But they have been regularly changed to suit the needs of the society."

Right! The way the rule for selection of the King and Lok-Rakshak were changed, Hetan thought. But he did not give voice to the thought. Instead he asked, "Did King Satyavrat create the concept of different classes?"

"No, it existed before him. But he removed the rigidity and allowed a person to change class based on his or her achievements or qualities. This was met with a lot of opposition, but he did it for the good. He had introduced many such reforms."

"What other reforms?"

"He was the one who came up with the rule of a single partner for both men and women. He also allowed women to work and not remain tied to the class of her husband or parents. This was also met with a lot of resistance. But over the years it was accepted."

"Do you agree with this?"

"Very much. Our society was initially patrilineal, and a woman's fate was tied to her partner or parents. Due to these reforms, women got a chance to have their own class status. Since then, many women have been selected for important posts and the female status in society has gone up. Now our society has started to become ambilineal. If you remember that day in the court Mangal was introduced as the son of Kalavati. But we still have a long way to go. But let's not digress, let's keep our discussion restricted to Dharmashastra. We can discuss these personal laws some other day."

Hetan nodded and asked, "What is the reason for having different rules for different classes?"

"Well, are all classes equal?"

"No."

"Then why should the rules be the same?"

"But for the same crime, why have different punishments for different classes? It is not fair."

Vishamadeva was impressed with the question. Hetan was applying his mind and not merely accepting what was written, which is what most people did. Vishamadeva took some time to answer, focussed on seating himself comfortably in his chair. He answered with a glint in his eyes, "Higher classes are powerful and rich. They can manipulate the judicial system itself. You remember the dispute in the courtroom that day – how an Utkrisht was trying to cheat a Yukth! That day he failed but some other day he may succeed. The system may fail, so giving milder punishment is a way to protect the lower class. Also, higher classes are educated and well-off, so they are not expected to commit crimes or cheat. They are on a higher pedestal, so that is why punishment is also higher for them."

Hetan did not look convinced.

Vishamadeva read the doubts on his face. He asked, "It appears you don't agree with the class system. Do you?"

Hetan hesitated. He pursed his lips. "Uhh."

"Don't worry. Speak freely. It is always good to discuss."

Hetan also sat down. He took some time to answer, "No, I don't agree with the concept of the class system. Please pardon me for saying so."

"Don't apologize. Tell me why you don't agree."

"It is an artificial division of society; makes one person superior to another. When God made us equal, who are we to create such boundaries!"

"Don't talk superficially. Think deeper. Did God really make us equal?"

"Yes, we all have two hands, two legs, two eyes, same blood... isn't it?"

"You are talking of physical attributes. Even here your argument is fallacious. It is said we get physical features of our parents and ancestors, so even physically we all are not the same. Someone is tall, someone is short. Some are very unfortunate. But for the sake of discussion, let's agree that we all are physically equal. Even then are we born socially and economically equal?"

"What do you mean?"

"I mean we are not born in the same economic and social structures. The societal and economic conditions are different across Lok or Rajya or Pradesh or even different villages. Where we are born influences us and makes us different. It is said that our previous lives' karma is the reason why God has made us different with each one having unique capabilities and potential."

Hetan nodded. "I agree that God has made us different. We can't change that. But why is there a need to assign a class? Why further create artificial differences? Can't we do without it?"

"I must tell you that even I used to think like this when I was young. But over the years I have come to realize that some sort of division becomes necessary for administration purposes. It helps in making suitable rules, tax laws and economic policies on the basis of a broad division. It is to serve this purpose alone and nothing else. It can never measure kindness of heart or tell how brave or loyal a person is. Let me try to explain it differently. Do we need the notion of money in our society?"

"Yes."

"Why?"

"Because it helps in the smooth transfer of goods. It also tells us the value of an item."

"But isn't that also an artificial division created by us to put a price for everything, including living beings? We are assigning prices to different items like fruits, meat, fish, swords, jewels, even water, and so on. Isn't it wrong to put a price on a living being like a cow or a goat?"

Hetan scratched his head.

Vishamadeva continued, "Remember that the price is set according to the quality and quantity of the goods. If a fruit is fresh or rare, it is valued more. So, the artificial division made by us is not inherently bad. It is to serve a purpose. The class system also gives a broad value to humans considering their profession or qualities and their financial status, that is, how much tax they are paying. It is based on the same principle. Based on your profession or wealth, you are assigned a class. If one does manual work or is a soldier in the army, he or she is allotted Nihsv class. If one is a small-time trader or shopkeeper or average rank in the army or small agriculturalist, he or she is treated as a Yukth. If you rise based on your talent and become a big landowner or a very senior official in the court or the army, you shall be given Utkrisht class. You can always go up or come down in class based on your actions, qualities and financial status. You don't remain stuck in one class. There is motivation to work hard and rise – an artificial reward."

Very softly, Hetan asked, "What about the Vanshaj? Why are they outside this scope? Why do they follow bloodlines?"

Vishamadeva was taken aback by the question. The look on his face hardened. He answered, with a raised voice, "For stability and loyalty. Only the Kings, Queens and highest-level officials are given a vansha title. You can't make anyone the ruler."

"But why? Himalia-Rajya does not follow the Vanshaj system anymore."

Vishamadeva's fist tightened. "They are trying it. We don't know if they will succeed in the long run. Whereas the Vanshaj system for the ruling class seems to have worked well. There may be ups and downs, but it has worked."

"It has become very rigid. It doesn't allow the best to become the King even among the Vanshaj. It did not allow you to become the Maharaja." Hetan realized what he had just said. The arrow had left the bow.

Vishamadeva's blood boiled and it rushed through his veins, ready to burst. A vein was pulsing at his temple. He responded, "It was my…" when a knock on the door interrupted them.

The door creaked open. A gatekeeper walked in. Vishamadeva swallowed his words. After exchanging greetings, he said, "Maharaja wants to see you urgently."

Vishamadeva looked at the sand clock. *So late. Something is not right.* He got up and walked out without a glance at Hetan.

◆

Dhananjay lay next to Padmini on the bed, trying to find sleep. She was in deep sleep, but he wasn't that lucky. He stared at the ceiling. The seed of doubt in his mind had grown bigger and it troubled him for the past few days. It was eating him up from inside. He had had a long tiring day, but the idea of sleep was absurd to him, one of those notions he knew from the outset was inconceivable. Every muscle, every joint felt weighted down with weariness, and yet he knew closing his eyes would do nothing.

He alternated sides. Unable to find peace, he crept out of the bed and went out to the big balcony overlooking the city.

He looked at the twinkling city, just like the glittering sky. It was a relatively dark night, with only two moons visible in the sky – a crescent moon and a full moon no bigger than a ball. He stared at the night sky speckled with stars and the sky stared back at him in all its vastness, like a ponderous book whose language he did not comprehend. Yet the stars seemed to be strung by an invisible string conveying a secret message to him. The universe speaks in mysterious ways, his inner voice said to him.

A cold breeze was blowing but he didn't feel it. His mind floundered like a helpless man in quicksand. The more he fights, the more ground he loses. Struggling merely expedites the inevitable defeat.

The prophecy of the Saptarishis was playing again and again in his head. And on it went in an unending loop. He closed his eyes and reheard it:

"Nakshatra are aligning in a manner which has never occurred before. It is changing from Dhruva Nakshatra to Ugra Nakshatra around the time of birth. If the child is born in Dhruva Nakshatra, he could become the saviour and bring prosperity to this entire Lok. But if the birth takes place in Ugra Nakshatra, he could be the destroyer."

He opened his eyes. The birth would happen around the time of Shivratri.

What is the will of God?

He felt a headache in his head. He clamped his eyes shut to rebuff the searing headache. It didn't help. He massaged his forehead with his fingers. It definitely didn't help.

His mind was filled with thoughts.

My Dharma is to Protect and Serve. No matter what the cost may be. My ancestors did that even though they had to make impossible choices. King Satyavrat did the unthinkable at great personal cost. This is the legacy of the Dhruvanshis.

I can't stand by and watch. I am a Dhruvanshi, the true King of Shivalik; its protection is my responsibility. I need to rise to the occasion and do what needs to be done.

Among these thoughts, something else the sages had said came to his mind:

Difficult choices lie ahead.

Suddenly, he shivered in the cold breeze. Some difficult decisions needed to be taken. Why else would the Saptarishis say so? He had a sudden realization:

the decision had to be now.

He walked inside and poured himself some wine in his goblet. He swallowed it in one single gulp. Some intoxication was required to muster the courage for what he was about to do.

Setting the goblet down, he hurried out of his chamber towards the small council meeting room followed by his Anga-Rakshak Karthik.

Before he entered the meeting room, he told Karthik, "Ask the Lok-Sevak and Lok-Rakshak to come immediately. I want to see them."

Very rarely did the King speak in such a tone. Bewildered, Karthik stood still looking at the King. *At this hour?* He waited for a few seconds to see if Dhananjay would change his mind. But the King was unmoved, and his eyes were cold. Karthik swiftly moved and instructed the gatekeepers to pass the message along.

In no time both Lok-Sevak Vishamadeva and Lok-Rakshak Simham walked into the room. Vishamadeva was in his usual white dress covered in a shawl. Simham was fully dressed in his leather outfit, which had a distinctive maroon cape reserved for his post. He even carried his sword, unsure of the purpose behind the late-night meeting.

Dhananjay's tense face conveyed the seriousness of the meeting. For a moment they looked at each other but none had a clue about what was going on. Together they said, "Pranam, Maharaja."

"Please take your seats," Dhananjay told them.

When they were seated, Dhananjay spoke, "A difficult choice lies before us."

"What choice, Maharaja?" Vishamadeva frowned.

"You both remember the prophecy of the Saptarishis? The day is getting near," Dhananjay replied.

Vishamadeva did not understand what Dhananjay meant. "But Maharaja, what can we do? We can't change destiny."

Dhananjay responded in a louder voice, "We cannot simply watch in case the child is born after midnight in Ugra Nakshatra. We have to do something."

Shocked, Vishamadeva gave Dhananjay an incredulous look. He shook his head. "Maharaja, I don't know what you mean. I hope it is not what I sense you are implying."

In agreement, Simham also added, "What is meant to happen, will happen

Maharaja, no matter what we do!"

"No, we can change it. The Saptarishis said that difficult choices lie ahead. Don't you remember?" Dhananjay said in an adamant tone.

"Yes, we remember. But what are you suggesting?" Vishamadeva asked.

Dhananjay himself was clueless about what to do. "That is the reason I have called you in the night. No one knows about it. It will remain a secret meeting. Let us put our heads together."

"Maharaja, I can't be a party to this discussion. It is a *maha paap* (grave sin) to even think of such things." Vishamadeva was clear in his mind. He raised himself from his chair.

Before Vishamadeva could stand up, Dhananjay stopped him, "I am the King of Shivalik. Its protection is my responsibility. One who wears the crown, bears it. You have taken the oath of life to serve me unconditionally, and to do as I say. Have you forgotten?"

The words threw him into the cage of his own words. Vishamadeva sat down with a bowed head and both hands on his lap. He was restless, yet his body was still. He closed his eyes and exhaled, swallowing his outrage.

"You think this is easy for me? But as the King I need to do what is best for my praja, for my kingdom. I have to think as a King, not as a father." Dhananjay tried to rationalize his point of view.

We can justify anything in our minds. That doesn't make it right, Vishamadeva said to himself.

Both the Lok-Sevak and Lok-Rakshak shook their heads in disagreement but they did not utter any words. Their hands were tied in this meeting.

After a long silence, Simham suggested, "Maharaja, we can take any decision after the birth, if the need arises. There is a good chance that the child may be born in Dhruva Nakshatra." He was hoping that the King would procrastinate on taking a decision and they would all get a safe, peaceful way out of this problem.

Dhananjay swivelled his head towards Simham. "No. After the birth, I will become a father, and will no longer be a King to my child. I know what I am saying now, I won't be able to say then. I will not be able to convince myself, forget convincing Maharani." Dhananjay's voice got heavy. He swallowed a lump in his throat and his jaw tightened. "If the child is born after midnight in Ugra Nakshatra, I want the child to be taken away and sent back to the Gods."

His eyes were wet and wild as he said this. Unable to look at the heart-wrenching distress on his face, Vishamadeva and Simham turned away from him.

"But what are we going to say to Maharani?" Simham asked.

After a moment of silence charged with emotion and sadness, he said, "I will tell her that the child was stillborn." Dhananjay wiped his tears as he spoke the dreadful words, "I hope the Gods will forgive me!"

They couldn't believe that the Maharaja would go to this extent.

However, what Dhananjay was saying made sense. If any decision had to be taken, it had to be now. After the birth, the situation would be out of control. The genetically coded love for offspring would take over. No one was capable of overcoming that.

"Maharaja, it will be a crime to change destiny." Vishamadeva made one more effort to make Dhananjay reconsider it.

"I disagree, Lok-Sevak. Not doing anything will be a bigger crime. The Dhruvanshis have made such impossible choices in the past. Only a true Dhruvanshi can understand this." The stress was on the word 'true'.

The words pierced Vishamadeva. *What do I know? I am not a true Dhruvanshi*, he grumbled in his mind.

There was a long silence.

Sensing no one was going to say anything, Dhananjay spoke once again, "Lok-Sevak, I want to give this responsibility to you. You do what's best according to your wisdom. I will never ask what you did."

Immediately, Lok-Sevak revolted, "No, Maharaja. I cannot do this." It was a big responsibility, probably too big, even for Vishamadeva.

Dhananjay tried to explain his decision. "You are the only one who can be trusted to make the *choice* – the right choice. We may fail when it comes to doing the unthinkable. Only you can do it. Your oath ties you to do what the King demands. Please agree." The King folded his hand in front of Vishamadeva. It wasn't an order but a desperate request from a helpless King.

"Maharaja is right. No one is better suited for this responsibility." Simham sided with the King this time.

"Shvetaveera! Jhanaviputra! Give me your word." Dhananjay demanded his promise because to Vishamadeva his word meant everything.

Vishamadeva closed his eyes and clenched both fists in despair. A disconcerting wariness swallowed him. Emptiness everywhere. Vishamadeva's chest heaved as he fought his panic. His heart was on fire, like a piece of it had been ripped apart; grabbed and yanked out. The sacrifices he had made, the life he was living, seemed meaningless. It was difficult to describe how Vishamadeva was feeling. He was broken!

Simham felt pity for Vishamadeva. To take a decision about the life and death of a new-born, helpless child and more importantly, live with that kind of action; it wasn't a task cut out for an ordinary person. No person other than Vishamadeva could make such a difficult choice.

He was born to make such choices.

◆

12

Vadhaka (Assassin)

BHUVAR - LOK

Thunder rumbled and lightning flashed in the night sky, but Srivijay was unconcerned. He rode his horse at a rambling pace, enjoying the warmth of the scented jasmine bushes lining the roads into the city. His mind stagnated, thinking about the day. A satisfying day.

The words of his teacher Sridhar-acharya had been his guiding force in agreeing to a trade settlement with the kingdoms of Salmala and Saka. *Respect is earned, honesty is appreciated, trust is gained and loyalty is returned.* He had taken a big risk by cutting down on taxes. It was his first big decision after becoming the Samrat. There was stiff opposition from his group of ministers. He remembered the fiery debate:

"Samrat, if we cut down on taxes, we will need to substantially cut down on army spending. In the next few years, we may have to cut down on recruitment as well. This will weaken our forces and make us vulnerable for attacks. We should have been consulted before agreeing to this!" Raksha Mantri (Defence Minister) Bhalla spoke bluntly.

Srivijay did not appreciate the direct remark. "What is the need to spend so much on the army in peacetime? We haven't seen a war in the last one century."

The reply did not go well with Bhalla. He gave the others a glance and looked away.

"Samrat, our treasury will get depleted in the long run. We don't know what is in store in the future. My duty is to ensure that the treasury should never reduce. Compromising could turn out to be disastrous. Samrat, please reconsider the proposal," Koshadhyaksh responded.

"I have given my word. There is no going back now." Srivijay's tone was

determined.

"Samrat, the decision to help neighbouring kingdoms for nothing in return goes against the duties of a King. We can't afford to be that magnanimous. Our duty should primarily be towards the interests of Jambu-Rajya," Mukhya-Mantri (Chief Minister) reminded.

"Who says we won't be getting anything in return?"

The ministers exchanged blank looks. Was there a secret deal they were not aware of?

"What do you mean, Samrat?" Bhalla asked. He wrinkled his brow.

"Our farmers have been complaining about floods due to change in the course of river Indravati because of excessive rain, or drought which dries up the river," Srivijay said.

No one understood where Samrat was going with this or what he was implying.

Bhalla rubbed his jaw in his trademark style.

Srivijay explained, "We were not able to do anything as these rivers flow into our neighbouring kingdoms and we can't afford to change the flow without getting into a water dispute, which can easily escalate into a war-type crisis. With the gesture of settling the trade dispute with the kingdoms of Salmala and Saka, we can now get them to agree to the construction of a dam on Indravati. They owe us and they know it."

There was silence.

"But how does that compensate our revenue loss, Samrat?" Mukhya-Mantri replied.

"The revenue loss will be temporary. As a Vardhan-vanshi, I am thinking long-term. More than three-quarters of our population depends on agriculture for which the lifeline is Indravati. With the construction of a dam, there will be less loss of crops. It will help us store rainwater as well. Over a period, the increase in production will compensate for the revenue loss. In fact, it may even rise higher than what we have lost today," Srivijay answered.

"Samrat, we are being too optimistic. Are we sure that the other kingdoms will agree?" Koshadhyaksh asked.

"Yes, they will. I am confident. With the blessings of Indra-deva we shall succeed."

And now, he was returning after the inauguration of the dam which was named *Indra-dhanush*. The neighbouring kingdoms of Plaksha, Kraunca and Pushkara agreed to his suggestion and the dam was constructed in record time under his personal supervision. The entourage which had all his important ministers and bodyguards, except the Queen, were behind him. Kaushiki was once again absent, skipping her duty as the Queen.

The farmers were happy. Everyone was singing praises for the Samrat.

He had a proud feeling of coming of age: a true Samrat, not a puppet managed by his own ministers. His face lit up with a high-spirited smile. The eaglet was ready to dive and rule the sky.

Another loud rumble in the sky woke him up from his reverie, he pulled the halter and galloped to the fort.

He had retired for the day when there was a knock on the door.

"Samrat ki jai ho." Hail the King. Anga-Rakshak Nirbhay spoke from the gate.

Srivijay went to the door. "Yes, Nirbhay, what is it?"

Thinking the Queen was asleep, Nirbhay whispered, "Samrat, a *guptchar* (spy) has come with important information."

"I will meet him," Srivijay replied to the amazement of the Anga-Rakshak.

"Yes, Samrat." Nirbhay rushed to convey the message to the visitors. He knew that urgent security related meetings were held in the private meeting room, next to the King's chambers.

Srivijay went to the wash basin and splashed some water on his face. The water was cold. It worked. He felt fresh. Then he quickly put on his attire and the crown.

He came out as if he was ready to charge on a battlefield.

In the meeting room only the guptchar and Raksha Mantri Bhalla were present. They both got up and said, *"Samrat ki jai ho."*

Srivijay took his seat. With a deep sigh, he gave a quizzical look and asked in light humour, "Tell me what is it? I hope nobody is planning to attack us."

A thick-waisted man in his fifties with close-cropped gunmetal grey hair, Bhalla made working for the security of the kingdom his life. He was shrewd and the job meant everything to him. With a serious face, he said, "Guptchar has come from Angaara. There is some development." His voice was raspy and ancient – the sound a snake would make if it could talk.

Srivijay got interested. His eyes became curious. Ever since Paulastya had attacked kingdoms in Bhuvar-Lok, as a policy they had left spies on the island to keep watch.

"I think Raakh is the new Tribal Lord. We put him there. He is not capable of raising an army with his ways. He is a fighter not a leader. His ambition does not go beyond Angaara," Srivijay said.

The guptchar, an ordinary looking man, spoke, "Samrat, Guru Shukracharya has taken a shishya."

This was big. Shukracharya had not taken a student for years. Guru Shukracharya was said to be even more skilled than Guru Bhaskar of Siddha-Lok. He was the only one capable of making a King – someone who could become *Trivikram*, the conqueror of the three Loks on Dhruva-Lok. Even Satyavrat had not achieved it. He left Angaara after defeating Paulastya. It was an impossible place to keep in control.

Srivijay's eyes widened. "Who is he?"

"His name is Vritra, son of Tvashta of the Shikavan tribe. Some call him Vichitra. He is four years old but is said to have the power of ten elephants."

Bhalla reminded Srivijay as he said, "Shikavan tribe was overthrown by Raakh with our help."

"Just a four-year-old child with no army, no home. He is no real threat," Srivijay retorted.

"Threats should be eliminated when it is easy to do so. Once he grows up, we may not have that option anymore." Bhalla tried to convince Srivijay with the way he saw the world.

Srivijay was outraged at the suggestion. "We are not child assassins. Let him grow up and then we will see. Let us fight like men and not cowards. I will be more than happy to fight him on a battlefield than to kill an innocent child. I can't go to such an extent."

Bhalla felt bad about the remark – *We are not child assassins*. He rubbed his jaw.

"We have done such things in the past," Bhalla reasoned.

"But never to a child." Srivijay gave a cold look, his voice stern.

Last time when he had agreed, he was very young. He had regretted it every day since then. He feared someday something bad would happen to him for this sin. And later on, the two miscarriages of his wife, he always held this to be the cause. This made her the way she was now. A befitting punishment by the gods, he believed.

Bhalla saw it in his eyes. Srivijay wasn't a child anymore who could be easily manipulated.

"Anything else?" Srivijay asked in his powerful voice.

"No, Samrat." Bhalla replied softly.

"Then the meeting is over." With these words, Srivijay got up and left the room.

Both Bhalla and guptchar got up and bowed their heads to the Samrat.

Srivijay stormed out and entered his room. He tried not to make any sound so as not to awaken Kaushiki.

"You are back early." Kaushiki's sudden utterance shook the silence of the room.

She sat up.

"You surprised me. Are you still awake?" His cheeks swelled into a big smile, which soon transformed into an ebullient laugh.

"It is not every day that you go to sudden security meetings."

"Since when do security matters interest you?"

"I get interested when I sense it could be important."

"Really? And how do you know it was important?" His tone was filled with sarcasm more than surprise.

"It's my sixth sense," she rolled her eyes as she said, "something I was born with."

"Well, you are wrong. It was nothing important. I think Bhalla is getting old."

This was the first time Srivijay had said such words about Bhalla. She asked, "Why?"

"He is getting scared of a four-year-old child."

"Really, a four-year-old child? I did not know he had a child."

"No, not his child. You know he is not married."

"But he can still have a child."

"Well, he doesn't. It is about a child at Angaara – a child with no army and no home. All because Guru Shukracharya has taken him as a student. And that scares him."

"Hmm…interesting. I heard he had retired after his favourite student, Vishvarupa, was found dead, probably killed a few years ago."

Srivijay's face changed colour. He remained tight-lipped, biting his lower lip.

Sensing something was wrong, she asked, "What happened? What are you thinking?"

Erasing his thoughts, he replied, "Nothing. So, you have heard of Shukracharya?"

"Yes, my Guru was very jealous of him. He never liked to hear Shukracharya's name. He used to say why such a learned man is on that island, teaching those tribals – who in turn attack here."

"Yes, exactly. Why does he do that? If he were here, we would have given a high rank and all the comforts of royal life."

"To some people such things don't matter. Not everyone finds peace in a life of pleasure. It's his choice, isn't it?"

"Maybe. And we have the right to make our decisions."

"So, what did you decide?"

For a moment, he thought she was asking about the decision he made five years ago. "Regarding what?" he stammered.

"That four-year-old child. What are you going to do? I hope you are not sending an army."

"I won't kill a child… Do you agree with my decision?"

"It doesn't matter whether I agree. Did your favourite Raksha Mantri Bhalla agree?"

"He may be old, but he is the one I can trust."

"You didn't answer my question, did he agree?"

"He has to. I trust his loyalty to the kingdom. He has served the Vardhan-vanshis for generations now. He is probably more loyal than me!" he said confidently.

"That's the problem: the one who is more loyal than the king cannot be loyal to the king," she replied.

◆

Bhalla returned to his chambers.

The words of Srivijay echoed in his head. *"We are not child assassins...* *Let us fight like men and not cowards."*

As the Head of Security Affairs, his job was to prevent a fight in the first place. He knew the Samrat was young and naive. Idealism may be a weakness of the Samrat but not his. After all, Bhalla had years of experience behind him. He knew very well that *a snake will always bite back.*

Ideas are great arrows, but there has to be a bow.

Bhalla thought carefully. Then he called the gatekeeper and instructed him, "Bring Surya immediately."

A man of medium build and ordinary looks with black hair – Surya was an average fighter in the army. But he specialized in a crucial aspect – assassination. He worked wonders in the shadows.

When Surya arrived, Bhalla started whispering, "This has to stay between the two of us. No one else can know, not even Samrat."

Surya was worried about the tone of his immediate boss and his heart beat rapidly.

"There is something I want you to do. It is difficult but it has to be done. It is in the best interests of the kingdom."

This scared Surya further. A multitude of thoughts went through his mind, but none reached his lips.

Bhalla told Surya his devious plan, "Our guptchars have informed us that there is a four-year-old child Vritra in Angaara. He is now a student of Guru Shukracharya, who is training him. When he grows up, I am sure he is going to attack our kingdom. He needs to be taken care of."

The words hit Surya hard. "But Bhalla-deva, this is not right. I have never killed a child before. I cannot do this." Surya tried to back out.

"He is not any ordinary four-year-old. They tell me he has the power of ten elephants. He is an asura."

Surya was still not convinced. "But deva this is adharma. I can't do this to a child, to a family, especially when I myself am about to become a father." He shook his head again and asked, "Does the Samrat know?"

"What is the dharma of a *rakshak* (protector), Surya?" Bhalla raised a question instead of answering.

"Loyalty to the kingdom always, at all cost."

"This is the cost, even if it means adharma. Our only duty is to protect the kingdom, no matter what." Bhalla appealed to the patriot in him. Patriotism is fierce as a plague, ruthless as a sword and as irrational as blind love.

"Killing an innocent is the biggest crime of all. I can't do this."

"What we have to do is morally indefensible but absolutely necessary. Someone has to drink the poison to save the world." Bhalla made a silent reference to Lord Shiva drinking the poison for the sake of saving the world.

Bhalla was an expert in playing with words. Dharma is built on understanding, and adharma thrives on misinterpretation. The distinction is subtle. He had twisted stories to meet his own narrow ends in the past.

Evil is a force that thrives on half-knowledge, which is much more lethal and dangerous. Very few can see through this evil design. Surya wasn't able to. He was now looking through the lens of blind patriotism.

He remained quiet. His mind overpowered his heart as he surrendered to the fragile logic.

✦

13

Janani (Mother)

SIDDHA - LOK

Vishamadeva walked back to his chambers, his gait slow and ponderous as if he had aged several years after the King's command. His eyes were grey due to both distress and tiredness. The die had been cast. The King had given a command and he had no choice but to obey. His hands were tied and there was nothing he could do. He felt a gnawing pain in his stomach. He had never felt so miserable or frustrated in his entire life. The walls and pillars mocked him as he walked past. He wanted to punch the walls or smash the pillars to vent some of his anger, but even that wasn't going to help. He knew. *Why me, Lord?* he screamed inside and continued wallowing in his misery.

Hetan was waiting outside the personal chambers of Vishamadeva, biting his nails in anxiety. *What was I thinking?* His outspoken tongue had probably gone too far. Was the string pulled taut enough to snap and destroy everything?! He was about to find out. He stood in attention as he saw Vishamadeva approach. Before he could apologize, Vishamadeva said, "We are done for the day," and walked inside. Hetan was perplexed. After lingering there for a while, he returned to his quarters.

Vishamadeva's wife, Gayatri was waiting for him. She was tall and lean with a lady-like elegance. Her skin tone was a lighter shade of caramel and her face framed by jet-black hair brimmed with youthful luminosity even at this age. It was an odd hour for a meeting; something must have been very urgent.

Taken aback by his defeated shuffle, her eyes flew open in shock. It was a look she had not seen for a very long time. He looked shaken to the core. She enquired, "What happened, dear?"

He was close to collapse, but he gathered his composure. "I can't say."

"Can't you tell me what it is?"

"Maharaja has commanded. I have given my word and I have to obey."

Gayatri didn't push him further. She understood him more than anyone. They both were living a life of punishment. For what crime even they did not know. They must have committed grave sins in their previous *janma* (life). Why would the Gods be that unfair?

She helped him sit on the bed and brought him a glass of water. His hands shook and she helped him take two sips.

"Can't you say no to the King?"

He remained quiet, thinking. "I can't," he replied sobbing, "it's my oath, my burden."

She understood, held his hand and said in a reassuring manner, "It is a burden which only you can bear."

He shook his head. "It is going against dharma. I don't know what to do."

"Honouring your word, your oath is the highest dharma, even if it means giving away your life. Who understands it better than you!" She hugged him.

Giving away one's own life is easy. It is taking an innocent life that tests your soul, he mumbled, not loud enough for her to hear.

"Don't worry. Just do your duty. The Gods will guide you." She again tried to comfort him.

"I no longer know what the Gods want." He shut his eyes and all he saw was emptiness, near and beyond. Suddenly, those dreadful words from his memory – *the curse of Dhruvanshis* – echoed in his mind again. Closing his eyes had made it worse.

He opened his eyes and took a deep breath. "I have made mistakes and they have come to haunt me. I took an unguarded oath. That is my sin and mine alone."

✦

He woke up before *brahma-muhurta* (dawn). He had hardly slept at night. The burden of the decision ahead was just too heavy for him to bear. The price of greatness was to continue making difficult decisions and live with them. The way sand continuously falls in a sand clock. After it is done, the clock is turned upside down to make the sand drip again. Is this what his life had become?

Vishamadeva got up, wrapped a white shawl around his body and walked out. There was someone to whom he could speak his heart out.

Gayatri pretended to be asleep. She knew where he was going.

With racing footsteps, he left the palace. The drowsy guards at the gate were surprised to see him at this hour but no one dared to question him or follow him.

The night was dark and still. As he walked, he thought of the past he had left behind. His father Sudarshan, the 105th Dhruvanshi, brought him to the palace and raised him as his own child. He named him Haridutt, the gift of God, but everyone called him Jhanaviputra, the son of Jhanavi. He had a deep bond with his father, a bond so rare that even the universe wouldn't let them separate from each other. It was his father he loved the most. He looked at the special sandalwood *wrist mala* (bracelet) in his left hand gifted by his father. The fragrance could still invigorate every pore. His face relaxed into a smile, and he raised his wrist to savour the moment with a whiff of its scent.

His eyes fell on the scars in his palm – a reminder of the terrible oaths he had taken in the name of his father. The oaths he could never break. They had altered not just his future, but everyone else's future as well! He earned the name Vishamadeva – a terrible god – as no ordinary human could or would have done what he did. In his eyes, the oaths were to save his family and protect the Dhruvanshis. Did it actually protect them? He wasn't so sure anymore. But they were his choices and he couldn't complain about it to anyone.

Destiny has a strange way of unfolding, he mused. He didn't know when it all started. He didn't know when it was going to end. All he knew was that it was his life and he needed to keep living, whatever it took and wherever life took him.

His path took him up a gentle elevation around the lazy meander of the river until he reached his destination – a secluded place on river Jhanavi. There were no settlements and the riverbank of palms, low bushes and yellow-bark trees nestled there in peace. The high muddy river had flooded the bushes on the banks. It was the lap of his mother – *Maa Jhanavi.* No one knew why she was his mother except that he was found there. And he had come to believe that over the years and formed a special bond with this place and he came here often to find peace and solace.

Today, he came to his mother, Maa Jhanavi, looking for guidance.

"Maa, your son has come." He closed his eyes.

Gradually his mother appeared in his thoughts. She looked like a nymph straight from the heavens – a slim, willowy woman with sharp features – a pointed nose, large eyes, small lips, and a well-defined neck. Strikingly, she had silver hair. She came near to him and said, "*Putra* (son)."

Her voice took root in his heart and mind. "Pranam, maa."

"Chiranjeevi bhava, putra. Why do you look so distressed?"

"Your son has been given another responsibility. The King has commanded me to change destiny. I may have to do the unthinkable to a newborn."

"No putra, you have been given the responsibility to decide destiny. Who else is better than you?"

His broken voice said, "Maa, what should I do?"

"You will know when the time comes. The moment will tell you. Leave it to the Gods," the mother answered.

"What if…"

Before he could say anything further, the mother in his vision replied, "You were born to make difficult decisions. You chose to be the Lok-Sevak when you could have wielded the Trishul and become the King. You even chose not to have a child. You made the decision for your wife, without even asking her. Isn't that the same as killing a child?"

"Maa, don't say that!" He closed his ears. In his heart he knew that she was right. This was his terrible past. "I selflessly did whatever I had to with the best intentions for my father and the Dhruvanshis."

"I know, son."

"Then why is all this happening?"

Maa answered, "The destiny changed when you made those choices. No matter how pure our intentions are, our decisions have consequences, many times undesirable, unexpected. Your decision will yet again decide the course of fate."

He fought back his tears.

"Your Maa Jhanavi will always be there with you, whatever you decide. Always remember that… Who knows? The decision might be an easy one this time."

He was relieved to hear those words.

She blessed him and disappeared. Jhanaviputra opened his eyes feeling much better, relieved.

Was he dreaming? Was he hallucinating? It did not matter. To him it was more than real. And that was what mattered!

He looked at his hands. The fate of Dhruva-Lok rested in them.

✦

14

Bhāgya (Destiny)

SIDDHA - LOK

It was late morning when Vishamadeva opened the creaking door and made his way into his study. Hetan had come in early. He got up and nervously said, "Pranam, Lok-Sevak."

"Pranam, Hetan," Vishamadeva replied, expressionless, without any hint of emotion on his face. Hetan sought relief in the fact that there was no fierce stare from the Lok-Sevak.

Vishamadeva stood at the high window and stared at the royal gardens outside. Summer was at its peak; nature was no longer smiling.

Hetan spoke with his head down, "I am sorry, Lok-Sevak. Please forgive me. It will not happen again." His tone was tinged in consternation. Vishamadeva neither turned nor spoke.

Questions pierced Hetan like arrows. How to seek forgiveness? How to undo what was done? How to turn the clock back? A slight bead of perspiration trickled down his temple. He bit his fingernail so hard that he ripped off the skin under it. Even hurting himself didn't help.

An ominous silence engulfed the room.

The metronomic clanging of the bell from the central clock tower, where time was maintained, drove frightened pigeons into flight and signalled the start of the second pahar of the day. It brought the room back to life.

Finally, Vishamadeva turned and said, "Don't bite your fingernails. It's bad for your nails, teeth, and in fact, for the entire body."

Hetan dropped his hand and nodded. He repeated his apology, "I regret what I said yesterday, Lok-Sevak. It shall not be repeated. Please give me one more chance."

Vishamadeva walked to the table and spoke, "You don't have to apologize for speaking what's in your heart, at least not in front of me...but be careful what you say in front of others. Life is not a storybook and nothing is in black and white. Life is messier than you realize. Seemingly perfect rules don't work in this imperfect world and, therefore, we are far from perfection. But I am glad to see that your heart is in the right place and you are able to stay true to it."

Hetan was elated but confused. To him they sounded like farewell. Vishamadeva's voice today was charged with emotion. Something must have happened last night in the emergency meeting.

Vishamadeva sat on his chair. He pulled out a quill pen and started writing on a blank scroll.

Hetan avoided looking directly at what was being written.

At last, Vishamadeva wrote his name at the bottom and placed the seal of Shivalik-Rajya. "I am appointing you as *Sahayak-Athapati* (Assistant Chief Judge) from today. Hope you will do justice to this responsibility."

Hetan's eyes widened in disbelief. It was a senior position in the palace. Fighting had never appealed to him. He had joined the army at his father's insistence. But things worked out on their own, for the best. *Destiny finds a way*.

"Ahem," Vishamadeva cleared his throat to break Hetan's wandering thoughts.

"I...I don't have words to thank you, Lok-Sevak. I never expected this," Hetan thanked him. He tried hard to control his excitement. "If I may ask, why me, Lok-Sevak?" He stared at Vishamadeva trying to gauge his reaction.

Vishamadeva let a twinkle of a smile crease his face. "You are not a yes-man. I like that." His reply was short and crisp. He got up and handed over the scroll bearing the official order.

Hetan felt goose bumps as he reached out eagerly to take the order. "Can I ask for one more favour, Lok-Sevak?" Hetan queried.

Vishamadeva frowned. "Yes, what is it?"

"I want your permission to continue my access to this treasury of books. Whenever I get time, I would like to come here and read."

"In that case, I will get you access to the grand library at the palace from where I brought these books. Have you seen it?"

"No, Lok-Sevak." Hetan's happiness knew no bounds. He touched Vishamadeva's feet in gratitude.

"*Yashasvi bhava.*" May you attain eternal success.

Vishamadeva left the room with a bounce in his footsteps. He had changed someone's destiny.

✦

Affectionately, Gayatri moved her soft hands across Padmini's forehead, "How are you doing, dear? Mitasha told me you were having shortness of breath after the morning walk."

"Yes, *badi-maa.*" The privacy allowed Padmini the freedom to address Gayatri intimately, unlike the way Dhananjay referred to her as Jyeshta Matashri. "Is it something I need to be worried about?"

"No, dear. It's quite common. Is that what's bothering you?"

Padmini fiddled with a lock of her hair and her eyes continued to remain blue.

Gayatri sensed it and asked, "You have been nervous lately. Is there something you want to tell me or talk about?"

Padmini chewed her lower lip. "It's nothing serious, badi-maa."

Gayatri wasn't satisfied but she didn't push her. "This is the time to be happy. We all are here with you. Don't be worried."

The silence stretched for a few seconds.

Padmini overcame her inhibitions and murmured, "Badi-maa, can I ask you something?"

"Yes, dear. You can ask me anything."

"Uhh," she hesitated again but she mustered courage and spoke, "badi-maa, do you ever regret not having a child?"

Gayatri's expression changed with the unexpected question. It was a sensitive topic and a very difficult one to explain. Most people never understood her. "Why do you ask?"

"I can't imagine how hard it must be for you. As a woman, it bothers me."

"It isn't easy but I don't regret it either. I chose to marry him. I knew what I was getting into."

"You agreed to marry him even after knowing that he wouldn't father a child?" Padmini wasn't sure if she heard it correctly. She could never contemplate such a thought.

"Our marriage was fixed. Then he took this oath. I still remember the day Jhanaviputra came to me and asked me to call off the marriage with hands folded in apology. He told me about the terrible oath he had taken."

"Then why did you decide to marry him anyway?"

"It didn't change anything for me. I loved him. I knew he was the man I wanted to marry. You don't come across such men often – brave, righteous, self-sacrificing – a true *nishkama-karma-yogi*. I couldn't let him go."

"How does one make peace with such a decision?"

"I don't need to. From where I see, there is no conflict. It was meant to happen."

"What was meant to happen?" Padmini was puzzled.

"Tell me, dear, what is the need to have a child?"

"Isn't that inherent in us? We need to propagate our vansha."

"I feel it's deeper. When we give birth to a child, we are giving a part of ourselves to that child. This way some part of us continues to live, even after we are gone. There is an unbreakable bond with your offspring."

"Right! That is why we have an embedded desire to have our own child."

"In fulfilling this desire, we remain stuck in the endless cycle of rebirth. Until the time comes when our soul is ready to unite with Brahma, in other words, to achieve *mukti*. At that stage, this desire ends. One no longer has any desire to live further. I feel his soul has reached that stage. His life is his legacy; he doesn't need a child for that. So, in hindsight, I feel he never would have fathered any children. Circumstances just made the inevitable happen."

"You really feel his soul is going to get liberated?" Padmini was befuddled with this perspective.

"My grandmother used to say that when the time for liberation nears, the soul is tested the most. So, when you get a feeling that a righteous one is leading a life of punishment for no apparent reason, the world is very cruel to him, even the Gods seem to be unfair, that means his time has come. That soul is going through the ultimate test before meeting Brahma. The cycle of learning is reaching its end. If you look at the life of Jhanaviputra, it just fits. That is his *destiny*."

Padmini took some time to understand this. Was this the way Gayatri's mind had made peace with the circumstances, or did she really believe what she was saying? She was not in a position to judge Gayatri. How could she?

This was the first time they had discussed this. Should she also do the same? Padmini cleared her throat and said, "Badi-maa, there is something I need to tell you. Please don't tell anyone."

"You know I won't, dear," Gayatri assured her.

Padmini told her about the prophecy, the complete prophecy of her to-be-born-child.

Gayatri listened to her patiently. The prophecy made her uncomfortable too. Her mind started connecting the prophecy with the events of the previous night. There had to be a link. It wasn't easy to break a strong man like Jhanaviputra.

"Say something, badi-maa," Padmini said anxiously.

"Did something happen yesterday?" Gayatri asked.

"No, badi-maa. Nothing happened. I wanted to tell you this ever since we heard the prophecy."

Gayatri realized that Padmini was not aware about the previous night's meeting. She avoided telling her. "Ohh, dear. That must have been so hard all this time. Why didn't you say anything earlier?"

"I didn't want to trouble you. But I am very scared now... don't know what is going to happen," she whimpered.

"Padmini, don't worry about it. Whatever happens will be for the best. You need to believe that. Your son will be a Dhruvanshi. He will bring glory to Shivalik."

"What if the child is born..."

Gayatri didn't let her finish. She placed Padmini's hand on her own belly. "Feel it, Padmini. The child is already there, very much alive, moving and even hearing us. It doesn't matter when he or she will be born. Destiny is already written by the Creator."

Padmini slipped into a tranquil state. She closed her eyes to savour the moment. The touch helped in calming her troubling thoughts.

She felt a flutter and then a kick as if her baby was confirming what Gayatri had said to her. It filled her heart with happiness, and she felt an endless love for her unborn child.

The child was already there, alive. Nothing could change that.

✦

15

Krātha (Murder)

ANGAARA

Blood dripped from his dagger. His heart thumped, competing with the deathly stillness in the air. Surya had completed his mission. He had done the unthinkable. The body of four-year-old Vritra was lying in front of him with his throat slit. Blood was all over the floor. He felt a searing pain in his chest at the disgraceful sight. Surya closed his eyes as a choking desolation crept over him.

Suddenly, he heard a wild cry from behind him. He turned. It was dark but he recognized the voice. It was his wife Radha who was carrying his child.

"Radha, what are you doing here?" Baffled, he rushed to her.

"I followed you here. What have you done, Surya?" She screamed pointing her hand towards the little boy's corpse.

She collapsed to the ground. He held her in his arms. As his hands touched her belly, he noticed there was some thick fluid. To his horror, it was blood all over her stomach. Gripped with panic, he asked, "Radha, why are you bleeding?"

"I am paying for your sins," she replied as she started losing consciousness.

"Who did this to you?"

"You don't remember? It was you who killed our son. You destroyed everything."

Her last words shook his soul.

He sweated profusely. Tremors ran through his body. He convulsed uncontrollably, his body contorting with each tremor.

He sat up from yet another nightmare. It took a long time for the tremors to subside. He sat there. Still. Silent. His dreams were terrifying. One day, he had seen Radha deliver a blind baby. In another dream, the child was stillborn. These spine-chilling dreams had become his daily companion throughout the journey. He kept consoling himself saying 'do your duty'.

Surya had left his home, at a time when his wife needed him the most, close to her ninth month. Surya wanted to be with her but to him duty came first. He couldn't tell her where and why he was going. He was on a mission to take the life of a child when the Gods were about to bless him with one. The agony was eating his soul like a cannibalistic witch.

It took him three days to cross the sea and reach Wonder Bay on the north-eastern coast of Angaara. The place got its name due to the neon blue waves that made the surface waters glow mysteriously in the night. This was caused by bioluminescent phytoplanktons giving rise to electric blue radiance, but to everyone there it was an enigma – a magic spell by the powerful spirits on the island. Surya had never believed it until he saw it with his own eyes. *Nature is the greatest artist.*

As soon as he landed in Angaara, he tracked the helper from Asrasya tribe about whom the guptchar had told him. The helper was a short, lean man with an unkempt beard and straggly hair. Pretending to be a trader, Surya made a deal with him to guide him through the deep jungles and cross the central highlands in exchange for one gold coin.

Surya was well-trained to survive in the jungles with limited food and water supply. He had gone on many such missions in his kingdom, where he took care of notorious dacoits or rebels or many big cats in the forests on the Amargosa mountains. But this was very different, both the place and the mission.

"Have you been to this place before?" the helper asked.

"Yes, this is my second time."

"When was your first time?"

"Around five years ago. But I had not gone so deep inside that time." He remained silent for a while. "What is this strange-looking fortress?" Surya asked in amazement, and also to change the topic.

"Ah! These rugged, white-colour towers are limestone mountain tops which were said to be originally formed under the sea. Time and rain have slowly shaped these into a jungle fortress." After a brief silence, he said, "I have never been to Bhuvar-Lok. I hear that you people have built huge forts, dams and big cities."

"True, but they are nothing compared to the structures built by nature here." Surya appreciated the beauty of the place.

"Why do you want to go to the western side? You can get almost everything here."

"Looking for something," Surya said in a cryptic manner and maintained a dignified silence.

Initially, the helper assumed it must be some medicinal plant the visitor was searching for. The island was filled with them, which attracted traders from Bhuvar-Lok. But Surya didn't look like one. After some thought, he suspected something else was going on, but he did not ask any further questions. Many times, the less you know, the better. "You are a city man. I hope you are not scared of animals!" he said in a jocular manner to test his gut feeling. He couldn't control his instinct.

"Not really. I know one thing – that the animals are more scared of you than you are of them. If you do nothing to provoke them, you will be okay," Surya replied instantly.

This reply confirmed what he was thinking. But for some reason, Surya's demeanour did not bother him. He said, "I don't think you have seen the unusual animals here. Have you heard of Draak?"

Surya broke out in a sweat on hearing the name. He thrust a restive hand through his untidy mop of black hair. He had heard stories! He firmly believed that even though there was an element of exaggeration in those stories, they were mostly true. He flung his questions at him, "Does it exist? Have you seen it? I mean, isn't it a myth?"

"Not a myth; they are very real, though not many of its species are left anymore. They are known to stay towards the south and rarely venture this side. I have seen them a few times, but not lately."

Surya breathed a sigh of relief. "I hope we are not going to be that lucky this time."

After crossing the central highlands, he parted with his friend. Being in his company, his nightmares had stopped. That was a big relief. Surya learned many life-saving skills in these jungles from him, most important of them, how to find food! What was poisonous, what was not – skills that only a forest dweller knows, which is passed on through generations. He also learned about a few plants whose crushed leaves gave a smell that repelled the animals and insects. He remembered the words of his helper, "In these jungles, one is more likely to die of poisonous fruits or a snake bite than hunted by animals."

He was alone now.

The guptchar had described the location of the ashram in great detail. So, Surya reached close to the ashram within a couple of days of travel. Along the journey, Surya prayed to the gods for forgiveness. He and only he should be punished for the heinous crime he was going to commit. Thankfully, his nightmares did not return.

When he was close to the ashram, he camped on a surrounding hill. Shukracharya was a powerful yogic. If Surya got too close, he would certainly sense his chakra.

Now his nightmares returned. Surya shook his head to plan the job. He had to be extremely careful now, since his destination was close by.

He swung into action. He used his spyglass to monitor the ashram from the top of the hill before he went in.

Surya scouted his surroundings for food and water supply. He dug a hole for groundwater from an underground aquifer. To his delight, it worked. But there was no food source. The food he had saved from his journey would suffice for three days. So, he decided to camp for two days before making his move. Next, he needed a place to take cover from animals and store his food.

He chose a tree from where he had a good line-of-sight to the ashram. He took a long, straight branch fallen nearby and placed it against the tree at an angle. He positioned shorter branches perpendicular to the length of the long branch on both sides at roughly forty-five degrees to the ground. He covered this temporary structure with large leaves to make a hideout for the night.

As he watched the small ashram from his hideout, he saw Vritra for the first time. The boy looked remarkable. He was much taller than an average four-year-old. His big, oval face, long neck, pointed ears and wide eyes gave him a serpent-like appearance. His skin was pear green. He looked extremely strong and muscular. Certainly, this was no ordinary child, but he was still a child.

Surya let out a trembling breath.

In the morning, Vritra meditated calmly. The boy looked remarkable. The poise on his face was captivating.

After that, the boy practiced shooting with a bow and arrows. He missed his mark frequently. Satyavrat The Conqueror was the best-known fighter with this weapon. His *amogha* arrows never missed their mark. One-time Vritra aimed his arrow towards the hill and Surya ducked instinctively. *Has he sensed me?* He wiped the beads of sweat on his forehead with his thumb.

In the late afternoon, Vritra practiced fighting with a sword and shield, which was called *Takshaka*. This technique was named after the famed leader of the snake-worshipping Naga tribe of Angaara. The moves and postures resembled the way snakes attack – sudden and sharp. It was a popular technique across Bhuvar-Lok as well. Even Surya was very good at it. But the way Vritra moved, it was natural to him. With such a muscular and hefty body, Surya wasn't able to fathom how the boy moved so rapidly.

The light blue sky turned sooty, but there was no sign of rain.

Next, he trained with a *bhaala* (spear), which was a fighting technique called *Ballamsilat*. He struggled with it. It was clear that the boy had not used it a lot before. This was more popular in Siddha-Lok.

In the night came the real challenge. The fight with Agni. The dreaded challenge game of Angaara – Agni-Maru. Vritra applied mud and ash on his body. He looked nothing less than an asura. This training continued for the longest time. It was this fight he needed to win first before skills with other weapons would matter. Surya's heart skipped a beat many times watching this training. He knew the pain of fire-burn very well. But Vritra endured it. Surya was filled with admiration for this vichitra boy.

He looked at the sharp edge of his favourite dagger closely for a while. There was no honour in what he was about to do. If it had to happen, it had to be quick and painless.

✦

Vritra followed the same schedule the next day. Surya spent a lot of time studying the design of the hut and making plans. He contemplated, "After such rigorous training, Vritra must get really tired at night. That will be the perfect time to make my move."

At midnight, Surya began his descent to darkness. His heart and mind were in a battle. A pulse pounded in his temple; something twitched behind his left eye. He was going to rob the world of a fierce fighter. But there was no turning back now. He suppressed his feelings.

He stood outside the door of the hut. With his sharp dagger, he slid through a small opening on the door's edge. Patiently, he lifted the latch to unlock the door. He entered the way a feather would go through; without making any sound. Surya was colour-blind. But this deficiency had given him better night vision. He could perceive variations in luminosity that colour-sighted people could not. That made him special in the shadows.

He saw Shukracharya sleeping in the corner. Near his feet was Vritra. Surya held his dagger and stood next to Vritra.

✦

16

Druhī (Daughter)

King Yuyutsu of Kailash-Rajya reached the Nandi valley to meet the Saptarishis. His first visit. After the prophecy to Shivalik-Rajya nearly coming true and with his wife also with child, he couldn't resist visiting them.

It took him six days of travel to arrive at the ashram. He was exhausted. He struggled to breathe. The chill at this height froze his body. He rubbed his hands together as he came out of the carriage.

A big contingent followed him unlike the previous visitor, Dhananjay.

"Pranam, O Divine Sages. Please accept my greetings and bless me," he spoke loudly with a hint of arrogance and his head raised high.

The Saptarishis did not open their eyes. They were caught up in the past seeing something very significant.

Many devas had approached Lord Brahma, praying, "Hey Lord Brahma – the Creator of the Universe – there is a grave situation developing at Dhruva-Lok. Vritrasura has taken birth on Dhruva-Lok. When he grows up, he will be the mightiest of Asura warriors with unmeasurable powers and he will be invincible. We have come to request you to take away the powers of the child."

Lord Brahma replied instantly, without even bothering to consider their request, "I cannot do that. The child has been born in the karmic cycle of rebirths that continues eternally. I cannot punish him for nothing. You get rewarded or punished for your actions. How can anyone get the karmaphala before doing the karma?"

"But Lord, the balance of power has tilted significantly in favour of the asuras. No one will pray to us once he takes control. That will be an injustice."

"The mighty Trishul of Lord Shiva rests at Dhruva-Lok. He could possibly wield the Trishul and become unconquerable," another deva added.

Brahma frowned. "I see what you are implying. The balance of power has to be restored. Which one of you devas is ready to go to Dhruva-Lok to stand up against Vritrasura if the day ever came?"

The devas looked at each other nervously. Vritrasura was the most powerful asura warrior in the Brahmand. They knew they could not defeat him.

"Who wants to go?" Brahma asked again.

The devas stood there with their eyes lowered. No one came forward.

"It seems none of you wants to go. Hmm." Brahma paused, thought deeply and then continued, "There is only one deva capable of challenging him. He is in a way responsible for all of this and has to pay for his karma as well."

The devas were puzzled as they asked, "Who, Lord?"

"The King of Devas, INDRA."

Yuyutsu was embarrassed. He then folded his hands and bowed like a student meeting his Guru. Again, he repeated, "Hey Divine Sages, I, King Yuyutsu of the Yavana-vansha from Kailash-Rajya, have come to honour you and seek your divine blessings." This time his tone was humble and respectful.

The Saptarishis opened their eyes.

Yuyutsu felt elated and touched the feet of sages.

The sages raised their palm and answered, "Ayushman bhava."

Yuyutsu sat down in front of them.

Sage Vashistha asked, "What is it that you want to know, Kailash-Naresh?"

Yuyutsu said, "Hey Divine Sages, I only seek your blessings." After a brief pause, he uttered his real purpose, "My wife Devayani is with child. I want to know if my son will fulfil my ambition?"

Sage Jamadagni smiled and said, "Hey Kailash-Naresh, you have been truly blessed. *Devi* is coming to your home. You will become a proud father of a girl."

The blessing of a daughter made him sad for a brief moment. In front of the Wielder of the Trishul, it was too optimistic of him to hope that his son would be able to challenge him. He took a deep sigh and absorbed the prediction. In their family lineage, for the last three generations, no girl was born so it was felt that they were cursed. But with this news, he was delighted. His ambition was not blind.

"Bless my daughter, Divine Sages. Devi is coming to our family after a long wait." He said with genuine delight and tears of happiness filled both eyes.

The sages beamed in unison.

Sage Agastya added to the prediction, "She will be *shakti*. She will fulfil your ambitions and become a Queen. Your daughter will decide the fate of the world."

Whatever the clouds of disappointment Yuyutsu had, they disappeared before the beaming rays of the news.

This was yet another powerful prophecy by the Saptarishis. It meant that troubling times lay in the future. Great wars were coming. They could see the forces of darkness and light at play.

The seven sages returned to their thoughts, "Comet Shesha went through the sky a few years ago. It crossed at night, so no one saw it. Foreseeing difficult times ahead, Lord Vishnu had already arrived in his avatar to play his role, to fulfil the promise he had made to Dhruva."

✦

17

Hrīkā (Shame)

ANGAARA

Surya waited. His heart wavered. His wife Radha's face floated in front of his eyes. A tear dropped from his right eye and fell on the ground.

At that moment he realized that he couldn't do it. It was not worth saving the kingdom while sacrificing dharma. Life was meaningless without dharma. The heart had conquered the mind. Fate took a different course at that instant.

Before Surya could turn around, Vritra got up in a flash, snatched the dagger from his right hand and aimed it at Surya. The teardrop had turned out to be very dangerous.

Vritra shouted, "Don't move."

Shukracharya got up. With haste, he said, "Vritra, wait. Don't kill him. Take him outside."

Surya neither resisted nor tried to run away. He had surrendered. He wanted to be punished.

"Let him go, Vritra," Shukracharya said.

Vritra wasn't sure that he had heard correctly. He did not let go of the dagger aiming at the intruder.

"Let him go. He is not a threat, not anymore," the Guru repeated. Vritra lowered the dagger and moved aside to stay behind Shukracharya.

"Why didn't you kill him when you had the chance?" Shukracharya asked Surya.

Surya remained quiet.

"Answer me!" Shukracharya commanded.

"Guruji, I came to kill him, but I couldn't do this adharma," Surya said softly with his head bowed.

Vritra asked, "Who are you?"

He replied, "I am Surya from Bhuvar-Lok. I serve Samrat Srivijay of Jambu-Rajya."

"Did Samrat Srivijay ask you to murder Vritra this way – like a coward?" Shukracharya asked in an angry tone.

"No, Guruji. I was sent by Bhalla, his Raksha Mantri. The Samrat doesn't know anything," Surya replied.

The Guru looked at Vritra. Proudly, he said, "Your name has already reached Bhuvar-Lok. They are scared of you."

Vritra said, "We should kill him and send a message."

Shukracharya shook his head in disapproval and turned to Surya. "You are free to go. One small crack does not mean that you are broken, it means that you were put to the test and you didn't fall apart. Go back and tell them to stay away or fight like honourable men. Have you learned nothing from Satyavrat?"

Surya looked down, in shame.

"Next time blood will be spilled." Shukracharya said as his gaze moved to Vritra. He continued, "He was never going to kill you. Had he wanted to kill, you would have been dead already. And he is not meant to die here either. Someone is waiting for him. He still has a big role to play in the scheme of things. Let him go."

Vritra did not understand much but he remained quiet in front of his Guru. Reluctantly he moved and returned the dagger to Surya.

A surprised Surya bowed his head in extreme penitence. Tears were in his eyes, but they were not of shame. Shame is a soul-eating emotion; he was glad to be liberated.

He left quietly on the right path; knowing who would be waiting for him.

✦

18

Nirṇaya (Decision)

SIDDHA - LOK

Padmini was pained that the day of Shivratri had brought with it this time, not its usual air of joviality and gaiety, rather a state of uncertainty.

She returned from her visit to the Grand Shiva Temple in the capital. She visited it every *trayodashi* (thirteenth) day, Lord Shiva's day, without fail. Ever since she was with child, her prayers to Lord Shiva increased manifold. More the worries, stronger the faith.

Her child would be born any day now. Sanjeevani had been with her for the last few days. Even Gayatri and Dhananjay hadn't left her side. Someone always stayed with her.

Shivratri was tonight. If the prophecy was to be believed, it should happen tonight. It was few hours to midnight now. She hadn't gone into labour yet, and there were no signs of imminent labour either.

Padmini was resting on her bed, fearful that her prayers would not be answered. Dhruva Nakshatra had started in the morning and would continue till the end of the day. It was a beautiful view in the sky. If she didn't deliver by midnight, then it would be Ugra Nakshatra.

Every few minutes she asked Dhananjay what would be done in case their worst fears came true. But, Dhananjay repeatedly avoided answering her question by saying that it would not come true. His behaviour made her feel that something was amiss. She was sure that he was hiding something from her. But she loved and trusted him.

Sanjeevani came in to check on her for any signs of labour. "Vaidya Sanjeevani, how does it look? Will it happen today?" Padmini asked.

Sanjeevani touched her belly at various places. Then read her pulse. After a while, she said, "Maharani, it could happen anytime. It could be tonight, or tomorrow, or it could be after ten days. There is no way of knowing."

"Can we do something to help start labour pains?" Dhananjay inquired.

"No, Maharaja. There are some ways, but I doubt they really work. Let nature take its own course. What will happen, will be God's wish!" Sanjeevani replied.

The Queen started sobbing loudly.

Sanjeevani was startled to see such anxiety coming from the King and Queen. Had she done something wrong? What was the hurry? *It is their first child, so that must be the reason,* she tried to answer her confusion. Sanjeevani left the chambers thinking it was better to leave them alone.

Dhananjay wiped Padmini's tears. She looked straight into his eyes and whimpered, "Not much time is left to midnight. It looks unlikely that our child will be born in Dhruva Nakshatra."

He immediately consoled her, "You don't know that. There is still time. I have faith. You need to have patience."

"But I want to know – what will you do in case our child is born tomorrow?"

"I haven't decided anything." He tried to avoid the question, yet again. He hesitated, and Padmini could tell he was hiding something.

She couldn't control her thoughts anymore. "You are lying. I know you have decided." Then she begged, "Please tell me. I will not stop you. I just want to know. A mother deserves to know!"

Dhananjay had thought it best to keep it from her, but it was a mother's request. He relented, "Vishamadeva has been told to make *the decision.* Whatever he does, we will accept."

She was shocked that they were serious about the prophecy. But she had been prepared for this. Some part of her heart always knew it. She couldn't argue about the solution that Vishamadeva was given this responsibility. He was the one who had taken an unbreakable oath binding him to serve the King and the kingdom selflessly.

She cried out in her heart, *Bholeshankar! Mahadeva! Protect my child.*

Within a few seconds, she screamed loudly. It was not a cry of desperation or helplessness. She was in labour.

Dhananjay frantically rushed outside and called Sanjeevani.

Sanjeevani entered within minutes. As she walked in, Padmini screamed again. She realized that the child was on the way. It could be anytime now. "Maharaja, the child is coming."

Delighted, Dhananjay asked, "How much time will it take?"

"A few hours...maybe by midnight," she replied.

His happiness quickly turned into nervousness. He had thought it would be sooner. It was his first child; he had no idea how long it actually takes. All he could say was, "Please take care of her," before he left the bedchamber.

The day was here – a contentious cusp between past and future! Dhananjay knew whom to call next.

◆

The message reached Vishamadeva.

He felt choked for a moment. The time for decision was upon him and he wasn't sure what he would do. He could face a thousand arrows or put a thousand enemy men to death on a battlefield but the thought of killing a child pierced deep into his soul. It was at such moments that Vishamadeva hated his life.

Gayatri prayed to Lord Shiva. Then she put three horizontal lines on her husband's forehead. They stared into each other's eyes.

It was as if he was going to war. Well, he was. A much more difficult war.

Dharmayuddha.

She noticed his quandary. She asked, "Are you ready?" She had a fair idea of what lay ahead for him. Padmini had told her about the complete prophecy. Gayatri kept the secret sealed in her heart. She neither mentioned it to her righteous husband, nor tried to advise him. It was his decision alone. She was sure he would do no wrong!

His face was shadowed with pain; his eyes dilated, filled with fear; his mind turbulent with a whirlpool of possibilities, each more terrible than the last. Would the King withdraw his command? Unlikely now. Were the Gods going to have mercy on him? He hardly felt so. Was he going to do the unthinkable? He did not want to think. Would he break his oath? Never.

Seeing him lost in thoughts, she asked again, "Are you ready, dear?"

He shook his head, staring at her like a damned man who beheld the face of an executioner. His eyes reflected an intense sorrow burning deep inside his heart. "I have to be," he said, controlling all the muscles on his face to hide the predicament he was wrestling with.

"You are the wheel of dharma. Do the honourable thing."

He felt her words conveyed a coded message. He remained quiet. His silence asked, "Why?"

"If you uphold dharma when it is difficult, it shall protect you when it is impossible," she answered calmly.

It wasn't so simple. The fault lines were such. What was the right thing? It was difficult to tell.

Vishamadeva gave a forced smile.

"Jhanaviputra! Mahadeva is with you."

Without saying anything further, he left hastily.

✦

Vishamadeva stood alone outside the bed-chamber. He gave instructions that no one was allowed here. Lok-Rakshak Simham himself guarded the gates. Dhananjay was in his chambers controlling his nerves.

All were praying.

It was close to midnight. All he could hear were the screams.

There had been silence for a while. Vishamadeva looked out through a small window. The shadow of Dhruva-Lok covered the seven moons. Ugra Nakshatra had commenced. His anxiousness had almost peaked. He tried to catch his breath, to slow his thundering heart and to still the throbbing veins in his forehead.

The door opened. He felt a cold shudder in his spine and a line of sweat crawled down his nape. Sanjeevani came out and whispered in his ears.

He let out a deep sigh and asked, "How is the Maharani?"

"She is unconscious, but fine."

"Does she know?"

"She lost consciousness in between. She does not know anything."

"Come with me," Vishamadeva said and went inside knowing what he was going to do.

✦

Dhananjay was pacing in his room. Every hour dragged by with torturous slowness. His anxious hands were shaking as his desperation increased with every passing moment. It was already long past midnight. *The unthinkable must have happened.*

He was prepared for the worst.

Outside, owls hooted. That disturbed him even more.

At that moment, loud and rapid footsteps reverberated from the external corridor. Someone was coming. His eyes were fixed on the gate and his heartbeat was erratic.

Vishamadeva entered with a baby in his arms and a wide smile on his face. "Maharaja, the 108th Dhruvanshi has arrived."

The father came rushing to his son with tears of joy. The feeling of being a father was unmatched to any other emotion. Before he touched the baby, he looked at Vishamadeva for confirmation. It was obvious what he wanted to know.

"Maharaja, he was born before midnight in Dhruva Nakshatra. He is the future wielder of the Trishul."

Dhananjay took the baby in his arms and gently kissed him. He felt the touch of his fingers. The moment was precious. *He looks like his mother,* he thought. "How is Padmini? Is she ok?"

"The Maharani is fine. Sanjeevani says she should be awake in a few hours."

Dhananjay was relieved.

"What should we call him, Maharaja?" Vishamadeva asked.

"Jhanaviputra, you should name him. We owe you for everything." Dhananjay was serious as he passed this responsibility. This time it was an easy one.

Vishamadeva took the child in his hands and raised him high. Then he said, "Viraat!"

◆

PART II

19

Śrēṣṭha (Best)

Fourteen years had elapsed.

A bright summer sun played hide-and-seek with white puffs of cotton-like clouds. The whistling wind spread the news of the upcoming match.

In a circular arena overlaid with red mud, a huge platform was constructed for the King and Queen and other high-ranking officials attending the match. Every year, the King sent a senior official to represent him, but this year he would be here in person. The King was supposed to be impartial but this year he couldn't be, even if he wanted to.

It was unlike any other day. A big crowd had assembled on the ground around the arena to watch history being made. The air was rife with whistling and shouting as they waited for the match to start.

The two fighters entered the pit. Tension mounted their faces like a sullen mist. They were dressed in traditional duelling clothes: bare-chested with only a dhoti arranged in proper pleats, tucked in between the legs and tied in tight knots. They moved to pick a weapon of their choice. In the contest, popularly known as *Illangam*, the fighters were allowed to pick any weapon: sword, scimitar, spear, mace or axe. They were even permitted to change weapons during an ongoing fight. The taller fighter went for a sword and a shield. The shorter fighter, who was also the younger one, chose a six-foot spear – an unusual choice. Both were training weapons made of wood.

Both contestants were students of the same Guru. The Guru, a taciturn, hefty and bald man in his fifties, was seated along with the King and other officials. He was one among the best teachers of the Lok. After initial schooling, the students entered his elite gurukul at the age of thirteen, where they underwent five years of rigorous training, learning everything from fighting to administration to finance. But the focus was on grooming fighting skills. At the end of every year, he organized a three-day gruelling Illangam to select the best fighter with weapons. In the long history of the contest, no one had ever managed to stay champion for four years continuously. Five-year continuous champion was unheard of when no one had managed to be the winner for four straight years. This year a four-year champion could be possible. Today was the grand finale where a champion of champions would be crowned.

The opponent was a first-year student, who was both determined and focussed. It was a lifetime opportunity for him to prove his worth. No one doubted his skills, but he wanted to become a legend. Still, he was relaxed as no first-year student had ever defeated a final year student. As he stretched, his eyes fell on his senior who was nearly a foot taller and much more muscular. An uneasy feeling swept over him. He was trusting his agility but could he overcome sheer strength? No one seemed to think that. The expressive faces and murmurs of the crowd confirmed that. They were calling it a one-sided match. Over the last three days, he had impressed the crowd and they were cheering for him, until this match. Now, he was up against his toughest opponent – the reigning champion for the last three years. He knew bets were being placed against his victory.

Weapons in hand, the two fighters bowed to the King and Queen. The King blessed the younger one in his heart. It was no ordinary feat to reach the final; that made the King proud. He got up from his chair and raised his right hand to bless the fighters. Then he moved to a bell hung nearby and performed the ritual of ringing the bell to start the contest. The crowd cheered loudly.

The fighters took their defensive guard. They cautiously moved in a circle.

The elder fighter felt the pressure; he had a lot at stake and everything to lose. He was confident, but a tinge of queasiness surrounded him. A small mistake could be expensive. He wanted the younger one to strike first. But the younger one was not going for it. He knew his opponent was ready. He stood a chance only if he outsmarted the older one, so he settled into a low stance, waiting. His reach was longer; he had no reason to attack first. He taunted, "Come on. Are you scared of a first-year student?"

But the senior fighter was not easily manipulated. He barked a short laugh. He maintained his position and continued the occasional toying of his opponent's spear with his sword.

The crowd was getting restless; shouting and screaming rose in volume. They started calling the senior fighter's name. And then the crowd started a battle cry. "Attack! Attack!"

The senior fighter succumbed to the crowd pressure. He licked his lips, took a deep breath and lunged with a powerful swing of the sword from the top. The junior fighter countered it by holding his spear horizontally and blocking the sword. He gave a strong backward thrust, momentarily making his opponent lose balance.

Sensing an opportunity, the junior swung his spear from the left, then right and backed it up with a repeat of the moves. All were blocked. He had applied so much power that vibrations ran from the spear to his fingertips. It didn't work. Then he rolled to make a surprise swing parallel to the ground, almost touching it. His opponent was momentarily late to react and the spear pierced his ankle. Excruciating pain rippled across his leg. The senior wobbled, his legs struggling to hold him upright. He fell and the sword dropped out of his hand.

There was a stunned silence in the crowd.

The King clapped. The crowd joined.

The younger one used his spear to fling the sword out of his opponent's reach.

Snarling like a wild beast, the elder fighter rose and frowned. The match was not over. Far from it. He tightened his grip on the shield and waited.

The junior fighter knew this was his best chance to pull-off an upset win. His teeth bared in a feral grin; his eyes lit up in excitement. Impetuously, he went with many quick left-right attacks. But he got no success.

Frustrated, the younger fighter went for an over-the-top attack. A bold move. The senior was prepared and expecting it. He sat down and blocked it with the slightly tilted shield. The spear skidded and hit the ground. Immediately, the elder fighter got up and jerked his right leg at the stomach of his opponent. The junior fell backward and the spear slipped out of his hand.

The elder fighter raced to his sword and picked it up. He was back in the match. He breathed a sigh of relief.

The crowd hooted and clapped. Even the King appreciated the move. Both fighters were back on their feet with their respective weapons.

The sun parted company with the clouds and beat down on the arena. They both could feel sweat bead up on their forehead, neck, arms, chest, almost everywhere.

The younger fighter waited for the senior fighter to attack. He trusted his special instincts of reading his opponent. He drifted around his opponent, maintaining the same distance and let the spear dance hypnotically.

The elder fighter was outraged. His eyes turned bright red. He had had enough. He made repeated powerful thrusts with the sword and even swung his shield lethally. But the younger fighter read his moves. He blocked or avoided all thrusts. The choice of spear was working to his advantage. It helped him maintain distance. If it was sword-to-sword combat, his opponent would have had the upper hand.

The crowd was loving it. They hadn't expected the fight to last so long and be so close. Many in the audience began to cheer for the underdog.

The cheers got the elder fighter angrier and more restless. His jaws stiffened. His heart was pumping rapidly. His chest was heaving. He needed to get closer. He threw away the shield and picked up another sword with his left hand. Then he showed his skills in moving both the swords with ease. The crowd clapped in amazement.

This was it. The climax.

The younger fighter had not anticipated this. This move seemed to scare him.

The elder fighter charged at him. The younger fighter moved backward, but kept blocking blows from both swords and not giving up. The elder attacked with the right sword going for his opponent's head which was blocked with a strong vertical hold of the spear. The disguised follow-up attack came from below with the left hand. But to his surprise, the younger fighter blocked that one as well. The senior couldn't understand how his opponent had read the second move.

The junior attacked with a rapid rotation of the spear and disarmed his opponent.

Both the swords fell out of his hand.

The junior positioned the spear in a lethal attack stance but stopped it right before he could strike his opponent's head. The senior conceded defeat. The younger fighter had triumphed.

There was silence before the crowd broke into thunderous applause. It was the best match they had ever witnessed. No one had anticipated this outcome.

Both the fighters hugged. The senior congratulated his opponent and raised his hand in appreciation.

The crowd cheered, "Lakshya! Lakshya! Lakshya!"

Surya, a proud father, stood alongside many officials. In excitement, Samrat Srivijay walked to Surya and congratulated him, "Your son has performed a miracle. He is extraordinary."

"It is all due to your blessings, Samrat." Surya bowed and thanked Srivijay.

"No first-year student has ever been crowned champion. Today history is made."

"You made it happen, Samrat." Tears of happiness swam in Surya's eyes, in a perfect storm of joy.

Srivijay returned to his chair.

Sridhar-acharya, a man of few words who rarely praised anyone, got up, went to Srivijay and said, "Samrat, this boy is extraordinary. I have never seen a fighter read his opponent so well. If he goes to Acharya Brihaspati's Gurukul in Siddha-Lok, he could become the best fighter ever known."

Srivijay replied, "He is doing exceptionally good here. What is the need to send him so far?"

"Acharya Brihaspati's Gurukul is the best school on Dhruva-Lok, named after famous Acharya Brihaspati. Dhruvanshi Satyavrat was trained there and he was crowned the Ultimate Champion. He achieved excellence. If Lakshya goes there, he too might achieve the same."

Kaushiki, who was sitting next to Srivijay along with her son Aakash and daughter Meghna, asked, "Will they admit him? You have to be the son or daughter of a Vanshaj or an Utkrisht. In fact, it is difficult even for an Utkrisht to get admission there."

"Yes, it is sad that, over time, the gurukul has stopped entry to the lower classes even when the student is talented."

"Then why will they take him?" Srivijay inquired.

"Samrat, I will make a personal request. Acharya Bhaskar, the current head of gurukul, knows me. And if you recommend him, Acharya Bhaskar may make this exception," Sridhar answered.

Srivijay and Kaushiki looked at their ten-year old son Aakash. Two years ago, Lakshya had single-handedly saved the young Prince from an attack of wild dogs, risking his own life. It was their generosity and payback that the son of an average army official, a Yukth, got admitted into the best gurukul of Bhuvar-Lok.

She signalled approval with a long blink of her eyes.

"Lakshya is our best fighter. I will recommend him," Srivijay said loudly.

Lakshya went on his knees and folded his hands to Srivijay. In the blink of an eye everything had changed for him.

The crowd cheered, *"Samrat Srivijay aur Samragyi Kaushiki ki jai ho."* May King Srivijay and Queen Kaushiki be praised.

Surya placed his hand on his heart when he heard the shouts of the spectators.

Lakshya was born to do something extraordinary, he was sure of that now.

✦

20

Devaprayāga (Godly Confluence)

SIDDHA - LOK

The ancient stones of the arena glistened and shimmered under the morning sun. Colourful maple trees surrounded the huge structure. Each maple leaf resembled a Trishul with a *damaru*. The soft fragrance of lavender blooms enveloped the entire area with its soothing scent, perfect for a place of worship.

The chariot stopped. A fourteen-year-old Viraat, dressed in a white dhoti and blue kurta, got down along with Dhananjay and Padmini. Viraat was tall for his age and had a fair complexion like his father. His nose and jaw had the same delicate lines as Padmini's. Long, wavy brown hair rested peacefully on his broad shoulders. This was his first visit to the place where he was destined to fulfil the prophecy. Looking around with wide eyes and slightly trembling hands, he tried to control his excitement. *This place looks exactly how I thought it would!*

A huge circular stadium was built at this place with a seating capacity of more than twenty thousand people. It was a sacred place except for a few days when it became a fighting arena. Whenever a new Lok-Rakshak of any kingdom was to be chosen, a competition was held at this holy place. If anyone could wield the Trishul he would automatically become the Wielder – the Protector of the entire Siddha-Lok – a position even higher than that of the Kings. This hadn't happened in centuries.

Simham was already on the ground, setting up a security perimeter, supported by Karthik and his elite soldiers. Simham felt nostalgic coming to this place where he was selected as the Lok-Rakshak nearly fifteen years ago. After Dhananjay was controversially crowned as the King, the prestigious position of Lok-Rakshak became vacant. An open challenge was held. There was no Prince or a Dhruvanshi to compete for this title. He was lucky indeed.

He had vivid memories of that day. As per rules, any Vanshaj or Utkrisht could compete. His selection as the Lok-Rakshak made him enter the elitist class of Vanshaj. The position would remain with him till he retired or died. After retirement, he would be crowned King of a Pradesh. Five generations thereon, his descendants would get a vansha name as well. The five-descendent rule had undergone many alterations in the past where it was increased from initial one-descendent, to three-descendent and, later on, to five-descendent to restrict entry into the elite club. The vansha was named after the first person who entered the Vanshaj class. So, his descendants would be called Simha-vanshi, but till then they would be *Ardha-Vanshaj* – a sub-class among Vanshaj who do not have a vansha name yet. His name would outlive him. Imagining his legacy made him extremely proud.

Vishamadeva, Gayatri and Rajguru Kashyap stepped down from their chariot. Vishamadeva's beard touched his chest and it showed the passage of years. They opened their eyes, only to be blinded by the glare of the sun.

"It's very hot today," Gayatri said, as she shadowed her eyes.

"Yes, but he doesn't seem to feel anything." Vishamadeva smiled, pointing his hand towards Viraat.

"He's been training at Acharya Brihaspati's Gurukul under Acharya Bhaskar since he was four years old. He is used to a hard life and is immune to heat," Gayatri replied.

Kashyap intervened, "He is turning out the way everyone has expected. Guru Bhaskar tells me he is seemingly invincible at the gurukul and he has defeated even senior fighters with ease."

"Isn't that expected? He is the 108th Dhruvanshi. No one can beat him!" Gayatri praised Viraat.

"I wouldn't be so sure," Vishamadeva murmured softly. He knew no one was invincible, not even himself. There is always someone equal or more powerful. If there is light, there will be darkness. If there is night somewhere, there will be sunshine somewhere else.

"Look how overjoyed he is, brimming with youthful energy." Kashyap grinned.

"Why won't he be? He has waited for fourteen long years to visit the place where he is meant to fulfil his destiny," Gayatri said.

They moved towards him.

Viraat came up to them and asked, "Jyeshta Pitashri, why is the Trishul kept here, outside the city?"

Vishamadeva replied, "The Trishul is kept in a no man's land, outside the recognized borders of the three kingdoms – Shivalik, Kailash and Himalia. No one claims rights over this part. This is a pilgrimage point for us; a place to meet God. That is why it is called *Devaprayaga* – the place where King Satyavrat met Lord Shiva." After a brief pause, he explained, "The Great War with Paulastya came at a very heavy cost. You know that King Satyavrat lifted Lord Shiva's mighty bow *Pinaka*. He used it in fighting with Paulastya, who was also a great devotee of Lord Shiva. After the final arrow was fired that killed Paulastya, the bow Pinaka broke."

Viraat listened attentively. He had heard this story earlier but hearing it from Vishamadeva made him feel as if it was happening before his eyes.

"Why did it break?" he asked.

"Paulastya was among the best fighters known, highly skilled, also a very learned and educated man. Killing him made even Satyavrat sad. It is said that Satyavrat wished that he could have only killed the ego, arrogance, greed, anger of Paulastya and not killed his wisdom and intellect. But there was no way he could have done that. So, he had to kill a true devotee of Lord Shiva. The breaking of Pinaka symbolized that even the Lord felt mournful."

Kashyap spoke as they moved towards the gate, "After killing Paulastya, King Satyavrat came back and did penance for a year at this place."

"Why did he do penance?" Viraat asked.

"War is a scourge on humanity. Many people die, mostly innocents. He did penance for them," Kashyap answered.

"Then what happened?" Viraat inquired curiously.

"Finally, his prayers were answered, and Lord Shiva appeared before him. Satyavrat asked for another weapon as Pinaka had broken. Lord blessed Satyavrat with his beloved Trishul," Kashyap replied.

"Dhruvanshi Satyavrat installed it at this place for a worthy one to wield it when the time comes," Dhananjay said with pride as they inched closer.

Viraat looked at Vishamadeva and asked, "Jyeshta Pitashri, have you tried to wield it?"

Everyone turned their faces towards the Lok-Sevak. Vishamadeva smiled. "No, I am not meant to."

Naively, Viraat asked in a jovial tone, "Why don't you try today, Jyeshta

Pitashri?"

"I will never wield it. I will not even fight against anyone who wields the Trishul." The reply was stern. His expression became cold. It was not a joke to him. It was his oath, his sacred oath.

Padmini shook her head signalling Viraat to end the topic. They continued to walk and reached the giant gate of the stadium.

The guards opened the gate. Viraat entered first in excitement. He rushed ahead but stopped in awe as his eyes fell on the radiant, mighty, golden Trishul. He broke out in goose bumps and his spine tingled.

Everyone else folded their hands and prayed to Lord Shiva. Viraat remained frozen until he received a pat from Padmini.

"It looks unreal. What is it made of, Jyeshta Pitashri?" Viraat asked.

"Lord Shiva's Trishul is said to be made from matter from the Sun by Vishwakarma, the divine architect who created the world. It symbolizes the ultimate power against which even the gods stand no chance."

"Really?" Viraat expressed surprise.

"It is believed that this Trishul was used to sever the original head of Ganesha by Lord Shiva. Undoubtedly, it is one of the most powerful weapons in the *Brahmand*," Vishamadeva explained.

"Does Trishul have some special powers or is it merely a weapon?" Viraat asked.

"That no one knows, but it must have some special powers. Probably, Satyavrat knew about the powers but he never told anyone," Vishamadeva shrugged his shoulders as he replied. "Now, only the wielder will get to know. Maybe someday soon we will get to see its true powers."

Kashyap emphasized, "After King Satyavrat kept it here, no one has been able to move it, not even give it a nudge; forget wielding it."

Shravan, the priest of this sacred place, was a tall and thin man with a fair complexion and a long face. His family had served the Trishul for the last twelve generations. Since there was no settlement around it, the priest and guards stayed in a village about four kilometres away. Every single day, they were at the arena, taking care of the temple and its surroundings.

He greeted the esteemed visitors and applied tilak on their foreheads.

"What does *damaru* (two-headed drum) on the Trishul signify?" Viraat asked the priest.

"It signifies infinite power," Shravan answered loudly, with both hands raised high as if the gods were going to shower flowers at that moment. "The Trishul has infinite power."

Vishamadeva placed his hand on Viraat's shoulder and said, "Enough of your questions, Viraat. Go ahead. Try to lift it."

Viraat felt a heavy pressure build within him. He had not expected to lift it during his first visit. He swallowed hard. With a deep sigh, he stepped to the Trishul. It was the moment of truth.

Would he be able to lift the sacred Trishul?

◆

21

Aśruta (Unheard)

Night fell and life came to a standstill in the busy capital city of Samrat Srivijay's Jambu-Rajya. Radha was sitting on a mat in a dimly lit room chanting her daily prayers, when there was a knock on the door. Draped in a cotton sari with her hair casually bundled in a bun, she wore a big, round *bindi* on her forehead which already displayed a smear of *sindoor* at the parting of her black hair. Radha was in her late-thirties.

She got up and opened the door of her modest home – a small two-room brick house inside the colony for average ranked soldiers in the army of Jambu-Rajya. Apart from the prayer alcove, a jute cot, couple of bamboo chairs, kitchen utensils and mud *chulha* (stove) were the only occupants of the space.

It was her husband, Surya, standing at the door.

He was excited with the day's events. His son Lakshya had achieved what others only dreamed of achieving. Everyone was full of praise for him. He was the talk of the town. The King had announced what was *unheard* of. Lakshya would be sent to Acharya Brihaspati's Gurukul at Siddha-Lok for training!

Without saying a word, Radha went to the kitchen to cook dinner.

Surya had come with a box of sweets. He took a piece out of the box and kept it before Lord Bajrang and various nature gods. He offered a piece to Radha.

She resisted and moved away.

"What happened, Radha? Aren't you happy with what our son has achieved?"

"I am happy. Any mother would be! But what is the need to send him to

Siddha-Lok, so far away? He is getting a good education here. There is no need to separate a child from his family. I will not send him." She had no qualms in saying this.

"I know he is getting a good education here. But he is going to get the best training at Siddha-Lok."

"Even princes from Bhuvar-Lok do not go there. I will not send him away for four long years."

"In Acharya Brihaspati's Gurukul, students are admitted at the age of four and they are trained for fourteen years. Whereas our son is going only for four years. We should consider ourselves lucky. Don't you know that King Satyavrat, The Conqueror, got education there! You should be happy that our son is getting this once in a lifetime opportunity."

"Satyavrat was a Prince, a Dhruvanshi. He was going to become a King. Our son is the son of a commoner, a Yukth. They will not even admit him. And even if they do, he is not going to become a King. He won't even get a high position. Then what is the need to send him so far away?"

Surya's voice got louder. "You don't know that! Dhruva achieved what no one could imagine. Our son will also do something that no one has done before. He is going only for four years. It will pass in a flash."

"What if he doesn't return?"

"What do you mean by that?" He knitted his eyebrows.

"You know he is such a good fighter. What if they keep him at Siddha-Lok? What if they don't let him return?"

Surya was not going to allow her doubts to affect his decision. He would do what was best for his son. He would not let him be chained to a parent's love. He replied, "Then so be it. It will be an honour for him to serve at the kingdom of Satyavrat." On a sudden impulse, he added, "I will do anything for him. It is because of Lakshya that I am alive."

"What do you mean?"

He turned his face away.

Radha felt queasy, hearing such words from Surya. She pulled him around to face her and demanded, "You are hiding something. What is it? Tell me."

"I can't."

"If it concerns my son, I want to know. You can't hide it from me."

After some hesitation, he yielded, "You remember when you were with child, I was sent on a mission."

"Yes, I remember."

"I never told you, but the mission was to kill a four-year-old child in Angaara."

"A child! What kind of mission is that?" She felt outraged with the very idea. "How could you agree?"

"I shouldn't have gone but it was a command. Nevertheless, I couldn't do it. I did not kill the child."

Radha was relieved to hear that. But she sensed there was something more. "I was caught, and I should have died right there. But Guru Shukracharya let me go. He said that I was not meant to die there as someone was waiting for me. Now, I know what he meant. It was Lakshya who saved me. He is meant for some far greater purpose. I see Lord Bajrang in him."

Radha did not know how to respond. She had herself hidden things from him. Was this the right time to tell him?

At that moment, Lakshya entered the house. He was elated by the attention and praise that was showered upon him. But even he did not want to go so far away.

Lakshya said, "Pranam pitashri, Pranam maa." He bent down and touched his parents' feet.

Radha had tears in her eyes.

Lakshya said, "Don't cry, maa. I will not go anywhere leaving you."

Before Surya could say anything, Radha interrupted, "No, son. You have to go. No sacrifice is big enough for the sake of education. God has blessed you with skills. You have to do justice to them. We will come and visit you whenever possible."

"But maa, I don't want to leave you." He hugged her and started crying.

The sound of Lakshya weeping, the mention of the word 'purpose' by Surya and the thought of sending her son away brought back old memories. The ones she had kept hidden. Memories are your real companions; they never leave you.

She began to recall the incident with disturbing clarity.

She was ten years old and enjoyed showing her palm to sages to learn about her future.

Her father was the caretaker of the local temple. One day a very learned Sage Abhinav visited the temple. Radha took care of his needs as a daughter. Abhinav was very impressed with her devotion. When he took leave, he said, "Putri, I am very pleased with your devotion. My blessings are with you."

She raised her palms towards the sage and said, "Hey Rishivar, please tell me about my future, my marriage, my children."

Abhinav studied her palms. "Are you sure you want to know? Sometimes it is better not to."

"Please tell me, Rishivar."

"You will get married and your husband will be very devoted to you."

She felt elated hearing it. But she wanted to know more.

He remained quiet. But Radha kept staring at him with her inquisitive eyes. She wanted to know more. He continued, "You will give birth to a son. He is coming into the world for a lakshya (purpose). But ..."

He paused.

"Tell me, Rishivar. What is it? I want to know." Her heart palpitated, like a fish out of water.

"... he will die young."

She closed her ears to not hear his words. It shook her soul. "Rishivar, please say it's not true."

Abhinav closed his eyes. Radha got up and ran away.

Many times, wanting to know the future can have terrible consequences.

She had not told anyone about this, not even Surya. How could she? She had not shown her palm to anyone ever again. Radha had never wanted Lakshya to be a fighter. She did not initially let Lakshya go to any gurukul and tried to keep him close to her. But everything changed when he saved Srivijay's son and the Samrat rewarded him with admission at the best gurukul on Bhuvar-Lok. No one could hide the light of the sun, not for long. She could not control destiny.

"No, maa. I will not go," Lakshya pleaded again.

To keep such things hidden in her heart, to control her emotions and send her son away was very difficult for her, but Radha overcame her instincts. She knew that at some point, she had to let him go.

She said with a heavy heart, "Everything happens for a reason, Lakshya. A caterpillar is safe in its cocoon but that's not what it's born to be. It is in the stars. You were born for a purpose and meant for far greater things, which you can't reach by staying here. You have to go."

Surya added, "Go and achieve what is yet *unheard* and make us proud, son!"

✦

22

Nirvrtta (Ready)

Time went by as time must.

It was a cloudless blue day near the western coast of Angaara where the crashing waves of the turbulent Tethys Sea could be heard even from a mile inland. A mild evening sea breeze blew, making the tree leaves rustle like a whispering audience.

Vritra had been an exceptional student. He was now nearly six and a half feet tall; his swarthy, oval face with a long neck was handsome in a brutal sort of way. Muscles rippled under his skin like trapped energy ready to explode. Locks of brown-black, well-oiled hair fell to his shoulders, and he sported a heavy moustache on his lip. His wide eyes had the iciness of a crocodile and his stretched earlobes were pierced with circular brass earrings.

Over the long and excruciating years of training, he had mastered fighting skills with all the weapons, learned rare vidyas and gained unimaginable powers. However, he was yet untested. Today, the Guru had given him a task. He was up against a bull, not any bull but an Ankole-Watusi bull. A fully-grown bull weighed nearly five hundred kilograms and was characterized by exceptionally long and thick horns, which were more than a meter long, with a broad spread as well. The bull came in various colours but was usually red.

Pashakura – taming of an animal – was a popular sport here at Angaara. The tribes had mastered these skills over the ages. Among the animals, the most challenging one to tame was an Ankole-Watusi bull. Taming an elephant or a rhinoceros was comparatively easier.

Shukracharya was waiting for his shishya to return to the ashram after his victory. Ever since that assassination attempt, they had always been on the move; not settling in one spot for long. He couldn't risk it. After years of training, the day had come for one final test. It was a test of strength and agility, mentally and physically, to know whether the student was *ready*. If he succeeded today, then he would be ready for Raakh who was known to have killed an Ankole-Watusi bull with his bare hands. If the shishya returned with the body of the bull, he would probably succeed in his real fight that lay ahead.

The wild bull was grazing in a small field with low grass, surrounded by trees. These bulls moved in herds and never left their mates. They were short-tempered and also very protective of their calves and the herd. They disliked intruders in their zone.

Vritra felt lucky as the bull was alone today, away from his herd. To attract him, Vritra picked up a small rock. He was relying on his special skills with animals. Worry lines creased his face. He let out a puff of air and threw the rock at the bull.

The rock hit the bull on his nose. Irritated, the bull looked around. Vritra whistled to seek attention.

The bull roared and charged at him. The ground shook. The small pebbles around his hooves' defied gravity. Vritra could feel the vibrations penetrating his body. He quickly jumped to the right, avoiding a head-on collision and escaping narrowly. Even a brief contact would have been fatal. He breathed deeply to calm his racing nerves. The bull stopped, turned and grunted loudly. Vritra remained focussed and readied himself for the next round.

The bull charged with reflex, ran again and tried to dislodge the intruder with his big horns. This time Vritra blocked and held the bull with his horns. Both applied their strength. Impregnable vigour against unwavering determination.

At last, Vritra's legs skidded. The bull was much more powerful than he had anticipated. When he couldn't hold it any longer, he turned the bull's horns to the left and jumped towards the right.

Defeating this bull with his bare hands was unlikely. He picked up a huge wooden log, he had kept ready. The roaring bull raced at him again.

Vritra retaliated with his roar, which was louder, and sprinted towards him. They approached each other for the showdown. At the last moment, Vritra got down on his knees. He used all his strength and hit the bull's legs with the log. With front legs dislodged from the ground, the bull lost balance and slumped down on the muddy field.

Vritra wasted no time and jumped on the beast with the log in his hand and pinned him down with a strong hold on the neck. The bull's eyes bulged out of the sockets. The bull fought for a while before it choked with a rasping, dying moan.

✦

The Guru was waiting for his student to return. He couldn't sit, so he moved around his hut, his fingers playing absentmindedly with his string of prayer beads made of rudraksha seeds. Nervous energy gripped him. Killing required cruelty and a moment's hesitation could be the cause of one's undoing. Knowing his student, he feared Vritra might hesitate. He may not go all the way.

Vritra was his best student so far. He had exceeded his expectations. If Vritra wielded the Trishul, there would be no one to stop him. That day was far but within sight.

Shukracharya heard footsteps. He smiled and turned back. But to his horror it was the bull which stood in front of him. It was as if a tsunami had hit him.

After the moment of shock had passed, he looked carefully at the bull and saw a rope tied around its neck. Vritra came out from behind the animal. He leaned down and touched his teacher's feet. To his surprise, the bull also bent his neck down.

"You couldn't kill him?" Shukracharya asked.

"Kill only when it is absolutely necessary!" Vritra reminded the Guru of his own teachings. "Also, in the sport of *Pashakura*, it is forbidden to kill the animal."

Shukracharya did not like it. "It was not a sport but a test. Hesitation is a vice. This is a weakness your enemy will not share. They don't follow rules."

With folded hands, Vritra replied, "I did not hesitate, Guruji. It is my rule to give my opponent one last chance and I won't break it."

"You and your rules." Shukracharya scoffed in a frustrated tone.

"Everyone deserves one last chance. He accepted, Guruji."

"Are you sure that he will not attack you again?"

"He is not human. If he was, I would not have hesitated." Vritra smiled looking at the bull. To him animals were more trustworthy and loyal.

Shukracharya's face beamed with pride. The student had once again gone beyond his imagination. He was brave, compassionate and governed by rules. He understood how far to go and where to stop. But was he ready for Raakh? Strengths could turn out to be weaknesses at times. Against Raakh, there was no room for error because he wouldn't have a second chance.

He is truly worthy. But he is still not ready. He needs to know.

"We shall leave tonight."

◆

23

Sparśa (Touch)

SIDDHA - LOK

Viraat broke into a cold sweat. He had never anticipated that he would be asked to lift the Trishul today. All he knew was that Satyavrat had installed it and said that when the time comes a worthy one would wield it. Going by the prophecy of the Saptarishis, he was destined to wield it. When would that happen? What would it take to wield it? Was he worthy of it today? He did not know.

A thin sheen of perspiration covered his face. A line of sweat crawled slowly down his back. His hands were shaking. *What if I am unable to move it? Everyone will laugh and make fun of me!* Self-doubt clouded his mind. All his life, so far, he had lived under constant pressure and weight of the prophecy. He stood frozen.

Padmini could see his diffidence. She held his hand and slowly moved it towards the Trishul. Viraat looked at her with pleading eyes that clearly said, *I am not ready, maa.* But her eyes were reassuring him, *Don't worry, son. Trust the Lord. Surrender.*

Viraat took a deep breath and silently prayed to Lord Shiva one last time. His heart was pounding like the thundering hooves of a wild stallion. Fear flickered in his eyes. His lungs seemed to have stopped taking in air.

As his hands drew closer to the Trishul, all his doubts began to disappear like fog dissipating in sunlight. He slowly placed his hands around the mighty weapon and waited to absorb the moment.

All eyes, filled with curiosity and trepidation, were glued on him.

Viraat took one long breath, closed his palm and tried to move the Trishul. He felt as if a current ran through his body.

The Trishul shook slightly.

This hadn't happened in centuries. Viraat didn't go any further and abruptly snatched his hands away, not yet ready to go through with it. *The time hasn't come.* Relieved that the Trishul moved on his touch, he got down on his knees and did a namaskar to the mighty weapon.

The priest blew the conch.

The gatekeepers and soldiers stared in disbelief at what they had just witnessed, which soon turned into admiration for the young Prince.

Padmini hugged Dhananjay. She was unable to control her happiness. It was a dream come true. Remembering their other children, she said, "I wish Upendra and Soma were also here today." Upendra was four years younger to Viraat and Soma was their six-year-old son.

"They will also come here when their time comes. Savour this moment," Dhananjay responded softly.

Vishamadeva and Gayatri looked up with their lips quivering, eyes moist with joy. Things were finally looking good. The pieces of the puzzle were finding their right places. The sacrifices they had made were paying off.

Simham took out his heavy sheathed wootz sword, held it high and screamed Shivalik's war cry, "*Hara Hara Mahadeva.*"

Soon the chants of '*Hara Hara Mahadeva*' filled the holy place.

◆

24

Upakāra (Favour)

SIDDHA - LOK

It was one of those days on Siddha-Lok when daylight had lasted for nearly seven pahars. The sun was about to set, but the calls of birds were nowhere to be heard. The fluttering of butterflies had paused for the day. Moths were out early, humming and dancing around the flowering shrubs.

Every year the day arrived when it was time to return to the tough life at Acharya Brihaspati's Gurukul after one month of royal life in the palace. The vacation period had come to an end. It was not easy to stay away from the family and royal comforts. But royal blood meant that the rock had to be chiselled and polished. The training was meant to strengthen them both physically and mentally; any Prince or Princess needed both. Aindrita wiped her tears as she got ready to enter the gurukul.

"Pitashri, it will get dark soon. You should leave and reach the palace at the earliest. Maa will be waiting." She was worried about her mother. Devayani wasn't keeping well and did not come to drop her.

"It's not that late. Don't worry about your mother. She is safe in the palace." Yuyutsu did not want to go. He was more attached to Aindrita than his nine-year-old daughter Sivasri, who was still at the palace as the vacation period for younger children was longer. Yet he never let even a single tear escape from his eyes in front of Aindrita. He needed to be strong in this moment of weakness.

He asked her, "Have you taken all your belongings?" By belongings, Yuyutsu meant a small bag which contained her weapons and books.

"Yes, pitashri." Royal articles including clothes and food items were not allowed at Acharya Brihaspati's Gurukul. Acharya Bhaskar, the head, was very strict about the rules and discipline. No one was allowed to wear royal clothes.

No exceptions! All students had to be in the attire of a shishya, like a monk. Boys wore dhoti or kurta-pyjama while a saree draped like a warrior was the dress for girls. The colour was yellow or white. White symbolized purity and yellow represented knowledge.

She touched her father's feet. Before she could enter through the gates of the gurukul, her eyes fell on a race that had just started.

Six boys were running in a hundred-meter sprint. One of them raced ahead and the race finished.

Viraat locked eyes with Aindrita. In fact, he had started the race to impress her on her return. He admired her beauty. Draped in a light-yellow saree, she was tall with a slim, flexible body and porcelain skin. Her long golden-brown hair was plaited and artfully coiled at the back of her head. Her lips were crimson red, and they bordered rows of perfect white teeth. Her beautiful, black eyes were shadowed with long, thin and curly eyelashes, sitting under high-arch eyebrows. The dimples on both her cheeks further accentuated her beauty. Except for a crescent nose pin and ear studs, there was no other jewellery on her body. Her long neck stretched like that of a swan with a distinctive black mole towards the left.

Viraat was tall and handsome. His skin was light brown, very much like Aindrita's skin colour. His medium-long, brown hair touched his shoulders. Eyes were round and big. His eyebrows were quite thick. There was no hint of fat on his perfectly chiselled body.

Viraat came running to the carriage and passed very close to Aindrita. Their bodies did not touch but their minds and hearts came very close. Both their eyes had a slight pinkish tint. He deliberately avoided eye contact with her. His eyes were on Yuyutsu. He bent down and touched Yuyutsu's feet. "Pranam, Kailash-Naresh."

"Ayushman bhava, putra." Yuyutsu's face was all smiles. He always saw Viraat as a prospective son-in-law, as he was biased with the words of the Saptarishis.

Aindrita turned back and looked at them. She felt a rush of indescribable emotions. It was as if she was living out a beautiful dream.

"How are the Maharaja and Maharani?" Yuyutsu asked.

"They are good. They left yesterday."

"Is it true what I heard? You lifted the Trishul?"

Viraat blushed. He did not like to be treated as a demigod. But he was born with the gift, his liability. "No, I did not lift it. It moved very slightly." When news spreads, its version changes in every ear. So, most people heard that Viraat had lifted the Trishul.

Yuyutsu placed his hands on Viraat's shoulders. "You are meant to achieve greatness, son!"

Viraat was embarrassed. A life destined for greatness was not an easy one. He was relieved when the Trishul had moved, but it meant higher will be the expectations next time. He did not say anything.

"Vishamadeva has named you perfectly…Viraat," Yuyutsu said loudly.

For the first time, Yuyutsu saw Viraat and Aindrita standing together. To him, they looked like an ideal couple, like *Shiva and Parvati*.

In a tiny corner of his mind, a door opened.

His eyes looked at Aindrita and then they moved towards Viraat. He said, *"Dhanya ho, putra."* Be blessed, son.

Without saying anything further, Yuyutsu left with the thought in his mind.

Dhananjay and Padmini were sitting in their chambers. They had returned yesterday after dropping Viraat at the gurukul. They would have to wait for another year now before they could see their firstborn again. The rules of the gurukul stipulated that in an entire year, only a vacation of one month was granted after the student attains the age of fourteen. No other holidays were allowed. No visitations, except in emergencies like death in the family, were permitted.

Anga-Rakshak Karthik entered and said, "Maharaja, Raja Yuyutsu from Kailash-Rajya is here and wants to meet you. Lok-Rakshak Simham received him at the city gates and escorted him to the palace."

Dhananjay looked up in surprise. He had come unannounced. This was unexpected, quite unlike the visitor. "What is it about? Did he say anything?"

"No, Maharaja, he did not say anything. He insists on meeting you at the earliest."

Hmm. Dhananjay rubbed his beard for a few seconds. "Is he alone? I mean, is the Queen with him?"

"He has come with a very small contingent. The Queen has not accompanied him. Even the Lok-Sevak and Lok-Rakshak are not with him."

"Show him into the elite guest chamber with all courtesies. I will meet him there in half an hour."

"Yes, Maharaja. Should I ask the Lok-Sevak and Lok-Rakshak to be there?"

"No, I will meet him alone."

Karthik nodded and left with the message.

Padmini picked up a glass of water and handed it over to Dhananjay. She asked him, "He has come unannounced. What could this be about?"

"I don't know. It must be something personal. He is not among those to seek favours."

After finishing the glass of water and waiting for some time, he said, "I should greet him."

✦

Yuyutsu was not seated. He was walking back and forth in the luxurious guest chamber.

With a vaulted ceiling and an expansive marble floor etched with floral designs, the room was exquisitely decorated. Big, airy windows lined two sides of the walls with a view of the inner courtyard and were strung with netted curtains that waved gently in the evening breeze. Plenty of furniture adorned the room which reflected high-class luxury, perfectly matching its occupants outlook to life.

Dhananjay stepped inside. "King Yuyutsu, Shivalik-Rajya is proud to welcome you. If you had informed us about your arrival, we would have accorded you a grand welcome."

"That is very kind of you, Maharaja. There was no time to inform you. It was a sudden plan. I decided to come after leaving my daughter Aindrita at the gurukul."

They both hugged each other.

Dhananjay said, "Please be seated. What would you like to have?"

"Nothing, Maharaja. I have already eaten thanks to Lok-Rakshak Simham."

After they took their seats, Yuyutsu asked, "How is the Maharani and Princes Upendra and Soma? I met Prince Viraat at the gurukul."

Dhananjay knew this had something to do with Viraat holding and moving the Trishul. It couldn't be a coincidence that so soon after it happened, King Yuyutsu was on a surprise visit. He replied, "Maharani is good. The princes are also fine. We also dropped Viraat at the gurukul and returned yesterday."

"Yes, Princess Aindrita is also at the gurukul. Aindrita is only a few months younger to Viraat. They both know each other." There was a sense of eagerness in Yuyutsu's reply. His eyes had lit up.

Dhananjay nodded.

After a brief silence, Yuyutsu said, "I heard Viraat lifted the Trishul."

"Saying that he lifted the Trishul would be twisting facts. It moved very slightly."

"No one has been able to even do that." Yuyutsu knew it was not a small achievement by any means. "It is happening as the Saptarishis had said."

"The Holy Trimurti has blessed us." Dhananjay folded his hands in thanks to the Gods.

With some deep thought, Yuyutsu said, "I took your advice."

"What advice?"

"I had visited the Saptarishis as you told me."

"When did you visit? What did they say?"

"I visited them before Aindrita was born. The Saptarishis told me that a devi will be coming to our vansha. I won't lie that I wanted a son but now I feel God has done a favour by blessing us with a girl."

Dhananjay raised both his hands in praise of the Gods and Saptarishis. Yuyutsu added, "They also said that she will become a Queen."

"I know she will…a very fine Queen."

After beating around the bush, Yuyutsu finally said, "I have a *favour* to ask for."

Dhananjay narrowed his eyes. He had an idea where this was going. He feigned innocence. "What could we possibly give you, Kailash-Naresh?"

"It will be an honour if Aindrita gets married to Dhruvanshi Viraat and becomes the Queen of Shivalik-Rajya. It will be a union of two great kingdoms."

Dhananjay got up from his chair. He felt elated with the proposal. He held Yuyutsu in a warm hug. "You have spoken what we desired. We saw Aindrita at the gurukul last year. She will be the daughter we don't have."

"After Viraat and Aindrita pass out of gurukul, we will announce their engagement and after one year we can get them married. It will be a wedding that will be remembered for centuries to come."

"Looks like you have everything planned." Dhananjay laughed. "Let us hope that they both agree to our wishes," he cautioned.

Yuyutsu had no doubts in his mind. "I am sure they will. It's written by the Gods themselves."

◆

25

Anuchit (Unfair)

BHUVAR - LOK

It was an hour to sundown. Dark clouds eclipsed the capital city of Jambu-Rajya. The rain had ceased but squally winds continued to blow. The musty smell of petrichor filled the air. Surya reached his house with another man and invited him inside.

The man replied, "No, it's getting late. The weather doesn't look good. I will come tomorrow."

"You are right. Let me call Lakshya. Meet him." Surya called Lakshya outside. "Lakshya, this is Janak, a merchant of silk garments and millets and a good friend of mine. You haven't met him before. He is a frequent traveller to Siddha-Lok and Acharya Brihaspati's Gurukul."

"Pranam, deva." Lakshya bowed his head in greeting. Lakshya saw a fat man with big eyes and red face under a hefty beard. The man had thick, rubbery lips that looked ready to break into a laugh at the slightest excuse.

Janak gave a hearty smile. "So, you are the one who is going to Siddha-Lok."

"Thank you, Janak, for agreeing to take him to the gurukul," Surya said gratefully.

"I am happy to help. Do you feel they will admit him? I mean, I have been to gurukul many times. What I know is that their rules are very strict."

"Acharya Sridhar is very hopeful. There is no harm in trying," Surya replied, controlling his irritation. He repeated these lines to everyone who reminded him about the rules.

"I don't want the boy to get disappointed. But I will bring him back if they don't admit him," Janak said.

Lakshya kept quiet. It was gradually dawning on him that his chances were slim. He asked, "How much time will it take to reach the gurukul, Janak-deva?"

"Almost six days. It will take two days of travel by land to reach the east coast. Then one day of travel by sea to reach Siddha-Lok. And another three days by land to reach the gurukul," Janak answered.

"Won't the route through the Sumeru mountains be shorter?" Lakshya asked.

"Ohh, a person like your father can reach in three days, or even less, through those mighty mountains. But it is not for people like me. If I ever try to go through them, I am sure I will never reach." Janak chortled.

"You are forgetting about the sea-route through the western side," Surya intervened.

"The tumultuous waves will crush the boat in no time. West is the doorway to hell. Only my ghost will reach through that route," Janak guffawed.

The continuous laughter irritated Lakshya. He realized it was going to be tough travelling with Janak. He looked at his father and pleaded, whispering, "Do I really have to go with him? Can't you come?"

Surya mumbled to Lakshya, "Sorry, son, but you have to go with him." Surya couldn't tell Lakshya that Janak had agreed to take him for free. He needed to save a lot of money to fund Lakshya's schooling, travelling, clothing and it still wasn't going to be enough. Till now Samrat Srivijay had sponsored his schooling at Acharya Sridhar's Gurukul, so he had to only pay for food and clothes. Now, he would need to pay at Acharya Brihaspati's Gurukul. It was difficult to predict how much they would charge him as Lakshya was going to be a special case. He wasn't sure how to say this to Lakshya. *If the Gods have opened the door, they will find a way for us to get through it, if it's meant to be,* he said to himself.

"When do we leave, Janak-deva?" Lakshya asked.

"Tomorrow morning. Be ready."

◆

Later, Radha came to Lakshya and said, "I have packed food and some medicines for the journey. It is going to be a long trip."

"Neither pitashri nor you are coming with me. Please come, maa."

"No, Lakshya, we cannot. You know I can't travel so far. Don't worry, it is going to be okay."

Surya interrupted them and gave Lakshya a bag containing some money. "Lakshya, take this and keep it with you at all times. It has some money for your travelling, clothing and other expenses. You may need this in the gurukul."

Lakshya took the bag.

"I will send more money with Janak. You can send any message to us through him," Surya added.

"Are you not going to visit me?"

"Yes... yes... I will visit you whenever I can. It is a matter of four years. They will pass by in a flash."

Lakshya felt disheartened hearing it.

"This will cheer you up." Surya pulled out his favourite dagger and held it towards Lakshya. "Take this. Whenever you miss us, this will make you feel that we are close to you."

Surya had never allowed Lakshya to touch the dagger before this. Lakshya reached out for it and admired the steel.

"It is very close to my heart. So, don't ever lose it," Surya expressed his love for the dagger.

"It will always stay with me, pitashri."

There was one pressing concern in Lakshya's mind. "Pitashri, are they going to admit me?"

"We need to try. Hope is all we have and one should never give up without trying. Remember that," Surya said.

"And even if they don't admit you, it's not going to change anything. One way or the other, you will achieve what you are meant to. If one door closes, another door opens. And at the end, all the doors lead to God. The important thing is to keep walking. So, trust the Gods and yourself," Radha assured him.

✦

SIDDHA - LOK

Endless cerulean sky above and unending turquoise water below with its irresistible radiance gives eternal peace within. The thought came to Lakshya as he stood on the deck of the cargo ship, watching the world unroll before him. His worries, his very existence felt so insignificant. It was his first sea-travel and he was thoroughly enjoying it. The soothing ocean breeze ruffled his hair but kept his mind at ease. Seagulls squawked from far away. He arched his back, breathed deeply and let the gentle wind caress his face. He noticed a pod of dolphins jumping in and out of the water. Watching them, his happiness floated like the rhythmic waves of the sea, setting his soul free.

Contrary to his expectations, he enjoyed Janak's company. Janak was a very good storyteller and regaled him with tales about the history of Siddha-Lok and the glory of the Dhruvanshis. He narrated to him the legend of Satyavrat The Conqueror and his tales, the current Maharaja and yes, about the Trishul and the prophesied Prince. The mere thought of the existence of such a weapon gave goose bumps to Lakshya.

Janak forced him to taste fragrant, red wine. He termed it as the drink of gods. Lakshya had never tasted it before. The aroma seemed pleasant. The first sip gave him an immediate burning sensation as the wine passed from his mouth, down the delicate lining of the oesophagus and into his stomach. The tartness of the wine left a lingering, bitter taste in his mouth. A shudder ran through his body; he twisted his face in distaste. Janak insisted that he should take some more and savour it. "Let it linger on your tongue. It takes time to get used to the god's drink," he said. But Lakshya didn't take any further sips and moved away. "What is so godly about this thing?" he marvelled, confused.

The journey through the hilly terrain after landing at the seacoast was the most strenuous. Ever since he got off the ship, Lakshya could feel that the weather in Siddha-Lok was cooler than at Bhuvar-Lok. The people were also fairer, and dressed for cooler weather. The preferred clothing for the common folks here was kurta-pyjama or a v-neck buttoned top and dhoti by men whereas the women wore sarees or loose pants with a long tunic over it, or a dress called *puan* with a wraparound skirt and a full-sleeve top. This was in contrast to an angarkha or a loose pullover shirt by men and a saree by women at Bhuvar-Lok. Turbans were common at Bhuvar-Lok but not so much at Siddha-Lok. He felt the food was not that different, except it was less spicy.

After six days of the challenging journey through sea and land, Lakshya arrived at the gurukul.

The gurukul was in the foothills of the Sumeru mountain range. Janak left him at the gate of Acharya Brihaspati's Gurukul. The school was spread over an area of eighty acres, more than five times the size of his earlier gurukul. It was hexagonal and fortified by stone walls on all sides with entry gates at six corners. Groups of students were undergoing training under trees with multiple teachers and trainers. Around twenty students close in age were in one group and there were fourteen such groups. Huts, made of mud and bamboo, of varying structures and sizes, were spread across the complex. There were many mud pits for training inside a circular running track. Cows, horses and sheep were domesticated inside the complex.

Lakshya stood at the entrance for a while. The real challenge lay ahead. He had high hopes that Acharya Bhaskar would accept him as a student. There were no assurances that he would. Even after Samrat Srivijay and his Guru Sridhar's recommendation, it was still up to Acharya Bhaskar to decide his fate. Life was about a few special moments and this was one of them.

Before he could step inside, he noticed a match was about to start. It was four against one in a circular muddy pit, each one having a sword and a shield. The fight seemed *unfair* to him. In the centre, there was a student of his age. The other four were older to the one in the middle. The students outside the circular boundary were cheering, "Viraat! Viraat!"

This must be the prophesied Prince, Lakshya guessed. Viraat looked both handsome and fearsome.

The other four were ready in attack position. The trainer, standing outside the ring, hit the bell and the match commenced. Viraat moved swiftly. He did not wait to defend unlike Lakshya's style of fighting. He attacked from the word go and straightaway went for the weakest opponent on the right, catching him off-guard. The opponent fell out of the ring and was out of the match.

It was now three against one. Two opponents attacked Viraat from behind. He countered the move with his shield and sword held high. Seeing an opening, he kicked one of the opponents with his leg and then turned around the shield to knock the other one down with his elbow from behind. His lightning speed was a delight to watch. He had caught the two opponents unprepared. They both fell to the ground.

For the first time in his life, Lakshya felt jealous. He had never seen anyone move so fast, attacking like an angry tiger.

Viraat went for the last standing opponent. They crossed swords four times, but the fifth impact was so strong that the sword fell out of the hand of the fourth opponent. He conceded defeat by raising both his hands and moving out of the boundary.

The remaining two got up and moved on to the left and right side of Viraat. They were ready to attack from the sides, in tandem. This time Viraat was on the defensive.

He tightened his grip on the shield and sword and kept a careful watch on both of them through his peripheral vision. After completing two circuits of Viraat's stationary position, they pounced on him together. Viraat sat down and used his shield to stop the attack. With all his strength, he pushed the shield up, throwing both of them off balance. Viraat leaped on the one on the left and kicked him out of the boundary.

Now it was one against one. But everyone knew that the contest was already over, only formalities remained. Viraat threw away his shield and took the sword in his left hand to make it equal of sorts. The cheering of the students got louder.

The opponent slashed down at Viraat's head. Viraat countered by raising his sword high and striking horizontally. It was followed by quick moves from Viraat testing his opponent. But the opponent was ready for them. He was watching the sword carefully. Viraat knew that and it was exactly what he wanted. He held the sword with both hands and started wavering it rapidly. The opponent was unable to figure out from which side the sword would come. Confusing his opponent's mind was Viraat's biggest asset. He attacked suddenly and disarmed his confused opponent. The sword flew high up in the air. While the opponent's eyes went towards his flying sword, Viraat rammed a kick into his diaphragm, sucking out the last whiff of breath from his lungs. He fell far. Viraat caught the flying sword.

The contest was over.

Viraat bowed gracefully before the trainer outside the ring. He had hardly broken into a sweat.

It was followed by loud claps. In his mind, Lakshya clapped in appreciation. Viraat turned and they exchanged glances. But Viraat's eyes moved away not paying much attention.

Viraat along with the rest of the students returned to their classroom under a nearby tree.

Lakshya's confidence plunged after watching this expert display. He closed his eyes, remembered his parents and trudged inside overcoming his doubts. He had noticed a senior Guru in white clothes sitting under a banyan tree at some distance, watching the contest. Calmness, serenity, poise on the face of the Guru and his white dress separated him from others. He was neither fair nor dark, had a lean yet muscular frame and a long face with wide forehead smeared with a red tilak framed by a white U-shaped tilak. His light auburn beard frizzed well below his collarbone and his free-flowing long hair was caught up in a rudraksha-bead topknot.

"Pranam, Acharya." Lakshya touched the Guru's feet.

"Ayushman bhava." The Guru felt good with Lakshya's greeting. He saw his tired, orangish eyes. "You look exhausted. Who are you and what brings you here?"

"I am Lakshya, son of Surya from Jambu-Rajya at Bhuvar-Lok. I seek to become your student."

"Do you have a vansha name?"

Lakshya shook his head tentatively. He lowered his head and remained silent even though his rebellious inner voice fumed, *I am a Suryavanshi.*

"You have come quite far. What does your father do?"

"He is a senior soldier in the army of Samrat Srivijay."

"Ohh, he must be a Yukth." The Guru was disappointed and sad hearing it. His gurukul never took children of commoners as students. "This is a gurukul for the elite class, Utkrisht and above. You must know the rules!"

"I know the rules, Acharya." Lakshya pulled out contents from his bag and gave the letter of recommendation from Samrat Srivijay and the personal note from Guru Sridhar.

If it were a year ago, Bhaskar would have refused admission without reading the letter. But he was a changed man after a talented young boy committed suicide on being refused admission by him due to his lower class. Lakshya's face reminded him of that boy. Was life giving him another chance to correct the wrong? He broke the seal and patiently read the letter and the note.

Bhaskar appreciated Lakshya, "No King has ever recommended a lower-class student. Guru Sridhar thinks very highly of you. You defeated the best fighter of his gurukul, a fighter much older to you."

Trainer Sandesh, standing next to Bhaskar, intervened, "But fighters from Bhuvar-Lok are no match to fighters from Siddha-Lok. They are poles apart."

Bhaskar continued, "Samrat Srivijay has recommended you. This hasn't happened in my lifetime." A beaming smile soon turned into a concerned look. "Training here will be much more difficult. Are you ready?"

"Yes, Acharya. With the blessings of the Guru nothing is impossible."

Bhaskar was delighted with the reply. "Are you tired from the journey?"

Lakshya wanted to lie but he couldn't, he was visibly drained from the journey. "Yes, Acharya."

"Very well. You have to demonstrate your worth. Get ready for a duel. Your training starts from this moment."

Lakshya was bemused. He heaved a deep sigh, as if he had been asked to move a mountain. He stared at the Guru.

Bhaskar's stony expression did not waver.

Lakshya cleared his throat as he said, "But I can barely stand, Acharya. It won't be a fair fight." Maybe it was a clever ploy to reject him. A deep frustration churned inside him.

"Is death fair?" Bhaskar asked with a serious look on his face. He never liked to hear excuses.

"No," Lakshya answered sheepishly.

"Has life been fair to you?"

Lakshya did not need time to answer it. He snapped, "No."

"Then let this be your first lesson. Don't expect your life or your opponents to be fair. And always be ready for it. A champion fighter must be. Do you want to become a champion?"

"Yes," replied Lakshya loudly. *If the intention is to embarrass me, then I won't make it an easy one.* Charged up, he kept his bag down, untied his turban, wrapped it around his waist and rolled up his sleeve.

Bhaskar signalled for Sandesh to fight Lakshya. Many eyes from the classrooms turned towards this unexpected match in the making, with a stranger. By his looks it was evident to them that the stranger wasn't from Siddha-Lok.

"Which weapon do you want?" Sandesh sneered at him. There was no sympathy in his eyes; if anything, all his face revealed was disgust.

"Spear," replied Lakshya. He decided to stick with his last lucky weapon. Both fighters took a wooden spear in their hand. He did not know Sandesh was among the best with the spear.

They both bowed to Bhaskar. At a signal from the Guru, they turned their faces towards each other.

Lakshya's entire body was aching. His special skills needed him to be focussed, which he could barely do. But there was no backing out now. Overcoming all that, he took a defensive stance, holding the spear in his sweaty hands.

Sandesh did not waste any time and immediately went with powerful blows. Lakshya crouched and jumped to avoid the first two, but he blocked the next four attacks. Sandesh's speed and strength were too much for him to match. The impact of the next blow was close to his hand. It was so strong that the spear dropped out of his hands. Sandesh did not stop and gave him body blows on his shoulder and leg with the spear, and then plunged one end into his stomach.

Lakshya cried in pain, "Ahhhhh." Blood spilled from his mouth. The blow on the stomach was extremely painful.

Clearly, Sandesh's intention was to humiliate and demean fighters from outside Siddha-Lok. He was sending a message. Next blow was on the back. Lakshya collapsed on the ground. He appeared unconscious. Sandesh went near him and scoffed, "Not good enough."

It was over before it could get exciting.

Sandesh looked at his helpless opponent for a few seconds. Sensing nothing, he rested one end of his spear on the ground and bowed to Bhaskar, signalling his victory. Everyone in the audience cheered and clapped.

But Bhaskar's eyes were fixed on Lakshya. He knew the match was not over yet. He could see what no one else could – Lakshya's unique *chakra*.

Lakshya's fingers came back to life. His hand crawled to his spear on the ground. He opened his eyes and jumped up in a flash. He screamed, "*Jai Bajrang.*" Praise to Lord Bajrang. There was thunder in his voice and fire in his eyes, which had turned bright red depicting extreme rage. Some deep, hidden power inside him had woken up. It was the roar of a lion, an injured lion.

Sandesh was taken aback by the intensity of his rage.

The audience froze in silence.

Lakshya gathered all his strength and attacked head-on with his spear. Sandesh resisted with a strong horizontal hold. But the sheer force of the impact was so strong that it tore Sandesh's spear into two. There was no stopping him now. Lakshya probed Sandesh with a low shot. When Sandesh blocked it, Lakshya reversed the spear, stepped back and heaved a powerful thrust that knocked the broken spear from Sandesh's right-hand to the ground. Then Lakshya held the spear at its mid-point with both his hands and swung it rapidly, hitting Sandesh on the left wrist and disarmed him.

Lakshya was filled with so much rage that he readied for another powerful blow to his body, when he heard a command, "Stop!"

It was from Bhaskar.

Lakshya was breathing fire. Yet he calmed down and stopped the spear before it could pierce Sandesh. He looked into Sandesh's eyes for a few seconds, and dropped his spear.

Bhaskar got up and came to Lakshya. He wiped the blood from his mouth and gave him a hug. "Dhanya ho, putra. No matter how long or dark the night is, how *unfair* the world is, the sun will always rise. This gurukul is honoured to have you."

Bhaskar looked at Sandesh. "You felt that fighters from Bhuvar-Lok are not good enough. Why do you keep forgetting that Mahabali Bajrang was from Bhuvar-Lok? It's a lesson to the teacher – arrogance has no place here!"

In a soft voice, Lakshya said, "Acharya, I don't have enough money to pay for my schooling here."

"Don't worry, son. This gurukul is under the auspices of Shivalik-Rajya. They sponsor schooling for everyone here. Money is not going to stop you."

Lakshya kneeled and sought blessings from Bhaskar.

Viraat watched from the classroom. He got up and clapped in appreciation. His classmates joined him. Even Sandesh applauded with his head bowed.

✦

26

Pratikāra (Revenge)

ANGAARA

The Guru and Student strode along the edge of a cliff, breathing in nature's serenity. The sun rose in a pool of gold and pink, spilling light all over the land and over the fluffy white clouds in the sky. A gentle wind sighed and moved the treetops, making them dance to its tune.

This morning reminded Shukracharya of the day, fourteen years ago when he had seen Vritra for the first time. He had retired from teaching after the death of his last student, Vishvarupa. The death had broken him and left him without any more ambitions. He had decided to spend the rest of his days praying to Lord Shiva.

When he had seen Vritra, he hadn't been able to resist the child's enigma. It re-ignited his long-buried dream of making someone a Trivikram. The boy seemed worthy of it. He was compelled to make another attempt as the boy Vritra, was truly Vichitra – like no one else. Vritra had done extreme hard work and learned many rare vidyas from him. Shukracharya felt very proud of him.

Shukracharya knew that the boy had the mettle to achieve what no one had done before. Why else would Lord Vishnu take an avatar? The boy would need protection from the tricks of Lord Vishnu. He had already thought of a 'flawless' plan and put it into motion long ago. Even though he wasn't a devotee of Lord Vishnu, in fact, they were always at odds, he encouraged Vritra to pray to both Lord Shiva and Lord Vishnu. After so many years, he felt Vritra had become more devoted to Lord Vishnu. That must be the reason why Vritra's nature had become more of a preserver, not a destroyer.

He avoided killing and followed his own set of moral codes and rules. He spoke the language of Lord Vishnu. It troubled Shukracharya, and for that reason it needed to be changed. Shukracharya decided to take him back to his home.

After two days of travel, they reached the home-in-exile of Vritra's tribe. It was close to dusk. During the journey, the reminiscence of the past and cherished memories kept bringing the occasional smile on Vritra's face.

Vritra saw the hut from a distance. His mental image of the hut was blurred until then. He had left home when he was four years old, but the faces of his parents were still fresh in his memory. He had finally returned. He kept wondering how his parents would look now. Would they be very different? Would they recognize him? What will be the first word they would say? Would he breakdown in tears too? The questions kept bombarding in his head. He felt a pricking sensation in his feet. He cracked his knuckles in excitement. Emotions were running high. Yet he did not run towards his home. He waited for instructions from his Guru.

Shukracharya nodded his head and signalled him to go. But right before Vritra was about to head out, he said, "Be strong."

Excited, Vritra rushed towards the hut. Above the door, he saw a colourful wooden half-statue of a monster that had emerged from the sacrificial fire *Dakshinagni* – big wicked eyes, two large upper canines, bloodied tongue hanging out and fire in his giant hands. Vritra could recall it from his childhood memories. His mother had carved the statue. He ran his fingers over it with care.

He knocked on the door and called out, "Pitaji, Maa. Open the door. It's me."

After a while, the door opened. An old lady came out. She looked a lot older than her age due to the hard work she did daily. The lines around her eyes were deeply etched. Her hands were calloused. A smile appeared on her weathered face as she asked, "Who are you?"

Vritra did not recognize her. She did not resemble the portrait of his mother in his mind. Many years had passed, yet he was sure this was not her. "I am looking for my father and mother. They live here. Who are you?"

"My name is Kalina. I have lived here for the last two years."

For a moment, Vritra wondered if he had come to the wrong hut. But the statue on the door was carved by his mother. He said again, "No, my father and mother live here."

The lady asked, "Who are you? What is your name?"

"My name is Vritra."

"Ohh! You must be the son of Tvashta and Dana."

"Yes, where are they?" Vritra asked impatiently.

"They died a couple of years ago. There was a raid by Raakh and his tribesmen. Many died in that raid. Your father and mother were critically injured. They died after a few days. I am so sorry to tell you."

Vritra felt as if a lightning bolt had struck him. Coming back after so many years and no reunion, instead, this dreadful news!

He felt agitated. Bubbling with anger, he asked, "Why did no one tell me?"

Kalina was taken aback by the intensity of Vritra's eyes. She stammered, "No one knew where you were. Your father did not tell anyone. He did not want your training to be disturbed. They sacrificed even seeing you for one last time."

Her words broke a strong Vritra. His mind became a blank slate and his body went numb. The world around him was collapsing and his legs were trembling. The thought of meeting his parents had kept him going during the difficult training and years of separation. Now, he lost all purpose in life.

Every corner of the sky felt lifeless; awkwardly wearing a gloomy grey dress of clouds. It was as if the sun had lost the desire to set, the winds lost its agility. The trees stood in silence, paralyzed by the sudden jolt. Nature seemed oblivious to her own rules.

The tidings of Vritra's arrival spread fast, and many men and women of their tribe gathered around the hut. There was no murmuring, no talking by the crowd. Instead an ominous silence ensued.

The old lady went inside and brought back two urns. "Your mother told me to wait for you at this hut. This is what is left of them."

She handed it over to Vritra.

Vritra took them in his hand. All the memories came rushing to him. "This is how God has rewarded me for years of worship and hard work!" he simmered with resentment.

Vritra wiped his tears and turned back to leave, fuming. Anger was raging inside him. He started to walk back to the Guru to ask him why he didn't warn him. "Guruji said 'be strong'. He must have known." These words resonated in his head.

The old lady called him loudly, "You should know. Your parents told me to tell you whenever you return."

Vritra turned back and looked straight into her eyes.

"Agnipath!" she said.

Angaara is our motherland. Agnipath we shall tread. His mother's last words to him echoed in his head. He repeated it in his mind and tightened his fist.

A wave of desire for *revenge* swallowed him.

An old man came forward and sobbed, "They will never let us live in peace. I lost two of my sons in that raid."

Another woman whimpered from where she was standing, "They broke my husband's legs and left him to die. He kept crying in pain for many days. We had to put him to rest." She collapsed into the arms of a woman standing next to her.

A voice from behind said, "They will return once they get to know that you are back."

Vritra stood so still that they thought their words were falling on deaf ears.

A hefty man with broad shoulders and squinty eyes, in his early twenties, from the gathered crowd came forward and spoke, "My name is Kaitabha. We were waiting for you to return. The time has come to take back what is ours. We are with you."

Vritra stared at him, breathing heavily.

Kaitabha thought that his words were not reaching Vritra's ears. He cleared his throat. But there was no response. Everyone in the crowd exchanged confused looks.

The sky continued to be ominous. It seemed many devas and asuras had surrounded the sky to hear what Vritra was going to say. A distant rumbling of thunder finally reached Vritra's ears, making him come back to his senses. He looked around vaguely as if he did not know where he was.

Then, he addressed the crowd, "Assemble the men. It's time for payback." Kaitabha and other men yelled, "Yay!" with their hands raised in exultation.

Revenge is a monster. Once the monster awakens, it is difficult to put him back to sleep. And, a man driven by revenge is highly motivated. Vritra would never be the same again.

✦

27

Mitra (Friend)

SIDDHA - LOK

Parthiv was only four-feet tall. At the age of twelve, he was about one foot shorter than his peers. Short height was a disadvantage in fighting. Parthiv was a mediocre fighter. He came from the smallest kingdom of Himalia and was the adopted son of unmarried Queen Maitreyi. For all these reasons, the young boy did not have any friends.

He was either teased or ignored. No one was ready to befriend him. It was more to do with his birth than height. Most students came from Shivalik-Rajya where bloodlines and vansha meant everything. They were taught this from birth. The seed sown during childhood, only grows with time.

Parthiv was alone out there. The training was hard. The circumstances made it even harder. He saw everyone walking in groups, away from him. They were talking loudly – laughing and playing. No one was with him.

What cannot be changed, must be braved! he remembered his mother's words.

They were sent to the jungle to bring wood. Soon it would get dark.

As he started to walk back, a few logs of wood balanced on his shoulder tumbled to the ground. He sat down to pick them up. His eyes fell on an animal. A clouded leopard was hiding behind a bush, aiming at his prey. The shrewd leopard had his eyes set on his classmates. The distance between the prey and its predator was less than forty meters.

A chill ran through Parthiv's spine and froze his body.

✦

It was his first day in the class. He was admitted but the journey ahead was strenuous. To reach the level of his peers, Lakshya had a mountain to climb.

In the class, Lakshya was visibly different. Being from Bhuvar-Lok, Lakshya's skin colour was tanned.

Niyati was Aindrita's best friend. Turning her eyes towards Lakshya, she asked, "Who is he?"

Lakshya was on their right.

Harshika, sitting next to her, answered, "His name is Lakshya. He has come from Bhuvar-Lok."

Aindrita arched her brows. "That's why he looks different."

"Yes. I heard he is a Yukth, son of a commoner. But he defeated *Shikshak* (teacher) Sandesh in a one-on-one spear fight," Harshika added.

"Shishak Sandesh! What are you saying?!" Niyati showed surprise.

"Impressed with his display of skills, Acharya compared him to Bajrang-deva and admitted him."

Aindrita was surprised by the comparison. She looked carefully at Lakshya. She saw a long bruise on his back. *It must be from the fight*, she mulled.

"It will be interesting to see him fight Viraat," Harshika said.

"He stands no chance against Viraat," Aindrita replied impulsively, only to realize what she said. It was quite clear to everyone that Viraat liked her very much. Aindrita always denied any feelings for Viraat. But in that moment her tongue had slipped.

"You can't hear anything against him," they both giggled.

Viraat was sitting on the left side and Lakshya was on the right in the first row. Aindrita was in the middle, but at the back. She could see both of them. They both looked nearly the same height and build. Viraat was even fairer than her. Viraat's ears had golden rings as against Lakshya's wooden. *This is what separates them*, she thought.

Bhaskar entered the class. The students folded their hands in greeting.

Lakshya got up and said loudly, "Pranam, Acharya." He had followed the custom of Bhuvar-Lok.

Everyone else laughed. This was not the practice here. They greeted their Guru without standing up.

"Lakshya, be seated," Bhaskar said in a calm voice. "We will start with *kirtan kriya* of *Kundalini Yoga*."

Lakshya was not used to this style of yoga.

Bhaskar saw his blank and confused face. He explained, "Kundalini derives its name through a focus on the awakening of kundalini energy through regular practice of mantra, tantra, and yantra. It is identified as the most dangerous form of yoga because of the involvement of subtle energies. So, be careful."

Lakshya asked, "What does kundalini represent, Acharya?"

Bhaskar answered, "Kundalini represents spiritual energy or life force located at the base of the spine, conceptualized as a coiled-up serpent. Practicing it arouses the sleeping kundalini shakti from its coiled base through the six chakras, and penetrates the seventh chakra, or crown. This energy travels along the *ida* (left), *pingala* (right) and *sushumna nadi* (center) – the main channels of *pranic* energy in the body."

Bhaskar continued, "Lakshya, sit comfortably with a straight spine. Rest the backs of the hands on the knees. Inhale deeply and begin to chant aloud the mantra: *sa ta na ma*. On the syllable *sa*, touch the index finger of each hand to the thumb; on *ta*, touch the middle finger to the thumb; on *na*, touch the ring finger to the thumb; on *ma*, touch the little finger to the thumb."

Lakshya quickly took the position, copying others. He asked, "What does *Sat nam* mean, Acharya?"

"The mantra means 'Truth is my identity'. When you meditate on it in the form of *sa ta na ma*, you are meditating on your own higher self, your consciousness. Your consciousness is the sun, and the body and the mind are the moons. Without the sun's light, the moons cannot shine. Similarly, without knowing your consciousness, the body and the mind cannot discover their potential. This meditation helps in unleashing the hidden capabilities of your body and mind."

"What is consciousness, Acharya?"

Others in the class giggled at this basic question from Lakshya.

"Quiet. Gurukul is a place for seekers. Those who seek the truth, need to ask questions. The day we stop asking questions, we become a blind man on a dark road and that will be the doom of our soul."

It silenced all.

Bhaskar asked, "Aindrita, tell us, what is consciousness?"

It was an easy one. Aindrita replied, "Human Body is a chariot. Mind is the charioteer. Consciousness is the passenger. It is the real 'me', my real self. That is the ultimate truth."

"Why is it the ultimate truth?" Lakshya questioned. Aindrita fell silent. She did not have the answer.

Acharya said, "A pertinent question. Anyone?"

Everyone remained quiet.

Sensing no reply, Bhaskar asked, "What should be the essentials for the ultimate truth?"

He gave the students some time to think. After a while, Viraat raised his hand.

Bhaskar said, "Yes, Viraat."

He replied, "The ultimate truth should not be dependent on time. It cannot vary across places. It cannot be born, nor it should die – it should be permanent."

"Very good, Viraat. Can there be an untruth to such a truth? Niyati, what do you say?"

"No, such a truth cannot have an untruth," she answered instantly.

Bhaskar smiled and replied, "Only consciousness, our soul has such attributes. It is neither born, nor does it die. It changes bodies like we change clothes. There is nothing opposite to it. It does not have any form. It is *nirguna* (formless). Search for it is the ultimate goal, the path to liberation. This is the ultimate truth."

Everyone was mesmerized with the Guru's words.

Towards the end of the day, the students were sent to the jungle to get wooden logs for cooking and *havan*. The younger ones had gone to the eastern side and the elder ones went towards the north.

✦

Aindrita, Niyati and Harshika were walking together. Boys were in four other groups going in random directions. Lakshya was alone.

Lakshya climbed a mango tree with ease.

The girls were impressed. Aindrita was staring at him.

Lakshya's and Aindrita's eyes met for a brief moment. He had never seen such beauty. A strange emotion swept over him, which he had never experienced before. Aindrita looked away. Lakshya kept staring.

Niyati asked, "Where have you come from?" Aindrita wasn't looking, but her ears were tuned in.

Before he could reply, Harshika asked, "What does your father do?"

The question put him off. He was here for his skills and not because of his lineage. He was proud of his father. He snorted, "He is a senior soldier in the army of Samrat Srivijay."

"So, it's true that you are no Prince or even the son of a high-ranking official. You are just a Yukth," Harshika said in a rude tone.

Aindrita glared at her. *It's inappropriate to say it so bluntly to his face.*

Her tone made Lakshya scowl. The words did not go down well with him and he started treading on the branch. He was breathing heavily, apparently angry. His feet went off target. He lost balance, slipped and fell to the ground.

"Ohh, maa," he said as he got up.

Hearing the words, the girls let out an involuntary laugh.

"He cries like a baby," Harshika guffawed as she taunted him.

In the spur of the moment, a laughing Aindrita mocked Lakshya, looking at Harshita, "And you thought he could stand against Viraat. A commoner, after all."

Aindrita didn't realize that it was loud enough for Lakshya to hear. Her words were more poisonous to him than they were intended to be.

Words are so powerful that they can crush a heart or heal it. This time they crushed his.

He felt humiliated, more so because the remark came from Aindrita. All that he felt for her disappeared. *All that beauty is only skin-deep*, he grumbled.

He limped away hastily without looking back.

Seeing him walk away, Aindrita realized what she had done. She had not meant to hurt him, but it had happened in that instant. A slip of the tongue. It was unlike her to say something like that directly on the face. She felt like stopping him, but she stayed with her friends. After all, she had only called him a commoner; there was nothing wrong for the Vanshaj class to act this way.

"I think we should apologize to him," Niyati said to her friends.

"Forget it…I am not apologizing to him. I am a Vanshaj. Someday he might work for me. He should be used to it. Studying with us doesn't make him our equal," Harshika was quick to respond. It slayed Aindrita's emotions.

"We were wrong. We had no right to mock him. Acharya says that on the battlefield and in this gurukul, all are equal," Niyati said. She had felt something for him from the moment her eyes fell on him.

Harshika said, "This isn't a battlefield and we are outside the school. He should know that."

Aindrita remained silent during the whole conversation.

Niyati swallowed her anger. Lakshya was long gone. The damage was done.

It was getting dark. Lakshya wiped his tears. They would never accept him or be his friends. But he would prove his worth someday.

On his path, he saw a young boy staring at a leopard. Panic gripped him.

✦

28

Agni-Maru (Fire-Duel)

Something was different about the night. It was eerily dark even though five crescent moons were glowing in the sky. The wind was whooshing wildly making the trees bend over. The birds were twittering. Deep growls rolled through the jungle. The hidden nocturnal animals and birds were communicating in the dark, scared of the interlopers cruising through their territory flaunting their fire torches.

Shukracharya was satisfied. His student had received what was needed – motive. The reason he had taken Vritra there before the ultimate test. Vritra had never killed anyone. He would always hesitate and look for ways to avoid it. Tonight, he would need to shed that cloak of weakness. The question still lingered in Shukracharya's mind, *Will he?*

"Instead of leading a revolt, it will be better to challenge Raakh for an Agni-Maru contest – the dreaded game of the islanders," Shukracharya advised Vritra on the way. "Raakh will not be able to resist the challenge and it will be the easiest way to eliminate him. But there is a catch. In this game, two players go in but only one comes out alive. It requires a certain level of insanity and readiness to go all the way. The winner will automatically become the leader of the tribe. His tribesmen too will fall in line. It will be the first step in a long path that lies ahead for becoming Trivikram – the conqueror of the three Loks on the planet. Do you understand?"

Vritra nodded. He still had some grievance against his Guru for keeping him in the dark for so long. But he did not express his feelings. He accepted that the Guru must have had his reasons for doing so, but still, it hurt. He had no ambitions of becoming a Trivikram, in spite of the regular impetus by his Guru. It was not his dream and he had never been interested. His newfound aim was to avenge the murder of his parents and his brother. Justice had to be done.

They reached their destination.

Vritra took blessings of Shukracharya before going in.

Shukracharya raised his right hand and said, "*Vijayi bhava.*" Be victorious. Easier said than done, he knew.

Vritra and Kaitabha walked past the numerous tents and huts to reach the middle of the colony, from where their tribe and their families were uprooted. The remaining tribesmen were told to wait on the fringes, and they were to come after the duel was over.

At the centre of the settlement, there was a four-sided pyramid. It had a series of square terraces with stairways up each of the four sides to the temple on top. Sculptures of plumed serpents ran down the sides of the northern balustrade. On some days, the late afternoon sun striking the northwest corner of the pyramid, cast a series of triangular shadows against the northwest balustrade, creating the illusion of a feathered serpent crawling down the pyramid. Each step of the stairway was lit up with torches of fire.

Vritra asked, "Did Raakh make this structure?"

Kaitabha replied, "No. Raakh doesn't have the brains to build it, or even to maintain it. Look at the cracks developing."

"Then who had it built?"

"Your father used to tell us that this pyramid was originally constructed by Supreme Lord Paulastya centuries ago. But later, it was ruined and was in dire shambles. Then, your brother Vishvarupa, renovated it. He was the one who unlocked many secret doors in this structure."

"What is it called?"

"Temple of Asura."

"Asura?!"

"Asura means greatness, powerful or mighty. Asuras are the possessor of power. There is nothing good or bad about the name."

Vritra remembered Shukracharya's words, "Power is neither good nor evil. Its possessor makes it so!"

Vritra pointed his hand towards the top of the pyramid and asked, "What is at the top?"

"It used to be a temple with statues of the Gods. But Raakh removed them and made it his home. He put a throne there. He calls it the throne of Red Dragon. It is said that the top of the temple is at the point of the cosmic axis, a place connecting with the higher realms. Your brother used to meditate there I heard."

In front of the pyramid, there was a big circular ground overlaid with ash.

Vritra surveyed it with wide eyes.

Kaitabha said, "This, my friend, is the Agni-Maru pit."

It was time to take a step forward, into a path of no return. Vritra touched his forehead to the urns of his parent's ashes and handed them to Kaitabha. He also passed the statue of the monster from his hut. He sighed and moved to the centre of the Agni-Maru arena.

Vritra remembered the words of his late father telling him about the deadly game. "Agni-Maru is a traditional fire-duel sport. No weapons are used in the fight, except the Agni itself. It is fought inside a circle of fire. Maru means circle. Fire duels were fought for hundreds of years. Such a duel became a way to settle disputes. With its growing popularity, it became a way to select the tribal lord. Under traditional rules, the duel ended when only one player remained standing till the count of ten by the audience, regardless of whether the opponent was still alive or not. Before Raakh's ascent to power, Agni-Maru rarely resulted in a death. But under his regime, sparing an opponent's life became a sign of weakness rather than one of generosity or mercy. He stopped the practice of counting and instead burned every opponent of his to death. That's how he earned the name – Raakh. It is cruel and gruesome to watch. Nowadays, many call the sport as *Agni-Mrityu* which means death by fire. Some term it the circle of death, *Mrityu-Maru*. Whatever, it may be called, it is the way to absolute power."

Vritra looked towards the top of the pyramid and bellowed, "RAAKH."

Raakh was sitting on his Red Dragon throne eating dinner, his favourite goat meat, when he heard the scream. He did not bother to get up or pay any attention. Many maniacs or drunkards used to shout his name.

"Raakh, I challenge you to Agni-Maru," Vritra screamed.

The words caught Raakh's attention. No one had dared to challenge him in years. It was not some maniac or someone with a death wish hollering his name, but someone challenging him to a fight to the death.

He was both outraged and happy. The game was life to him. He dropped the bone in his hand, he was done eating. He clenched his jaw, took a deep breath and got up. He grinned briefly as he lay hands on his favourite gloves.

Vritra had come dressed. The attire during an Agni-Maru was loose-fitted trousers and gloves in the hands, while being bare-chested and barefooted. The gloves were made of special material. Fire was put on the outside of the gloves, but it caused no harm to the hands. Players used the fire on the gloves to hurt and burn their opponents.

Raakh stepped down from the temple of asura.

Vritra was six-and-a-half foot tall but he looked small in front of his rival, who was nearly seven-foot tall. Both were extremely well built. It would be a well matched contest.

As soon as the word of a duel got out, everyone assembled near the Agni-Maru pit. There was only one question in everyone's mind – *Who has come to die?*

Everyone was staring at Vritra like he had a death wish.

Raakh took some ash in his hand and rubbed it in his palms. Then he clapped to let it fall out. He asked, "Who are you? Never seen you before."

"I am Vritra, son of Tvashta."

"Which tribe?"

"Shikavan."

"Hmm. You seem young. What's your age?"

"Eighteen."

Raakh said loudly raising his right hand, "Old enough to die." The voice roared, so powerful it shook the ground.

The crowd cheered. It meant Raakh had accepted the duel. "Do you have any last wishes?"

Everyone became quiet to hear it.

Vritra smirked. "Don't worry, I will make it quick."

"Very well. Let's begin." It was followed by loud laughter.

Two men came rushing and poured oil in the circle around the pit. Both the fighters took position inside the circle. They both put on their gloves.

A lady came with a *mashaal* (fire-torch). She ignited the oil in the circle. The circle of fire started burning.

The duel began.

✦

29

Vīra (Brave)

SIDDHA - LOK

Parthiv's eyes were on the leopard. He had a quick decision to make, whether to scream or stay quiet. Being alone, his chances of escaping the leopard were slim. If he did nothing, one of his classmates would be wounded or worse, killed.

To make matters worse, a sly voice in his mind stated, *they scorned me merely for what I am, maybe they are getting what they deserve!*

With that thought, he swallowed a lump in his throat.

Brave conquers not just his foes but his own ego and fears as well, his mother's words rang in his head.

His head hung low in shame. The urge to be brave rushed through his veins. He overcame the inhibitions even though it felt like signing his death sentence. Do your duty without fear, he thought.

After some hesitation, he shouted, "Leopard! Run! Sharnish, Harsh, run…" His classmates were alerted before the leopard could start his sprint. They ran.

The leopard looked at his spoiler with fiery eyes. He was quick to realize that his new prey was weak and alone. He changed course and started his sprint.

Parthiv picked up a log in his hand. He decided to fight. A bad choice. But running was also not going to win it for him, he knew.

When the leopard was close enough, it leaped upon Parthiv. Parthiv tried to block him with the log in his hand. Luckily for him, the leopard's mouth went straight into the log.

I made a huge mistake. This will not end well.

The leopard struggled to bite him. Foiled by the log, he jumped aside.

Parthiv knew one more attack was coming but he did not know what to do.

The leopard was getting ready to jump but suddenly a rock came and hit him in the eye. He grunted in pain. Leopard looked around and saw another human staring at him.

Lakshya shouted, "*Jai Bajrang,*" and ran towards the injured leopard. He had his father's dagger in his hand.

Now, the leopard was alone but had to fight two humans. The wounded leopard panicked, and fled the scene with a loud roar.

Lakshya went to Parthiv and asked, "Are you alright?"

"I'm fine." He dusted the dirt from his clothes.

"That was foolish of you taking on a leopard alone. What were you thinking?" Parthiv remained quiet. He still looked a little shaken.

Lakshya knew what had made the boy do the unthinkable. What he had done was very brave and it had saved his classmates. "But it is what true warriors do!" Lakshya said patting Parthiv on his back.

"What is your name, brave friend?"

More than 'brave', it was the word 'friend', which brought a smile on Parthiv's face.

"I am Parthiv from Himalia-Rajya."

"I am Lakshya from…"

"I know. I heard what you did yesterday."

The words were very comforting. Lakshya smiled as well. "What were you doing alone here?"

"I came to collect wood. I am not good at fighting, so no one is ready to be with me or be my friend."

Lakshya said, "Well, you have one friend now. And, who says you are not good at fighting? You are a brave heart, that's even more important than being a fighter. The one who refuses to back down, is someone I don't want to fight with."

This incident made Lakshya forget his sorrows.

A friendship began that would last until one of them breathed his last breath.

✦

30

Prathama (The First)

ANGAARA

The stage was set. In a few moments, the deadly clash between two powerful asura warriors would begin.

Raakh, a scary-looking bald man with a bulbous head and beaked nose, stared at Vritra with an unblinking gaze. He was trying to read his opponent. He saw the burn marks on Vritra's body. He asked, "Have you fought Agni-Maru before?"

"No."

Raakh grinned. "So, it's your *first* fight. Who gave you the idea to fight me?"

"You ruined my family, took everything away. I am going to make it all even today by sucking the life from your body."

Raakh spat on the ground showing his contempt. "I will enjoy watching you burn, you overconfident pig!" Raakh said as he lit up his gloves with the fire in the circle. He punched his gloves together and got ready.

Vritra followed. He had laid his trap. Shukracharya had advised him to make Raakh extremely angry early on. Anger clouds judgement and makes one predictable.

Both were in position.

The bugle sounded.

Raakh rolled his hands forming a circle of fire and pounded at his opponent's chest.

Vritra retreated and saved his body from the punch and the fire. With a reflex, he did a somersault and kicked Raakh on the chest. It was a risky move exposing his pants to the fire, but it worked. Raakh lost his balance. Vritra drew the *first* blood.

The crowd was shocked at the sheer audacity of the move. Raakh was outraged and gave a thunderous bellow.

He put his hands together and blew so hard that it was like he had breathed a deadly fire-bolt. It was his ultimate, deadliest move. Vritra managed to dodge it narrowly. The years of training had prepared him for this. Raakh had used his best move too early, when the opponent was still fresh. It was a mistake, but anger does that to one.

Raakh followed it up with three more such bolts. Vritra rolled in the air and dodged them repeatedly. His agility was exceptional.

The audience watched with their mouths agape.

Agitated, Raakh and Vritra went at each other. They locked horns like two wild bulls, throwing punches at each other. Vritra took a few on his body and he returned them with equal intensity. Raakh was surprised and frustrated to see his opponent endure pain so effortlessly. His fire-punches were not having the desired effect.

A sudden push from Raakh made Vritra fall on his back. Raakh tried his trademark fire move again.

Vritra rolled on the ground and made a slender escape. Then, he got back on his feet with a kip-up. A glazed insane fury loomed inside his eyes. The intensity of the look made the hair stand up on Raakh's arm, and for the first time, he feared him.

Outsmarted in the duel so far, skill abandoned Raakh. He readied yet another fire-bolt move. It had never failed him before, and he hoped it wouldn't fail him this time. But this match was different. His former opponents were never so agile and muscular.

Vritra was waiting for this moment. All of a sudden, he did a spinning-roundhouse-kick and it connected. Raakh wasn't prepared. It hit his skull hard. He fell on his knees with blood from his mouth spattered on the ground. All he could hear was a loud ringing in his ears. An unbearable high-pitch tone. His mind had lost control of his body. He collapsed on the ground.

The crowd stood stupefied in utter disbelief. No one had anticipated this end.

Vritra screamed, "Count." He was sending a message – telling everyone that he was different.

The audience exchanged confused looks and realized that Vritra was seeking to revive the forgotten rule of the game.

Kaitabha shook his head. He did not understand why Vritra was playing by the rules. What was he going to achieve by giving a chance to a monster like Raakh, who followed no rules? It was foolish.

The crowd started counting. "One… Two…" Raakh remained unmoved.

"…Ten."

Vritra declared, "The duel is over! I am …"

Before Vritra could finish, he was blinded by a sudden heap of ash flung on his face.

Vritra was blinded for a few heart-stopping moments.

Raakh got up, punched, and kicked Vritra. Vritra's return punches were in vain. Raakh easily blocked or dodged them. He continued with his blows.

Finally, Vritra was down.

Luckily the fire in Raakh's gloves had extinguished while he was lying on the ground.

"The duel gets over, not by counting, but when I say so," Raakh announced. The traditional rules of the game meant nothing to him. He had changed the game. To him, there was only one way to win a duel. A barrier Vritra wasn't ready to cross.

The crowd cheered. They chanted Raakh's name.

Raakh walked near Vritra and started knocking him with repeated body kicks. Vritra extinguished the fire in his gloves, curled into a ball and wrapped his hands around his face. Blinded, Vritra had no options but to bear Raakh's body kicks. Bracing himself on the ground, Raakh kicked out and hit him in the chest and belly. He followed with many shots to the shoulder and face. As Vritra rolled, Raakh kicked him on the spine. That hurt the most. He rolled back to take the blows on the ribs. The pain from his chest washed through his body to the tips of his toes and fingers. His breath was coming in choking spasms and the air was getting blocked in his lungs.

Punching, kicking, Raakh's teeth bared triumphantly in the darkness. After the non-stop mayhem, he spat bloodied saliva on Vritra's face as he delivered his last, tired kick. Vritra was motionless.

Raakh trudged to the edge of the pit to re-ignite his gloves; to get back his weapon in the game.

Hesitation is a vice. This is a weakness your enemy will not share, Shukracharya's warning played over and over in Vritra's head. He had already committed the mistake of not listening to his Guru and playing by the rules against an unworthy opponent. *Those who live by the rules of the jungle do not understand the rules of the civilized world,* his inner voice said to him. His rules needed to be altered. It was as if Lord Vishnu had spoken to him. He opened his eyes. Some vision had returned to his eyes, but everything was still blurred. He was bleeding intensely and his whole body was throbbing with pain. His hearing was impaired.

Hazily, he saw Raakh returning with fire in his gloves. Raakh stood over Vritra's legs to deliver the killing blow, to spew fire on Vritra's pants to end it. Right at that moment, Vritra kicked him in the crotch. The move was against all rules of the duel. But it hardly felt wrong. This was not a sport, it was a game of life and death, of survival. And, there are no rules in the fight for survival. Now, Vritra understood this more than ever.

Raakh did not see it coming. Making a guttural sound, he bent forward, but he could not protect his crotch with his hands because of the fire in his gloves. Vritra screamed as he threw a solid punch on Raakh's face and everyone could hear his nose break. Blood spilled out of his nose down the sides of his face. Raakh collapsed in a free fall on his back under the pull of gravity. He couldn't say a word as he gritted his teeth in pain.

The crowd had fallen silent for a brief moment. Soon, the members of Raakh's tribe abused Vritra for the unethical move. They called him, "A crook! Loser!" But the others remained silent. They knew Vritra was only reacting, not acting. The outsider wasn't at fault.

Vritra raised himself up. He could feel the renewed stream of adrenaline build up in his bloodstream. He remembered the strategy of Shukracharya. They had discussed it in depth before coming for the match. It had worked well till he had made the error in judgement and ignored his Guru's advice.

Raakh lay there on the ground, gasping for air. Slowly, he returned to his senses as the pain subsided. His nose was swollen, and it hurt when he touched it.

They were both up.

Discomfited, Raakh threw away his gloves. He grabbed his nose between the thumb and index finger of his right hand. He closed his eyes and snapped it, to straighten his broken nose. He hollered with pain as the blood splattered from his nose on to the ground. He opened his eyes and looked back at Vritra. His eyes glowed red in fury. "You scoundrel. Get ready to die," Raakh said in a belligerent tone as he twisted his face in disgust.

In the crowd, Raakh's tribesmen screamed the name of their leader. Others were silent. They did not know which side to pick.

They charged at each other. Without the gloves, Raakh was now relying on sheer strength as he got ready with his powerful fist-hammer to knock Vritra's head from the top. Vritra did not stop and used the opportunity to jump, rotate in the air and deliver a roundhouse-kick on Raakh's bulbous skull. He was like a flying snake. It was a truly breath-taking sight.

Raakh's hammer remained frozen; it did not materialize. His nervous system couldn't bear the jolt.

It was Shukracharya's advice, "Due to Raakh's height, no one has been able to test him with kicks to the head. So, he considers it his strength and will never be prepared for them. Your strength becomes your biggest weakness at times."

Vritra threw a kick to the neck. A precision knockout punch. It chopped the carotid artery along the side of the neck, the vessel most responsible for bringing blood to the brain. Extreme pain, disorientation, and loss of consciousness – its immediate outcome!

Raakh stood paralyzed.

Vritra re-ignited his gloves and then rotated so rapidly that he appeared like a ball of fire. The ball hit Raakh's face and then on the stomach.

Finally, he put Raakh's trousers on fire. By now Raakh was non-responsive. Vritra's strategy of using sudden kicks worked. That was the advantage of having Shukracharya on his side. Raakh wasn't used to such a fighting technique.

The match was over and everyone in the audience waited with bated breath.

Vritra could end the practice of killing his opponent and leave him alive, in spite of what had happened earlier.

He lifted Raakh's body like a weightlifter. Many in the crowd shouted, "Kill him." Very few screamed, "Mercy."

Only one word came to Vritra's mind. *Agnipath*. The monster in him had woken up and there was no such thing as mercy in the fire in his eyes.

Vritra flung the half-burning body into the Agni-Maru circle, giving a literal ending to Raakh.

There was pin-drop silence.

Agniparvat exploded loudly in celebration. Vritra had tasted his *first* kill.

✦

31

Asi (The Sword)

Time is a stubborn illusion, as elusive as our consciousness. It constantly accompanies us from birth till death, and maybe even beyond. It can neither be seen nor controlled, yet you know it is there. Time never stops for anyone, but some moments do slow it down. It is these moments that become a memory and define life. Four years had passed without time slowing its pace. Now the last days in the gurukul were here and time would soon become a memory.

Trainer Sandesh was standing next to Bhaskar in the Guru's hut. Today the Guru would announce the ultimate challenge, which was conducted very infrequently. Sandesh knew that the real competition would be between two students. Bhaskar had never let the two fight in the pit against each other after one unforgettable incident a few days ago.

One cloudy, chilly morning, the Guru had put both of them in the pit to duel with a metal sword. Sandesh hoped Lakshya would lose. Both were in position, ready to attack. Aindrita was praying for Viraat. But in her heart, she knew it would be a close contest. As they moved and attacked each other with their swords, a loud thunder splintered the sky, and sheets of rain poured, like a cloudburst, drenching the gurukul. Bhaskar stopped the duel. When Sandesh tried to argue for the match to continue, he had only two words to say, "Not today."

Perhaps the day has finally come, mused Sandesh.

Bhaskar finished his morning prayers in the small temple in his hut, which had an Om symbol and a statue of Acharya Brihaspati. Apart from the temple, there was nothing much in the hut, except a mat for sleeping, and a wooden box for clothes and personal belongings. The statue of Acharya Brihaspati was the symbol of power in the room. He was the first to get the title of *Acharya*. The elite teachers had found their way out of the class system long ago. They were the keepers of knowledge and were very close to the Vanshaj, so they had negotiated a separate title of *'acharya'* from the Kings, which was considered classless. They were independent except for one thing that tied them to the class system. It was total loyalty and allegiance to the Vanshaj class. Both needed the other to maintain dominance. Over time, the result of this alliance was that the entry of the lower classes to the gurukul was discontinued.

Bhaskar moved towards the mat on which he slept daily. Pointing his finger towards the mat, he instructed, "Sandesh, dig here."

Sandesh was confused. "Dig here. But why?"

"Do as I say. Since when have you started questioning me?"

"Forgive me, Acharya."

Sandesh brought a spade and started digging. *What could be here? Must be something of very great importance. Why else would Acharya keep it so close, yet hidden?* The sweat covered his entire body. It started dripping from his forehead. But he didn't stop.

Thud! Suddenly, the spade hit something, a wooden object! Sandesh stopped; his eyes lit up with excitement and he looked at Bhaskar.

"Take it out."

Sandesh carefully pulled out a big box. "What is it, Acharya?"

"You will know. Please carry it for me to the class."

The box was heavy. He could feel some mystic energy around the box as if some deep power or something unnatural was inside it. Sandesh walked behind Bhaskar; his heart beating rapidly.

They reached the class where everyone was seated in their usual positions.

Bhaskar looked at the students, especially his favourite. Then he spoke, "Today will be the last day of your training. I am very happy with the way you have all performed."

There were smiles on all faces. It was very rare for them to hear praise from Bhaskar.

Their eyes fell on the box Sandesh was carrying. Sandesh placed it by Bhaskar's feet.

Viraat asked, "What is in the box, Acharya?"

Bhaskar smiled. He opened the box and took out its contents.

It was a shining blue sword. The kind of sword that could easily cut through metal like water.

The Guru held the sword in his hand. "It is no ordinary sword – it is *Asi*, the sword."

He explained, "Asi is the first weapon ever created."

All the students were in awe, seeing the shining blade. It was unlike any sword they had seen.

Lakshya asked, "Who made this sword, Acharya?"

Bhaskar held the sword high in his hand and answered, "Millions of years ago, Devas approached Brahma, the Creator of the Universe, and protested against the unjust rule and evil doings of the demons. Hearing the protest from the Devas, Brahma collected sacrificial objects and proceeded to perform a grand sacrifice with the foremost of the sages and Devas at a small island inside Brahma Sarovar.

During the course of the sacrifice, a dreadful creature sprang from the midst of the sacrificial fires, scattering flames all around. It was as though a moon had arisen in the midst of the stars. He was coloured like a deep-blue lotus. His teeth were sharp and terrible, stomach lean and skinny and stature very tall and slim. He had enormous energy and power. At the same time, Dhruva-Lok started shaking, there was turmoil in the oceans, volcanoes erupted, the forceful winds swept through the land, the trees fell and meteors blazed through the skies. Brahma declared, 'The being I have conceived is *Asi*. It shall effect the destruction of the enemies of Dharma'.

Upon hearing this, the creature assumed the form of a blazing sharp-edged sword, glowing like flames. This sword was the primordial weapon created by the Lord for the destruction of evil. The name of the sword is Asi, the personification and the primary energy behind all weapons ever created.

The sword was born in *Krittika Nakshatra*, Agni is its deity, *Rudra* is its high preceptor and whoever holds this weapon is assured of victory, and has absolute power over any weapon ever created, as Asi is the primordial source of energy behind all weapons."

Viraat was concerned. No one had mentioned this weapon to him. It was always stories of the Trishul. He asked, "Is it more powerful than the Trishul, Acharya?"

To this question, even the Guru did not have an answer. He shrugged. "I don't know." Bhaskar paused and added, "Remember, these special weapons cannot be used by anyone. To whoever I give it, that person will become the wielder of this weapon. Only when you willingly give this weapon to someone or if some other person defeats you in a duel, then the other person becomes its rightful owner and its true powers can be unleashed by that other person alone."

Viraat asked, "Do such rules apply to the Trishul as well?"

"It should. These are not ordinary weapons. They choose their wielder and respond only to their rightful owner."

Finally, the Guru revealed why he took out the sword from its resting place, "You all know about the ultimate competition at the gurukul."

Everyone except one knew about the ultimate challenge. It was the contest that Satyavrat had won in record time.

Lakshya did not know. He thought it must be a fighting challenge. He looked towards Viraat knowing that he would be his opponent. After that unforgettable incident and thinking it was against God's wishes, Bhaskar never made them fight against each other. *Maybe Acharya was waiting for the ultimate challenge*, Lakshya deliberated.

"This ultimate challenge is held when I feel that someone is capable of completing the task. This time the competition is special as many of you are capable of completing the challenge. Therefore, I have decided to give a special award to the winner of the ultimate challenge – the *Sarva Shrestha Shishya* will receive the sword of Asi as a reward," Bhaskar elaborated.

Viraat, Aindrita and Lakshya had their eyes glued on the sword. They all wanted it at any cost and were ready to go to any extent. Whatever it may take!

Who was going to succeed?

✦

32

Upaśāntin (Tame)

ANGAARA

"We have done the impossible – uniting more than a thousand tribes spread across Angaara. Who would believe that!" Kaitabha applauded, his voice celebratory.

"It took longer than I expected. And, we still have a long way to go," Vritra replied in a nonchalant tone. He did not give out any strong emotion. His eyes were set on one target – make the betrayers from Bhuvar-Lok pay!

"Don't say that. Four years is a very short time considering what you have achieved. Even Paulastya wasn't successful in pulling this off. You have the biggest army on Dhruva-Lok at your command. We are ready to tame the world and bring it to its knees."

"Not yet. The men need weapons and training before we can start our ascent. You go and check the progress of training. I will meet the Guruji and join you later."

The sky was breathing fire. Like the hottest part of a smith's fire, the sun was blazing reddish-yellow on the horizon. The clouds were like a spray of paint thrown carelessly on a canvas.

Vritra went to the Temple of Asura to meet his Guru. He was expecting that today the Guru would give his approval to commence the war. After the duel with Raakh, he had followed Shukracharya's advice and not questioned him. He trusted his Guru's words more than ever. He reached the top of the temple where Shukracharya was meditating.

"Pranam, Guruji," he said as he touched the feet of Shukracharya.

The Guru opened his eyes and said, "Ayushman bhava. Take your seat."

Vritra sat on the Red Dragon throne. The throne was carved out of a big silver-grey granite stone, which was painted in red and black. The roaring head and the curling tail of the dragon boasted as the armrests. The left wings of the dragon served as the backrest. Unlike other thrones, this one was neither tall nor deep, but wide enough to seat five persons with ease. Even though no precious stones were embedded in it, the throne was truly magnificent.

"Guruji, as per your wishes, I have united the tribes and raised my army. Now, I have nearly one hundred thousand warriors behind me. Their training is progressing well. Weapons are being cast. We should be ready to move on Bhuvar-Lok within a few months."

"Are due precautions being taken as we had discussed?"

"Yes, Guruji. The weapon development and training is being done with utmost caution. The spy network of Bhuvar-Lok kingdoms has been demolished in the last four years. Now they get to hear what we want them to know. So, they are under the impression that I am no different than Raakh, with no ambitions beyond this island."

Shukracharya swept his beard to and fro with one hand. "Alright. The number of warriors is enough but you need something more."

Something more! Vritra was puzzled. "What more do I need?" he frowned.

"Victory in a war is never about the number of warriors. It is about conquering the minds of your adversaries. The enemy should fear you. They first lose the war in their mind and then on the field. Fear is a grave – it buries one alive."

"They will fear me after they see me. They feared me when I was a child," Vritra reminded his Guru about the assassination attempt in his childhood.

"You are mistaken. You are strong but still flesh and blood. They have the Trishul given by Lord Shiva. As long as they have that, they will not fear a human. Unless… they see you as a God."

Vritra did not understand the meaning behind the Guru's words. "I cannot get my hands on the Trishul without reaching Siddha-Lok. Before that I need to defeat Bhuvar-Lok kingdoms."

"You can get something that will send chills into the minds of your enemies. Instead of fighting they will run from the field."

"What is it, Guruji? What do I need to do?"

"You need to tame Draak."

Vritra felt a wave of panic sweeping him off the floor. He did not fear animals, except this one. His jaw dropped. He had heard stories from his mother. No one could go near Draak.

Draak was a flying lizard, a dragon – a fire breathing, dangerous creature spewing forth torrents of flame. She was the last of her species surviving on the planet. She lived south of Angaara, which was called Andhaka – a place where only a blind would go.

Many had not seen Draak in years.

"It is time you use your special skills with animals," Shukracharya spoke in a rich throaty voice.

Vritra raised a brow and marvelled, "Does Guruji know?"

"Yes, I know."

Vritra got down on his knees, with folded hands. "But it is impossible to control Draak."

"We are tested not to show our weaknesses but to discover our strengths." Shukracharya took some time and continued, "If you want to achieve greatness, you need to overcome your fears first. To be Trivikram, you need to do the impossible, something unimaginable…something that tells your enemies that you are no less than a God."

Vritra swallowed. "She hasn't been seen in years. Is she even alive?"

"Yes, she is alive. She is difficult to spot. But she is waiting to be *tamed*."

Difficult to spot! How could it be with such a size? Vritra wondered.

Vritra had already climbed a mountain to unite the tribes and keep them together. Now, he was told that he was not even half-way done. And the next part seemed ten times more tough and dangerous. His army was big enough to crush Bhuvar-Lok kingdoms. Taming Draak was insurmountable. He made an effort to change Shukracharya's mind. "I could die trying to tame her," Vritra opined.

"Death is not the enemy; it is inevitable. Fear is the real enemy. Never be its slave."

"Will it not be too big of a risk, Guruji?" Vritra argued.

"Well, not doing so, is also a risk. Look at your own face at the mere thought of a dragon! Now imagine how your enemies will feel at the sight!" Shukracharya replied nonchalantly.

Vritra remained quiet.

Shukracharya could read Vritra's troubled mind. He gave a wry half-smile and added, "When this is done, there is one more task that needs to be accomplished. I will tell you when you return."

There is more! Vritra let out a deep sigh. *How high does this mountain go?*

✦

33

Sarvaśreṣṭha (The Ultimate)

SIDDHA - LOK

"The ultimate challenge will start an hour before sunset tomorrow evening," Bhaskar announced.

Lakshya asked, "What is the challenge, Acharya?"

"I was coming to that. The task is to climb the Sumeru mountain and reach the Neelkanth peak. You can carry weapons of your choice. The more the number of weapons you carry, the slower you will get, so choose them carefully. However, you won't be allowed to carry any food. You have to find it on your own. There is no compulsion; those who wish to participate, can take part in this challenge."

The students looked at each other.

Viraat was unmoved, his eyes fixed on the sword.

Bhaskar added, "Satyavrat did it in two days. Since then, many have completed the task. But no one has come close to Satyavrat's record and has not even succeeded in completing it in three days. But I feel this year one of you would make me proud and become the rightful owner of Asi." He showed the glittering sword again. "There you will take blessings of the Saptarishis and that will be the end of your training. I will be waiting for you at the top. At my request, Maharaja Dhananjay and many Kings from other kingdoms are coming to witness and bless the winner."

Hearing this Viraat's eyes widened. He felt an added pressure to win. Losing wasn't an option anymore.

Lakshya realized why Maharaja Dhananjay and other Kings were coming. To witness Viraat being crowned as the Sarva Shrestha Shishya. *They all treated me as a commoner, never respected me. It's time I prove myself.* Lakshya tightened his fists and readied himself for the challenge.

Aindrita thought that she stood a good chance of winning the competition. She was special. She could fight blindfolded, based on sound and vibrations. Even Viraat and Lakshya couldn't match her in that. She was very skilled in climbing as well and no one had stamina like her.

It was a fair challenge to all.

The Guru cautioned, "Students have died in this challenge before."

Waves of panic washed over the students. The Guru's blunt words hung over their heads like a menacing cloud.

"You will be alone out there. Enter the challenge only if you feel ready for it. You need to be very careful and remember your training to succeed in this challenge. Nothing is more important than life," Bhaskar summed it up.

✦

The challenge started one hour before it turned dark. This unusual timing gave the challengers an option to let the night pass at the gurukul and start early in the morning, or take a risk and venture out in the darkness.

Only five final year students consented to participate in the contest. Aindrita, Viraat and Lakshya decided to head out that very evening. They made their way out through the different gates of the gurukul. The other two, Rudra from Himalia and Chitra from Shivalik, decided to start early next morning.

It had been few hours since the challenge commenced. The night was turning foggy, as dense, white, mist enveloped the surrounding forest. Viraat walked downhill on a rugged path along the edges. When he looked back, the trail had disappeared. There was no going back now. He needed to find a place to stay for the night. He was still in the foothills, so chances of finding a place were good.

A faint sound reached his ears. Alert, he tuned in to listen and locate the direction from which it was coming. It was a tiny tintinnabulation, probably from the bells tied to a domestic animal. The sound was coming from a place near a gorge. It was dark, but he followed the occasional clinking. As he closed in, he realized it was coming from a small settlement. Relieved, he reached the place quickly and decided to spend the night in the small village. The villagers welcomed him after they got to know he was a Dhruvanshi.

Early next morning, the fog was lifting up over the gorge, when Viraat woke up. It was so peaceful that it felt magical. The weather was perfect for walking – warm with a light cool breeze. Walking along the edge of the gorge, he heard the gentle sound of the stream flowing. The river was emerald green in colour. Different type of flora was scattered everywhere. It consisted largely of tall cypresses, most of them many centuries old, kermes oaks and maples in the upper reaches of the gorge. Lower down there were pines, oleander and chaste tree shrubs. Lizards and chameleons sunbathing beside the path scurried away into the dry leaves as he walked by.

The hill people told him about a secret route through a cave which was called "the devil's neck". A dark and steep path but it was the quickest way to the other side of the big mountain. Viraat did not have the experience of exploring caves but he decided to take the unknown route. Some risks needed to be taken if he wanted to be the winner!

He lit up a fire torch and went inside. It was dark and damp. A mammoth colony of bats clung to the roof, while thick piles of moss carpeted the floor. He treated the wind as his compass and continued on the uneven terrain. His pace remained slow as he had to watch his step in the slippery moss. Viraat thought he had made a mistake but he continued walking, trusting the advice of locals. It was humid inside and he was sweating profoundly. From climbing to belly crawling, all had to be done in pitch dark. Finally, he saw a light at the end and made his way out. At the end of the cave, he saw something that made his eyes pop out. *'Satyavrat was here'* – the message was carved on the rock. Thrilled, Viraat jumped in the air discovering that he too had used the path taken by Satyavrat. For the first time, Viraat believed he could beat, or realistically, equal Satyavrat's record. He pulled out his knife and chipped on the rock below the engraving – *'Viraat was here too'*.

As he emerged, he raised his fist in victory. Certainly, he had saved nearly two pahars of time and plenty of energy by journeying across the devil's neck. This devil wasn't so bad, he grinned, a slight dimple dotting his left cheek.

Outside, it was an even more picturesque scenery. But there was no time to cherish it. More than the journey, the outcome mattered.

✦

One day had gone by since the challenge commenced.

Deep gorges, narrow cliffs, cold rivers, wild animals – the route had everything. As she climbed up, the silence of the jungle and cold winds were frightening. It was mentally exhausting and physically demanding.

Nearly half of the climb was done. But the toughest part lay ahead. The thinning air would make the climb more challenging. There was no way of knowing where the other challengers were. Everyone took a different route. They were not supposed to work as a team, and everyone respected it.

Aindrita had a decision to make: take rest at night or continue her climb? She wanted to prove herself. No girl had ever won it. Bhaskar had told her before he left the gurukul, "If any girl was ever going to win this challenge, it would be you."

Taking the words of the Guru as a sign, she decided to take the risk. In the night, wild animals would be difficult to spot and avoid. She lit a torch. She looked around and continued walking briskly.

A couple of hours had passed. She had covered a lot of distance. She was happy with the decision, a calculated risk. The thought of winning the competition was dreamlike. It brought a smile to her tired face. Her eyelids refused to get heavy in spite of the lack of sleep.

Suddenly, there was a crackling noise followed by a howling sound. Another howl echoed it. Then they howled in unison. It meant an impending attack from a pack.

She looked around and spotted gleaming eyes in the dark. They were closer than she had thought. She threw the torch and scurried to a nearby tree. The howling and grunting increased rapidly.

She noticed a windmill palm close to her. She leaped on it and made her way up like the expert climber that she was. It was an essential skill that was taught to everyone at the gurukul. The continuous howling made her hands shake with each step up the tree. There was no scope for error. Any mistake and it would be her end, a very painful one as well. She had gone halfway up the tree. She was in a safe zone. All she had to do was to hold on till the wolves gave up.

She gripped the trunk of the tree and took a deep breath.

Out of nowhere a squirrel came running down. She panicked and her grip on the trunk loosened. Her hand slipped and her feet fumbled. She fell hard.

She landed wrongly with a sharp pain shooting up her ankle. The wolves crept closer and the terror hit her like a great wave rolling in – sudden, concrete hard and cold.

In matters of survival, it usually require a split-second decision. Every moment of inaction was an invitation to death. She had to act quickly.

She took out her bow and arrow. Carefully listening to the grunts, she shot an arrow in the dark. It hit. The wolf cried in pain. She fired another arrow. Nothing happened. Then another. Same result. The trees were sheltering the wolves. One down but it was not enough to scare the pack.

The wolves came close to her. She could see them now. They surrounded her. The time to pull, fix, aim and fire arrows was not there. She pulled out her sword and got ready to fight. She was shivering with fear. The end was here. She had never expected to die fighting animals. She always imagined it to be on a battlefield.

One wolf jumped on her. She ducked and hit it with her sword. The wolf collapsed and did not get up. She gasped. *That's two down. I have a chance.*

The remaining six now trapped her in a small circle. They kept poking at her. She swung the sword, scaring them. She had no idea which one would jump on her first. Eventually, one of them jumped on her which she tried to block but it bit her hand. Luckily, she was wearing leather bracers, so it did not hurt her, but the sword fell from her hand. She had no moves left. Whatever stones she could find, she threw it at them in desperation. Beyond this, fighting was useless. She gave up.

Out of nowhere, an arrow hit the alpha of the pack, and then another and then one more. The arrows were perfectly aimed. There was a flurry of arrows.

The wolves were alarmed by the surprise attack in the dark. They looked back but the burst of arrows continued. With the alpha down, they retreated and fled in haste.

Who was it? she exhaled, relieved.

✦

Aindrita sat on the ground, looking around. She wrapped her arm around her knees, drawing her legs up to ward off the chill. Five minutes elapsed but no one came. She did not know who saved her. To whom she owed her life?

She could feel her rescuer's eyes on her, still watching her.

Finally, she decided to get up and move ahead. She needed to find a safe place for the rest of the night. Her ankle was hurt due to the fall. She tried to walk but it was painful. She slipped and fell. She cried in pain, "Ohh, maa."

She removed her leather footwear to take a look at her injured ankle, when she heard footsteps approaching. Someone was coming. It was dark and she couldn't see who it was. She asked, "Who is it?" Her voice quavered.

There was no response.

She could see the outline of her rescuer's body – the breadth of his hunched shoulders, the tilt of his head. The person came close, bent down and squinted at her ankle. She saw the face and recognized him. It was Lakshya! Nothing had changed between them since the incident on his first day. They had never talked after that. *Of all the people, it had to be him!*

He touched her ankle. It was swollen. He broke the silence, "Try to move your toes. Are you able to?"

She tried. She was able to move them.

"It means nothing is broken," Lakshya said.

"Was it you? You saved me?"

Lakshya did not answer.

The silence in the forest around them gave her the answer.

Aindrita had mocked and laughed at him when he had fallen. Now she was compelled to take his help after a similar fall. Karma has a unique way of working.

He opened his bag and took out a small container. He extracted a thick paste and applied it on her leg.

"What are you applying?" she asked.

"It's an herbal medicine. This should help."

She had a burning sensation in the inflamed area, followed by a soothing relief. She asked softly, "You are a vaidya as well?"

"We commoners have some specialties. We have to learn these things in our simple lives... don't have the luxury of calling vaidya to our homes."

It was a sarcastic remark which she immediately understood. She felt bad hearing his tone. Clearly, he hadn't forgotten their first meeting. Chastened, she fell into silence.

It had taken immense courage and determination for Lakshya to come this far, suppressing his emotions, his tears. He had faced day-to-day discrimination. It was years of piled-up anger and vexation that had spilled over. Emotions can never be subdued indefinitely. They have to be conquered. He couldn't do that. But soon, Lakshya realized it was a rude thing to say. It wasn't her fault; it was the fault of her upbringing. He regretted what he had said and tried to change the conversation. "You need to rest for a few hours before you can resume climbing. Let me take you to a safer place."

He offered his hand. She did not accept the offer and tried to get up on her own. He moved his hand away.

She tried to move ahead on her own. As she took her first few steps, she slipped but Lakshya swiftly caught her up in his arms before she fell. Their eyes met for the second time in all the years they had been students together. The world stopped for a few seconds. Her breathing turned heavy and Lakshya could see her pulse beating in the hollow of her neck. Their eyes began to change colour and both of them closed their eyes in a bid to hide their feelings from each other. With regret and reluctance, he let her go.

They looked away from each other.

Lakshya took the first step towards conquering his emotions. Forgiveness. He said, "I am sorry for what I said. Please hold on to me and let me take you to a place where you can rest."

She reached out for his hand this time.

Devoid of anger, the softness and warmth of her hand sent goose bumps across his body. His heart was pounding. He avoided reading her; he was scared to know.

They walked in step with each other.

She spoke, "I am sorry for what I said that day. I am really sorry. I wish I could *unsay* it."

"That's alright. That was a long time ago." He smiled in a reassuring manner.

They came to a weeping willow tree whose large branches spread out in long, flowing tresses offering concealment. He went down on his knees and cradled his palms together. "Use this to climb up and stay hidden until morning. I will be down here."

"You should go. You should not lose because of me."

"Nothing is more important than life," he repeated the last words Bhaskar had said to them.

◆

Aindrita woke up to the hues of a reddish-purple sky at the break of dawn, when birdsongs filled the air.

She watched Lakshya asleep under the tree. He was sleeping comfortably as if on his mother's lap, with a gentle and innocent smile on his face. Thoughts gushed and tumbled, like the ripples in a lake before silently dying in despair. She regretted how she had behaved with him all these years.

She tested her ankle and gave an incredulous gasp when she could move it without pain. She climbed down.

The movement woke Lakshya and he sat up, fully alert and on guard. He asked, "How are you?"

"Much better."

"How is your ankle?"

"There is some tingle. But I can move on my own at least. Your medicine did wonders." Her face lit up saying it.

"I am happy it helped."

After a brief silence, he asked, "Are you hungry?"

"I am starving."

Lakshya took out some walnuts he had saved while climbing and offered them to her.

After eating, they started walking. He walked two steps ahead of her. She followed slowly. They walked, both in deep thought, till the end of the first pahar of the day.

Lakshya's smile grew wider as they covered the distance. He didn't know what was happening to him. Whatever it was, it was new. The feeling was lovely, like a cool breeze in the hot sun.

Aindrita sat on a knee-high rock to rest, but only her body was at rest. Her mind was in a turmoil.

Lakshya sat on a similar rock some distance away. She looked at him and said, "You should get going. I am fine now."

"Are you sure?"

"It is safe now. Animals won't come this far up. You are losing crucial time walking with me. This way you won't win."

"If I am meant to win, I will win, no matter what."

"But I won't like it if you don't win on my account."

Lakshya blushed at her remark. She had changed. He was about to leave when he recalled that Aindrita was out of weapons. She had lost her sword and bow in the dark, last night. He took out his father's dagger and extended it towards her, "Take this. You will need it. It has the blessings of my parents."

She took it without any resistance. "Thank you."

As he began to walk away, she asked, "Why did you save me after what I did to you all these years?"

He turned and replied, "My friend Parthiv says that the brave conquers not just his foes but his own ego and fears as well."

In that instant, she felt he was a truly deserving Sarva Shrestha Shishya. He was not like she had always imagined. Her personal biases were misconstrued.

She asked him, "Do you forgive me?"

"For what?" He already had. "My mother says when someone hurts us, we should write it down on mud where rains of forgiveness can take them away. But, an act of goodness should be engraved in stone where no rain can ever erase it."

A bright smile lit up Aindrita's face. She understood what he meant.

His words left her in strange admiration of him. Her perspective towards commoners changed. Aindrita felt as if she was sinking into something deeper than the ocean.

✦

Lakshya walked swiftly. He doubled his speed to make up for the lost time.

He rested for a few hours in the night and again started his ascent.

By afternoon the next day, he could see the Neelkanth peak. Parts of the climb were very slippery and narrow. He hadn't been able to break Satyavrat's record. If Satyavrat had started with them, he would have finished the challenge the previous night.

He decided to run the last two hundred meters of the climb. He gasped for air when he finally reached the top.

There were nearly thirty people there. They must be the Kings and senior officials who had come to see the end. Everyone cheered and clapped for him.

Lakshya went straight to Bhaskar and touched his Guru's feet.

"Well done, Lakshya. I am proud of you."

Lakshya looked at him in anticipation of the result. *Did I win?*

Bhaskar pressed his lips and replied, "You came a close second." Lakshya saw Viraat holding the sword Asi. *Ohh!* "You missed by a couple of hours," Bhaskar told him.

Losing is one thing but losing by a wafer-thin-margin is heart breaking. The feeling is unbearable. Lakshya slowly walked towards Viraat. He touched his heart with a fist, bowed his head, and said, "Congratulations, Prince. You deserved to win."

Viraat reciprocated the gesture of mutual respect used by warriors at Siddha-Lok, especially after a good fight. "Thanks, Lakshya. I was lucky," Viraat replied in a graceful manner.

They kept looking into each other's unflinching eyes.

Lakshya blinked first. *You were born lucky*, he mumbled in his mind as he walked away, distressed.

✦

PART III

34

Gurudakṣhiṇā (Preceptor's Fee)

SIDDHA - LOK

By nightfall, the other students had not reached the peak. Viraat was joyous as he fenced with the sword. "It's mine. I still can't believe it."

Dhananjay took it from him and admired the workmanship. "It looks stronger than a wootz steel sword. Even the sword of Vishamadeva is not so heavy and sharp. It is something else and you truly deserved it."

"Why did Jyeshta Pitashri not come?" Viraat asked.

"I wanted to take you around the kingdom on the way back. We will visit all the prominent Pradesh in Shivalik. Vishamadeva had to stay back to administer the kingdom in my absence."

"What is the need to visit now? I want to go home. We could have gone later."

"Son, I want to pass this crown of burden to your head soon. You should get to know the kingdom you have to rule. Everyone in the kingdom is eager to see the prophesied Prince. It's time to give them a glimpse."

The entryway of the temporary tent structure opened and Dushyant, Padmini's younger brother and Viraat's uncle, entered. Dushyant ruled Shivalik's Mandhak-Pradesh, which was gifted to him by Dhananjay after his marriage to Padmini. Rules were bent by Dhananjay to make Dushyant an Ardha-Vanshaj, so that he could be made the King of a pradesh. The rule was amended to give the Maharaja unfettered power to make anyone a Vanshaj.

Dushyant was clean-shaven with short curly red-black hair and his bushy eyebrows met over the nose. His face was strong with a rawness to it – high cheekbones, a thin nose and peculiarly arched nostrils. His teeth protruded over the lower lip. As he stepped inside, he uttered, *"Maharaja ki jai ho."*

Viraat welcomed and hugged him. "Uncle, so nice of you to come."

"This is the least we could do. You have made the whole of Shivalik-Rajya proud. I have sent a message to your mother. Entire kingdom will be celebrating," Dushyant said proudly.

"Look at the sword, uncle."

Dushyant folded his hands and prayed to the primordial sword. "I had heard of this but never believed it existed. How did Acharya Bhaskar get it?"

"After creation it was passed to Lord Shiva, who later gave it to Lord Vishnu, who in turn passed it to Acharya Brihaspati. Then we heard it was lost. It is surreal to see it emerge again. And now it is in the hands of another worthy warrior," Dhananjay said holding Viraat's forearm with pride.

He asked his father, "It is the first weapon created by Lord Brahma. Is it even more powerful than the Trishul?"

Dhananjay understood what was troubling his son. He assured him, "There is no way to know. But the Trishul is Lord Shiva's favourite weapon. Nothing can be mightier than that."

Viraat's anxiety abated with these words.

"There is nothing to worry about. Both the weapons are with us. In front of the might of Trishul and Asi, no one will be able to stand against you. You will take our kingdoms to heights unheard of. You will go beyond King Satyavrat," Dushyant said in excitement.

"Don't get so excited," Dhananjay steadied Dushyant. "Let's sit down."

Dushyant asked Viraat, "Who is the lad that came second?"

"Yes, who is he?" Dhananjay said.

"His name is Lakshya. He is from Bhuvar-Lok," Viraat answered.

Dushyant asked, "Which kingdom in Bhuvar-Lok? Who is his father? What does he do?"

"Jambu-Rajya, I think. He is the son of a commoner, a Yukth. His father is a soldier in Samrat Srivijay's army."

"Ohh."

The word 'Yukth' put an end to any further questions.

"He did exceptionally well for his lineage," Dhananjay muttered.

◆

It was a dark night with none of the moons visible, as if they were deep asleep in their blanket of clouds. Lakshya had no desire to be lulled to sleep that night. He was resting outside his tent with a rock supporting his back, though he longed to lie under a tree – the way he had slept a couple of nights back. It was a night that stayed in his mind. But tonight, there was neither Aindrita nor a tree in sight. He was oblivious to everyone around – lost in his thoughts, invisible. As expected, no one paid him any heed. No one remembers the runner-up. He was beginning to understand the harsh reality. He stared at the Dhruva star shining like a bright jewel in the sky. He asked the star, "I worked so hard. I did everything in my reach. So, why did I not win?"

A handsome man, middle-aged, with a medium-dark complexion having a bluish undertone, came up to Lakshya and said, "You must be Lakshya. Why are you sitting alone, son?"

Lakshya was engrossed in his thoughts, but he quickly regained his composure. He wasn't expecting anyone to come and visit him. Even more surprising was that the visitor knew his name.

Lakshya scrutinized him as he stood up. The golden crown on the head of the visitor held a *mayura-pankh* (peacock feather) rather prominently. The man was irresistibly attractive, and his countenance was angelic. His face was long with a high and sloping forehead, bow-like eyebrows, straight-edged nose, bulging, well-cut lips and a square chin. His soothing eyes were long like petals of a blooming lotus with a pinkish tint – *kamalnayan*. His lips were purple, and his whole face was beaming with a wide, delightful smile! The smile was enchanting, and his voice was mellifluous and velvety with perfect accent and diction.

He was wearing an asymmetric marigold silk dhoti-kurta with a kavacha which had the symbol of an endless knot engraved on it, both on the front and the back

The man's clothes were glittering with jewels and precious gems. He had gold anklets and bracelets on both arms. The man was not carrying any weapon, but he held a flute.

Lakshya replied, "I don't know anyone here. My family isn't here. They were not invited."

"Why do you think so?" the man asked.

"They stay very far in Bhuvar-Lok," Lakshya replied with a grimace.

"Oh, you are from Bhuvar-Lok, the land of Bajrang Bali." A bright smile beamed on his face.

Lakshya felt good hearing the name Bajrang from someone else.

The visitor said, "You made the entire Bhuvar-Lok proud. As far as I can recall, I don't think anyone from there, has achieved what you have."

"But I still lost," a dejected Lakshya said.

"Did you lose unfairly?"

He thought and then answered, "No."

"Did you give your best?"

"Yes, I did," he answered instantly.

"Then you have triumphed, son."

Lakshya looked at him, slightly confused.

"More than winning, giving your best is more important. One who is not corrupted with victory, or dejected with defeat, is a true winner," the visitor explained.

"Are you saying I should not think about winning?"

He patted Lakshya's back. "No, son. The thoughts of winning should be your guide till the challenge. After that, the outcome doesn't matter. All you should care about is the lessons learnt. If that is done, you have won and there is no reason to be depressed."

The visitor knitted his eyebrows. He asked, "Is there something you would have done differently in the challenge?"

This question threw Lakshya into a thoughtful silence. There was only one reason for his failure. Aindrita's face floated before his eyes with her soulful eyes and dimples on her cheeks. After deliberation, he answered, "No." This time there was a beatific smile on his face. The storm of self-doubt and defeat had settled in his mind.

"Then you should be happy. Chin up!" The visitor lifted Lakshya's chin.

"I feel it is better not to dream. It hurts a lot when they are not fulfilled. Emotions make us weak."

"No, son. 'We are artists, karma is our brush and life is the art.' Emotions are the colours on this canvas of time. They make life worth living. With the right emotion at the right time, the art will be beautiful. Not all dreams come true but always keep your heart open to dreams. For as long as there's a dream, there is hope, and as long as there is hope, there is meaning to life."

Lakshya absorbed the words.

The visitor added, "Had Dhruva not dreamed, he would not have achieved what he did. Never forget that."

Lakshya asked, "What is your name, deva?"

"Madhav from Mayura-Pradesh, an autonomous region in Kailash-Rajya. Some call me a cow-keeper. Some call me *Mayuradhish* (Lord of Mayura)."

Lakshya realized the peacock feather must represent the symbol of Mayura-Pradesh.

"Are you a King, deva?" Lakshya thought Madhav must be a Vanshaj.

Madhav let out a small laugh. "Far from it. To me, I am another you, and you are another me. We are all connected by this endless knot... Aren't we? So, it really doesn't matter who I am or to which class I belong." He turned and left abruptly, leaving Lakshya baffled at the wisdom behind his words.

✦

Aindrita arrived the next morning. Viraat forgot himself so far as to dash to her. "I was waiting for you," he said, forgetting that her father King Yuyutsu was standing next to her.

She smiled and said, "Congratulations. I heard you won."

"Yes, he did," Yuyutsu replied.

Viraat folded his hands. "Pranam, Kailash-Naresh. My apologies! I did not see you."

"There is no way anyone else could have won," Yuyutsu praised his prospective son-in-law. The way Viraat and Aindrita looked at each other, it appeared to Yuyutsu that his dream would certainly come true.

There is someone who almost did. Aindrita felt bad that Lakshya had lost. She felt worse after hearing that he lost only by a thin margin. She blamed herself for his defeat and had no idea how to fix it. She swallowed around the guilt rising in her throat.

"Come, I will show you the sword Asi." Viraat was obviously thrilled and wanted to share it with her.

"What is the hurry? Let her take some rest, Prince Viraat," a voice came from behind them.

They all turned.

Aindrita ran and hugged the person who had spoken.

Yuyutsu introduced the visitor, "This is Madhav, my distant cousin from Mayura-Pradesh in our kingdom. He came last night."

"Pranam, deva," Viraat ventured cautiously.

"Pranam, Prince."

"Please call me Viraat, deva."

Madhav was pleased. "You truly are what they say about you."

"I don't know what I am. The blessings of my parents and Guru have made me whatever I am."

Madhav smiled. "After centuries someone has finished it in less than three days. That's remarkable."

"But I still couldn't beat King Satyavrat's record." Viraat tried to play it down.

"You should be happy that you walked on his path." Madhav winked.

Viraat was confused. *How does he know?* Before he could say anything, Madhav said, "Viraat, please show us the sword. We are excited to see it."

Viraat was delighted that they asked about the sword. He went into his tent to bring it.

Madhav looked at Aindrita. She had a sombre look on her face. There was sadness engraved on it. Concerned, he asked, "What's wrong, Aindrita?"

"Nothing," she replied mirthlessly.

A troubled Yuyutsu asked, "What is it, Aindrita? You know I cannot bear to see you unhappy!"

Viraat had returned with the sword but he stood quietly listening to the conversation.

Dhananjay and Bhaskar also came and joined them.

Aindrita told them, "I was attacked by a pack of wolves in the night. I would have died had Lakshya not come and rescued me. My leg got injured and he treated it."

She removed her footwear and showed them. "He protected me in the night and stayed with me till I could walk on my own." Fear of the danger she faced with the wolves was written all over her face. After a deep sigh, she said, "Had he not stopped to help me; he probably would have won. He did all that in spite of the fact that I never treated him fairly during the training and mocked him for his humble background. Yet he helped me and saved my life." Madhav noticed that she used the words 'humble background' instead of 'Yukth'. Something in her had changed.

Viraat's excitement disappeared. He too felt bad that he never gave Lakshya the respect he deserved at the gurukul.

"I will reward him with gold," Yuyutsu said loudly. "The kingdom of Kailash is indebted to him."

"No, the reward of gold is not enough. I have something else in mind," Dhananjay said.

✦

When Lakshya came out of his tent, he was surprised to find everyone assembled outside.

Dhananjay said, "Son, we all know what you did. Your bravery deserves to be rewarded. From this day onwards, you will be my Anga-Rakshak." Karthik, his Anga-Rakshak, could not accompany him due to his rapidly deteriorating health.

Viraat and Yuyutsu were pleased with the announcement.

The burden on Aindrita's heart eased. She smiled softly.

This unexpected, unanticipated command from Dhananjay astounded Lakshya. It was a big position, considered as an Utkrisht post. The title of Anga-Rakshak was next to the Lok-Sevak and Lok-Rakshak in terms of rank. He was going to start his career as an Utkrisht. It was an honour, an elevation that Lakshya could not even imagine in his dreams. But he was in a fix. Lakshya went down on one knee and bowed his head. He said, "I am honoured, Maharaja. But please pardon me, I cannot stay at Siddha-Lok. I have to go back to my kingdom. I owe it to my *janmabhumi* (motherland)."

Bhaskar understood the dilemma in Lakshya's mind. He replied, "We understand your perplexity. I will make it easier for you. Accept this position as my *gurudakshina*, Lakshya. The debt of Guru is bigger than the debt of janmabhumi."

Lakshya opened his mouth to defy him but he closed it without uttering a word. He couldn't say no now. The notion of gurudakshina was very sacred. It was meant to show respect and gratitude to the Guru. There was no way he could have refused to pay the Guru's fees, whatever it may be.

Lakshya nodded his head saying yes.

Dhananjay extracted out his sword and laid it on Lakshya's head. "Take a pledge that as the Anga-Rakshak you will protect the King and Queen of Shivalik and their complete lineage with your life and soul. You will guard them day and night, during peace or war, from enemies within or outside, at all cost. You shall always endeavour to bring glory to Shivalik."

Lakshya took the pledge.

The small, informal ceremony made him the Dhananjay's bodyguard.

Then, Dhananjay raised him to his feet and hugged him. Everyone was overjoyed. While this was happening, the remaining two students – Rudra and Chitra reached the peak and finished the challenge.

Lakshya looked at Aindrita standing at the back, watching in silence. Her eyes were alternating between Viraat and Lakshya, waves of unsettling thoughts filling her mind.

Bhaskar said, "It is time for all of you to get ready to take blessings from the Saptarishis. Whatever the Saptarishis say to you, that is for you and you alone. No one else will be there. We will leave within an hour."

After everyone left, Viraat went to meet Lakshya alone in his tent. He folded his hands and said, "Lakshya, I will forever be grateful to you for what you did to save Aindrita's life."

Lakshya put his hand over Viraat's folded hands and replied, "I did my duty, nothing else. You too would have done the same."

"You are the real winner."

Impulsively, Viraat hugged Lakshya and uttered, "Please forgive me if I have ever hurt you."

"There is nothing to forgive, Prince. I am humbled by your kind words."

"Don't call me Prince. Call me Viraat."

Then Viraat did the unthinkable. He extended the sword Asi towards Lakshya and said, "This sword belongs to you. You are its rightful owner. I want to gift this to you. Please don't say no."

Madhav watched from a distance. He was impressed with Viraat's gesture. *Love indeed brings out the best in humans.*

The offer left Lakshya bewildered. His mind and heart couldn't comprehend that someone could do such a thing.

The decision sealed their fate.

✦

35

Yātrā (Journey)

ANGAARA

It was dark outside with incandescent stars blinking in the moonless sky. "Kaitabha, you will be the Lord in my absence. You have to ensure that the training continues, and weapons production is not interrupted," Vritra said to his trusted friend and the commander of his army.

"My Lord, what do you mean by 'my absence'?"

"Guruji has asked me to do something. I need to go somewhere alone."

"Alone. But why? After such a long time we have a lord who can keep the tribes united. Without you, they might start fighting again. Leaving them all of a sudden will send a wrong message."

"That is the reason I am putting you in-charge. I will return very soon."

Kaitabha had played an important role in unification. His eyes rolled. Concerned, he asked, "But for how long?"

"A few weeks, maybe, I am not sure."

"If you don't mind me asking, what is so important that Shukracharya has asked you to do it alone?"

Vritra contemplated whether to tell him or not. He had to tell someone in case he did not return. "You can't tell anyone."

"You know I won't."

"Guruji has asked me to go to Andhaka at the southern end of Angaara."

Kaitabha let out a deep sigh of disapproval. "Unthinkable creatures dwell in that forest. You know only a blind goes there; never to return. Why there?"

"To tame an animal."

"Which one?" Kaitabha could guess which one, but he asked to be sure.

"Draak."

"Draaaaak! Are you nuts?" The very sound of her name shook Kaitabha's soul. "It can't be tamed. It will burn you before you even go near it." Kaitabha had never understood Vritra's special skill with animals. He thought it was due to his physical strength that he tamed them so easily. Vritra did not tame but controlled them, which Kaitabha did not know. The mere idea of taming Draak sounded foolish to him. "It sounds like you are inviting *Yama-raja* (God of Death) to your home."

"I can't disobey the Guruji's command. If he thinks I can, I have to try."

"But…"

Before Kaitabha could say anything further, Vritra raised his hand, signalling him to stop. "Success doesn't come to you; you have to go to it. I will leave tomorrow morning."

"Do you know where to go? It is a vast, uncharted area. Who knows what other dangerous animals live there!" Kaitabha said, obviously concerned.

Andhaka, the south of Angaara island, was an unknown world. It had forests so dense that even sunlight did not reach the ground surface. Trees were so tall that they got lost in the fog. The riverbanks had the richest flora and fauna, and it was inhabited by many unseen species of animals.

"If it's meant to be, I will find my way," Vritra consoled him.

"Don't go alone. At least take me or someone with you."

"No, I will go alone. You are needed here, in my absence."

Vritra hugged his friend. It was to end the conversation and his concerns.

"You don't have to worry about here. Just return as soon as possible," Kaitabha replied realizing there was no convincing his friend.

◆

Three weeks had passed since Vritra left. The journey had been tougher than he had imagined. If there was anyone in the world who could survive in this part of the island – it was the vichitra boy, Vritra.

He stepped out of the raft he had used to travel this far. River Japurá, the longest river on Dhruva-Lok, was the spine of Angaara island. It was also the fastest way to his destination.

It was close to dusk. Owls hooted, and something far away hissed like a chorus of snakes. He needed to find a place to rest.

The land was a marshy swamp. He walked carefully to avoid slipping. The ground squelched under his boots as he walked.

His senses alerted him to a predator around. His neck tingled. He turned slowly. A crocodile jumped out of the water, straight at him, with its mouth wide open baring the numerous teeth inside. The crocodile was ten feet long. Vritra landed on his hips and retreated rapidly in the muddy land. He was in the crocodile's territory. There was no time to rely on his special skills. He had no other option but to counterattack.

Nothing helps your chances more in close combat than a knife. Swiftly, he pulled out a knife from his boots. The crocodile opened his mouth and moved to get a hold of his leg. Vritra rolled back and then stood on his feet. *Offence is the best defence.* With this thought, he jumped on the crocodile trusting the knife in his hand.

They struggled. The crocodile moved wildly. But Vritra's grip was strong. He used all his muscle power to keep the crocodile tightly reigned in. Vritra turned and the crocodile was on top of him, upside down. He used his knife to cut open the soft, squishy belly of the wild beast. Then he repeatedly stabbed him till the reptile bled out.

He lay next to the body of the crocodile, breathing hard and gulping air. The adrenaline still gushed through his veins.

"The hunter is hunted. The beast had chosen the wrong species to prey upon; the cause of his undoing," he thought.

◆

For the next two weeks, Vritra kept moving around. Animal growls and bird whistles filled the air. He kept walking, looking for clues – giant footprints, trampled trees, swaths of burning forest or burned skeletons. *There is no way something that big could sneak around. Right?* But not a single sighting of Draak. He had no idea which direction to take, and what to look for. He was losing hope. Was it possible that Draak had died? No one had seen her in years. As crazy as it may sound but in reality, hope was among the worst of all evils as it kept adding to the torture with no surety of outcome.

It rained heavily and frequently because of which he remained immobile for a large part of the days. The rains were different here. The raindrops were the size of a berry. The rain came down fast and hard. It felt like a barrage of pebbles had been catapulted from the sky, as if someone wanted to prevent him from proceeding further.

For a long time he had been sheltering in a cave. There were no signs of the rain stopping.

Frustrated, he came out of the cave and started walking in the rain. He no longer cared about getting hit by the pebble-sized raindrops. Vritra had lost track of time and all sense of direction. It seemed impossible that Andhaka could be so deep and wild. Towering trees on all sides formed a canopy above his head. He kept walking in a senseless manner.

He reached the coastline. It was the southern tip of Angaara island kissing the mighty Tethys Sea.

He stood in silence for a few minutes, absorbing the enormity and serenity of the ocean. Then he went down on his knees and screamed. It was a cry louder than the trumpet of an elephant or the roar of a lion.

The rain abated into a slight, misty drizzle, almost as if Vritra's cry had scared it away. Rays of sun pierced the sky forming a magnificent rainbow across the horizon. When the echoes of his cry faded away, there was complete silence except for the background symphony of the waves. The foamy ocean waves swayed rhythmically, landing with soft swishes on the beach.

Finally, he heard the growl of a dragon. It occurred to him that it was the rain which had kept Draak in hiding. With the sun shining, Draak would be out flying.

He followed the sound. From a cave close by, Draak came out. She was at least fifty feet long, snout to tail – a monster snake with the wings of a bat. She was truly the serpent King. The red gold beast opened her wings and moved with grace. Her scales gleamed in the sunlight. According to lore, each one of those scales carried poison strong enough to fell a grown man in seconds. Her teeth and claws, big and razor-edged could easily rip through a wootz steel armour. Chocolate-brown fiery eyes with endless pools could zoom in from hundreds of meters away and her ears could sequester sounds from one another. Her sense of smell could effortlessly identify most creatures by scent alone. Her tail was long and sharp as a sword and it could split a human into two. It was nature's monstrous and deadliest weapon!

The magnificent bird spread open her wings; a thrumming sound came from her jaws and nostrils, along with wisps of smoke. She shuddered and flapped her wings and started flying. Draak flew as if she was trying to string the rainbow in the sky. Her colour changed to blue – the colour of the sky.

This bird can camouflage as well! Vritra stared at her in astonishment. That must be the reason she was spotted so rarely. Was there any skill left in the animal world which the bird did not possess?

With Draak away, Vritra ran to her cave under the cover of darkness. He saw many skeletons and skulls of various animals. There were numerous black marks inside the cave – burn marks.

The journey was successful. But the mission was not accomplished yet. Vritra needed a plan to tame her. It won't be easy. One mistake and he could be burned to ashes.

Vritra climbed a tree near the cave and waited for her to return.

When Draak returned to her cave, she waited outside. She could feel the presence of a foreign smell.

She looked around but noticed nothing.

Without wasting any time, Vritra jumped and landed perfectly on her long neck, her only blind spot.

Draak got angry and she breathed fire to burn every living thing around her. She struggled. But Vritra was in a perfect position. All he needed to do was to grip her tightly.

This annoyed Draak further. She ran and became air-borne, hoping that the sheer speed and air drag would make the intruder fall. Vritra continued to hold her firmly with his big hands.

Flying on the dragon was the most amazing experience ever for Vritra. Up high, the air was freezing cold; the dragon's cold body felt warm.

Vritra's creased forehead finally relaxed. Tension subsided. It was time for him to use his special skills. He moved his right hand towards the forehead of Draak. He closed his eyes, and whispered in a language which the creature understood, "*Shantayati.*" Calm down. Yes, he could talk with animals.

Draak resisted. She kept squirming.

It took a long time, but he overpowered the mind of the dragon. Draak calmed down and returned to the ground. The creature had been tamed.

The *journey*, to the unknown, far away, proved to be fruitful. The ultimate power of nature was in his hands.

I am no less than God!

✦

36

Pratyāgata (Returned)

SIDDHA - LOK

"Pranam, Jyeshta Pitashri and Jyeshta Matashri." Viraat bowed and touched the feet of Vishamadeva and Gayatri. Even though they were like his grandparents, Viraat always referred to them in the same manner as his parents.

"Ayushman bhava, putra." Both blessed him one after the other.

Vishamadeva raised him and hugged him with affection. "You remind me of my youth."

"I wish to be like you, Jyeshta Pitashri," Viraat said.

"No, putra. You are a true Dhruvanshi, the rightful heir. Don't ever wish to be like me."

Viraat had hit a raw nerve. Some wounds never heal. Gayatri hurriedly held Vishamadeva's hand and changed the topic. "You have made us proud by earning the coveted title of 'Sarva Shrestha Shishya'."

Viraat smiled proudly.

He asked, "Jyeshta Pitashri, was this challenge conducted when you were in the gurukul?"

"Yes, it was conducted," Vishamadeva replied.

"How long did you take to finish the challenge, Jyeshta Pitashri?"

"Ohh, I don't remember now. It's such a long time ago. My memory is fading. Not as fast as you, that much I remember." It was obvious he did not want to answer.

Viraat did not push him. "I should go and meet maa. I came to seek your blessings first."

"You should have gone and met her first. Only a mother knows the sacrifices she makes," Gayatri said in a heartfelt tone.

Viraat rushed to his mother's chambers.

✦

Mitasha hurried to Padmini's chamber. "Maharani, the Prince is coming."

Padmini picked up the pooja plate. Mitasha helped her light the lamp to get ready to welcome her son.

Dressed in his princely clothes, Viraat entered the chambers. He had a crown on his head – the crown of a Prince. Golden armour and jewels decorated his body. He looked like a mighty warrior.

Padmini applied *teeka* on his forehead and did an *aarti* with the lamp.

"Maa, bless me." Viraat bent forward to touch his mother's feet.

She raised him up and hugged him. "My blessings are always with my son. I cannot tell you how happy I am. Finally, you are back in the kingdom, never to return." Her delight was infectious.

Viraat smiled.

He said, "They crowned me Sarva Shrestha Shishya."

"You are a Dhruvanshi. I never had a doubt. I am sure no one would have got close enough to win?"

"Well, someone got very close."

"Who? That is not possible!" The expression on her face changed abruptly.

"His name is Lakshya. He is the son of a soldier from Bhuvar-Lok. He saved Princess Aindrita from an attack by a pack of wolves. This slowed his climb. If he had not stopped, he could have been the winner."

Padmini said, "He saved Princess Aindrita! We are indebted to him. I would like to meet and personally thank him."

"Pitashri has already rewarded him. He made Lakshya his Anga-Rakshak."

"Where is he from, you said?"

"From Bhuvar-Lok."

"What does his father do?"

"He is a soldier in Samrat Srivijay's army."

"Ohh. So, he must be a Yukth. Your father has indeed rewarded him fittingly, directly making him an Utkrisht. I will thank him again when I meet him."

She led him to a seat.

"Now tell me what did the Saptarishis say to you?" She was desperately waiting to hear this. Her life had changed after visiting them. For this reason, her impatient, inquisitive eyes did not blink for a long time. She bit her lower lip.

Viraat travelled in time to recollect his meeting with the Saptarishis.

Sage Gautama looked at a nervous Viraat, "What is bothering you, young Prince?"

Viraat asked, "O Divine Sages, there is only one question that bothers me. When will I be able to wield the Trishul?"

Sage Vashistha replied, "Prince, you were born to wield the Trishul. The power is within you. Nothing can stop you when the time comes."

Viraat did not understand what the Sage meant when he said that the power was in him but he was relieved to hear the rest of it. "But, when will that day come?"

"Don't be so impatient, Prince. Lord Shiva had blessed that when the day comes, the worthy will wield it. Nothing comes before its time and when it is destined. Wait for the day to come, when you lift it for the right reasons," Sage Agastya replied.

Sage Atri added, "Trust the Lord. Wait for your destiny, as the destiny of the entire Lok depends on it."

The sages closed their eyes.

Viraat bowed his head.

Viraat's mind returned to his mother's question. He said, "This is what the Divine Sages said to me. I haven't told anyone else except pitashri."

Padmini was flooded with relief on hearing this. She raised her eyes heavenward. *Om Namah Shivaay.* She asked, "What did they mean that the destiny of the entire Lok depends on it?" Her features sharpened.

"I did not ask. To have an entire Lok depend on me is a heavy burden."

"Yes, don't think about it. Just do your duty. Time is the greatest Sage. It will answer all our questions."

Their discussion was interrupted by Dhananjay walking inside. He spoke as he approached them, "Did you talk with your son about his marriage?"

Viraat blushed.

"I was about to." Padmini continued, "Viraat, we want to get you married soon."

He avoided the topic. "Marriage not so soon. Not before I become the Lok-Rakshak."

Dhananjay rebutted quickly, "Simham still has a few years left until retirement. But we have decided to get you married within a year. We have already fixed your marriage."

Viraat was shocked and his face turned pale. Suddenly, he felt like choking. His heart pounded. All he could say with a lot of hesitation, "With whom?"

Padmini said, "King Yuyutsu from Kailash-Rajya has offered his daughter Aindrita's hand in marriage. We have consented. But if you don't agree, we can still decline."

Instinctively, Viraat stood up and uttered, "No, no, that is not necessary." Realizing he had given away his true feelings, he altered his response, "Your word means everything to me. I agree with whatever you have decided." His cheeks turned red in shyness.

Dhananjay and Padmini looked at each other, delighted and relieved with his approval.

"We will announce the union between our two kingdoms on your birthday."

Viraat felt dolphins jumping in his stomach. His fair skin reddened even further.

They were interrupted by the sudden clatter of a spear falling on the floor.

Dhananjay asked, "Is everything alright, Lakshya? What happened?"

The clatter brought Lakshya to his senses. Emotions never follow reality. Even when you know the impossible cannot be made possible, it still hurts. False hope is cruel; it burns you from inside. With his head bowed, he came inside, and said, "I beg your forgiveness, Maharaja. It slipped from my hand."

Padmini left her seat and went to him. "You are Lakshya."

"Yes, Maharani."

She held his hand. "What you did was truly brave in saving Princess Aindrita! You have done a great favour to this kingdom. We shall always be indebted to you."

"No, Maharani. I did what anyone would have done. It was my dharma."

"Don't call me Maharani. You are of Viraat's age and you have studied together. I am like your mother. Call me Matashri." She put her hand over Lakshya's head with endearment. Her eyes were pink in motherly love.

Lakshya realized she meant what she was saying. He felt as if his mother Radha had touched him. It had been such a long time since he had seen her. He said, "I cannot Maharani. I am your servant."

"Son, to me you are not."

Dhananjay interjected, "Lakshya, you have to obey the wishes of the Queen."

"Yes, Maharaja."

Lakshya bowed down and touched Padmini's feet.

She said, "I am your mother now. And a mother can ask for anything. You can't say no."

"Yes, Matashri. You can ask for anything from me."

It never crossed his mind that one day she might actually ask for something.

✦

37

Heraka (Spy)

SIDDHA - LOK

"How could you let the Maharaja take such a hasty decision, without any verification or background check?" Vishamadeva was visibly upset. He took security matters very seriously, even though they strictly were not in his domain of work.

Simham defended himself, "Maharaja offered him this position. I could not question his decision in front of everyone. Later, I tried to make him reconsider but he wouldn't listen. Karthik's health is failing, so that probably made the Maharaja take this decision hastily."

"We cannot have a stranger, especially someone not from our kingdom, so close to the King. It's too risky."

Simham nodded and replied, "He said no to the position. But Acharya Bhaskar termed it as his gurudakshina. Acharya will not put anyone dangerous close to the Maharaja. But, I will keep an eye on him."

Somewhat appeased, Vishamadeva asked, "Hmm... What do we know about him?"

"He is from Bhuvar-Lok. His father is a soldier in King Srivijay's army. But my informants tell me that his father could be a spy or an assassin."

Vishamadeva, a man driven by the compulsion to protect the Dhruvanshis, shook his head. "This is not good. He is a threat. This could be a big conspiracy to eliminate the Dhruvanshis."

"But King Srivijay doesn't have such a reputation," Simham reasoned.

"Not everything happens with the King's approval. You know that very well. His Raksha Mantri Bhalla is a notorious fellow. He has performed devious deeds in the past. King Srivijay overlooks such acts of his."

Simham scratched his beard. "I agree with you, Lok-Sevak. We need to be careful. He could be a spy."

✦

Lakshya was standing guard outside the Maharaja's chambers carrying an eight-foot long spear and a heavy sheathed sword. He donned the heavy black armour required of the Anga-Rakshak, and a blue cape with the emblem of Shivalik-Rajya. He hated the heavy armour and the cape.

He had been in Shivalik for a few months now and was looked upon as an outsider. He felt alone in this place. Dhananjay, Padmini and Viraat were very nice to him.

It was late in the night. His head drooped as he stood. Suddenly, he was jerked upright by a stealthy sound from inside the chamber.

He had the authority to enter the Maharaja's chamber unannounced and he crept in.

The room was in shadows. He gazed around in the dark. The Maharaja and Maharani were sleeping. There was nothing out of the ordinary. Maybe it was the wind.

His eyes went to a hook in the balcony that was used to climb walls. He looked around the room again and noticed a silhouette behind the curtain. Someone was in the chambers.

He took a protective stance before the bed where the Maharaja and Maharani were sleeping. "Show yourself, you coward," he said.

Two masked men came out with knives in their hands. One of them whispered, "Are you Lakshya?"

"Yes."

"Samrat Srivijay has sent us to kill the King and the Prince. He said you will help us."

"I don't believe you. The Samrat will never do such a cowardly act."

"We have a sealed letter from the Samrat. Take a look yourself." The man handed a letter from his pocket.

Lakshya noticed the seal. It was the seal of Jambu-Rajya with a thunderbolt symbol.

Dhananjay had woken up and was listening to the conversation.

Lakshya replied, "I don't care if it's a letter from Lord Bajrang himself. My sworn duty is to protect the Maharaja. That is my dharma. I will not stand down. Surrender immediately."

"You think you can defeat the two of us?" the man chuckled.

"If you doubt it, come and try me," Lakshya invited.

The intruders felt agitated. The man replied, "Very well, you die with them."

They threw the knives at him. Lakshya deflected one with his spear. But the other knife hit the breastplate of his armour. He was lucky that the armour was made of metal, and that he was wearing it.

They pulled out their swords.

Dhananjay said, "Lakshya, don't kill them. I want them alive."

Lakshya got ready with his spear, "Yes, Maharaja."

They both attacked him with swift moves. Lakshya stopped them with a strong horizontal hold and pushed them back.

The intruders were no match for his defensive skills. Lakshya threw his spear at the stomach of the one on his left, aiming at the unprotected area. He avoided throwing it from the sharp razor side. The intruder collapsed in pain.

Lakshya pulled out his sword. The other intruder rushed towards him, swinging wildly, but Lakshya deflected the attacks with ease and kicked the attacker, who fell on the chair.

Quickly, Lakshya disarmed him and placed the sword against his neck.

Padmini lit the torches in the room.

At that instant, the door opened and Vishamadeva and Simham rushed in with five guards.

Simham instructed the guards, "Take them down to the dungeon for questioning."

The guards obeyed and took away the attackers.

Vishamadeva helped Lakshya pull the knife from his armour.

He asked, "Are you hurt?"

"No," Lakshya replied.

This was his first meeting with Vishamadeva. For some reason, Vishamadeva had never met him before. Lakshya assumed it was because of his birthplace. But the more he heard about Vishamadeva, the more he felt there was another reason.

Vishamadeva stared at him with wide, unblinking eyes. The curtains in the room fluttered in the breeze. He said, "Well done, son. Now go and take rest for the night."

This praise made Lakshya feel as if he was melting into a warm pool of happiness. He bowed to the Maharaja and left the chambers.

Dhananjay looked at the Lok-Sevak and Lok-Rakshak in anger and said, "Are you both satisfied now?"

There was no reply.

Padmini was confused. *Why the sudden outburst?* She had rarely seen her husband raise his voice in front of Vishamadeva. Curious, she asked, "What is going on?"

"They thought Lakshya was a spy of King Srivijay of Jambu-Rajya. So, they had planned this test."

Simham answered, "It was for your safety, Maharaja."

"I told you that Acharya Bhaskar seconded his appointment. He deserves our trust."

Vishamadeva was quiet.

"That is our job." Simham once again explained.

"Are you satisfied now?" Dhananjay asked.

"Yes. He is not a spy," Vishamadeva said in a loud voice and walked out.

◆

38

Bhasma (Ash)

It was one of those gloomy days when the sun played hide and seek with menacing grey clouds. Humidity hung in the still air, preparing for a torrential onslaught.

"This is a nice sword." Kaitabha examined the sword from all angles. Then he swung it in the air. "It's lightweight as well. You are a good blacksmith."

"Thank you, my Lord." The blacksmith was relieved. He was new in this line of work. Being fat, he was not good at fighting. It was essential to be useful in the time of wars.

"Can it withstand a heavy sword?"

"I don't know, my Lord. This is the first one with the new alloy that I have created."

"Very well. Make a few more of these and get them tested."

Someone called Kaitabha.

He turned and looked.

Prachanda, a lean man in his late-forties with a fleshless face and fighting a losing battle with baldness, came running to Kaitabha and told him, "Tribes of Rishvan and Dola have started fighting again. Only you can stop them." Prachanda was the trainer with swords and an expert in the fighting technique *Takshaka*. He was from the Naga tribe.

Getting the Rishvan and Dola tribe to stay together was an impossible task. With Vritra not in sight for nearly six weeks now, the fissures had started to emerge. The fragile unity was beginning to collapse.

Kaitabha took his sword and rushed to the place where the conflict was going on. He reached the training camp where fighters from both tribes had gone berserk. The silver lining was that they were fighting with muscles and not weapons.

Kaitabha screamed at them to stop.

Nobody listened or cared. Maybe they did not hear him.

"STOP!" Kaitabha screamed louder this time.

The fighting stopped. Many men were bleeding profoundly. "Get away from each other," Kaitabha ordered.

Kaitabha looked at Prachanda. "Take the injured and get them treated."

The leader of the Dola tribe, Gaara, a tall, hefty man with his face covered in blood, came forward and said, "We are leaving. We will not work with them."

"Vritra will be mad. He will bury you here when he gets back," Kaitabha threatened.

"Where is he, huh?" Kaitabha was silent.

"We last saw him sail south through Japurá. There is only one way it goes… to Andhaka… to Death," Gaara revealed.

Prachanda looked at Kaitabha in surprise. He asked, "Is this true? Why did he go there?"

Gaara spat blood from his mouth and said, "Doesn't matter. He will not come back. Things will go back to the way they were."

"No one is going anywhere as long as I am here. Vritra is going to come back. And you better watch your back," Kaitabha retorted.

Gaara laughed. "What will he do to me? Today you watch what I am going to do to you." He picked up an axe and a sword lying on the ground.

At the sudden turn of events, Prachanda pleaded with Kaitabha, "My Lord, we better leave. They are mad. We are outnumbered. We stand no chance in front of so many of them."

"I am not going to run. You tell Suketu and his men to come here. I will hold them till then."

"But they are too many for you to hold them off."

"Don't worry. Just go."

Prachanda ran as fast as he could.

It's time to see how good this sword is. Kaitabha swung the newly-forged sword.

Gaara rushed with the axe and sword. Kaitabha also ran towards him.

Kaitabha swung his sword first. Gaara stopped it and then swung the axe. Kaitabha sat down and avoided it narrowly. Gaara used all his strength and swung the sword from top. Kaitabha brought his sword in between to block it.

Unfortunately, the freshly forged sword wasn't strong enough to withstand the impact of a heavy metal. It broke into two.

Everyone laughed.

Gaara kicked him and Kaitabha landed on his back three feet away.

Kaitabha got up quickly, and tried to find a new weapon. But he was surrounded by men of the Dola tribe. There was no escape. *Where is Suketu?*

"I told you. Now get ready to be slaughtered."

Kaitabha tried to get out. But he was kicked back by the men encircling him. They had surrounded him like a pack of wild dogs. Two men snatched his arms and twisted them behind his back.

Gaara punched and kicked him several times. He enjoyed every bit of it. "I will kill you today, you weirdo." Gaara was referring to Kaitabha's squinty eyes, which could move independently of each other.

Kaitabha could feel his facial muscles grimacing in unremitting pain in his bloodied face. He clenched his eyes shut.

Gaara picked up his axe. He spat on Kaitabha as he asked, "Any last words?"

Before Kaitabha could say anything, they all heard something. The laughter stopped and all turned back towards the sound. Nothing. There was no one.

As they returned to their victim, a loud growl came from the sky. They looked up with fear. A huge bird flew over their heads.

Someone shouted, "It's Draak. Run."

The mere sight of Draak sent them into a panic. Many ran into hiding. Others watched, frozen with fear at the jaw-dropping spectacle. The men holding Kaitabha released him and ran away.

"Vritra is here," Kaitabha announced it aloud before collapsing on the ground.

Everyone noticed that Vritra was sitting on the dragon, riding her like a horse.

Gaara dropped his weapons in surprise. He blinked twice. It was beyond reason, but real. Impossible, but true.

Draak swooped down from the sky and landed in front of them. She growled menacingly. From behind her body, Vritra's face emerged.

Gaara stood alone. His heart sank. He fell on his knees with his hands folded seeking forgiveness.

"Forgive me, Supreme Lord."

Vritra looked around. The bloodied face of Kaitabha angered him. He said, "There is only one punishment for insubordination, for treason. The one who digs a hole, is buried in it."

Vritra gently pressed on Draak's neck and whispered, "BHASMA."

The dragon croaked, roared, and charged. A column of yellow flames from her mouth billowed over Gaara, and burnt him down to ashes in seconds.

The chilling silence came back again, as several people broke into a cold sweat and shivered against the most powerful weapon in anybody's hands – fear.

✦

39

Upakṣepa (Hint)

Siddha - Lok

"Maharaja, Kailash-Naresh will be arriving shortly," Lakshya informed the King.

With a nod from Dhananjay, Lakshya closed the door and took his usual position outside.

"Let us welcome them personally at the palace gates," Dhananjay said to his wife.

"It is against tradition. As per protocol, the Lok-Sevak receives them at the gate."

"Some traditions should be broken to signal the importance of the relationship. After all, very soon we will become relatives. Tomorrow is Viraat's nineteenth birthday. It will be memorable."

Dhananjay looked at his outfit in the full-length mirror. Padmini placed the crown on his head.

"They are not coming on your birthday," she teased him.

"I don't care. It is my son's first birthday after returning from the gurukul. It will be a day everyone will remember. I want it to be perfect."

"And it will be, with the grace of Lord Shiva."

◆

Drums were beaten loudly. Flowers were showered at every step. Soldiers stood on either side as far as the eye could see, giving the visitors a royal salute. Elephants trumpeted, horses neighed. It was a grand spectacle.

Yuyutsu, Devayani and Aindrita walked regally, full of smiles at the grand welcome.

Aindrita was dressed in a gorgeous flamingo-pink *odhani* over a skirt and bodice. Her slender waist and navel were clearly visible like a vortex in the calm ocean. She had kept her look minimalistic with nearly no-makeup. She had put on pink bangles and a pair of *mujris*. The sheer elegance of the Princess attracted admiring glances. She said to her parents, "So much pomp and glory?"

"This is not for my welcome. They are welcoming their next Queen," Yuyutsu said to her, eyes brimming with joy.

She didn't hear her father's words because at that moment, her eyes found Viraat. Spellbound at the sight, she did not want to blink in case the vision disappeared. Viraat was standing next to the King and Queen in his royal attire. He looked regal. With his dazzling smile and a crown on his head, he looked like a demi-god.

Dhananjay gave a warm hug to Yuyutsu. Padmini applied tilak on Devayani and Aindrita's foreheads.

Padmini took some kohl from her eyes using her ring finger and moved to apply it on Aindrita's neck. "You are very beautiful. This is to save you from any evil eye." She saw the mole on Aindrita's neck. "The gods have already given you natural protection from any evil eye."

Viraat's smile grew wider. Dushyant, who was standing beside Viraat, whispered, "She is a perfect match for you."

Viraat and Aindrita looked embarrassed to see each other, out of their gurukul and dressed so differently.

Dhananjay asked Yuyutsu, "Please accept our greetings, Kailash-Naresh. I hope you had no inconveniences during the long journey?"

"Not at all," Yuyutsu replied.

Yuyutsu went up to Vishamadeva and Gayatri, and touched their feet. He was followed by Devayani and Aindrita.

Gayatri gave a warm and affectionate hug to Aindrita. "You are indeed beautiful, truly a goddess."

As Aindrita hugged Gayatri, her eyes finally found Lakshya who was standing on the side-lines. He looked important in his armour but nothing compared to Viraat.

She smiled. But Lakshya stiffened and did not return her smile. His hands were clasped behind him, his shoulders eloquent with tension. She saw a hint of redness in his eyes, even from the distance. His gaze accusing her of crimes she could not fathom.

Was he angry with her for some reason? Aindrita raised her eyebrows in the universal what-is-the-matter expression and was met with his stony gaze.

Madhav came up to Viraat. "How are you, Prince?"

Viraat leaned down and touched his feet. He said, "Pranam, deva. We are privileged that you have come on this occasion."

Madhav hugged Viraat and said, "Honour is all ours. I wouldn't have missed such an auspicious occasion for anything."

"Only a birthday, deva."

"Important events are going to unfold here."

Viraat was confused. *Does he know about the engagement?* It was a closely guarded secret and the announcement was meant to surprise everyone. A grand alliance was being forged.

Vishamadeva interrupted them, "Let us go inside. Viraat, take our honoured guests to their rooms."

Viraat led them to the interiors of the palace, through the well laid-out royal gardens spread across thirty acres. The grass was recently cut. The aroma of the flowers in the garden was soporific. Numerous birds were chirping. As they strolled, a family of peacocks walked past them oblivious to their presence. The harsh crackles of hornbills startled them and everyone let out an involuntary laugh.

The palace was constructed facing east, allowing its inhabitants to pray to the Dhruva star and the Sun-god at the crack of dawn, most days. The rectangular palace was double the size of the one at Kailash-Rajya. It was a four-storey stone structure with marble domes and had a 108-foot six-storey tower in the centre. The four-storey stone building of fine grey granite with deep pink marble domes had a facade with several expansive arches and two smaller ones flanking the central arch, which was supported by tall pillars. Above the central arch was a sculpture of Dhruva with the emblem of Shivalik in the background. The palace had two hundred and fifty-six rooms surrounded by large gardens on all sides. Many fountains, pillared terraces, courtyards, and columns lines were spread across the palace.

Aindrita looked at Lakshya as she walked past him but he deliberately avoided her gaze.

Lakshya was about to fall in step behind them, when someone touched him on his shoulder.

He turned. A bright smile wiped the dull mood off his face.

"How are you, son?" Madhav asked.

"Pranam, deva."

Madhav gave him a hug and said playfully, "I think you needed one."

"It is good to see familiar faces in a sea of strangers."

Madhav asked, "How have you been?"

"With your blessings, I am well." He was not. His face conveyed it.

"Something is not right. What happened?"

Lakshya's smile turned fake. "Nothing. It's been a long time since I have gone home." What he said was true, but that was not the reason for his dullness.

"Don't worry. Something tells me that you will meet them very soon." Madhav seemed to hint at something.

"Maharaja has told me to go home after the wedding."

"You are getting married?" Madhav pretended to be surprised and teased him. "No, not mine...after Prince Viraat's wedding."

"Ohh. But still I feel you will meet them soon."

Before he could dig further, Madhav said, "Go quickly, the Anga-Rakshak cannot be so far from the *anga* (body) he has to guard."

"Yes, deva."

"I will meet you later," Madhav said as Lakshya hurried to catch up with the King.

On his way, Lakshya was interrupted yet again by a familiar voice. Someone called, "Lakshya, wait."

A woman's voice! He looked at the direction from where the call had come. It was Niyati.

She said, "It's good to see you. How have you been?" Her eyes were hooked on him and they did not move away from his face even for a moment. She wanted to envelope him in a warm embrace, but she couldn't do that in such a public place. She kept her emotions in check.

Niyati was dressed in a purple sari and she looked enchantingly attractive. Lakshya was momentarily smitten by her almond eyes. "I am good. How about you? You look different." And remembering his place, lowered his eyes and said, "My lady."

She chuckled. She could see he was still learning the royal etiquette. "Yes, I am different. I am now the Queen of Sangrur-Pradesh."

"I heard about it. You had to leave midway from the gurukul."

"Yes, due to the untimely death of my father. As I was the only surviving child, I had to take up this huge responsibility."

"You are the first Queen of a Pradesh in Shivalik. You have changed the tradition. I am sure you will do total justice to the title."

"Well, you are the first Anga-Rakshak of Shivalik who wasn't even born here, purely due to your talent. That's a far bigger achievement."

Talking to her brought a smile to Lakshya's face. But at that moment, Lakshya saw Dhananjay was about to move inside the palace.

"I have to take leave of you now, my lady."

"I understand. Go ahead."

As he walked away, she let out a deep breath. Her heart refused to slow its frantic beat.

✦

Viraat took Aindrita to her room. Viraat wondered what thoughts filled her mind right now? What dreams come to her at night? Did she like him, or even better, love him? He had no idea.

He had taken special care of her room's decoration, hoping to impress her.

The ambience of the room conveyed beauty and joy. As she took a deep breath, fresh lavender soothed her senses. The room was diamond shape with grey porcelain floor tiles. The high walls had been painted a soft cerulean. There were grand columns with inset panels depicting flowers made from semi-precious stones. The rosewood bed was neatly made with a red silk quilt. There was a feeling of luxury and peace in the room.

"I hope you like the room," Viraat said.

"It's perfect," Aindrita exclaimed smiling. Viraat felt a spark of excitement.

"It has a very good view. Come, I will show you." Viraat held her hand. Her heart did a somersault.

She liked the way Viraat was making an effort to impress her.

The view from the balcony was breathtaking. It had a direct view of the Grand Shiva Temple.

At that moment, Aindrita saw something strange moving in the sky. Her eyes became wide. "What is that?" She pointed her hand swiftly. "Did you see that?"

"What?" Viraat looked towards the sky but saw nothing.

"It was something flying in the sky. But it disappeared into the clouds."

"Can you describe it?"

"It was white and looked like an elephant with wings. I have never seen anything like that before. Or maybe it was just a fast-moving white cloud. I don't know."

"I know what you have seen. It is for real. I have also seen it a few times, but no one believes me. It always disappears in the clouds before you can get a good look."

"Exactly! A cloud never moves so fast. Hope it was for real." She stared at the clouds, willing it to reappear.

Suddenly, there was a meow sound. Excited, Aindrita hurried into the room and lifted the cat, stroking the silky hair fondly. It meowed in recognition. "You are so beautiful. Where have you come from, you cute little thing?"

"Never seen her. I think she is a stray," Viraat said.

"She looks friendly. Look at the way she is so comfortable in my arms. She's used to being around people," Aindrita said in a caring manner.

Viraat brought some milk in a bowl and placed it on the balcony. The cat jumped and started lapping the milk.

"The cat has found a new home. She will remind me of you when you are not here." Viraat's impish grin spoke volumes about how he was feeling.

The cat purred in agreement. They both laughed.

After a while, Viraat said, "This is the first time you have come here. If you need a tour of the palace or the city, I will take you around. Just let me know."

She put on a drowsy face and replied, "I am too tired for that today. But I would love to go tomorrow."

"Tomorrow is difficult. There is pooja in the morning, followed by many functions and ceremonies."

"The day after?" She gave one of her endearing smiles which caused the dimple in her right cheek to deepen in the sun's play of shadow and light.

Viraat's face lit up.

They looked into each other's eyes. The moment stretched until his eyes began to turn pink. Hers did, too.

Madhav coughed at the entrance to the room. They both looked at him and turned away as if they were caught.

"I hope I am not intruding at the wrong time," Madhav said.

"Pranam, deva. No-no, I was just leaving," Viraat replied, hastily.

"It is a beautiful room with an excellent view."

"Very honoured guests have come," Viraat looked at Aindrita as he replied.

"Indeed. Very rare that so many Kings get together." After a brief pause, Madhav said, "It's a big day tomorrow. I heard some big announcements are expected. Please tell us what to expect?"

"I don't know, deva. Maharaja and Jyeshta Pitashri decide everything."

"The prophesied son is going to be crowned Prince tomorrow. Not a small occasion by any standard." Madhav toyed with him.

"I don't know, deva. Do you believe in prophecies?"

Madhav moved away without answering. He had a mischievous smile on his face.

"Do you, deva? Do you believe in prophecies?"

Madhav turned back and replied, "I believe in karma, son."

"That's not the answer to my question, deva."

"Acharya Bhaskar has trained you well."

"Still not answering my question, deva."

Aindrita listened intently.

"You won't let it go?" Madhav shook his head gently.

"No, deva," Viraat answered as a curious but adamant teenager.

"What is a prophecy, Prince Viraat?"

There was a long silence. Madhav answered his own question, "The purpose of prophecy is not to tell the future, but to make it."

"I don't understand. What do you mean?"

"Let me put it differently – a prophecy is a prediction of the future by observing the past karma and relating them with the present and future circumstances and the nakshatras."

"Do nakshatras decide so much?" Viraat asked.

"Nakshatras don't bring a guided or directed change. They lead to forces that influence our mood, our emotions, the way we act. But it is ultimately we who have to act through our free will. That choice is always with us."

"You seem to imply that it's just a prediction which may not necessarily come true?"

"That depends on who is making the prediction."

Aindrita interrupted, "What if the Saptarishis are making the prediction?"

"Then I will take it very seriously. They see what no one can. They reveal what needs to be told in the large scheme of things, nothing more, nothing less."

"Do you mean to say certain things are destined to happen in a certain way?" Aindrita asked restlessly.

"Tough question. Who knows what destiny is? I don't think even the Gods have control over it. I see destiny as a river flowing through its natural course, towards the ocean. Our actions and determination are like obstacles in its path which can force the river to meander, or at times even alter its course," Madhav replied. He paused and added, "But destiny, like a river is very elegant. The river always finds a way to meet the ocean in some way or the other."

Viraat breathed a sigh of relief.

Aindrita shifted in discomfort. The words of the Saptarishis rang in her ears.

Madhav added, "Remember nothing is predetermined and certain, not even birth. Everything has been created by us through our actions. The past never leaves and karma is supreme. It comes back like a boomerang when you least expect it."

✦

The day had been endless. Lakshya retired to his quarters, relieved that he had not run into Anidrita again. He missed his parents a great deal today. Imagining his home made him ache with loneliness. He sighed. His stomach rumbled making him realize he was very hungry. He reached for a glass of water and drank it in one long gulp. Before his hand could reach the food kept on the side-table, there was a knock on the door.

He wanted to be alone, so he did not answer. The door creaked open on its heavy, rusted hinges.

Aindrita tiptoed into the room. She was wearing a sea-green top with a long skirt draped over with a shawl. Her hair was neatly braided, as usual.

Lakshya was perplexed. It was late for a lady to come to this side of the palace. *How did she even find it?* He did not know how to react. "What are you doing here, Princess? Are you lost, Princess?"

"Stop calling me Princess," she shouted at him.

Lakshya stood silent.

"Why are you avoiding me?" Aindrita asked.

"I am not avoiding you. I know my place in the real world. Servants cannot equal their masters."

"I don't believe this. You saved my life and I will be your friend till my last breath. It is engraved in stone."

Some guards walking by, stopped and tried to peep in on hearing a feminine voice.

Lakshya closed the door. "I think you should leave. It is not appropriate for you to be here at this hour."

"Tell me what's wrong? Are you not happy here? Don't they treat you well?"

"I am very happy. The Queen treats me as her own son, Viraat as a friend. Everything is perfect."

"Then what's wrong?"

"Nothing is wrong. Why are you assuming something is wrong?"

Something had been bothering Aindrita ever since she had returned from Nandi valley after meeting the Saptarishis. Her mind was in turbulence. She said, "Can I ask you something?"

Lakshya's heart beat faster. Reluctantly, he replied, "Yes."

"What did the Saptarishis say to you that day?" Her voice was soft, but her expression was tense.

"Why?" His eyes narrowed. "Why do you ask?"

"Just tell me. I want to know. Please," she insisted.

"Nothing significant. Difficult choices need to be made. Such cryptic words." He chose his words carefully.

"Ohh." She was disappointed.

"Why do you ask? What did they say to you?"

"Nothing." She walked towards the door.

She remembered why she had come. She pulled out the dagger Lakshya had given her during the challenge and returned it to him. "I think this should be with you."

He took it. The dagger was no longer in a leather case.

She added in a sweet voice, "It is said we Yavana-vanshis have a heart of gold. I got a gilded scabbard made for it. I hope you like it." She looked expectantly at Lakshya.

Heart of gold. It means you don't have a heart, his inner voice smirked. He did not say a word.

She started to leave, to head back to her room.

Was he okay? Was he settled? In a word, no! The pull by love into its orbit is too strong for anyone to resist. When it lets you go, it leaves you with all the pain. It makes you fall directionless. He was crashing. He could no longer control his temper. The unbearable torment had warped his mind. He blurted, "I know what the Saptarishis must have said to you." She turned. "That you will become a great Queen of Shivalik-Rajya."

Her face hardened. She wasn't impressed with the tone. She replied angrily, "Is that what you think?"

"Don't pretend that you don't know. Tomorrow they will announce your engagement with Prince Viraat. I know."

"Who told you this?"

"I am the King's bodyguard. I have ears." Lakshya was more rattled thinking that she could lie so smoothly. The pain in his voice was palpable.

Lakshya scowled as he held the door for her to leave and looked away.

Aindrita was flustered. She stormed out without looking at him. She needed some answers.

Niyati was standing outside at some distance. She had come to meet Lakshya. She saw Aindrita walk out of Lakshya's room. A strange emotion stopped her, and she stood there, frozen. She had a feeling that she was too late. A minute later, she left in silence.

✦

"Maa, is this true? Why did you not tell me?" Aindrita shot questions at her mother, as she paced into the room.

Devayani was surprised at her daughter's accusatory tone, something she had rarely heard directed at herself. Something was not right. She asked, "What are you talking about?"

"That tomorrow you are going to announce a union between me and Viraat?"

Devayani said, "We thought you liked each other."

"But you should have asked me before making such a big decision for my life."

"Marriages are not discussed with children in our kingdom. Parents decide what is best for the child and the kingdom. You know marriages play an important role in deciding the ties between kingdoms. You have known this since childhood." Devayani gave her a reproving look.

Aindrita's irritation swelled at her mother's judgemental tone.

"And your father said that he gave you a hint this morning and you did not object," Devayani chided.

"What hint?"

"He told you that Shivaliks were welcoming their new Queen."

"I don't remember pitashri saying any such thing."

"Do you not like Viraat?"

Aindrita's body stiffened with the question. "It's not like that."

At that moment, Yuyutsu returned to his chambers after the grand dinner. He heard the last two lines on his way in.

"What is going on?" he asked.

"Nothing important. We were just talking." Devayani tried to cover up the discussion with a chuckle.

Aindrita blurted, "Pitashri, how could you fix my marriage without even telling me?"

"I did it in your best interest." Yuyutsu was bewildered at the turn of events. He added, "Viraat is going to wield the Trishul. The Saptarishis had said that. You will become a great Queen; you are destined to."

Aindrita knew what the Saptarishis had told her. It was her destiny.

"If you are not happy, I will cancel the engagement announcement," he said.

"No, pitashri. That will not be necessary," Aindrita replied with a heavy heart and left the room abruptly.

Yuyutsu was relieved to hear it. It would have been a big embarrassment; his plans would have been ruined.

"I hope you were not serious when you said that you will cancel the engagement?" Devayani asked.

"I wasn't. It's too late for that. I wanted to know what was going through her mind."

"I never asked this but why did you fix Aindrita's marriage with Viraat? Are you prepared to let her stay away from you? And what about the future of our kingdom? We don't have a son," Devayani said.

"It is in our best interest."

"How?"

"I see Shivalik as a threat in the future. Till now Dhananjay, a crippled and incapable King, is ruling it as a nominal head. Vishamadeva is the real King and he is not an aggressor, so, there was nothing to fear. But once Viraat takes over, I know things will not be the same. Power intoxicates men. It ignites the urge to dominate and compels you to abandon self-restraint. Viraat won't be able to resist the temptation." He sipped a glass of wine and continued, "This marriage will safeguard our future. I will crown Sivasri as the Queen of Kailash. Himalia-Rajya has done it, so even we can do it. Thus, the Yavana-vanshis will have control over both the kingdoms and our future will be secure. Marriages have and will always be the bloodless way to conquer. If I can't become a Chakravarti King myself, I will be a kingmaker. Through my daughters, I will live my dream."

Devayani was taken aback by his words. All along, she had assumed his love for Aindrita was driving him, but instead it was the security of his kingdom and his desire to be a Chakravarti King. "I thought you had forgotten about your dream."

He gave a crooked smile. "Never. If I can't conquer by blood, I will conquer by mind. It's in my blood."

"What do you mean it's in your blood?"

"Not many know that our roots go back to Angaara. We originally belong to the Yavana tribe, who settled here ages ago."

A snake can shed its skin but it never forgets to bite.

✦

40

Prastāva (Offer)

ANGAARA

It was one of those days when the sun shines hot, yet the wind blows cold. Summer in sunlight, and winter in the shade.

Prachanda said to Vritra, "Supreme Lord, our armies are ready. Training is nearly finished. We have weapons in sufficient quantity."

"Hmm." Vritra responded with a wide smile. On the contrary, Kaitabha had a concerned looked on his face.

Vritra saw it. He asked, "Kaitabha, what are you thinking?"

"There is a problem."

"What problem?"

"We don't have enough ships to take our armies, horses and other animals to Bhuvar-Lok. We could only make a hundred ships in all this time and they are not strong enough to take us safely. We don't have the skills needed to make big ships."

"How many big ships and small boats do we have?"

"We have around two hundred big ships and around five hundred small boats. They are not at all sufficient to carry us across. Also, we won't be able to withstand attacks from the powerful navies of Bhuvar-Lok kingdoms, Salmala and Saka."

Shukracharya was listening to their conversation.

"Guruji, what should we do? How should we cross this ocean?" Vritra asked, concerned.

"Alliance."

Vritra's brows furrowed deeper. "With whom? The kingdoms of Bhuvar-Lok will never form an alliance with us."

Ever since Paulastya had attacked Bhuvar-Lok kingdoms and wreaked havoc, they had become permanent enemies of Angaara. Even years of peace was not enough to regain trust. They had not forgotten Paulastya.

"That was before you had Draak. She is the game-changer and will compel them to reconsider. Show them."

"That's why you asked me to tame Draak!" Vritra said.

Shukracharya said, "Kaitabha, Prachanda, give us a moment. I want to talk to Vritra alone."

"Yes, Guruji." Kaitabha and Prachanda did their salutations and left.

"Vritra, I had told you about one more important task to be done after you tame Draak," Shukracharya said.

"Yes, Guruji. I remember. What do I need to do?"

"It's something very important which only you can do. It's related to my former student and your elder brother."

"My brother Vishvarupa!" Vritra exclaimed, bewildered. After a moment, he asked, "What is it, Guruji?"

"The correct question is 'where is it?'"

BHUVAR - LOK

Kaitabha was sent as a messenger to the coastal kingdoms of Salmala and Saka. Put together, the two kingdoms had more than five thousand ships.

King Bali of Salmala and King Ugrasena of Saka were good friends. Bali ruled the north-east side and Ugrasena occupied the south-east of Bhuvar-Lok. Both were seated in the council room of Saka's fort. They had assembled there after the arrival of Vritra's messenger.

"Glory to kingdoms of Saka and Salmala," Kaitabha said loudly.

"Introduce yourself," Bali told the messenger in a strident tone.

"I am Kaitabha from the Buluwai tribe of Angaara. I am the messenger of Supreme Lord Vritra."

"Supreme Lord," Ugrasena smirked and continued, "to which tribe does this Vritra belong?"

"Vritra is the son of Tvashta from Shikavan tribe."

They had heard about Tvashta.

"What makes him Supreme Lord?" Bali asked.

"He is a student of Guru Shukracharya. He has successfully united more than a thousand tribes of Angaara. At this point of time, he commands an army of more than one hundred thousand Angaara men."

The number surprised both Bali and Ugrasena. One hundred thousand Angaara men meant nearly one hundred fifty thousand men of Bhuvar-Lok.

"You have come here to threaten us?" Ugrasena asked.

"No, on the contrary, Great Kings, Supreme Lord Vritra proposes an alliance."

Bali asked, "What kind of alliance?"

"He wants to become Trivikram – the conqueror of all three Loks on Dhruva-Lok."

Ugrasena leered as he said, "He cannot even come here and he dreams of becoming Trivikram. You think he can conquer Siddha-Lok. No one can climb the Sumeru mountain or stand against their army or navy."

Bali added, "They have the Trishul as well."

A confident Kaitabha replied, "You don't know what Vritra has!" They both raised their eyebrows.

"What does he have?" Ugrasena asked.

"Vritra wants to meet both of you and show it."

Ugrasena did not like cryptic replies. He said, "Why didn't he come directly then?"

"Supreme Lord intends to meet you very soon. That is why I have come to fix a place for the meeting. I am the commander-in-chief of his army. This shows how much importance he attributes to you, Great Kings."

"Why should we meet him? How do we know it's not a trap?" Bali questioned.

"He will come and meet you alone at a place of your choosing. All he desires is to meet you at the earliest."

Bali and Ugrasena looked at each other.

Bali replied, "Alright, we will meet him on the fourteenth day from now at Vishram Rock."

Vishram Rock was the place where Satyavrat had rested on returning to Bhuvar-Lok after defeating Paulastya. It was right after the ferocious Great War – a war to be remembered, which could have gone either way.

Ugrasena narrowed his eyes and added, "We hope he won't be wasting our time."

Delighted, Kaitabha said, "Hey Great Kings, he will make an offer, you can't refuse."

✦

Winter had come. It was a stormy day. Winds were blowing at full speed and clouds covered the sky, not allowing the sun to shine through and making it a very cold afternoon.

Both Bali and Ugrasena had been standing at Vishram Rock for an hour now. Twenty of their best soldiers protected them. They did not intend to walk into a trap.

They waited. But there were no signs of any ship, or boat, or any activity. "How is life with three wives at the same fort?" Ugrasena asked.

"It's messy. They keep fighting for some reason or the other."

"I told you to keep them in different forts. The way I have done it," Ugrasena chuckled.

"I tried. But they insisted on staying in the main fort. I should have never brought them there after marriage."

A thunder detonated in the sky. All of them lifted their chins skyward. It seemed the game of hide and seek between the sun and the clouds would get violent.

Bali looked through a sailor's spyglass. "No sight of him."

"He fooled us or the coward decided not to come," Ugrasena said as he moved his hand over his head.

"Let us leave. Don't want to get caught in a downpour," Bali decided.

They had no idea that a blizzard was on its way to hit them. They got back on their horses to ride out.

"King, look at the sky." Rishabh, Ugrasena's bodyguard, a man in his late twenties with a simple personality but sharp, confident almond eyes, told his master.

Ugrasena gazed at the sky. He saw nothing. "What? There is nothing."

Rishabh did not reply.

Ugrasena looked towards Rishabh, who was staring at the sky, frozen.

Both Bali and Rishabh's mouths remained wide open as they saw Draak flying in the sky. *That's impossible!* They squinted into the distance and realized Vritra was riding her. He looked like a demigod challenging the laws of nature.

Rishabh screamed, "Soldiers get ready to fight." The hands of the elite fighters shook as they reached for their spears.

Draak circled above them a few times and glided to the ground. Her colour changed from grey to her natural red-gold. This astonished everyone even more. All eyes were glued to the beauty, both out of fear and admiration. Steam came out of her nostrils. She roared like a lion and bared her dirty yellow teeth.

The soldiers fell back a few steps with trembling feet, instead of moving forward. They had their spears pointed towards Draak. But the conviction wasn't there. Their hands and legs were shaking, their eyes were filled with fear, blood drained from their faces at the sight of the dragon hissing at them. They had only heard of this monster bird, but it was the first time they were seeing it. They had no idea how to fight this fierce beast.

She had ruined Ugrasena and Bali's plans. The tables had turned. Vritra slid down from his perch.

There was a loud thunder in the sky. The wind picked up with a vengeance. Bali and Ugrasena came out of their spell. They swallowed hard as they got down from their horses.

"Thank you for coming, Great Kings. There is no need for your soldiers to raise arms. We are friends. Please ask them to lower their weapons," Vritra said authoritatively. He could see fear in their eyes. He knew he was in charge.

Scared, Ugrasena said in a shaky voice, "Stand down."

The soldiers were more than happy to relax. One of them wiped the thick layer of sweat on his forehead.

"What is it you want?" Bali asked. His voice shook.

"We can help each other. I have what you want and you have what I need."

"We know what you want. But what do you have to offer us?"

"After I become Trivikram – the undisputed Lord of Dhruva-Lok, you will become absolute Kings of Bhuvar-Lok. You will have complete control over the sea trade and full profit from the business." Vritra twisted the ends of his newly grown heavy moustache.

Money always appealed more to both Bali and Ugrasena. Vritra had their attention now. He rightly brought it up at the insistence of Shukracharya.

"Can we discuss it among ourselves?" Bali said to Vritra.

"You can discuss among yourselves as much as you want. But I want to know your decision before I leave."

Ugrasena and Bali went away and started deliberating their options.

Bali said, "With this dragon and an army of a hundred thousand Angaara soldiers, there is no way he can lose. If we join him, it will be the biggest army ever."

"He hasn't given us a choice. If we say no, he is going to burn us alive here."

"That's true. He has played us."

"Let's use it to our advantage then."

"By agreeing to his terms, we will become undisputed Kings of Bhuvar-Lok. Defeating Srivijay should not be that difficult. Let us put a condition that our army will not go to Siddha-Lok. Whether he wins or not, it won't matter to us."

"Yes, we will rule at Bhuvar-Lok either way."

"We shall enter into a peace treaty with whoever wins."

They returned to the spot where Vritra was standing with Draak. "What have you decided, Great Kings?" he asked, his voice dangerously kind.

Bali took the lead and said, "We accept your offer. We have only one condition."

Vritra wrinkled his brows. "What condition?"

"Our armies will not go to Siddha-Lok to fight beside you."

Vritra considered it for a few seconds. He still wasn't convinced of going to Siddha-Lok himself. But he had not voiced his misgivings to his Guru. He had plenty of time to decide. "Alright, but I will need your sailors and ships."

"Our ships and sailors are at your disposal as long as you need them," Bali said.

"We have a deal then. It will be an alliance that will rule Dhruva-Lok for centuries to come."

"Yes, Supreme Lord," Bali and Ugrasena said together.

Vritra grinned noting that Bali and Ugrasena already referred to him as 'Supreme Lord'. Draak was indeed a game-changer.

✦

41

Mṛtyu (Death)

Everyone had assembled at the Grand Shiva Temple, waiting for the rituals to begin.

"We will start with *rudra-abhishek* of Lord Shiva," Rajguru Kashyap announced.

"What is it?" Viraat asked.

"Rudra-abhishek is the holy bath that is dearest to Lord Shiva. It is said to please Lord Shiva and is the most powerful way to worship and seek his blessings."

"Why is Lord Shiva called Rudra?"

"Lord Shiva is very benevolent. He allowed the request of Lord Brahma and Vishnu and created eleven immortal beings: Kapaali, Pingala, Bhima, Virupaksha, Vilohitaa, Ajesha, Shavasana, Shasta, Shambu, Chanda and Dhruva. As he created Eleven Rudras, he is addressed by this name."

"What will be done?"

"Powerful hymns and mantras are chanted and various aromatic liquids and sacred items such as milk, honey, sandal paste, *belpatra* are offered during this pooja."

The pooja commenced. The first half of the day was over along with the rudra-abhishek. The sacred fragrance of sandalwood powder, honey, camphor, *ghee* and turmeric pervaded the surroundings as the gurus chanted sacred mantras and poured the mixture into the fire.

After that, Viraat was formally accorded the title of Dhruvanshi.

It was followed by lunch. The food was cooked in the temple and was served on banana leaves to the guests inside the temple premises. Food was distributed to the poor outside in vast numbers.

All the high-ranking officials of Shivalik-Rajya, many Kings from the different provinces and all esteemed guests sat in rows. Yuyutsu, Devayani and Aindrita also sat opposite Dhananjay.

Lakshya stood behind Dhananjay. Aindrita and Lakshya looked at each other.

The difference in their status was evident. "Come, sit here," Padmini said to Lakshya.

"No, Maharani, I will eat later." He referred to Padmini as the Maharani in front of everyone. He only called her Matashri when no one else was around.

"I said sit here," Padmini ordered like a mother.

"Yes, have food with us. We shall always be indebted to you for what you did," Yuyutsu said.

"Please come, Lakshya," Viraat said.

Viraat had treated Lakshya like a true friend. Always referred to him by his name or as a friend.

Hesitantly, Lakshya joined them.

Aindrita was pleased with Viraat's gesture. She smiled graciously at him. Her whole face blossomed, like a newborn flower.

◆

The beautiful city, decorated for the celebrations, gleamed in the twilight hour. The sky was lit up in hues of pink and orange. An air of festivity blanketed the entire city. Everyone was happy at the prospect of the marriage announcement of the Prince. The news had spread due to the arrangements.

Aindrita was getting dressed for the evening function. She had to look perfect, so she had picked a traditional blue silk saree. Gold and diamond studded jewellery graced her neck, ears, and hands. A matching *bindi* embellished her oval face.

She was lost in her thoughts. Her pace of dressing up had come to a near halt. Suddenly, the harsh crackles of the hornbills in the balcony became louder. She looked outside, irritated. The clamour was unpleasant, as the shrieks got unbearably louder. Were the birds trying to say something to her?

Devayani came and placed a golden, crystal tiara on her head.

"You look no less than an angel. You shall be the most beautiful Queen ever."

"Let us go maa and get this over with," she said, "and what is wrong with those birds?"

Mitasha, Padmini's maid, ran into the chambers and said, "Pranam Queen, Pranam Princess, there is a message from Maharaja Dhananjay."

"What is the message?" Devayani asked.

"This evening's event is cancelled."

"Why?" Aindrita got up and asked in total shock.

"There has been an unexpected death," Mitasha replied.

"Oh, God! Who has died?" Devayani asked.

"Lok-Rakshak Simham has died," Mitasha spoke in a rush.

"Ohh." Devayani's mouth remained half-open.

The maid left the room after salutations.

Aindrita removed the tiara from her head. She started removing the jewellery. It was difficult to say how she felt – relieved or sad.

Yuyutsu came into the room from the balcony and saw Aindrita taking off her jewellery. It rattled him. He asked, "What happened?"

"Lok-Rakshak Simham has died. The function has been cancelled," Devayani replied.

"This is highly shocking. He seemed to be fine in the morning. I should go and meet the Maharaja."

✦

In the emergency meeting room, there was an eerie silence. Vishamadeva, Dhananjay and Viraat were in the room deliberating the news of sudden death.

Lakshya stood outside.

Stroking his beard, Vishamadeva said, "This is unexpected. I smell something foul."

Dhananjay replied, "Vaidya Sanjeevani said that he died of a sudden heart failure. There is no foul play."

"We should think about what to do next," Dhananjay said.

"There is nothing to think about. The post of the Lok-Rakshak cannot be left vacant for long. We will have to organize the competition at Devaprayaga within fifteen days," Vishamadeva replied without any hesitation.

The words brought a thin smile to Viraat's face. He was looking forward to the day.

Outside, Yuyutsu reached the meeting room and asked Lakshya, "Is the Maharaja inside?"

"Yes, an emergency meeting is going on."

"Please tell the Maharaja that I would like to meet him."

"Yes, Kailash-Naresh."

Lakshya went inside. He came back after ten seconds. "Please go inside, Kailash-Naresh."

Lakshya opened the door for him. Yuyutsu scampered inside. Dhananjay got up. "Welcome, Kailash-Naresh."

"Maharaja, is this sad news true?" Yuyutsu asked.

"Unfortunately, yes."

"That's shocking indeed. Life is so unpredictable."

"Yes. We will have to postpone the engagement announcement by a few days. I hope you understand."

"Yes. Yes, Maharaja. I understand. But a few days?" He did not understand.

"We will be organizing the competition for the selection of the Lok-Rakshak at Devaprayaga within fifteen days. We will announce the engagement after Viraat wins the competition."

"That will be a perfect day for such an auspicious announcement." Yuyutsu's happiness returned.

Viraat was pleased with the turn of events. Bad news is not always bad for everyone.

✦

42

Sahāyatā (Help)

BHUVAR - LOK

"Is it really happening?" Srivijay asked.

Raksha Mantri Bhalla replied, "Yes, Samrat. The movement of ships has started." His answer came with a raspy cough.

The atmosphere in the room was tense. Queen Kaushiki and young Prince Aakash were also present for this emergency meeting. The Queen had started taking interest in matters related to the kingdom ever since the news of a possible war had come up. The main reason was concern for her children and their safety. It was a mother in the meeting, not a Queen.

"What are our options?" Srivijay asked.

"We can attack Saka and Salmala kingdoms before the armies of Vritra land on Bhuvar-Lok," Bhalla answered.

"Are our armies prepared to attack?"

"The movement of the army will take ten days. We expect stiff resistance as the terrain doesn't suit us. They just need to wait till the armies of Vritra arrive."

"Can we burn their ships?"

"That is difficult now, Samrat. My spies tell me that they are being guarded day and night. Also, they have nearly five thousand ships scattered across the coast. It will be difficult to achieve this."

"What do you propose?"

"Samrat, with due respect, I had proposed to kill him years ago but you refused. Now, the snake is here to bite us. We took care of his elder brother Vishvarupa and we had many years of peace. I wish we had done the same to him as well." Bhalla was agitated, his tone almost accusatory.

Kaushiki's ears perked on hearing this. Her eyes fluttered. Srivijay had never mentioned anything about Vishvarupa.

Srivijay's face became guarded. "What is done, cannot be undone. We should think about what to do now." Srivijay absorbed the outburst without mentioning any specifics.

"I hear he has a dragon as well," Bhalla revealed.

There was a long silence. Srivijay pressed a hand to his brow at the troubling word. "A dragon! It's ridiculous. That's a rumour; they are spreading lies to scare us," Srivijay said.

"It's not a lie, Samrat. Many claim to have seen it."

"And the dragon is in his control?" Kaushiki interrupted. She sounded alarmed.

"Yes, he has control over it. We don't know how he did that. They call him Supreme Lord and he is on a mission to become Trivikram," Bhalla answered.

Srivijay heaved a deep sigh. It was overwhelming to hear that the odds were so much against them. "So, what should we do?"

"Let's send a message to other kingdoms at Bhuvar-Lok and start preparing for war. Our best chances are when we are defending the fort."

"We have never lost a battle here," Srivijay said enthusiastically.

"Yes, Samrat. We have never lost here, and we shall not lose ever. We have the blessings of Indra-deva." Bhalla wasn't as confident as he sounded.

"Send messengers to the other four kingdoms. We need to fight together and with Indra-deva's blessings, we shall succeed."

Before everyone could leave, Kaushiki suggested, "We should call for help from Siddha-Lok."

Srivijay's eyes widened, and Bhalla gave a small exclamation of dismay.

Bhalla instinctively responded, "Why will they come here to help us?" He folded his arms disapprovingly.

Srivijay sat down. He agreed with Bhalla and nodded. "They didn't even come to help King Satyavrat. They are safe across the mountain. Sumeru mountain protects them. Why will they help in our matters?"

"But we should try. There is no harm in trying. We should seek whatever help we can get. Also, they have the Trishul. Maybe this is the defining moment for which it is there. If they come with it, the morale of our army will be unmatched," Kaushiki argued.

Srivijay thought about it for a while. "You are right. You never know. They have a strong navy and excellent fighters. Siddha-Lok will be Vritra's next target. It is in their interest to ally with us."

Bhalla rubbed his jaw and said, "I'm not hopeful that they will come. I don't want to rely on false hope."

Srivijay reasoned with him, "I agree with you. But there is no harm in trying. We need to send a messenger."

"If we are sending a messenger, it is better to send Prince Akash to convey the importance we attribute to their support," Bhalla suggested.

Kaushiki, as a protective mother, interjected, "We can't send Akash so far away to an unknown land. It is not safe anymore."

Srivijay gave it some thought. "Akash is too young for this. Sea-route is no longer an option. We will have to go through the mountains. I have someone else in mind."

Bhalla asked, "Who?"

"Let us send Surya. His son, Lakshya, is Maharaja Dhananjay's Anga-Rakshak. Personal relations can do wonders at times," Srivijay proposed.

Bhalla thought for a few seconds. "It's a good choice. He can cross the Sumeru mountain. Lakshya can help convince Maharaja Dhananjay. Maybe for this reason, he is there. Hopefully this time he will succeed."

Srivijay did not understand the last line but he ignored it. "Exactly. It can't be a coincidence. God works in mysterious ways."

✦

Surya bowed his head and said, "Glory to Jambu-Rajya and Samrat."

Srivijay acknowledged the greeting and replied, "Take your seat, Surya."

Bhalla was also in the room. He had side-lined Surya after his failure in the last mission. Surya was surprised at the unexpected meeting with Srivijay, especially the timing. Would it be another assassination attempt?

"You know that war is upon us," Srivijay said.

"Yes, Samrat. We shall fight till the last breath."

"That we will. But, there is something more you can do."

"I will do anything, Samrat."

"I need you to go to Shivalik-Rajya at Siddha-Lok and convey a message to Maharaja Dhananjay."

Surya waited.

Bhalla took over and said, "We are outnumbered in this war. We have around twenty-five thousand soldiers. They have an army of more than one hundred thousand men. We need their help."

Surya nodded.

Srivijay explained, "There is a special reason I am sending you. Lakshya is Maharaja Dhananjay's Anga-Rakshak. He can get you a personal meeting with the Maharaja. Let's hope they return our call for help."

The thought of meeting his son made Surya smile, but he bit on the insides of his cheek and nodded again.

"Sea-route is no longer available. You will have to go through the mountains," Bhalla said.

"Yes, Bhalla-deva, the route through mountains will be shorter. I will reach in less than three days."

"Time is of the essence. They will also need time to mobilise their army. Travel as fast as you can," Bhalla added.

Surya rose to take leave.

"We look to hearing good news from you. All our hopes are on you to perform this miracle," Srivijay concluded.

"I will do my best, Samrat."

✦

Srivijay returned to his chamber in the night. War was upon them. Everything was at stake. If he won, he would become a legend, more than what his ancestors had achieved. He would become the first among the Vardhan-vanshis. The prospect made him feel alive and energised.

He removed his jewelled turban and lay on the bed; his footwear dangling in the air.

Kaushiki was awake because something else was distracting her. It had been bothering her since the meeting that morning. Knowing the truth wasn't going to help in any way but she needed to know. She licked her dry lips. Fragmented words tumbled from her mouth, "Can I ask you something, dear?"

Srivijay sat up leisurely. "Of course, what is it?"

"I heard in the meeting today… Is it true that we had something to do with Vishvarupa's death?"

Srivijay hoped she wouldn't bring it up. He frowned. "I won't hide it from you anymore. I hoped it would never come up. Since, it has, I will tell you everything."

She reached for his hand.

Her touch gave him strength. "You know I was made the King at the age of fifteen. An age when I was not ready. A few months after I was crowned, a messenger arrived."

"Messenger? From where?"

"From Angaara sent by Vishvarupa. The messenger said that Vishvarupa extended his friendship to Bhuvar-Lok kingdoms. Since we were the largest kingdom, he reached out to me first. He was uniting the tribes and they were falling in line. He wanted to develop and educate Angaara tribes. He wanted to trade with us and people-to-people contact to grow. He sent us a big box as a goodwill gesture."

"That sounds like an honest attempt."

"But Bhalla argued that people of Angaara could not be trusted. His spies informed him that Vishvarupa was very intelligent and potentially dangerous. He knew very rare vidyas and had created many powerful and magical weapons. He was trained by the great Shukracharya himself. Bhalla said it could be a big conspiracy or a master plan to conquer Bhuvar-Lok. He advised me to use this as an opportunity and order his assassination. Nip it in the bud."

Kaushiki's palm covered her mouth in shock. "Oh, God. And you listened to Bhalla?"

"I did not agree. But that night, I had a dream…it was more of a vision. Indra-deva appeared and told me to assassinate Vishvarupa. He said Vishvarupa was working for the welfare of asura and that he would soon lead an army to conquer Bhuvar-Lok. His friendship was a trap. Nothing but a ploy to fool us."

Srivijay closed his eyes and relived his dream. "I don't know. It felt real, very real. Trusting my vision as divine intervention, I ordered the killing of Vishvarupa. I knew deep down it wasn't an honourable thing to do. So, later when Bhalla brought the same proposal for Vritra, I ordered him not to commit this crime."

Kaushiki disagreed. *If you had killed Vishvarupa, you should have gone all the way and killed his brother Vritra as well. Always eliminate the danger completely.* "You say he was so intelligent and powerful. How did you assassinate such a man?"

"Two of our best assassins went disguised as my goodwill messengers. He thought we had accepted his friendship. He let his guard down. In the night when the opportunity arose, they killed him in his sleep."

Srivijay cupped his eyes with his palms.

She could see that Srivijay regretted it. It was a grave sin to betray someone in the guise of friendship and that too as a guest. He was very young then and was susceptible to Bhalla's manipulation.

"What's done is done. It was probably the right thing to do at that time," Kaushiki consoled him with a white lie and changed the topic. "What was in the box he had sent as a goodwill gesture?"

"We never opened it. We feared it was something dangerous – poisonous gas, some vicious chemical, or maybe a magic potion. So, I had it locked up in the dungeons, never to be opened."

There was something queer about the box. What could be inside it? She wasn't convinced it would be something dangerous. Kaushiki's curious mind wanted to go down to the dungeon and open the box right away. But this was not the time. Her husband would not agree.

Maybe later.

✦

43

Sabhā (Meeting)

SIDDHA - LOK

The sun was high in the cloudless sky, and the winds were wild and freezing. The uncertainty in the air carried signs of change. The winds were shifting.

Lakshya was on guard outside the Maharaja's chambers.

A gatekeeper came and said, "A messenger has come from Jambu-Rajya of Bhuvar-Lok."

At the mention of Jambu-Rajya, Lakshya tried to contain his excitement. "Who has come? What is the name of the messenger?"

The gatekeeper tried to recollect the name. "An army officer...someone by the name of Surya. He says he has a message from Samrat Srivijay for the Maharaja."

Lakshya almost cried with unexpected happiness. *What Madhav said, has come true!* "He is my father. Where is he?"

"He is in the visitor's waiting room."

Lakshya entered the Maharaja's chambers on winged feet and said, "Pranam, Maharaja. Pranam, Maharani."

Padmini responded, "Lakshya, how many times have I told you to address me as Matashri when you are in this room? I like it when you say that!"

"Pranam, Matashri," Lakshya said.

"What is it, Lakshya? You look very happy," Dhananjay asked.

"Maharaja, a message has arrived from Samrat Srivijay of Jambu-Rajya. The messenger is my father."

Dhananjay got up immediately. "It will be a privilege to meet him. Let's go right away."

"Wait. Put on your crown, Maharaja. Don't be in such haste." Padmini gave the crown to Dhananjay.

Lakshya was unable to control his nerves at the prospect of meeting his father. *Indeed, what Madhav had said, has come true!* he thought.

✦

Surya was not sure if he would get an audience with the Maharaja and had settled in for a long wait in the waiting room. However, wonders were never to cease. Very soon, Surya was summoned to the council room. He had not expected to see his son wielding such influence over the King.

Surya was led to the council meeting room and seated. It was an airy chamber, sparsely decorated.

After a while, Vishamadeva and Viraat entered the room and sat down. Vishamadeva guessed the purpose behind the visit. He was quiet, deep in thought, deliberating strategy.

Their reverie was broken by the dwarapala, who announced the Maharaja's arrival.

All rose from their seats when Dhananjay entered. Surya saw his son. He felt extremely proud seeing Lakshya in his formal outfit. He looked like an elite fighter, which he was. Lakshya wanted to rush towards his father and touch his feet. But he controlled his instincts. He blinked long and slow and bowed his head.

Vishamadeva was ruminating on various strategies. The meeting was going to be a fateful one.

Surya folded his hands and said, "Pranam, Maharaja."

"Welcome to Siddha-Lok, Surya," Dhananjay replied.

Surya was pleased with the way Dhananjay referred to him by his name. "Please be seated."

"After you, Maharaja."

Lakshya left the room to stand guard outside.

"So…what message do you bring?" Dhananjay asked as he scratched his stubble.

Surya stood and unrolled a scroll. "Maharaja, this is a personal message from Samrat Srivijay."

"Glory to Shivalik-Rajya.

O Great Dhruvanshi, King of Kings, Maharaja Dhananjay.

We are the two greatest kingdoms on Siddha-Lok and Bhuvar-Lok. Our vansha is the reason for the long-lasting peace on our Lok.

But today, we are threatened by a common enemy. The tribes of Angaara, led by a tribal Lord Vritra, are uniting once again to endanger our freedom. He aspires to become Trivikram.

Long time ago, Paulastya tried to do the same. But he was stopped by an alliance of King Satyavrat from Siddha-Lok and Mahabali Bajrang of Bhuvar-Lok. It was an alliance of hearts and minds. Together they defeated him and restored peace.

Enemy is at our gates. Our brothers from Saka and Salmala kingdoms have betrayed us and joined the enemy. We are heavily outnumbered. We seek your help in this hour of need. Together we can defeat them.

It will not be forgotten, ever!

Samrat Srivijay."

Surya bowed and handed over the scroll to Dhananjay.

Dhananjay read it and handed it over to Vishamadeva. Vishamadeva did not read it. He asked, "How big is the army of this Vritra?"

Surya replied, "They say he has about one hundred thousand Angaara soldiers. It is also rumoured that he has a dragon."

Dhananjay eyebrows narrowed. He winced and rubbed his temples. "What do you mean he has a dragon?" He felt a shiver, his nostrils flared slightly as he contemplated his options.

Viraat's ears pricked.

"Rumours say that he has tamed a dragon," Surya explained. Dhananjay's legs trembled. He placed his hands on his thighs and pressed down.

Unperturbed, Vishamadeva asked, "How big is your army?"

Surya answered, "We have around twenty-five thousand men."

Vishamadeva looked at Dhananjay. "Maharaja, we should discuss this privately."

Dhananjay leaned forward and replied, "There is nothing to discuss."

No one understood what he meant. They waited for him to elaborate. Dhananjay gave a sardonic smile. "It is not our problem."

Both Vishamadeva and Surya were surprised to hear this from the Maharaja. Viraat settled his features to show no expression. It was best not to get involved in security affairs, especially with the elders talking.

"But Maha..." Before Vishamadeva could complete his sentence, Dhananjay raised his hand and stopped him.

"We have this problem because their kingdoms of Saka and Salmala have joined the enemy. They are providing Vritra with ships, using which he is coming here."

"That is why we are asking for help, Maharaja," Surya replied. This wasn't going the way he anticipated.

"I will not risk my soldiers in your internal war." His voice was brisk with irritation.

"But Maharaja, if Vritra succeeds in defeating Jambu-Rajya, his next target will be Siddha-Lok. It is in our mutual interest to fend him off together and eliminate the threat."

"We will fight him when he comes here. I have a responsibility towards my kingdom and its praja. I will not unnecessarily risk the lives of my soldiers."

Surya realized there was no convincing Dhananjay. His mind was already made up.

Vishamadeva gazed at Viraat, signalling him to convince Dhananjay to at least discuss the issue. Knowing the King's ways, he understood that the words of the Prince would carry more weight.

In a soft tone, Viraat said, "Father, please let..."

Dhananjay rebuked him, "Quiet, Viraat. You are too young for this. I know what I am doing." The thought of a fire-spewing dragon and love for his son had got the better of the King's judgement. He was crippled. Vishamadeva was old and Simham was no longer there. The responsibility to lead the battle would fall upon the young Prince. He did not want his young son to go and fight a dragon when he was yet to wield the Trishul. Faced with a dragon, would even the Trishul be enough? These fearful thoughts had pushed him down this road.

Viraat obeyed and did not try to persuade his father.

Without Simham, Vishamadeva needed someone to support him. That's why he had brought Viraat. It did not work. He made a last-ditch effort. "It is not in our tradition to refuse help to anyone who comes to our door."

Dhananjay was prepared for this. He countered, "The only help I am willing to offer is to provide them refuge here at Siddha-Lok. They can leave their homes and come here. We will fight him together from my kingdom. We have better chances of succeeding."

"How can we abandon our motherland, Maharaja? She will not forgive us." Surya beseeched with folded hands.

"I want to help but I cannot leave Shivalik unprotected and send my army to fight alongside you. What if he attacks here first?"

This clinched the argument. It was hard to argue after that.

"I am very proud of you," Surya said gleefully.

"It is all due to your blessings, pitashri. How is maa?" Lakshya asked his father. They were in Lakshya's room.

"Your maa misses you a lot."

"Why didn't you bring her?"

"Lakshya, you know, I came for official work."

"Ohh, yes."

"Next time I will bring her. Tell me about your life? Are they treating you well?"

"Yes, pitashri. They all treat me very well."

Surya was delighted to hear it. "When will you come home?"

"After Prince Viraat's marriage."

"Hmm. When is the marriage?"

"It will happen soon, I think," Lakshya answered. His face lost its cheer at the thought.

"I heard that the selection of the Lok-Rakshak is this week."

"Yes, after three days. Tomorrow we will leave for Devaprayaga. Why don't you stay back and watch it?"

"No, I have to give Maharaja Dhananjay's message to the Samrat. The sooner, the better. Particularly since the return message is not as expected. They will be waiting."

"Why exactly did you come here? What was the official work?"

"I can't tell anyone."

"So secretive that you can't tell me?"

"It's politics."

"Why would Samrat Srivijay send you for political matters?" Lakshya was not convinced.

Surya realized his son was no longer a child who could be distracted with a play of words. He tried to give a more satisfying answer. "I mean...its politics about purchase of weapons. I can't give more details. Be assured, it's nothing serious," Surya avoided telling the truth to Lakshya. If Lakshya got a whiff that Jambu-Rajya was under attack, he would certainly leave everything to fight beside them. In his heart, Surya knew that defeat was imminent unless some miracle happened. He didn't want his son to die for nothing. He might be useful when war knocks on the doors of Siddha-Lok. Battles may be lost but the war should be won.

"Okay." Lakshya let it go.

"I should get going," Surya said.

"Stay for one day at least with me."

"No, son. I need to reach as soon as possible. It's urgent."

Surya got up and gripped his son in a fierce hug. Then he said, "Always remember that you have our love and blessings...And, everything that happens is happening for a reason. You are meant for some far greater purpose...Never forget that!"

Lakshya was perplexed by the choice of his father's words. He did not know how to respond. "Yes, pitashri. Tell maa I will come very soon." Then, he touched his father's feet.

Surya closed his eyes in agony. He wondered if he should tell Lakshya the truth. His son should know. But eventually he decided not to. He opened his eyes and gave all the blessings he could gather.

This could be the last time he was seeing his son.

✦

44

Preraṇā (Inspire)

Prachanda was at the peak of a steep cliff near the coast, looking at the numerous ships. He was on a horse.

"How many have come?" he asked.

The man in-charge of loading the ships, answered, "Two thousand. The loading of food and weapons is almost done. As soon as we finish and they set sail, the next two thousand will take their place."

"When can the first lot leave?"

"Tomorrow morning."

Prachanda was happy with the progress. He pulled on the halter and rode back.

◆

"My Lord, everything is going as per plan. The first fleet will be ready to leave tomorrow morning. And the day after, the next fleet will leave." Prachanda briefed the commander-in-chief, Kaitabha. "My Lord, why don't we attack Siddha-Lok directly? A surprise attack will catch them unprepared."

"Why don't you leave the strategy with Supreme Lord and Guruji?"

"I just thought…"

Kaitabha interrupted him, "Our soldiers are not used to sea travel. It will take longer to reach Siddha-Lok. Have you heard of sea-sickness?"

"No, my Lord."

"Siddha-Lok has a strong navy as well. You do what you are good at."

"I beg forgiveness, my Lord."

"Get the soldiers lined up tomorrow morning."

"Yes, my Lord."

Kaitabha walked to the Temple of Asura where Vritra stayed with Shukracharya. Draak stayed in the rear of the temple. No one except Kaitabha dared to go near her.

He climbed the stairs, lost in thought.

"Supreme Lord, we are ready to leave tomorrow morning."

Vritra saw some concern in Kaitabha's face. He asked, "What bothers you, dear friend?"

Kaitabha answered, "The soldiers have never left this island. There is some hesitation to leave their homeland. Also, they are tired from long preparations for the travel ahead."

"But they don't have a choice. Either they go or they die."

Shukracharya intervened, "Vritra, for every problem, the answer is not death or fear. They are on your side. What they need is motivation, some inspiration! Everyone needs it from time to time."

"Inspiration...hmm."

"Don't ever forget that."

Vritra asked Kaitabha, "Is my weapon ready, the way I had instructed?"

"Yes, Supreme Lord."

Vritra turned his face toward Shukracharya and said, "Guruji, please come with us and see how we avenge the injustice done to us."

"No, Vritra. I have shown you the way. Now it is up to you. Fulfil your destiny."

"Please, Guruji. I need you."

"Don't worry, Vritra. I will come, if the need ever arises." Shukracharya smiled.

✦

The sun had woken and the land below that its rays kissed, was teaming with activity.

Kaitabha and Prachanda stood on the hilltop looking over the huge army. Thousands of fire torches glowed.

The normally calm Tethys sea was turbulent today. Strong winds were spiralling inward and the waves smashed against the rocks in anticipation.

When dawn broke, all eyes were glued to the distance. A tornado had formed far away in the ocean. Draak was in the sky, encircling the tornado with Vritra on her back.

The soldiers stared in amazement. Many had not seen Draak before this.

Even the waves slowed their onslaught.

Kaitabha cheered with his sword raised, "Vritra! Vritra!"

The army followed. The din was louder than the thunder of the Agniparvat.

Draak closed in, circled above the army and landed on the cliff. Vritra stepped down. A black-brown interlaced special armour, like the scales of a snake shielded his entire body. The armour had a golden dragon engraved on it in the front. The terrifying dragon was screaming and flouting her wings. Vritra's long hair was tied in a knot at the back for the first time. He looked like a scary yet elegant serpent.

In his hand, he held a seven-foot black Trishul made specially for him. He wanted to be seen as the One True Supreme Lord in the eyes of his men. He screamed,

"My brothers, our time has come. They say we are uncivilized, not capable of fighting together. They have merely used us for our vast resources and not allowed us to grow. Repeatedly backstabbed us. We are going to achieve what no one had thought was possible. It is time to show them the wrath of Angaara, a place and people long suppressed by them.

The final injustice was killing my brother in the most dishonourable manner. He wanted peace and they betrayed him. We will make them pay for their crimes.

Soon we will take our rightful place on the Lok.

Angaara is ready to rain fire."

He paused to catch a breath.

"We are born for a purpose. I have found mine. Are you with me?"

The soldiers screamed as loud as they could with their weapons raised high, "Yes."

Vritra stuck the black Trishul in the ground. He put on his Agni-Maru gloves and lit fire on them. He gazed at Draak and said, "Ahi, at my signal." Vritra had given her the name 'Ahi'. Ahi nodded, acknowledging the instruction from her master. Vritra opened his arms towards heaven. From behind Vritra, Ahi reared her head and spewed fire towards the sky with her wings open. It created the illusion of a Trishul made of fire. A breath-taking, heart-stopping spectacle!

Vritra looked heavenward and shouted, "Angaara is our motherland. Agnipath we shall tread…Agnipath…Agnipath… Agnipath."

Everyone joined in the chants of 'Agnipath'. It became their war cry.

The soldiers were charged up.

Vritra looked at Kaitabha and asked, "Will this keep them inspired?" Amidst unending screams, he replied, "For a long time, Supreme Lord." The tornado was ready to hit Bhuvar-Lok.

The Second Great War had begun.

✦

45

Varaṇa (Selection)

SIDDHA - LOK

The fateful day had come. The weather had remained unusually chilly and the winds were signalling an upcoming storm. Dense clouds covered the orange horizon. Even the land was wild that day. Mild tremors shook the trees, sending ripples down the water bodies and agitating the birds. Something was amiss.

Vishamadeva returned to his room in the waiting area to take some rest after overseeing the arrangements at the arena. He felt worn out. In the absence of Simham, the security and safety of everyone at the arena fell on his head.

Gayatri, who was already in the room, caressed his forehead. It worked like magic in taking away his stress. "Don't stop," he said.

There was a knock on the door. "Come in," Gayatri said.

Vishamadeva's chair was facing away from the door. He did not bother to turn around.

The door opened and a man whose age was a brush over forty entered.

He was wrapped in saffron garments like a monk and had dishevelled hair with a long untrimmed beard. He swayed in fatigue and his body exuded a foul smell.

The man bent down and touched Gayatri's feet. "Pranam, Jyeshta Matashri."

"Ayushman bhava." Gayatri did not recognize the strange looking man.

The man's voice brought a smile to Vishamadeva's face. He stood, turned around and said, "Welcome, son. You have returned."

The man touched Vishamadeva's feet.

"Yashasvi bhava," Vishamadeva blessed. He raised the man to his feet and hugged him. The man felt he was at home.

"Gayatri, don't you recognize Hetan?"

Gayatri exclaimed, "Hetan, you look so different! You have lost a lot of weight. When did you last eat?"

Hetan gave a faint smile.

"You have returned on a perfect day," Gayatri said.

Vishamadeva added, "Yes, a perfect occasion for you to come back."

"I was on my way to the palace when I heard about the untimely death of Lok-Rakshak Simham and that the selection of the Lok-Rakshak was going to happen today. I also heard that Prince Viraat will be participating. Such a day should not be missed," Hetan explained.

"You have returned after many years. I hope you found what you were searching for?" Vishamadeva asked.

"Yes, Lok-Sevak. I stayed with the Saptarishis for seven years. I learned a lot from them. I am grateful to you for showing me the way and also, allowing me to go," Hetan thanked Vishamadeva.

"Anyone who treads on Dhruva-pada finds his own way. I did nothing. In fact, I thought you might never come back."

"The Saptarishis asked me to go back to Shivalik."

"Why?" Vishamadeva frowned.

"I don't know. They told me and I obeyed."

The wrinkles on Vishamadeva's forehead deepened as he contemplated. *The timing is odd.*

"I haven't seen Prince Viraat for many years. I missed seeing him when he had come to meet the Saptarishis after the ultimate challenge. People said that he had moved the Trishul," Hetan said.

"Yes, that happened five years ago. He could move it slightly, but it was truly amazing. We hope he lifts it today," Gayatri responded.

"If he wields the Trishul, he is going to be crowned the Wielder — the Protector of entire Siddha-Lok. That must be the reason for a lot of excitement among the gathered crowd. People have turned up in huge numbers. It is going to be a memorable day. I can feel it," Hetan replied.

"There is one more reason. Prince Viraat will be engaged to Princess

Aindrita from Kailash-Rajya after his selection. This announcement will also be made," Gayatri told him.

"That's why there is electricity in the air too!" Hetan smiled.

Vishamadeva was still lost in his thoughts. The prophecy of the Saptarishis from his last visit was playing in his mind. Gayatri touched his forearm and said, "It is time. We should go, dear."

Vishamadeva dragged his thoughts back to the room. "Yes, right! It is time. Hetan, join us in the arena."

Hetan nodded.

✦

In the recent days, Viraat's slumbers were fraught with disturbing dreams. Last night, the Dragon Lord had come face-to-face with him. The army of the Dragon Lord had attacked Siddha-Lok in full force. Fireballs rained from the sky. His men butchered the combined armies of Siddha-Lok kingdoms. The cries of wounded men filled the battleground. The dragon spewed fire and burned down everything in its path – men, trees, horses, everything. It was mayhem. All hope was on Viraat's shoulders. This was his moment. He tried to wield the Trishul. But even when everything was at stake, he failed to lift it. It had let him down. Was he not worthy of it? He broke into a cold sweat recalling his failure. The pressure of uncertainty engulfed him. The day for which he had waited all his life, was upon him but he did not feel ready. *What is going to happen today?* Even the comforting words of the Saptarishis were not to enough to calm his mind.

Madhav entered. After the exchange of greetings, he asked, "How are you feeling, son?"

Viraat's eyes spoke volumes.

"Why so nervous?" Madhav asked.

"I don't know what will happen."

"You wanted this day, didn't you?"

"Yes, deva, but why do I feel I am not ready?"

"In life, many times our struggle is with ourselves, and self-doubt is the most potent weapon of the enemy within. It appears you are waiting for something. All you need is a push of faith, a leap of belief."

"Um-hmm."

"Do you trust your abilities?"

"Yes."

"Then you don't need to worry. Trust yourself. It will be for the best."

Viraat smiled briefly.

Sensing Viraat was still in doubt, Madhav added, "A bird sitting on a tree is never afraid of the branch breaking, because her trust is not on the branch but her wings. Remember that."

Viraat felt much better, but not completely out of the quicksand of doubt.

Madhav left the room.

After fifteen minutes, Padmini entered. "Viraat, what are you doing here, all alone?"

He looked away and said, "Maa, what if I am not able to lift it today?"

"Then it will happen some other day. Don't ever forget what the Saptarishis said. You will wield it when the right time comes. King Satyavrat lifted it when he was much older than you."

"I know maa but I want it to happen today."

"What is meant to happen, will happen! Today, you will be crowned the Protector of Siddha-Lok or the Lok-Rakshak of Shivalik-Rajya, either way. Our blessings are with you; nothing is greater than that."

Dhananjay walked into the chambers along with Vishamadeva and Dushyant. "Are you ready, son?" Dhananjay asked.

"My nephew is always ready. Today is his day," Dushyant answered for him.

✦

The rush of visitors kept the guards on their toes. The arena was full but many still waited at the gates for entry. No one had anticipated these high numbers.

The arena was packed. The west side was allotted to Kailash-Rajya, the east side for Himalia-Rajya. Visitors from Shivalik-Rajya occupied the south side, directly in front of the Trishul, which was placed on the north of the arena for centuries. There was no seating area on the north side. A temple was built there.

The announcer moved to the centre of the arena and declared:

"Everyone welcome Dhruvanshi, King of Kings, the One True King, Maharaja Dhananjay with Maharani Padmini, Lok-Sevak Vishamadeva,

Dhruvanshi Prince Viraat, and other esteemed dignitaries."

Loudest cheers came when Viraat's name was mentioned.

They entered and sat down in their respective places. Dushyant sat beside Viraat.

"Today we are privileged that Acharya Bhaskar has also graced the occasion."

Bhaskar rose from his seat. His former students clapped with enthusiasm. Viraat and Aindrita stood up and applauded. So did Lakshya.

"As you all know, we have gathered here today to select a Lok-Rakshak for Shivalik-Rajya. The rules of selection are as follows:

Any Vanshaj or Utkrisht who wishes to become the Lok-Rakshak has to raise his hand before the bell is rung three times. That person will go and try to wield the Trishul. If that happens, there will be no contest. That person will become the Wielder, the one true Protector of Siddha-Lok with blessings from The Holy Trimurti.

In case the person is not able to wield the Trishul, then that person will have to defeat his challengers. Anyone from Shivalik-Rajya can challenge the contestant. All he needs to do is to raise his hand before the bell is rung three times again.

Both the fighters will fight in the manner they agree. Whoever remains standing till the count of ten will be declared the winner. The duel stops if one player surrenders.

This will continue over the days till the last man remains unchallenged or undefeated. The winner will be crowned as the Lok-Rakshak of Shivalik-Rajya.

Maharaja has entrusted Lok-Sevak Vishamadeva with the responsibility of the judge for any dispute that may arise."

There were loud cheers from the audience that went down in volume until there was a hush of anticipation in the arena.

◆

Lakshya stood on the side-lines looking at Aindrita. A sharp pain prickled his heart. He was sure he would leave his post after her marriage to Viraat and return to his homeland. It would not be prudent to stay so close and serve under her.

"What are you looking at, son?" a voice said from behind.

Lakshya recognized the voice. It was Madhav. Without turning, he said,

"Pranam, deva. Why do you always surprise me from behind?"

Madhav laughed. "I decided to be behind the curtains in this life."

"Sorry, deva, I don't understand."

Madhav stood next to him, and said, "Forget it. What were you looking at?"

Instinctively, Lakshya's eye went towards Aindrita and then he looked away. He replied, "Nothing." Madhav noticed it.

The announcement came, "Ring the bell."

First bell.

One hand went up and everyone in the crowd felt ecstatic. Normally, the Prince came last, so as not to be tired, in case, there are many challengers. But Viraat was confident of defeating anyone or any number of challengers. His eyes shone with conviction.

Everyone admired the confidence of the Prince. They screamed, "Viraat! Viraat!"

Aindrita clapped with gusto.

"We have our first contender: this year's Sarva Shrestha Shishya, Dhruvanshi, Prince Viraat," the announcer said loudly.

Madhav asked Lakshya, "What do you think? Will he be able to lift it?"

"I don't know, deva. You are good at making predictions," he replied, remembering that the forecast about meeting his father had turned out to be true.

"As they say he is born to do it. If it is the will of Lord Shiva, he will. Let's see," Madhav answered.

Dhananjay and Padmini's lips moved in prayer.

Viraat stood near the Trishul. There was pin-drop silence in the entire arena. Every eye was fixed on him. Shravan, the temple priest was ready with the conch in his hand. Today could be the day.

Viraat wrapped his hand around the Trishul. His nervousness had peaked.

Aindrita's heart was in her mouth.

Everyone took a deep breath and waited. Hearts beat faster, legs shook in excitement.

As Viraat applied strength, Trishul moved slightly, yet again. He tried to lift it with all his power, unlike the last time. But, he was unable to wield it.

"AHHH." A wave of disappointment went through the crowd. They applauded. At least they witnessed some movement of the Trishul. Their belief in the prophecy became stronger.

At that moment, Madhav asked, "Lakshya, why did you not go to Bhuvar-Lok?"

Lakshya was astonished with the unexpected question. He raised an inquiring eyebrow. "Why, deva? Why should I go there? Did something happen?"

"Ohh! You don't know," Madhav said.

"What don't I know?" Lakshya felt a shiver run through him upon seeing Madhav's expression.

Madhav looked down at his feet.

"What's wrong? Please tell me, deva...please don't talk in riddles." Lakshya's heartbeat raced.

"I heard that a tribal Lord Vritra from Angaara is planning to attack Bhuvar-Lok very soon. Samrat Srivijay is heavily outnumbered and they face a certain defeat. Some messenger had come to Shivalik-Rajya seeking help, but Maharaja Dhananjay refused to intervene."

Now, Lakshya realized the purpose behind his father's visit. *Why didn't pitashri tell me?* "Why did the Maharaja refuse to help?"

"That only he knows. You are the Anga-Rakshak. I am surprised you don't know about it. You should have been the first to know."

Anger roiled inside Lakshya. Refusing help in the time of need! Lord Bajrang had helped them and they refused to pay it back. He felt betrayed by Shivalik-Rajya and the Dhruvanshis. His eyes fell on Viraat. "Did Viraat agree with the decision of the Maharaja?"

Madhav shrugged his shoulders. "I don't know."

Lakshya's mind rebelled with thoughts. *They call themselves Dhruvanshi! They don't understand its meaning.*

But what could he do? The thoughts of the coming war on his motherland engulfed him. His eyes began to turn bright red. He wanted to leave everything and walk out.

The announcement came, "Is there a challenger?"

Viraat stood in the centre of the arena, looking around.

First bell.

Madhav asked Lakshya, "Are you still wondering what you can do?"

Lakshya looked at Madhav, confused. It seemed that the world around him had come to a halt. Realisation crept into his mind in slow, tentative steps. A bead of perspiration trickled down his temple and Lakshya swiped it with his thumb.

He gazed at Aindrita, whose eyes were on Viraat. He was already bitten by the pangs of love. Jealousy is a silent poison that follows unrequited love. It was slowly invading his mind and heart.

Lakshya's eyes wandered towards Padmini. Her eyes were closed in prayers.

Then he looked at Dhananjay, who was in an extremely cheerful mood seeing no contender.

Second bell.

They refused to help. What was the use of having the Trishul, when it was not used to destroy evil? There was only one way to change that. The volcano was ready to erupt. The heat of lava ran through his body. His jaws tightened.

Lakshya clenched his fist and slowly raised his hand.

◆

46

Trishul (Trident)

SIDDHA - LOK

The announcer looked at the raised hand, and he croaked, "WAIT!"

The hammer in the hand of the person hitting the bell stopped right before contact.

It was a shocker. Totally unexpected. Everyone looked around to see the challenger. All eyes were searching for the one who had dared to challenge their Prince.

Very few recognized him. Some identified him with his armour. *He must be the Maharaja's Anga-Rakshak.* The word spread rapidly and the arena buzzed with possibilities. The audience hushed one another, not wanting to miss anything.

The reactions were varied.

Lakshya! Viraat could not comprehend this sudden turn of events. *Why?* His body stiffened; he gritted his teeth. Yet, he looked brave and determined. He straightened his spine and raised his chin.

Vishamadeva did not know what to make of this development. He guessed the reason for Lakshya's defiance. If anything, he was happy. *It's good to be challenged. The Lok-Rakshak should not be selected unopposed. Viraat will be tested. He will have to earn it.*

Padmini was puzzled. *Why, Lakshya?*

Dhananjay felt agitated. He pursed his mouth as if he had bitten into a spoilt papaya. His eyes were as unforgiving as a snake's. *My own bodyguard, my servant challenging my son. I gave him everything and he pays me back with this. What a betrayal!*

Bhaskar was happy because today was the day a tiger fights a lion.

Hetan knew there was something more going on than what met the eye.

Niyati was astonished. *What have you done, Lakshya!*

Madhav smiled.

Aindrita stood up in numb shock and went to the edge of the seating area, overlooking the arena. She knew which side her heart was on, it was her mind which was refusing to accept it. What the Saptarishis had told her did not make sense anymore! *Who is going to win? Wait…Can Lakshya possibly wield the Trishul?*

Lakshya was unable to shake off the feeling that he was being watched by everyone in absolute hatred.

The crowd yelled, "Boooooooh."

They were not happy that a commoner, an outsider, was challenging the Prince of Shivalik for the coveted title of the Lok-Rakshak of Shivalik-Rajya. With such an orthodox mindset, how could they let this happen!

Many in the audience screamed, "He is an outsider, a *firangi* (foreigner). He cannot compete." It surprised many that the term 'firangi' was used for Lakshya which was a derogatory term used to refer to unwelcome outsiders. The common term was '*videshi*', which wasn't considered demeaning.

The murmuring grew louder; it was pretty persuasive.

The announcer looked at Dhananjay for instructions. He cleared his throat and waited for the signal. But Dhananjay looked at Lok-Sevak Vishamadeva, and so did the others.

Vishamadeva sat deep in thought. He looked at Viraat and Lakshya in turn. After weighing the options before him, he ended the dilemma in everyone's mind. "The challenger's *karmabhumi* is Shivalik. He is an Utkrisht by virtue of his post. He meets all the requirements to contest. Let the challenge begin." His stern voice silenced everyone, including the Maharaja.

The announcer sneered, "The challenger may try to wield the Trishul." The spark in the announcer's voice had died.

Life has been unfair to me all along just because I wasn't born a Prince. Everyone has been unfair to me. I had to fight and earn everything. It is today that I change my destiny, Lakshya's mind swirled with these thoughts.

"Control your anger. May Lord Shiva bless you," Madhav said.

Madhav left and moved away to the place where he was needed next.

Lakshya dropped his weapons. He removed his headgear and dropped it on the ground. Then he untied his blue cape. He knew that he would no longer be the King's bodyguard after this act of revolt. He would be thrown out of the kingdom. But he no longer cared. There was nothing left for him to lose. *If I am defeated, I will go and fight for my motherland. If I win…* Lakshya himself had no idea what he would do with a win. He had not thought it through. Sometimes our impulses are too strong for our judgement.

With deliberate steps, he entered the arena and moved towards the Trishul. He stood in front of it. The sparkling Trishul looked other worldly from such a close distance. He went on his knees and folded his hands. He bowed to the mighty weapon, his head pressed to the ground and his hands flat. He could hear the beat of his own pulse in his ears.

He jumped back to his feet and his right hand moved towards the Trishul.

The priest was ready with the conch, in case the extraordinary event happened. Everyone watched with interest, but they all had one thought in mind: *He can't.*

Aindrita prayed.

Lakshya looked at her one last time. He wrapped his right hand around the weapon. With closed eyes, he thought of the Lord. He waited and got ready to lift the Trishul. Taking a deep breath, he applied all his power for a long time. But it did not move!

Even though he didn't believe he could wield the Trishul, an intense feeling of disappointment crept over him as he released his breath.

The crowd roared with laughter and derision. Aindrita felt sad.

Viraat was relieved. A cloud of doubt did shadow him for some time.

◆

The announcer swallowed a lump in his throat. He had to ask a tough question, but he did not know how to. Finally, he mustered all his courage and spoke, "Prince Viraat, as a Dhruvanshi, do you want to fight him yourself or do you wish to have a substitute who fights on your behalf?"

Hearing this question, Dhananjay held his crippled arm, as he remembered that the rules for appointment of the Lok-Rakshak had been amended at his insistence. He wanted to be selected as the Lok-Rakshak before he became the

King as per the custom. The glory of the Dhruvanshis had to be kept intact. That was all he cared about. He had chosen Vishamadeva as his substitute. No one dared to fight him and Dhananjay was appointed as an unchallenged Lok-Rakshak.

Viraat stared at the announcer and replied, "No substitute. I will fight him myself."

The crowd cheered hearing that the Prince was going to fight on the strength of his own muscle and blood.

The announcer said, "The match will start after the challengers decide how they wish to compete."

Both fighters stared into the other's fiery eyes.

Viraat said, "I considered you as a friend and you betrayed me," he lied as he continued, "but still I am happy you challenged me. No one will ever question my selection after this."

Lakshya did not respond.

Sensing no rebuttal, Viraat asked, "Which weapon do you want to fight with?"

"How about without weapons? The way it was done in earlier times."

Viraat liked the challenge. "Alright. No weapons. It sounds fair. I owe you for saving Aindrita's life… consider this as repayment."

Viraat removed the piece of cloth around his neck. Lakshya removed his left-over armour.

✦

Both fighters were bare chested. Lakshya was in black baggy pants whereas Viraat was wearing a light brown dhoti.

Dark clouds covered the sky indicating that everyone from Indra-Lok had come to watch the contest. Heavy winds blew as if many other gods rode on it to the arena. The clouds turned an ominous charcoal gray over the arena.

Looking at these signs, Vishamadeva was restless. He had a bad feeling since the morning. And it was getting worse.

Viraat and Lakshya faced each other.

The hammer hit the bell, and the match commenced.

The crowd had already picked their favourite and the chants of his name echoed, "Viraat! Viraat!"

The challenger and the challenged stood with their fists raised to their ears, their elbows raised to their shoulders – in a typical offensive stance. Both moved around in a circle for a while. They relied heavily on their special skills, but in a fight between equals, more than skills, the will matters. Viraat was skilled in attacking and Lakshya was an excellent defender. It was a match written by the Gods.

Viraat jumped in and gave back-to-back punches and kicks. Lakshya avoided them. Viraat was surprised that it did not work.

Like wild bulls they locked horns with their hands. They tried to push each other in a show of strength. Both of them applied all of their muscles but neither was able to push the other.

Viraat abruptly changed course, instead of pushing, he pulled Lakshya and then used his right leg to kick on his opponent's stomach. He caught him off-guard. Using his elbow, he smashed Lakshya to the ground. Viraat had the first laugh.

The audience erupted in whoops of appreciation.

Viraat waited for Lakshya to get up.

Lakshya got up slowly and in a flash attacked using both his legs and arms. Viraat stopped all of them with ease. The counterattack from Viraat was equally well blocked by Lakshya. Finally, Viraat used his right hand and left leg combination for a row of kicks and punches. All of a sudden Viraat used his disguised left hand to go for Lakshya's nose and it connected. Blood splattered on the ground. The punch from his left hand was as strong as his right. It was followed by a sidekick directly on Lakshya's chest. Toppling a few times, Lakshya fell on the ground like a lifeless tree.

Vishamadeva was impressed with the move.

The crowd loved it. They chanted, "One… Two…Three…Four."

Pain rippled across Lakshya's chest. He was puzzled by what was happening! His nose felt a piercing pain. He had never felt this way. Never! As he wiped the blood, his eyes found Aindrita. Her mouth was covered with her left hand in disbelief. Lakshya lifted himself with care.

He needed to regain composure. Madhav's advice rang in his head: control your anger. He took a deep breath and forced himself to focus. With his anger calmed, he concentrated and awakened his kundalini energy. His eyes changed to green.

Viraat decided to finish it quickly. He ran towards his opponent and went with a reverse kick. He swung hard.

But to everyone's surprise, Lakshya stopped the move and grabbed Viraat's leg in mid-air with his hands. Then, he turned the leg strongly. Viraat's body rotated and he fell to the ground. It was a bad move, a wrong choice by an overconfident Viraat.

Lakshya waited for Viraat to get up.

Both charged at each other like two angry rhinoceros. Not two, only one, since Lakshya kept his anger in check. It was a no holds barred attack now. They hit each other with repeated blows, punches, kicks, elbows, with whatever they had. Some were blocked but many blows connected. Neither stopped.

The crowd kept alternating, not able to decide who was ahead.

Viraat had a cut near his left eye, swollen and bleeding. Lakshya had a bloody nose. Blood oozed from their cut lips and blood was dripping everywhere. Both were tired, but they kept hitting each other. They were exhausted; their hearts pounding hard, failing to get enough oxygen for their bodies. Their vision blurred and their legs trembled.

Who would collapse first? Neither was giving up. It was a question of who wanted it more.

Finally, both punched each other on the left cheek bone with their right hand at the same time. Lakshya and Viraat fell on their backs simultaneously, like a log cut into two by a heavy blow from an axe.

This was it.

The counting started. This time they counted slowly. Both players needed time. There could not be a draw as per rules. "One."

They breathed heavily. Unimaginable pain engulfed them. Their faces were completely swollen, covered with red and black marks. Neither of them made an effort to get up.

"Five."

Viraat was the first to show some movement. He turned sideways and started to get up.

"Six."

A few in the crowd shouted, "Come on, Prince." Lakshya opened his eyes and looked towards Viraat. Viraat was halfway up by then.

"Seven."

Lakshya tried to get up but he couldn't. He was down completely, again.

"Eight."

Viraat was on his feet.

All eyes were on Lakshya.

Lakshya made one last effort. He couldn't feel his body parts. But he managed to get halfway up.

"Nine."

Viraat prepared to celebrate his victory.

In an impulse, Aindrita shouted, "Come on, Lakshya."

Shocked, Viraat looked at her. Did he hear her right? He felt as if she had slammed into him. It is never easy to accept rejection. Love is a door to insanity, a raw emotion capable of driving out the best as well as the worst in humans. Jealousy and outrage made their way through the open door. From crimson red, his eyes changed to bright red.

Lakshya applied his left-over strength and got back on his feet.

Just then the crowd screamed, "Ten."

"Did he get back on his feet before ten?" Some voices in the crowd raised the question.

The announcer looked again at Vishamadeva. It was a close call and the match could be declared over.

The discussions in the crowd were growing.

Dhananjay turned his head towards Vishamadeva for his decision. "I think it's over," Dhananjay whispered.

Vishamadeva did not look back at Dhananjay. He was someone who could not be easily swayed by reckless emotions. The reward of victory was high, so it had to be conclusive. He didn't let the monster of pride swallow him. Vishamadeva disagreed and held, "It's not over till it is over without any doubt. The match continues."

Dhananjay was not happy with the decision, but there was nothing he could do.

Viraat was visibly upset. He kicked dust off the ground. He shouted in anger, "That's enough. We will fight with weapons now. I gave you a fair chance, but you failed."

Viraat turned to his uncle.

Dushyant moved swiftly and threw the sword Asi towards Viraat. He caught it and swung it in style, slashing the innocent air in front of him. The engraving on the blue sword had lit up as he held it.

Lakshya had refused to accept the primordial sword from Viraat that day. He regretted it now more than ever. His fate was sealed.

Defeat seemed inevitable. But he would not give up without a fight. Lakshya rushed to the weapons area. He picked his favourite spear. His best hope was to disarm Viraat and take control of Asi. He needed to change his strategy to make that happen. As he turned, he locked eyes with Aindrita, who was beseeching with her eyes to end it. But he wasn't going to surrender, even if it meant dying today. There was no return from the path he had chosen. He would go all the way.

Both were in the centre of the arena, again.

The audience was mesmerized at the sight of Asi.

Both players were ready to resume the match. Before Viraat could make his move, Lakshya jumped on him with continuous strikes, aiming for his wrists. He moved swiftly; it was a delight to watch. Viraat kept blocking or avoiding. Finally, Lakshya gave a thrust and succeeded in hitting Viraat's right wrist with a heavy blow, and the sword Asi fell out of Viraat's hand.

This was the golden moment that could tilt the balance in his favour. He pushed Viraat back with a couple of wild swings. The crowd, especially Dhananjay, had their hearts in their mouths, in disbelief. Dhananjay got up from his seat.

The Trishul and Asi were at equal distances from both of them on either side. The moment froze for a few seconds. They looked at the celestial weapons and then at each other.

Wasting no time, Lakshya went to pick up the sword.

For a moment, Viraat considered going towards the Trishul. A risky leap of faith. But a sliver of doubt, made him go towards Asi. He was not willing to risk losing the sword. He did not have much time and he needed to do something exceptional. He did a few quick somersaults and snatched Asi right before Lakshya could get his hands on it. Lakshya watched his last ray of hope fade away. He should have pushed Viraat back further. It was too late.

As expected, this time Viraat made the first move. Lakshya countered the attacks. He prevented four swings of Asi, but on the fifth one, his spear split into two.

Dushyant signalled the soldiers to block access to the weapons. He wanted it to end soon. It was enough embarrassment that the match had lasted for so long. Moreover, any challenge to the Prince and Dhruvanshis should be crushed to send a lasting message.

Viraat saw the spear split but he did not stop. His pride was wounded, and it could only be soothed by a brutal death. He swung Asi at an unarmed Lakshya.

Lakshya avoided the sword and ran towards the weapons area but he was stopped by the soldiers.

The crowd had tasted blood and they shouted, "Kill him! End it!"

Hetan was troubled at Lakshya's plight. He pleaded with Vishamadeva, "Lok-Sevak, this is madness. Stop it or allow him access to a weapon. It is unfair to attack an unarmed opponent."

Before Vishamadeva could say anything, Dhananjay overruled him, "The match will not stop. This is my decision. He can surrender if he wants to live."

Not accepting the Maharaja's command, Hetan tried to move inside the arena but was stopped by the soldiers.

Vishamadeva watched in silence. One tear escaped his eye and ran down his face.

Lakshya ran around the arena searching for a weapon. The crowd jeered at him. He looked towards Aindrita. She mumbled, "Lakshya, please surrender." She was crying openly now, her mind spinning at the horror of Lakshya's death. But Lakshya was on the bridge of life and death, and he chose death. Time was running out.

She closed her eyes and hid her face in Madhav's arms who was standing next to her. She repeated something in her heart.

Viraat looked at Aindrita's teary face. The tears added fuel to his rage. He could feel the blood gushing in his veins.

Lakshya felt his end was here. He looked at Madhav one last time and smiled. *I won't surrender and will die with a smile if that's what the Gods are wishing for today.*

Madhav was closely watching everything. But he couldn't stop any of it. So, he turned his eyes away. His face was as emotionless as a rock. His eyes never changed colour, but, at that moment, even they wavered.

Viraat came forward and swung his sword.

Lakshya barely managed to avoid it and he fell in front of the Trishul.

His parents' faces flashed before his eyes. His final moments. As a last resort, he grasped the only weapon around – the Trishul. Viraat swung Asi hard at Lakshya to end the match.

Suddenly, the crowd went silent and all air was sucked out of the arena.

The unexpected silence made Aindrita open her eyes; scared that the unthinkable must have happened.

What she saw stunned her beyond belief. Lakshya stood there, holding the Trishul in his hand and blocking Asi!

Boom! A lightning bolt pierced the heart of the open sky. The loud thunder tore through the golden light meeting the Trishul. The clouds parted, paving the way for sunlight to bless the Wielder of the Trishul. The winds whooshed in honour, the water bodies danced with gusto, the ground shook in celebration and the tree leaves rustled in admiration.

For a moment, everything seemed frozen in time. The sight astounded everyone in the arena.

Dhananjay fell back on his chair.

Padmini fainted.

Vishamadeva got up from his chair in shock. The words that always haunted him, hammered in his mind:

"The Gods will not forgive you. I will not forgive you. Your love will become the curse of Dhurvanshis. You shall pay. Your coming generations shall suffer and pay for this injustice. This is a dying, innocent man's curse on all of you…"

The next part of the curse was even more sinister,

"And there is only one way it would end – on your death-bed."

Memories come back in bits and pieces, but not this one. It kept bouncing inside his head. The reverberation ebbed slowly, leaving him both cold and weak.

✦

47

Netrapaṭa (Blindfold)

SIDDHA - LOK

Pushed by an unbelievable force, Viraat fell on his back in disbelief. The sword Asi fell out of his hand. His worst fears had come true. When he came back to his senses, he felt like an empty slate. His lifelong dream had been snatched away in a moment. Viraat was no longer sure if he was awake or dreaming. Someone had stolen his thunder, and it made no sense.

Everyone in the arena were on their feet. There was an eerie silence of anticipation.

Amidst all this, Lakshya stood with the mighty Trishul in his right hand. Strong winds were blowing his hair about his face. The sand whirled beneath Lakshya's feet. The scars and blood on his body glimmered like precious jewels and made him look like a herculean demigod. Only one question was bouncing in his mind, "Is this for real?"

The announcer was stupefied. He felt as if he had lost his voice. He swallowed a very heavy lump in his throat.

The reverie was broken by the priest Shravan, as he blew the conch. He had readied for this moment his entire life. Even he had never dreamed that it was meant to happen this way.

He was joined by a loud thunder and lightning in the sky.

Queen Maitreyi of Himalia came forward, went down on one knee and bowed her head. Seeing her, the residents of Himalia followed. The entire east side of the arena was on one knee, with their heads down. It meant only one thing.

"Our salute to the Wielder, the Protector of Siddha-Lok blessed by Lord Shiva," she announced.

The murmurs in the crowd went up exponentially. It was chaos. One of the kingdoms had shown its allegiance. The smallest kingdom never believed in bloodlines or prophecies. They believed in what they saw. To them, the Wielder of the Trishul was the Protector of Siddha-Lok. As prophesied. Period.

Confusion spread across the arena. The others were waiting for the decision of their respective Kings. All eyes were on Dhananjay and Yuyutsu.

Dhananjay stuttered, "This doesn't make sense. How can he wield the Trishul?"

"But he has, Maharaja," Vishamadeva replied.

"What about the words of the Saptarishis? You were there. Does it mean nothing? They can't possibly be wrong. Can they?"

"The Saptarishis had said Viraat is destined to wield the Trishul. They never said he would be the *first* to wield, or the *only one* to wield it."

The words silenced Dhananjay. He frowned deeply, his nerves throbbing across the side of his wrinkled face. For the second time in his life, he faced the agony of blasted hopes and shattered dreams. His heart was crying for Viraat thinking of his son's plight. Finally, he spoke, "He is not the *true* wielder of the Trishul. He is a deceiver."

The crowd around him gave him puzzled looks. How could anyone deceive the Trishul?

The winds stopped in disbelief.

"We can't accept him as the Protector of Siddha-Lok. As per the rules, he was supposed to wield it when he was given the chance to do it, before the start of the challenge. He failed to move it, not even slightly. We all saw that. Then, he had lost the contest. He was disarmed by Dhruvanshi Prince Viraat. It happened before our eyes. The contest ended at that moment."

The technicality raised by Dhananjay made some voices agree with him.

Then, Dhananjay played the card that was more likely to work with other Kings and nobles. "He is an outsider, not even born in Siddha-Lok. He belongs to a lower class too. We can't possibly accept him as the Protector of Siddha-Lok and bow before him."

The last words made the crowd agree with Dhananjay wholeheartedly. "The Maharaja is right," many screamed.

"I know what the Saptarishis said to us. Dhruvanshi Viraat would wield it to save the Lok. The Trishul has moved whenever Viraat has put his hands on it.

He is the one true wielder. And today if we accept this deceiver, an outsider as the Protector of Siddha-Lok, it will be the worst service to the Gods. He is not the true Wielder of the Trishul and he never will be. The Gods are testing our faith and I will not fail them."

The Kings of other provinces joined the Maharaja in the chorus.

He had lost.

He is a deceiver. An outsider.

Viraat is our Lok-Rakshak.

Vishamadeva tried to interrupt, "Mah–"

Before he could complete his sentence, Dhananjay raised his hand and silenced him. Slowly, he whispered, "Follow your King, your oath."

That stilled the only voice of reason in Shivalik.

"If anyone does not agree with me, prepare for war. You are either with us or against us. The battle lines are drawn," Dhananjay warned. He made his decision loud and clear. "My ancestors had taken an oath to never raise weapons against anyone on this holy land, except during the contest. Dhruvanshis are true to their words. So, I am letting him live. He can leave the Trishul and return to where he came from...where he belongs."

With these words, Dhananjay abruptly left the scene. Padmini dutifully followed her husband.

Bhaskar slowly walked behind them. His gurukul had sworn total allegiance to Shivalik. He had no choice but to follow the King.

Dushyant moved inside the arena and picked up Viraat and his sword. They too left the ground. Viraat's head had sunk to his chest. His mind was too befuddled, and he was too exhausted to think clearly right now.

Niyati's heart wanted her to stay back, but her mind knew she couldn't openly rebel against Dhananjay. It was too big of a decision to take impulsively. She also walked out.

Vishamadeva stood in his place as the last person from Shivalik. Lakshya looked at him and bowed his head in respect. A faint smile came on Vishamadeva's old, distraught face. He raised his hand in blessing. As a caged eagle, he too left after that.

All eyes now turned to Yuyutsu. He did not know which side to take. He didn't want to displease Dhananjay and make an enemy. A war he knew he could never win. He held Aindrita's hand, but she resisted.

"If you have any respect for me, don't make a scene. This isn't the time to debate." Her father's voice was unusually stern, and it stifled her arguments.

Madhav nodded, signalling her to follow her father's instructions. Unwillingly, she left with her father.

Himalians too walked out without any argument.

The arena was deserted as each group abandoned it. Instead of celebrations, there was an atmosphere of mourning.

The only persons left in the arena were Madhav, Shravan and Hetan.

Shravan held an aarti plate with a glowing lamp on it. He slowly swung the flame around Lakshya's face. With total devotion, he applied teeka on his forehead. "They may be blindfolded. But I am not. You are the Wielder, the Protector of Siddha-Lok – the one chosen by the Lord," Shravan said.

Madhav placed his hand on Lakshya's shoulder.

Lakshya asked, "What happened, deva? How is this possible?"

"I don't know. You tell me. You are the one holding the mighty Trishul," Madhav replied.

"It doesn't make sense. How can I possibly wield the Trishul?"

Madhav smiled. "It never makes sense until it happens. Accept it. The sooner the better."

"But they are not going to accept me!" Lakshya said despairingly.

"They fail to see through the drape of emotions, their weaknesses...the boundaries they have created."

"What will happen now?" Lakshya asked with disquiet in his eyes.

Wordless, Madhav turned his face towards the Trishul. A strong, reviving wind slammed into his face. He had no control over destiny, the detour it had taken. After a momentary silence, he answered, "What is meant to happen!"

Shravan blew the conch again, stirring the waves of changing times, and announcing the start of the Second Great War.

✦

*GREAT WARS HAVE BEGUN... WHO SURVIVES, OR DIES?
THE STORY CONTINUES IN ...*

THE FALLEN GOD

GLOSSARY OF INDIAN TERMS

(in alphabetical order)

aarti	a ritual part of worship in which light is offered to the deity
acharya	teacher
agni	fire
agnipath	a difficult path; literally the path of fire
anga-rakshak	bodyguard
astra	a weapon which is released from one's hand
asura	a class of power-seeking divine beings in the Vedic period
athapati	chief judge
avatar	incarnation
ayushman bhava	may you live long; a blessing
badi-maa	elder mother; a form of address
bhaala	spear
bhumi	land, soil
bindi	a coloured dot worn on the forehead by women
brahmand	universe
chakravarti	world emperor
chandan	sandalwood
chiranjeevi bhava	wish you an eternal life; a blessing
damaru	a small two-headed drum, symbolic of Lord Shiva
deva	a class of benevolent divine beings in the Vedic period; also, a form of address
devi	goddess; also, a form of address
dhanya ho	be blessed; a blessing
dhanyavad	thanks

dharma	literally 'what is established or firm'
dharmayuddha	a righteous war
Dvapar Yuga	third of the four Yugas
dwarapala	gatekeeper
graha	planet
guptchar	spy
gurudakshina	preceptor's fees
halahala	the poison created out of churning of the ocean by Devas and Asuras
Indra-deva	the god of rain and thunder
janmabhumi	motherland
jyeshta pitashri	elder father; a form of address
jyeshta matashri	elder mother; a form of address
karma	the effects of a person's actions that determine their fate in this life and the next incarnation
karmabhumi	the land where one works
karmaphala	the results of your actions
kavacha	shield
koshadhyaksh	treasurer
kundalini	divine energy believed to be located at the base of the spine
lok	region
lok-rakshak	protector of the region; post of the commander-in-chief of the military
lok-sevak	servant of the region; post of the chief advisor to the king
maa, matashri	mother, a form of address
maharaja	king
maharani	queen

mantra	a 'sacred utterance' in Hinduism
mantri	minister
moksha	liberation from the cycle of death and rebirth
nakshatra	constellation
naresh	king
navgraha	nine heavenly bodies or deities
pahar	unit of time (normally equals three hours)
pitashri, pitaji	father, form of address
pooja	the act of worship
pradesh	province
praja	citizens
pralaya	cataclysm or dissolution
pranam	respectful greeting
putra	son; a form of address
raja	king; a form of address
rajya	kingdom
rajguru	royal priest
raksha	defence, protect
rishivar	sage; a form of address
rudraksha	a seed that is used as a prayer bead
sada saubhagya-vati bhava	good luck always; a blessing
samrat	emperor
Satya Yuga	first of the four Yugas; the age of truth
shakti	strength or power
shastra	a weapon which is used by keeping it in hand

shesha-naag	king of snakes and one of the primal beings of creation; associated with Lord Vishnu
shishya	student, pupil
shivratri	a festival celebrated in honour of Lord Shiva
sindoor	vermilion
suraksha-kavacha	defensive shield
Surya-deva	the sun god
tapasya	meditation
Treta Yuga	second of the four Yugas; the age of mankind
tathastu	amen
tilak, teeka	a mark on the forehead
Trimurti	triad of deities, typically Brahma the creator, Vishnu the preserver, and Shiva the destroyer
trivikram	the one who made three strides
Varuna-deva	the god of water
vaidya	doctor
vayu	wind
vichitra	strange
vidya	knowledge
Yama-raja	the god of death
yashasvi bhava	may you attain eternal success; a blessing
yuddha	war